RELICS OF POWER BOOK 3

THE NAMELESS GOD

EMMA L. ADAMS

PROLOGUE

Naxel Daimos trod across the flagstones, the staff of Astiva in his hand. The indistinct shapes of pillars rose on either side of him, supporting a high, arched ceiling. This chamber might have belonged to a temple or a palace once, judging by its size, but at the present moment there was nobody here except for himself and two deities.

The realm of the Powers had initially been challenging to adjust to, but by now, he was unbothered by the hazy surroundings or the lack of any definable beginning or end to any of its features. While the pillars looked solid to his eyes, when he reached out to touch one, his fingers passed through the surface as if it were made of naught but cloud.

As for the floor… admittedly, he tried not to think too hard about the solidity of the nebulous grey haze beneath his feet in case the mere thought sent him tumbling into some dark oblivion. Regardless of its foreign nature, the realm of the Powers was an improvement on the human world in several ways, such as its lack of noise and the absence of irritating disturbances.

Except, that is, for the two man-sized birds that waited for him in the middle of the chamber. Like most deities, their forms were fluid and shifted according to their whims, which were frequent and many. For the sake of ease, he called them by their chosen names, Xeale and Kyren. At one time, it might have surprised him that the deities would offer a human their loyalty so readily, but in truth, winning them over had been no challenge for him. They'd witnessed him save Orzen from imprisonment in this realm and give him a human body, and the mere hope that he would do the same for them was enough for them to bow their heads in subservience.

Nearing the two birds, he addressed them. "Any news?"

"The humans are moving as you expected," said Xeale, a male deity who took the form of a grey dove. "They've taken the village and swiftly set up a barrier against intruders. They believe they're acting on the orders of their own deity. Poor fools."

Kyren gave a high-pitched laugh, which made Daimos's brows twitch. The female deity, who'd adopted the appearance of a large raven, shuffled closer to him. "It is precisely as you planned, master."

"Please cease your fawning," he told her. "It's an embarrassment to all of us."

"Of course." Kyren dropped her simpering tone. "We also brought you more trinkets."

"Show me."

The two deities took flight in a shower of feathers that vanished before they hit the ground. Daimos followed their flight across the chamber until they came to a pile of objects, most of which appeared to be junk to mundane human eyes—buttons, rusted knives, shoes, and other garments. *Relics.* None were as impressive looking as the crimson staff in his hand, but they'd suffice for his needs. Like the staff, they were tools, nothing more; he'd long since learned the difference between Relics that held a consciousness of their own and ones that did not. The deity whose power resided in his staff had never whispered in his ear as Orzen had, but he had no need of a deity to guide his hand any longer.

Now, Daimos commanded the deities with his own hand instead.

Xeale shuffled closer to him. "Is there a particular target you have in mind?"

Daimos considered the question. "Not at the moment. I already have the Changers, in addition to my spies... though I didn't expect the old Sentinel to be so hard to pin down."

"She's a wily one," said Kyren, a hint of displeasure entering her voice. "When we served Orzen, she tried to trick us into helping her escape."

And succeeded, if I'm to believe the rumours. Daimos cared nothing for the deities' loyalty to him; he was under no illusions that they served him for any reasons but for the sake of their own survival.

No illusions... He chuckled at the irony of the phrase as he surveyed the Relics in front of him, their power undiminished despite their long years of abandonment. He could afford to lose a few tools, but he would never place his trust in a deity. Orzen had helped him, true, kept his arrogance in check at a time when it might have been a costly mistake—but he had no need to limit his expectations.

Orzen wasn't dead—despite their longevity, the gods *could* die, as Daimos had learned recently—but with his Relic imprisoned within the domain of the nameless Shaper, he might as well be. As for the Changers... it was galling to have to ally with those who'd botched Orzen's mission so badly, but he needed them ready in case his adversaries pulled another unexpected feat of trickery. Between the Sentinel's family and his old enemy, Arien Astera, there was entirely too much potential for another disaster such as the one they'd caused in the Isles of Itzar.

That wouldn't do. Not when he stood on the brink of forcing the people of Aestin to remember the wrongs they'd done his family and to repay that debt in blood.

As for Zeuten, he'd known nothing of their nation or its Sentinel protectors until they'd aided Astera against him and seen to Orzen's end, but the ties between Zeuten and Aestin were close enough that it seemed almost inevitable for their fates to be entangled. It would be immensely satisfying to see them brought to ruin at his hands... with a little help from the Great Powers.

Daimos looked upon the Relics of the deity of illusions and smiled.

1

Zelle brought the staff down on the gremlin's head, stunning it mid-flail, before picking it up one-handedly and tossing it out the open window. The gremlin, which resembled a human child formed of a papery substance with needle-like teeth and claws, yowled once before vanishing from sight out of the stone tower.

Gremlins were frankly the least of the problems plaguing the Sentinels' outpost, but they were among the few Zelle was able to handle. Being magical constructs and not living creatures, they felt no pain and consequently elicited no guilt when she caught and tossed each one out of the tower. Two large eagles watched the gremlins tumble from the window with curious eyes, as did Chirp, the wild dragonet who'd formed a strong bond with one of her companions.

"Another one." Grandma shoved a struggling gremlin into her hands, which Zelle shoved out of the open window to join the others. "I don't see the point in throwing them out when they'll reappear by the morning anyway, personally."

"I prefer not to have constructs creeping around me while I'm sleeping." Zelle yanked the window closed with a firm hand.

"Too right." Aurel lifted her auburn head from where she lay sprawled in an armchair near the fireplace. She'd collapsed into it as soon as they'd entered the tower and had barely moved since. Zelle didn't blame her, given that they'd spent almost the entire day travelling home from Itzar and had little expected to arrive in Zeuten to find Aurel's home surrounded by elite assassins.

Their narrow escape to the Sentinels' outpost in the mountains of the Range ought to have exhausted Zelle, too, but restlessness stirred beneath her skin and prompted her to search the various corners and cabinets for more unwelcome guests. Addressing her grandmother, who occupied the second armchair, she asked, "Is the Shaper conjuring the gremlins in response to what's going on down in the village, do you think?"

"No," Grandma replied shortly. "For the Powers' sakes, girl, sit down. You're making me twitchy."

In the corner, Evita jumped at the Sentinel's sudden command. The tall, lanky former assassin had been hovering near the window without taking a seat, no doubt keeping an eye on her dragonet companion, who was now too large to fit through the doorway and had to wait outside with the eagles they'd borrowed from their hosts in the Isles of Itzar.

"Grandma, don't yell at people. One of us needs to keep an eye out for trouble." At least the elderly Sentinel must be feeling better than the last time Zelle had seen her, after she'd been injured in the attack from the warriors from Itzar who'd captured Aurel. She looked better, certainly, the colour having returned to her tanned face, despite her recent escapades in dodging the Changers.

What a mess we've landed in this time.

The old Sentinel gave Zelle a disgruntled look. "The assassins aren't going to fly up here this close to nightfall. They know they won't get in, and it'd be a wasted effort."

"So was taking over Tavine, for the Powers' sakes."

Granted, the Changers believed themselves to be following the orders of Gaiva, the creator goddess and one of the three Great Powers, but Zelle knew that to be untrue. Not least because she'd *seen* Gaiva's remains scattered around Itzar less than a day prior to their arrival home.

No, it was another deity entirely who influenced them, one who'd allied with the man who'd been partly responsible for their visit to Itzar to begin with. Naxel Daimos, Rien's sworn enemy, and now possibly the most dangerous man in the known world.

I imagine Daimos intended to send a message. The voice, which came from the staff Zelle had propped against the wall next to the window, spoke clearly in her mind, unheard by any of the others.

Zelle gave a short laugh. "Unless he really wanted Aurel's priceless junk collection."

"Hey, there are some real valuables in there," Aurel protested. "Not to mention most of my clothes. You didn't think to pack any of them, Grandma?"

Grandma Carnelian shot her a withering look. "I'm sorry I didn't have time to pack any of your nice dresses while I was evading arrest. It's lucky I was able to bring any food and supplies, let alone frivolities."

Sensing an argument brewing, Zelle stepped in. "Did the Changers just take Tavine? Not Randel as well?"

"No, but they knew I was staying with the Reader," Grandma answered. "We're their targets. Some of the villagers might have tried to resist, but who would dare to challenge the orders of the Crown?"

"It's not the Crown *or* Gaiva. It's Daimos." When Zelle spoke the name, she saw their other companion shift on his feet out of the corner of her eye, his attention sharpening. Rien, who stood near one of the bookcases in the corner, had remained silent throughout their conversation, but she could never forget he was there.

"No doubt he planned this carefully," Rien said, his voice barely accented despite not being a native Zeutenian speaker. Tall and broad, he had the medium-brown skin of an Aestinian and wore his long, dark hair in the fashion of their upper class.

"Exactly," Zelle said. "The Crown Prince doesn't keep a close eye on the Changers, and the success of Orzen's takeover proved to Daimos that they're the perfect route through which to reach the Sentinels. His Royal Highness is probably safely in his palace, planning his next societal function, utterly oblivious to all of this."

Aurel gave a snort. "You aren't wrong, but I'm surprised there are any Master Changers left after Orzen slaughtered them all."

"True." Daimos seemed to have no end of resources and allies, though—including, allegedly, a Great Power. "I doubt that's much of a concern to him. He has what he needs."

Who knew what the deity of illusions might be capable of? Zelle *hoped* Daimos only had a Relic and not the aid of Invicten Himself, but nothing was certain when it came to the Great Powers. The last fragment of Gaiva's consciousness was confined to a Relic buried inside the Isles of Itzar, and the nameless Shaper had been imprisoned here in these very mountains by the other deities, but Invicten was an unknown entity.

Rien met her gaze, his tense expression indicating that he'd caught the direction of her thoughts. "As soon as he realised that we had the support of the nameless Shaper, I bet Daimos changed his strategy to focus on finding the others. He'll have sent his spies to scour the far edges of the world, no doubt, and ordered Igon to ensure Gaiva never left the Isles."

Zelle inclined her head. "Worse, we don't even know what kind of magic Invicten's Relic bestows upon its wielder."

"You *are* standing near the most extensive source of information concerning the Powers on the continent," Grandma told her. "In case you've forgotten."

Zelle hadn't, but the Sanctum was the Shaper's domain, prone to making her lose track of time. What if Daimos intended to attack the outpost the instant she turned her back on the others?

He won't. The staff answered her unspoken thoughts.

"So you do know where he is," she muttered.

No. I can sense anyone who comes into the mountains, though, and he isn't here.

"Does that include the Changers?"

They are not in my domain.

Aurel cleared her throat. "Let us in on your one-sided conversation, Zelle."

"There's not much to say." Zelle lifted her gaze from the staff. "The staff says Daimos isn't in the mountains, but it isn't able to sense his actual location. Or the Changers, even though they live in the Range."

"They have Relics of their own," said Grandma.

In the window seat, Evita startled then tried to cover up the motion by picking up a book. Everyone pretended not to notice she'd opened it upside down. "I'm not—the cloak isn't a Relic."

Aurel shrugged. "It's got magic inside it, which makes it a Relic according to every definition of the word."

"I haven't a clue which deity it belongs to," Evita protested. "The Changers taught me that Gaiva's magic was inside it, but it's not the same as those Relics the islanders carried."

"Well, it's on our side," Aurel said. "For what it's worth."

Evita didn't answer, but Zelle was inclined to agree with her sister. Not only could the cloak render the former assassin close to invisible, but she'd even used it to fly. That made it a Relic in Zelle's eyes, but Evita had known nothing of magic before Orzen had invaded her small village on Zeuten's southeastern coast and razed it to the ground. If she wanted to believe the cloak was nothing like the capricious and dangerous staffs that Zelle and Rien carried, then it did no harm.

"Speaking of Relics." Grandma indicated the swirling marks that now covered Zelle's hands and wrists. "What exactly is that?"

Zelle tugged down her sleeves, wishing she'd kept on

her fur coat, but the old Sentinel was sharp enough to have spotted the change in Zelle without any prior indications. "It's my godsmark."

She'd never uttered the word before, not in reference to herself, but a hush followed, and every noise inside the room appeared to quieten, as if the Sanctum itself was paying close attention.

Grandma broke the silence. "A foolish decision, if you ask me."

"I didn't have a choice." Annoyance stirred within Zelle. "The Shaper and I had to join forces to fight against Igon, and the only way to survive was to bind myself to the staff like an Invoker and their Relic."

"And you didn't feel any different afterwards?"

"We were in the middle of a battle," Zelle said. "As for now, I don't feel like raising continents from the ocean, if that's what you mean."

The Shaper, the stories told, had created the very lands on which humanity lived and walked. She had been formidable enough to prove a threat even to the other Great Powers, if Her eventual imprisonment within the Range was any indication. Zelle hadn't made her choice lightly. Her aunt Adaine, who'd raised her, had always made it clear that the Powers weren't to be trusted to act in the interests of humanity, but if there'd ever been an opportunity to turn back, it had long since passed.

Zelle's hand curled around the end of the staff. "I'm going into the Sanctum. Anyone else want to come?"

Rien surveyed her. "I would if I was certain of finding what I was looking for."

"You might be surprised." The Sanctum lacked for knowledge on nothing except perhaps recent history;

Zelle's ancestors had stopped bringing in new texts a few centuries after they'd departed Aestin and settled here in the mountains some thousand years prior. "I don't know about you, but I want to know more about this god of illusions."

"Agreed." Rien lifted his crimson staff. *Right, he wants to know more about his own deity.* Rien's own ancestors—the Asteras, one of the most prestigious families in Aestin—had once maintained contact with the Sentinels, but evidence of their past communications had been destroyed along with his house when Daimos had slaughtered his family. Rien had managed to find a replacement for the Relic he'd lost in the carnage but no information pertaining to his current Relic, which Zelle had believed to be a myth until the nameless Shaper had placed it in his hands.

"No thanks," said Aurel. "I'll go back to the village and see what the Changers are up to."

"No, you will not," Grandma told her. "It's dark. At least wait until morning before you take unnecessary risks."

"Does that count all the times *you* went wandering in the forest with the Changers sniffing around the village?"

Zelle was more than happy to leave them bickering and make for the stairs ahead of Rien, climbing up to the short corridor that led into the Sanctum. "I give them less than a day before they're at one another's throats."

"Not so different to when we were all staying in the Reader's house, then." He caught her up easily, his movements elegant enough to make her feel unrefined. Despite the weeks he'd spent in Zeuten, living in relative anonymity, he carried himself like a noble no matter how he dressed, including the Itzar-made furs he currently wore.

"There's less space here, though." Like Aurel's house, the outpost contained a collection of artefacts gathered by generations of their family but not much in the way of comforts for human habitation. With five of them present and only two bedrooms, one of which belonged to her grandmother and the other which would be claimed by Aurel, Zelle suspected she and Rien would find themselves sleeping in the living room—together.

She'd have to think on that one later. Rien showed no signs of that particular dilemma having occurred to him and indicated the door ahead of them. "Except in there. How big *is* the Sanctum?"

"Haven't a clue." The staff's magic warped the space inside the tower and could even create passages leading to the opposite side of the mountain if the Shaper desired. Regardless, Zelle hoped that unlike their last visit, the books wouldn't wipe their pages clean when Rien tried to read them, and the doors wouldn't seal themselves against him.

"And yet this is all we have." Rien stood distractingly close behind her, and Zelle's hands fumbled the bolts on the exterior door. She wished he'd take a step back, but she couldn't think of how to ask him without admitting how he'd flustered her.

The staff groaned. *Preserve me from this nonsense.*

A flush heated her cheeks. *Stay out of my thoughts, Shaper.*

"Zelle?" Rien asked. "What is it?"

"Just thinking about where to start," she evaded. "We need to find out as much as possible about the Great

Powers, especially Invicten. Then we can figure out what we're up against."

Daimos must have obtained Invicten's Relic somehow, but he couldn't have joined forces with the deity directly without surrendering the other Relic he already carried. That Rien already knew, and she didn't need to remind him that the other Relic in question had once been his.

Nor did could she afford for either of them to be distracted. Zelle finished unbolting the locks in silence and opened the door to the Sanctum.

2

Rien walked after Zelle into the short corridor connecting the Sanctum's exterior door to the interior one, behind which a clawed instrument hung from a hook on the wall. Zelle took the instrument in hand before unlocking the inner door and leading the way into the main part of the Sanctum.

An archway shadowed them, inscribed with runes in the old language the settlers of Zeuten had once shared with his own ancestors. A thousand years of separation had driven the language to evolve in two separate directions, but if he racked his memories of his childhood linguistic lessons, he could make out some of the words.

"Three… then beginning," he read.

Zelle halted. "I didn't know you understood the old text."

"Not all of it, but I'm guessing it doesn't actually say 'leave while you still can.'"

She flashed him a smile at the reminder of her comment during their first visit here, when she'd suggested the archway was marked with a warning. At the time, he'd been surprised that she'd speak to him in such a familiar manner, but it hadn't taken long for him to realise she hadn't had a friend to talk to in a long time. And while he'd been missing his memories at the time, he'd recognised something in that loneliness.

A shuffling noise in the background caused Zelle's shoulders to tense. "Thought so."

Raising the clawed instrument, she left the archway and went in search of the intruders. Oakwood shelves lined each wall, interspersed with alcoves containing torches that stayed lit no matter how long the place went without visitors—no doubt because of the nameless Shaper. He often forgot the gremlins lurking in the shadows were a product of the Shaper's magic, too, though he and Zelle dispatched them with ease, tossing out of the windows opened by levers some resourceful past Sentinel had installed between the shelves.

With the gremlins taken care of, he and Zelle walked until they came to a door inset with a metal ring. There, Zelle halted. "Do you want to ask the book for what you need?"

"You aren't going in there yourself?"

"I'm going to speak to the Shaper directly," explained Zelle. "I think it's the quickest way to get the information I need."

She was probably right, but the notion of splitting up in the Sanctum didn't appeal. He reminded himself that the Shaper wouldn't do Zelle any harm and said, "I agree."

Zelle tugged on the metal ring, opening the door to reveal a room the size of a small cave. Atop a pedestal in the centre sat a book with a cover as bright as a jewel, and

Zelle stepped aside to allow him to reach it. "I shouldn't be too long, but you should take this. Just in case."

He took the clawed instrument she offered him. "You're making me have second thoughts about parting ways."

"Really?" She blinked as if surprised. "I wouldn't advise you to come with me to see the Shaper. She threw *me* off a cliff once, remember?"

"That was a joke." Only half true, but he hadn't anticipated her reaction to his remark. "Not a great one."

"Oh." Her gaze lowered. "That's all right, then."

What was that? he berated himself. He hadn't meant to imply that he wanted to stay by her side like an infatuated youth, but she seemed to have taken the comment that way, and he wished he hadn't spoken at all. Heat crept to the tips of his ears, and while Zelle's face had flushed, too, she said nothing, ducking out of sight.

Rien opened the book sitting atop the pedestal, and its pages expanded to fill his vision, prompting a familiar dizzying sensation of looking upon a visual that ought by rights to be outside the boundaries of his perception. The towering pages supposedly listed every book in the entire Sanctum, which should also be an impossibility, but hardly more so than the entirety of the Sanctum's many corridors fitting inside a small stone tower.

Really, it was surprising that nobody in Zelle's family had guessed the nameless Shaper's involvement sooner. No other deity had power over the very nature of reality itself. Though if Zelle was anything to go by, the Sentinels held the view that some questions were best left unanswered. Not an illogical approach, given recent events, and Rien had certainly had his own perspective upended since he'd lost his link to Astiva.

While his original deity had been a loyal companion, Rien had since faced the reality that not every deity thought of humanity the same way—including, perhaps, the one whose power resided in his current Relic. As far as he could work out, the founders of Zeuten had brought the Relic here to the mountains, but his knowledge ended there. For that reason, he would leave it to Zelle to gather information on Invicten and intended to focus his attention on his own deity instead.

Rien focused on the text filling the pages and addressed the book. "Find me a text that contains information about the children of Gaiva, especially Zierne."

Zierne, like Astiva, was one of five children of the creator goddess Herself. While all of them had departed this realm countless years ago and left only their Relics behind, the other four had remained in Aestin. How, then, had Zierne's Relic come to be on a separate continent to Astiva and his other siblings? It was not simple curiosity that drove him, but understanding his new Relic might well prove necessary to his own survival.

On the page, spiky letters formed words in modern Zeutenian—*Children of Gaiva*—and he committed the name of the book to memory as he stepped away from the pedestal. The towering pages disappeared while the book returned to a more ordinary size.

Leaving the pedestal, Rien went in search of the book he needed, keeping the clawed instrument Zelle had given him ready in case any more gremlins appeared. Since the title was in the part of the Sanctum they'd already cleared out, he found the right shelf without being ambushed.

Crouching down, he retrieved a dusty volume with careful hands. The leather-bound cover had faded with age, but he made out the title: *Children of Gaiva.*

Rien opened the book, finding a spot in an alcove under a lantern that enabled him to read the sprawling text on the yellowing pages. *This is the history of Gaiva and Her five true children, fathered by Invicten.*

Invicten? That might be of interest to Zelle, though the book's overall focus appeared to be on Gaiva's children and not their parents.

A sudden clattering sound came from nearby, and Rien snapped the book closed. Raising the clawed instrument, he rounded the corner and stopped short when he saw Zelle. She faced the stone wall and gripped her staff in a hand that was aglow with blue light from her fingertips to her sleeve. From her frazzled manner, he could discern that her visit to the Shaper had not ended in her favour.

"Are you all right?" he asked.

She blew out a breath. "The Shaper doesn't want to talk to me about Invicten and told me to do the research for myself."

"Didn't the Shaper *witness* that history?"

"Not the part after Her imprisonment, which covers several thousand years." Zelle turned away from the wall. "I can learn the basics from a book, true, but the Sanctum's texts won't tell me anything about the present day either. Did you find anything useful?"

He held up his own book. "*Children of Gaiva.* There's one mention of Invicten in the opening section, but I haven't read the rest."

"I wanted recent history, ideally." The glow from the

staff had dimmed while they spoke, and when she lowered her hand, he could almost fool himself into believing she no longer bore the mark of her new allegiance with the Shaper on her skin. "I knew it was unlikely that I'd find any, but it'd help to know if any humans have previously held Invicten's Relic."

"Assuming there isn't more than one Relic, and that they all have the same abilities." He spoke the pessimistic words automatically, though he'd been trying to avoid thinking of the possibility of Daimos carrying *multiple* Relics of Invicten. One was quite enough to handle on its own.

Zelle's brow twitched. "Powers, don't even start with that. All right, I'll see what's in here."

As she made her way to the room with the pedestal, Rien waited under a lantern and once again opened *Children of Gaiva*.

Five children there were, and they were born in harmony. Astiva, Mevicen, Venzei, Lauvet, and Zierne.

Before he could read further, Zelle stepped down from the pedestal. "The Sanctum only recommended a single book. It had better be a good one."

He followed her past rows of shelves, reading one-handed as he did so. *But the peace was not to last, for one of their number was jealous of the humans Gaiva had created.*

His foot caught on a stone, and Zelle shot him an amused look over her shoulder. "If you're not careful, you'll walk into a pillar. I *might* have done that a few times when I came in here as a child."

He lowered the book. "I'm surprised there's any appropriate reading material for a child in here."

"There isn't, but my grandmother never cared what I

did as long as I didn't get in the way," she said. "She reasoned that it was marginally less dangerous than letting me run wild outside on the mountain paths, which was a fair assessment."

"Despite the gremlins hiding in the shelves?"

"I learned to deal with them."

Not for the first time, it struck her how radically different their upbringings must have been.

Losing her parents at a young age coupled with not being chosen as Sentinel meant Zelle would have spent a lot of time alone, while he'd always been surrounded by a sea of relatives and acquaintances. "And your sister?"

"My sister was too young to care about a bunch of boring old books," she said. "Ah—we're in the right section."

After skimming the titles on the shelves, Zelle retrieved a volume that was simply titled *Tales of the Three.* "Myths aren't exactly what I had in mind, but the Sanctum usually sends me in the right direction."

"You mean the Shaper," said Rien. "Her magic must guide the recommendations, right?"

"Yes, but it's not… coordinated, I suppose I'd say." Her brow scrunched up. "Or maybe it is, but it doesn't feel that way when one part of the Shaper just berated me for being too lazy to do my own research."

"And the other gave you a book."

She studied the cover for a moment. "A book I've already read, in all likelihood."

The Shaper was known for being inscrutable, but Zelle had more control over the Sanctum than most, so he could understand her frustration at the lack of certainty.

"Do you remember it containing anything useful on the nameless Shaper?"

"No, but everyone knows the stories. They're written over the walls in here, in fact." She indicated the symbols carved into the stone, worn away by time. "The three Great Powers were here before humanity walked the earth. *Three there were, in the beginning. The first gave us life. The second gave us thought. And the third, who shaped the world itself, gave us our legacy.* I don't remember the rest."

"They're in a different order to the one we're taught in Aestin," he observed. "The Shaper created the land, then Gaiva created life, and then Invicten gave certain beings consciousness. Your tale starts with Gaiva, then Invicten..."

"It doesn't matter what order they appear in," Zelle interjected. "They're symbolic, besides."

"Symbolic?" he echoed.

"We don't—look, not everyone believes the Great Powers actually created the entire world *and* everything that lives in it," said Zelle. "I certainly don't, anyway."

"You don't?" Did *he?* He'd always taken the story as true in a broad sense, but he hadn't thought on the specifics. He certainly hadn't imagined he'd ever end up in the company of someone with a connection to one of those Great Powers themselves.

"I believe the three Great Powers have some level of control over the elements of this world," said Zelle. "I *don't* believe they're the sole reason for any of humanity's accomplishments."

"I suppose not." From her tone, he sensed that his comment had annoyed her in some way. "The Great

Powers left the world a long time ago, and I'm sure there's more than one way of interpreting their history."

"Especially when certain deities refuse to answer our questions." She gave the staff a scowl. "One would think they would be a little concerned there might be another Great Power walking around this realm and on the side of our enemy at that."

Rien didn't *think* Daimos had the real Invicten—not simply a Relic—at his command, but given that the nameless Shaper had turned out to be imprisoned here in these very mountains, anything might be possible. "I hope that book gives you some direction, then."

"So do I." She tucked it under her arm and began to walk towards the exit. "And yours. Learn anything interesting?"

"Allegedly, Gaiva's children got into a fight because some of them were jealous of *humans*."

"That's well-known, isn't it?" said Zelle. "I mean, it stands to reason that they would see the other living beings Gaiva created as rivals for Her attention. That's what I was taught, anyway."

He certainly hadn't been, but as far as his family was concerned, the only one of Gaiva's children that mattered was Astiva: a benevolent friend to humans and his family's greatest ally. He might have to do some more reassessing if he wanted to uncover the truth of Zierne's history with Astiva and their other siblings.

They returned to the downstairs room, where Grandma Carnelian had fallen into a doze in her armchair. Aurel, meanwhile, had pulled out a pack of Relics and Ruins cards and was sipping a dark liquid from a glass.

"You brought *wine?*" Zelle stared at her sister. "You think now is a good time to get drunk?"

"If we're going to be stuck here, then I'd say yes, it certainly is." Aurel put down her glass on the floor. "Relax, I don't have enough to get drunk on. Speaking of which, we'll have to do a supply run in the morning."

"We have food and water," said Zelle. "We don't need unnecessary luxuries, especially when there are people down in the village who'd happily see us captured or worse."

"True, but we don't have to rely on Tavine any longer." Aurel shuffled the deck of cards. "We have eagles, remember? We can fly anywhere we like."

"Are you forgetting the Changers might spot us from the sky?"

Rien let their argument fade into the background and returned to his spot next to the bookcase to read the new volume he'd collected from the Sanctum.

Gaiva's children's arguments with the humans grew more intense, and finally, one of them lost patience altogether. Zierne, second of Gaiva's children, decided that the only way to win back Gaiva's affection was to get rid of the humans who had infested the world altogether.

He looked up sharply, his heart lurching. The stories couldn't possibly be verifiable, given that they'd taken place before any written records, but would Zierne himself back up the claims that he'd once been jealous enough of humans to want to stamp them out of existence? Unlikely, given that they had no way of direct communication, but the notion of being despised by the being to whom he owed his life made his skin prickle.

He read on, the words blurring as he skimmed the text

as quickly as his comprehension of written Zeutenian would allow. Zierne, it seemed, had developed a number of schemes to drive the humans out of existence but had been thwarted each time by none other than Astiva. The eldest of Gaiva's children had begged his brother to leave the humans alone, but Zierne refused to relent. When tensions had escalated between the siblings, Zierne had extended his threat to Astiva himself, and war had broken out among the gods.

He looked up to see Zelle approaching him. "You look like a gremlin just poked you in the ear. What is it?"

He scanned the room, where Grandma Carnelian continued to sleep in her armchair and Evita and Aurel sat on the rug playing a game of Relics and Ruins. None were paying any attention to him or Zelle, but he hadn't the faintest clue how to begin to tell her that *Zierne had allegedly been jealous enough of humans to declare war on his own siblings. Voicing the book's contents aloud inside the Shaper's domain seemed a bad decision when his allegiance with his deity was shaky enough already.*

"Wars between humans and gods are unpleasant," he evaded. "Have you checked your book yet?"

"Did you know Invicten fathered Gaiva's children?"

"Not until I read this." He held up *Children of Gaiva.* "That explains why those five deities are stronger than the other lesser gods. What else does it say?"

"That Gaiva and Invicten had a huge falling-out and ran to opposite ends of the world to get away from one another."

"Maybe that's how Gaiva ended up in Itzar." He shook his head. "This is all speculation, though, isn't it? Thousands of years have passed since then, and the only certainty is that Daimos has one of Invicten's Relics. We don't even know what he can do with it."

"We can guess," Zelle said. "The deity Himself is shown as a trickster who was fond of leading humans astray. According to the stories, He disguised himself as a human after His argument with Gaiva and seems to have wandered the continent playing practical jokes on anyone unfortunate enough to run into him. Most of those involved creating illusions or unleashing visions for the purposes of sowing confusion and dissent."

"Trickery and illusion seem accurate to me, given that someone convinced the Changers that Gaiva Herself ordered the Sentinels' capture." By 'someone,' he meant Daimos or one of his associates, though there was no telling whether the man himself had ever set foot on the continent at all. Last time, he'd sent Orzen in his stead.

"True," she acknowledged. "I find it hard to believe the Senior Changers were so easily taken in after seeing the real Gaiva's Relic, though I doubt She spoke to them directly."

He inclined his head. "After Orzen, I would have hoped they'd be wiser to their vulnerable position. To find the truth, though, I think we'll have to go and see what's going on in their camp with our own eyes."

From the worried expression on Zelle's face, he knew she'd had the same thought. "Agreed. If they don't show their faces tomorrow, we'll go directly to them."

3

Evita woke early the following morning, feeling cold and bruised. Overnight she'd rolled out of the window seat onto the hard wooden floor, and the fire had burned itself to ashes. A chill breeze swept through the downstairs room of the Sentinels' outpost, and while the window was closed, Zelle had had to climb over her every time she wanted to get rid of an unwanted magical construct that had shown up during the night.

Compared to sleeping on the floor of a cave as she had as a novice Changer, Evita thought the tower was positively luxurious by comparison. Of the two bedrooms, one had been taken by Grandma Carnelian and Aurel and Zelle had briefly tussled over the other. Zelle had insisted that it ought to go to Rien, as a foreign guest, but Rien himself had argued otherwise. In the end, Zelle had been forced to cave in and let Aurel take the spare room, while she and Rien each lay in an armchair under the thick furs they'd bought from Itzar.

All things considered, Evita had slept in worse conditions, even if she did have to deal with the way Zelle and Rien acted around one another when they assumed she wasn't paying attention. If there was one thing worse than being around two people who were madly in love with one another, it was being around a pair who had yet to acknowledge their feelings and consequently turned every interaction into a game of second-guessing. They'd be talking as normal, and then one would make a comment that made the other blush or look away, and Evita would wish that she'd slept outside instead. Despite having no desire to participate in anything similar herself, Evita wished one of them would take the next step and get it over with.

Since both of them were currently sleeping, Evita quietly climbed back into the window seat. When Aurel appeared on the other side of the glass and waved at her, Evita startled and nearly slipped out of the seat again. Sheepishly waving back, she grabbed her shoes and slid her feet into them before hurrying out of the tower and closing the door behind her.

Aurel's auburn hair hung in damp curls, as if she'd recently immersed it in water. "I'm glad one of you is awake. Grandma must have tired herself out yesterday. She's usually up way earlier than this."

Evita scanned the skies for the dragonet and spotted his reptilian shadow chasing the eagles around the mountaintops. "You wanted to go and get supplies from Tavine?"

"Once my grandmother wakes up," Aurel replied. "Trust me, she'll have my head if I sneak off without telling her. Anyway, there's a mountain stream around the back of the tower if you want to have a proper wash. It's not exactly a luxury inn, I know, but it's all we've got."

"Thanks." The journey the day before had left Evita sweaty and dirty, though she'd had more pertinent concerns than taking a bath.

Evita went back into the tower to fetch some clothes from her pack and grabbed her empty water skin before making her way to the stream Aurel had pointed out. She didn't need to worry about anyone watching her, because the area was as remote as possible and the only obvious route to the outpost was a rickety wooden bridge at the foot of the path that sloped downhill from the tower. Not even the Changers would have risked crossing the bridge, and as far as she knew, they were unaware of the hidden tunnels within the mountain that were accessible to the Sentinels. Convenient, and no doubt the reason they'd survived the night without an ambush.

The stream's water was freezing, so Evita washed as quickly as possible before changing into fresh clothes. She then filled the water skin and slaked her thirst, shivering in the cold mountain air and wondering why adventuring always seemed to involve so much discomfort.

Their escape from the Changers had put Evita's decision on her future to the back of her mind too. Aurel had hired Evita as her cleaner and servant prior to her capture at the hands of rebels from Itzar, but it had always been a temporary position to enable her to scrape together some cash after Orzen had left her with nothing of her former home. Aurel had since suggested that Evita might be more suited to making use of her unexpected gambling talent, as she'd demonstrated a lucky streak at the tavern in Itzar while playing cards with the locals, but now her luck had come to a decisive end, and her future was murkier than ever.

That's assuming I survive, added a pessimistic voice in the back of her mind. She'd come close to death too many times to count in recent weeks and getting on the wrong side of the deities was considerably riskier than a simple game of Relics and Ruins.

Now thoroughly wide awake, she returned to the tower, where Aurel waited at the top of the sloping path, watching the eagles chase one another around the cliffs. "They seem to like it here."

Evita studied the swooping birds for a moment. "I thought they were going back to Itzar. Don't they belong to the islanders?"

"I think they're just well trained, like Chirp."

"He's trained, but he's also loyal." She'd saved the dragonet from being devoured by a wyrm during her first—and only—Changer's trial, and Chirp had become attached to her immediately. He'd since returned the favour several times over, and she doubted she'd have had as much success training him as she had if not for that foundation of mutual trust. "Also, we did cause rather a lot of trouble in the islands, so we could do worse than return their eagles."

"That was Zelle's fault, mostly," said Aurel. "She's the one who broke Gaiva's rock into a million pieces."

"She also enabled most of the population of Itzar to access Gaiva's magic. That's probably enough to make up for flooding the Isles and breaking their most treasured possession."

Aurel shot her an amused look. "If you ask me, she ought to unleash the same sort of mayhem in Aestin. It'd solve Rien's problems more efficiently than anything else. And ours, if that elusive Daimos character is there and not here."

"Don't forget the Changers," Evita reminded her. "Do you think they'll be waiting to ambush us at your house?"

"Haven't a clue." Aurel's tone sounded unconcerned, but a hint of wariness tensed her shoulders. "I'd wear that cloak of yours, though."

"Of course I will." Evita's cloak would render her unseen, but risking capture solely for a few trinkets struck her as a bad idea. Not when they also had an opportunity to learn how widely the Changers' influence really stretched. "We should take Chirp too."

"I'll see if my grandmother is awake." Aurel returned to the tower while Evita waved at the reptilian beast to get his attention.

Abandoning the chase, the dragonet flew over and chirped a greeting as he landed in front of her. Chirp had grown dramatically in the two months or so that they'd known one another and was now large enough to comfortably carry two people on his back.

"Want to come with me to the village?"

The dragonet bumped his head against her hand, which she assumed meant "yes." The beast seemed to understand her speech, though the reverse wasn't true, and he seemed as happy to spend time with her as she was glad of his company.

Behind her, the tower door opened, and Grandma Carnelian emerged. One hand rested on a walking stick that she'd taken to carrying as a replacement for the staff that Zelle had claimed for her own, and her wrinkled face reflected disapproval. "Aurel said you want to go to Tavine."

"She wants to get some things from the house," explained Evita. "I can use the cloak to sneak around and see what the Changers are doing or listen in on some conversations between the villagers at the tavern."

"Last I saw, the Changers took over the entire tavern themselves," the old Sentinel growled. "I don't know what they did to poor Marita, but the girl was shaking like a leaf when they left."

"They want Aurel, not me, right?" Evita considered this unwelcome development. "Should I go alone?"

"I'd like to see you talk Aurel out of anything she's set her mind to." Grandma Carnelian tutted. "Stubborn, she is."

I can see where she gets it from. The Sentinel's warning was clear, but Evita herself had no other way to make herself useful. She couldn't read, so helping Rien and Zelle hunt for information on the Powers was beyond her. Her only other skills stemmed from her assassin's training, while she was the only one of their number not in possession of a Relic. *No, the cloak doesn't count,* she told herself. Zelle had claimed otherwise, but the cloak had been on loan from the Changers before she'd decided to keep it for herself, and besides, didn't one need to *choose* to claim a Relic?

"Stop scaring her, Grandma." Aurel's voice drifted through the tower door. "It's not like we're breaking into the Changers' base."

"You could stand to be a little more prepared." The elderly Sentinel addressed her granddaughter. "For instance, it might help you to know that their guard shifts outside the front gates change every four hours, starting at midnight."

"That means the people on duty now will be groggy from lack of sleep." Aurel emerged from the tower with a large pack in one hand. "Though they're Changers, so physical discomfort might not bother them."

"It doesn't," Evita confirmed. "Also, they believe they're serving Gaiva, so they'd happily spend their days shovelling cow dung if they thought the deity wanted them to."

Aurel gave a snort of laughter and stepped aside to allow Evita to enter the tower. Seizing on the chance to get away from the old Sentinel, she walked into the outpost and found that Rien and Zelle were both awake, each studiously not looking at the other. Ignoring the awkward silence that emerged when she entered, Evita returned to the window seat and retrieved her pack.

"You're going now?" Zelle asked. "To the village?"

"We are." Aurel poked her head through the open door. "We'll be back within the hour. Wait at least that long before you send out a search party."

"Don't joke," Zelle insisted, but Aurel had already withdrawn from sight.

Evita hefted her pack over her shoulder and waved goodbye to Zelle and Rien before leaving the tower. Grandma watched, hands folded on top of the walking stick planted in front of her, but she made no move to stop them from approaching the dragonet.

"We can both fly on Chirp," Evita told Aurel. "He can carry two of us quite comfortably now, and we'll be less conspicuous."

Aurel walked up to the reptilian beast. "He knows where to go?"

"Of course." Evita stroked his nose. "We can land in the forest. He'll blend in easier that way."

Evita climbed on the dragonet's back and helped Aurel scramble up to sit behind her, her heart lurching at the already significant drop at the side of the mountain path. When the ground dropped away beneath them, she gripped Chirp's neck until he grumbled at her.

Aurel noticed, leaning forward. "I can look down and help navigate if you like."

Glad to have someone with a head for heights on her team, Evita gave a mute nod, turning her gaze to the overcast sky instead. The clouds didn't make it any easier to figure out if any Changers might be watching her, but they reached the other side of the peaks without being challenged.

After they'd reached the path where the Sentinels' cave lay hidden, they flew lower, over the thick pines surrounding the village until they found a gap in the canopy through which they could descend without causing too much of a disturbance. Helped by Aurel's whispered instructions, Evita directed Chirp to follow one of the forest paths until they reached the back of the village. They'd avoided the front gate where the two Senior Changers had accosted them during their last visit, but she held her breath when the dragonet landed, stirring up a flurry of leaves.

Evita pulled up the hood of her cloak to hide her face, while Aurel used the bushes and undergrowth as cover to approach the village from behind.

"Have you done this before?" Evita whispered to her.

"Of course," replied Aurel. "I lived with Grandma as an apprentice. I've lost count of the number of times I had to sneak into the house after a late night at the tavern when I was a teenager."

And more recently, if what Evita had witnessed in the weeks that she'd spent living in the Reader's house was anything to go by. She had no chance to reply, however, because two Changers came into view near the fence, their silvery cloaks rippling from their shoulders.

Evita held her breath, but the patrol walked past without appearing to notice they weren't alone. When she was certain they'd passed out of hearing distance, she continued towards the back fence near the wide stone house Aurel lived in.

Aurel held out a hand to stop her from walking any farther. "I'll go in alone. You go around the front and see what the Changers are doing."

"Are you sure?" she breathed. "They might come back."

"They won't get past the fence." Aurel's confident tone brought back the rather unpleasant memory of Orzen taunting Evita from the other side of that very same fence. Even he hadn't been able to get inside the Reader's house, though, so Evita reluctantly gave in.

"Be careful."

She left Aurel and followed the path of the two Changers they'd seen earlier. Evita's cloak would enable her to walk through the centre of the village without being seen, in theory, but she took care to tread lightly. On swift feet, she passed rows of stone cottages that comprised most of the village until she came to the spot where the newly constructed fence curved around a corner. At the front gates, the two Changers she'd seen patrolling were conversing with Briony and Verne, a pair of Senior Changers she'd met beforehand. From the glimpse she caught of their faces, both looked rather tired after an early-morning session of watching for trespassers, but as one of the trespassers in question, she had little sympathy for them.

"Nothing?" asked one of the newcomers, whose silvery cloak strained across his broad shoulders.

"No," replied Briony. "Strange. I would have expected them to be too impatient to wait until morning, and they must know it's riskier for them to come in daylight."

"Hasn't stopped that old woman from wandering around," remarked the second newcomer, a woman with bristle-short hair who carried a bow and arrows slung over her shoulder. "You let her slip through your fingers again yesterday, didn't you?"

"She didn't even use magic," grumbled the broad-shouldered man. "She's escaped, what, four times now?"

Grandma Carnelian. She certainly hadn't used magic, given that Zelle held her staff. Evita couldn't hold back a grin at the mental image of the Changers chasing the old woman around the forest without being able to catch her.

"Never mind her." Briony stifled a yawn. "A supply cart is due to arrive today, so we need to make sure nobody sneaks out while the gates are open."

Their conversation turned to mundane matters concerning running the village, though Evita had to remind herself that the Changers weren't *supposed* to be in charge. Tavine received most of its supplies from the larger towns nearby, so if the Changers had taken control of their supply lines, they were effectively holding the entire village hostage for no good reason.

A cloaked female Changer interrupted their chatter by jogging into view and breathlessly halting next to the gates.

"I saw movement in the Reader's house," she announced.

Evita's heart lurched. *Aurel.*

"Are you sure?" Briony sounded unimpressed. "She wouldn't be that foolish, surely."

"Yes, she would," said the male newcomer. "She's a drunk and a spendthrift, from what I've heard. No doubt she couldn't resist picking up some of her pretty dresses to take into hiding with her."

A spasm of rage shook Evita, and she clenched her fists to avoid giving herself away. That his guess was right was beside the point. She cast a wild glance around and spotted the dragonet's scales glinting in the nearby bushes. *I have to warn her.*

"We'll wait outside the door, then," said the female newcomer. "She's bound to come outside eventually for one of her trips to the tavern. I guarantee it."

A second jolt of anger hit her, and Evita began to make her stealthy way towards Chirp's hiding place, sticking to the shadows despite the cloak hiding her from sight. Aurel might be protected while she was inside the house, but she couldn't stay in there forever, and Evita wouldn't put it past the Changers to try any means of trickery to lure her outside.

She halted next to the dragonet's scaly leg and leaned to whisper in his ear. "Get Aurel out of the house. Come back for me later."

Chirp made a displeased noise, but at Evita's insistence, he vanished in a rustle of leaves. Evita remained crouched in the shadows, holding her breath, tensed for the sound of flight.

Instead, a hand seized her cloak and dragged her out of the bushes.

4

Zelle yawned, dunking her hair underneath the waterfall fuelling the mountain stream in an attempt to wake herself up. She'd stayed up late reading the book she'd removed from the Sanctum by the light of the fire, and the intermittent disturbances from gremlins and other magical constructs had made it hard to settle down to sleep. In the armchair next to hers, Rien had been perusing his own book, his gaze roving the page with intentness and an occasional furrow of the brow, as if the text displeased him. Zelle might have asked for the details, but she hadn't wanted to wake the others. Now Aurel and Evita had left, though, she found herself putting off the moment when she had to be alone with him again.

After pulling on a clean tunic and a pair of trousers and shrugging into her fur-lined coat, she retrieved the staff from where she'd propped it up against a nearby rock and circled the tower to the front door.

The staff itself had maintained a frosty silence whenever she asked any questions pertaining to whether the

Shaper would be willing to talk to her today. Taciturn though the staff might be, Zelle hadn't expected the Shaper to shut her out altogether when she'd asked for the details of Her history with Invicten. One would think that the threat of another Great Power would be enough to prompt a helpful response, but the Shaper had left her to read between the lines of a book instead.

Outside the tower, Grandma paced up and down, looking askance at the spot where the dragonet had taken off with his two passengers.

"They'll be fine," Zelle told her grandmother. "If they run into trouble, the dragonet will be able to help them escape."

"Exactly." Rien walked into view. He must have found another river to wash in, judging by his dripping wet hair and clean shirt. Even dressed in travelling garb as opposed to the attire of an Aestinian noble, he retained the air of someone who was used to always presenting an impeccable front.

"What are you going to do with yourselves while those two are on their ill-advised trip, then?" asked Grandma. "Did you find anything useful in those books of yours?"

"Not exactly," Zelle admitted. "Rien, did you?"

He was silent for a moment as though mulling over his words. "I found little information relevant to the present, but that was to be expected given the age of the texts in the Sanctum."

"I'm sorry our resources aren't up-to-date enough for you, Arien Astera."

"Grandma!" said Zelle. "Our resources *are* several hundred years out of date. When was the last time anyone brought any new texts to add to the Sanctum?"

"At least a century ago, and that hardly matters." Grandma dismissed her words. "The books won't help you. They're just words."

"The Shaper's magic is rooted in words," Zelle reminded her. "I thought you knew that."

For once, we are in agreement, commented the staff. *I would not underestimate words, Sentinel.*

Grandma's gaze sharpened, indicating that she'd heard the staff speak too. It shouldn't have surprised Zelle that Grandma had no faith in the Sanctum to give them anything of use—she might be the current active Sentinel, but she had no interest in the theoretical parts of the role and had always preferred roaming the mountain paths to poring over old texts. Even Zelle, despite her childhood fascination with the Sanctum's ancient tomes, had never considered this place to be the main source of her family's power.

Not until she'd learned what—or who—lay imprisoned inside the mountains.

"I am sorry if I offended you, Sentinel." Rien spoke up before Grandma could snap at Zelle as well. "The fact is, I was rather hoping not to have to travel back to Aestin to find any documentation of how Zierne's Relic came to be in Zeuten."

Zelle could understand his frustration. If her own readings had taught her anything, it was that there was a gaping hole between the era when the deities had interacted with mortals and the current era in which all that remained of them were the Relics they'd left behind. No documentation gave any specifics of what event connected the two, and until she managed to pry the truth out of the Shaper, she could only guess at how they'd become estranged.

"What about the deity of illusions, then?" She directed her question at Grandma. "*His* Relics weren't brought here at any point, right?"

"The Relics of Invicten haven't been seen in over a thousand years," the Sentinel replied. "The same as the other Great Powers, except for Gaiva. As well you know."

"We thought *our* Relics came from Gaiva," Zelle reminded her. "Instead, they turned out to belong to the nameless Shaper. The texts don't reveal everything, do they?"

"That was what I was trying to tell you," Grandma growled. "Words can lie."

Turning her back on them, she stomped into the tower. Zelle and Rien exchanged bewildered looks and then followed her through the door.

Scooping up *Tales of the Three* from the armchair where she'd left it, Zelle flipped open the book. "The stories in here might have no meaning except in a metaphorical sense, but I assume the Shaper wanted me to read this version of the falling-out between the three Great Powers for a reason. I just wish She'd tell me what it is instead of being oblique."

"Maybe talking it through aloud will help you puzzle it out," Rien offered. "It can't hurt."

"Skipping over the part about the creation of the world…" Zelle sat down in the armchair and turned the pages. "The text says that humanity was the actual cause of the schism between the three Great Powers. Humans were Gaiva's creation, and Invicten grew jealous of them for stealing Gaiva's attention."

"Really?" Rien's brows rose. "That's not so different than what it says in *Children of Gaiva*... except it says Gaiva's children were the ones who grew jealous of humanity, without mentioning Invicten."

"Don't interrupt," Grandma reprimanded him. "You can make comparisons later."

Zelle hadn't known her grandmother was paying any attention, but she continued. "Allegedly, Invicten finally grew jealous enough of humans to use His divine influence to cast a spell on them. The power of illusions warped their minds into seeing one another as enemies and dividing into factions from where they'd once lived in harmony. When those new hostilities erupted into wars, Gaiva was devastated. She sent Her children to convince the humans to make peace with one another, but they were unsuccessful. After that, She did not involve Herself with humans again."

Rien picked up his own faded leather textbook. "There are similarities with the stories in here, except that instead of Invicten, it was supposedly *Zierne* who grew jealous of humans and started warring with them, forcing his own siblings to take up arms against him."

"Zierne?" Was that what had been bothering him the previous day? Accurate or not, learning that one's deity might have waged war against humanity was bound to be a shock. "My book doesn't mention him. It just says that Gaiva's children took sides among the various groups of humans and got involved in the wars that eventually resulted in the gods departing the world..."

"Does it give any details on the last part?" he asked. "The wars?"

"No," she said. "The book is mostly about the Great

Powers, and that's where their involvement with humans ended. There's no mention of the Shaper being imprisoned by the other Great Powers, nor whereabouts Gaiva or Invicten went afterwards. The Great Powers alone know the truth."

A pointed look at the staff yielded no response.

"Did your stories say that Invicten *created* illusions to turn the humans against one another?" Rien asked. "That sounds like the spell currently afflicting the Changers."

"I thought so too," she said. "I hope Evita and Aurel manage to find out what's going on down there."

Maybe the Changers had been inclined to fall for the ruse because of their prevailing belief that Gaiva had initially given them their powers, but she had to wonder where *those* stories had started. *Tales of the Three* contained no mention of Zeuten at all, let alone which Great Powers might have once roamed the continent. While Zelle herself didn't believe the tales of the deities were true in a literal sense, the Shaper was certainly here, and not being accurate to real history didn't mean the stories held no truth.

"Exactly," agreed Rien. "The Changers don't know they're being manipulated or coerced, as they did when Orzen was pressuring them into serving him. They believe wholeheartedly in their quest."

"Because they think they're serving the Crown. Fulfilling their duty. There must be a way to convince them otherwise." Zelle racked her brain for her admittedly rusty knowledge of Zeuten's policies on foreign magic users. "When they tried to have Rien targeted for being an illegal Invoker, they were going by the same policy that says that anyone who brings a hostile Relic into the country is as good as declaring war on Zeuten itself."

Grandma gave a snort. "You'll have a job and a half proving that to anyone, given that Daimos most likely isn't even here."

Zelle scowled at her. "Thanks for the support. If Evita and Aurel find out how deep his influence runs, it'll be a starting point, but if Daimos *is* here, then we have bigger problems than the Changers."

You don't say was the staff's contribution.

"You're being quiet." Zelle faced the staff. "Considering you *witnessed* some of this history for yourself, one would think you'd have a comment to offer."

I did not.

"You didn't witness it?" She frowned. "You and the Shaper are the same, right? Don't you have the same memories?" She'd assumed that must be the case, though she'd never asked directly. The Shaper might be split into three pieces—or four, if you counted the Book of Reading—but Zelle had thought they shared a mind, at the very least.

The staff, however, didn't answer.

"What's the staff saying?" asked Rien.

"It's giving excuses as to why it can't tell me anything." Zelle's eyes narrowed at the staff's knotted wooden surface. "Who created the staff, anyway?"

Not the first Sentinels, who hadn't even known the nameless Shaper's magic existed within the staff when they'd picked it up. At some point, though, someone must have had direct contact *with* the Shaper to detach some of Her magic to put into a Relic.

I already answered that question.

The sound of rustling came from behind her, and she spotted a gremlin creeping up on their packs, no doubt looking for mischief. Marching over to it, she swung the staff with rather more force than necessary, and the gremlin deflated like a squashed frog.

While she one-handedly opened the window, the staff whispered in her ear. *There are books detailing how to create a Relic in the Sanctum, if you truly want to know the specifics. I have not prevented you from accessing that knowledge.*

"Oh, but telling me yourself is too much hassle?" Zelle threw the gremlin outside and slammed the window shut before turning back to Rien.

He raised a brow as if confused by her outburst. "If you're talking about creating Relics, I can give you some details on the process, but I can't speak to the differences between creating one from the magic of a Great Power rather than a regular deity."

"Right." Zelle lowered the staff, mildly embarrassed. It wasn't Rien she was angry at, so she calmed her tone. "I doubt the Great Powers are mentioned in the official documents detailing Zeuten's policies on foreign Invokers, either, but there must be a way to convince the authorities that the Changers were mistaken in thinking Gaiva was giving them orders."

"I seem to remember the last time you tried negotiating with the Changers, two of your number ended up being kidnapped," Grandma commented.

Zelle's jaw tensed. "Last time, we didn't know what was going on until it was too late. This time, we know exactly who's behind this, and while the Changers themselves are oblivious, there's someone else we can tell."

"And who is that, exactly?"

"The Crown Prince, of course." When Grandma laughed, she pressed on. "The royals are supposed to command the Changers. Officially, anyway. They're also allied to the Sentinels. If we tell them the Changers are under a hostile spell, they might be able to intervene."

"There's merit to going through the official channels," acknowledged Rien. "I didn't do the same when I returned to Aestin because I wanted to avoid drawing unnecessary attention, but perhaps I should have."

"You mean the Emperor?"

From what Rien had told her of his brief trip back to Aestin, he'd kept his presence quiet, simply paying his respects to his family and settling their affairs before returning to Zeuten. He'd come here in search of Daimos, in fact, but now they'd established that his enemy wasn't present in Zeuten, he could theoretically leave at any moment. Yet he hadn't. Zelle didn't know if Rien was simply trying to make up for betraying her trust once beforehand or truly did believe he could make more progress towards taking down Daimos from staying in Zeuten, but she was glad he was here.

Rien inclined his head. "I thought about speaking to him, but at the time, I didn't know if Daimos was still in the country or not."

"If you'd alerted the Emperor, you'd have painted another target on your head," Grandma added. "The same will result if you visit Saudenne. Mark my words."

The beating of wings outside interrupted Zelle's reply. Aurel and Evita were back. Good timing, because Zelle wanted an outside opinion on her plan from someone who wasn't biased. Meaning Evita, not Aurel, since the latter would likely be as amused as her grandmother about Zelle's suggestion that they'd get anything resembling help from the royal family of Zeuten.

When the door opened, however, Aurel hurried in alone. Breathless, she slammed the door behind her. "They caught Evita. The Changers did."

"They did?" Zelle's heart sank. "How?"

"They spotted me in the house," she mumbled. "The dragonet helped me escape, but Evita must have sent him to rescue me instead of her. Powers above, this is my blasted fault."

"Yes, it is," Grandma agreed. "I warned you."

"Grandma," Zelle warned. "You were lucky not to get caught yourself yesterday."

"I at least picked an inconspicuous manner in which to approach the village."

"The Changers can fly, so there's no way to entirely avoid them," Zelle pointed out. "Besides, they were watching from the ground as well as the skies."

"I suppose at least it was the assassin they caught and not you, Aurel," said Grandma. "They won't harm her, since she used to be one of them."

"You don't know that," Aurel insisted. "What's got you all riled up, anyway?"

"Grandma has decided our winning strategy is to hide in the tower until the country tears itself apart," Zelle told her sister. "I suggested we send warning to the Crown and tell them their Changers have been compromised for a second time."

A calculating expression crossed Aurel's face. "Maybe this will inspire the Crown Prince to get off his royal arse and help out."

"That's what I thought." Relief at Aurel's acknowledgement bolstered Zelle's resolve. "Isn't it worth getting in contact with someone who might be able to lift the Changers' control over Tavine without any bloodshed?"

"Agreed." Rien took a decisive step towards the door. "I imagine it's common practise to send a letter announcing our visit in advance, but we can't risk the Changers intercepting the message."

"Exactly." Zelle ignored her grandmother's derisive laughter in the background. "If we take the eagles, we'll be able to get back and forth from the capital in a comparatively short time anyway."

Aurel eyed her. "Didn't you just tell me the Changers were watching the skies?"

"They are, but that won't change if we wait," said Rien. "I agree with Zelle. The sooner we warn the Changers' commanders the better."

Heartened by his support, she turned to her grandmother. "We'll be back within a day, one way or another."

For now? It was time for her to take Rien to meet the royal family of Zeuten.

5

Gaiva's tits, I'm in trouble, thought Evita.

The Senior Changers hauled her up the narrow wooden stairway to the upper floor of the tavern, which Briony and Verne had picked out for their interrogations. Poor Marita, who owned the tavern, hadn't been able to do a thing to prevent them from marching in and taking over, and no doubt wasn't being compensated nearly enough for her trouble. She was far outnumbered, though, with two Changers standing guard on the other side of the door while Briony and Verne accompanied her inside the room.

"That beast of yours is quite the remarkable creature, isn't it?" Briony sat opposite her on the hard wooden floor with no apparent care for the discomfort. "How did you tame it?"

Evita said nothing. Maybe they wanted to know if Chirp intended to come and rescue her, which he might, but she'd have to get out of this room before she could find him.

"Answer the question." Verne sat down on a blocky chair that looked as uncomfortable as the floor but still gave him a height advantage over Evita. "Or else we'll have to be less accommodating. We generously offered you a chance to join our ranks, and instead you chose to use the skills we taught you as a Changer to commit crimes against the nation."

"It's not a crime for the Reader to go into her own house, and I'm her assistant." She had an inkling that wasn't what he meant by *crimes against the nation,* but if she stalled him by feigning ignorance, she might win an opportunity to escape. "As for how I tamed the dragonet, he saved my life, and we trust one another. That's all there is to it."

Maybe it was a mistake to share that information, but she had far more important secrets inside her head than her bond with Chirp.

Verne's thick brows drew together. "Had you stayed in Zeuten, you might believe differently. Gaiva Herself has honoured the Changers with Her blessing."

Briony dipped her head. "She gave us orders, and we will honour Her word."

Evita had had quite enough of this nonsense. "You went to Itzar yourself, didn't you? Did you pay a visit to the Blessed?"

"We are asking you questions," said Briony. "Not the other way round."

"If you *did* see the Blessed, then you'll have seen Gaiva's Relic," Evita went on. "Gaiva serves the people of Itzar. She never came here. You're being played by another deity."

Indignation rippled across Verne's features. "You know nothing of our bond with Gaiva."

"What did you actually see?" Evita pressed. "How do you know for sure that She is the one giving the orders? It's not the first time a deity has deceived someone into thinking they were someone else entirely. I've seen it myself, with Orzen. How can you have fallen for the same trick twice?"

"Enough." Verne climbed to his feet. "I will not be mocked by someone who betrayed both the Changers and her country at the same time."

"She has not seen what we have." Briony's gaze flickered with something that resembled pity. "She doesn't understand."

"Believe me, I do." Unfortunately, Invicten's magic must have conjured up a convincing illusion to have fooled the entirety of the Changers' ranks. "If you can show me proof, I'll gladly change my mind."

Briony's mouth pressed together. "Master Drazer is a busy man, but he might be willing to discuss the matter with you at the base."

Who is Master Drazer? Was he human or deity? Last time, Daimos had sent Orzen to give orders to the Masters, but this time he wasn't using fear and desperation to influence them, and the Changers' unshakeable devotion to a deity to whom they'd already owed allegiance might prove trickier to undo.

"She *is* mocking us," Verne snapped. "Don't forget she already turned down our offer of a promotion before she flew away with the Reader to visit those primitive islanders."

"I went to *rescue* the Reader," Evita corrected. "Also, the people of Itzar are allies of Gaiva, and they aren't using Her magic to hassle innocent villagers and try to kidnap the Sentinels."

"How dare you?" Briony rose to her feet to join Verne. "We were kind enough to extend the hand of friendship to both the Sentinel and her granddaughter, both of whom rudely refused our offer and attacked us."

"That's not what it looked like to me." Evita looked stonily up at the pair. "You ambushed us without warning and prevented the Reader from going into her own house."

Granted, Chirp had taken a few swipes at the Changers during their escape, but they hadn't been undeserved. Perhaps reasoning with these people had been futile from the start.

"I see you're determined to believe your own stories." The flicker of pity came into Briony's eyes again. "You'll see when you visit Master Drazer that your assumptions are mistaken."

A spasm of fear shot down her spine. Abruptly, she had the intense desire *not* to set eyes on this Master Drazer person, whoever he was. Orzen had slaughtered the former Masters, after all, and if they'd hired someone worse in his place, she wanted no part in it.

"You work for the Crown, don't you?" Evita groped in her mind for anything that might make them reconsider their unquestioning belief in Daimos's lies. "Did the Crown Prince tell you to do this? Or are you ignoring his orders?"

"Not at all," said Verne. "It was the Crown Prince who

sent Master Drazer to bring us Gaiva's message to begin with."

Evita's mouth fell open. "He did?"

She hoped they were mistaken, because if the people ruling over the entire country believed that Gaiva Herself had come to give them orders, then they were in far worse trouble than she'd suspected.

I have to get out. She couldn't let them hold her hostage here when the others were unaware of the extent of the danger Zeuten might truly be in. She might not have any weapons, but the Senior Changers hadn't tied her up or restrained her... and neither had they taken her cloak.

"Yes." Briony's expression reflected pious righteousness. "You must see that the sensible and right choice for you to make is to hand your friend and her grandmother over to us."

"Hand them over?" she echoed. "I don't *own* them. Besides, I thought you wanted to form an alliance with them, not take them prisoner."

Verne's eyes narrowed. "They have to answer for their violence towards us."

"And then?" Evita projected her best attempt at an impression of innocent inquisitiveness. "What do you plan to do when you have them?"

"That is for the Crown Prince to decide, as is right for enemies of the country," Verne told her.

Evita sat back, her heart swooping downward. *Enemies of the country.* Like her. Except they'd dragged her up here to give her this speech anyway, in the hopes that she'd surrender her allies.

As for how they expected her to do that? An idea occurred to her, and Evita rose to her feet.

"I'll see what I can do."

"Excuse me?" Briony's shoulders tensed. "Where are you going?"

Evita flashed her a bright smile. "To ask the Sentinel to accompany me to visit the Changers, of course."

Plainly, their plan had been to "fetch" the Sentinel themselves, but she had the advantage of having surprised them. On swift feet, she made for the door and shouldered it open. A muffled yelp on the other side told her she'd hit one of the guards from behind.

"I'm terribly sorry," she said blandly. "Got to go— urgent mission."

And with that, she clattered downstairs, yanking up her hood to hide her face before emerging into the lower room.

"Behind here, quick." The tavern owner beckoned Evita to join her behind the counter. Her momentary surprise faded in an instant; despite being hidden from sight, she'd made enough noise to rouse a sleeping cow from the other side of a field, and it was no surprise that Marita had noticed her presence.

Evita ducked behind the counter, while Marita tutted at the sound of thundering footsteps overhead. As usual, the tavern owner wore her grey hair tied back, while her face appeared more lined than it had when Evita had last seen her. Motioning to Evita to stay hidden, she crossed the tavern and opened the front door just as the Senior Changers and the guards came running downstairs.

Marita let the door close behind her and faced the guards, one brow raised. "What is it?"

Briony stalked across the tavern, her footsteps echoing on the wooden floor. "Where is she?"

"Who?" asked Marita. "I haven't seen anyone."

"Don't play the fool," Briony growled. "You must have *heard* her, at least."

"I heard someone, yes." Marita's matter-of-fact tone gave nothing away. "Whoever it was, they went straight outside."

"Then step aside," ordered Verne.

He and the other guards barrelled past her and through the tavern door. Evita waited until the last one had departed before raising her head. "They're gone?"

"Yes, and you're in trouble, aren't you?" Marita returned to her side.

"We all are," Evita whispered. "How could they take over the entire village?"

"Gaiva's will, allegedly," said Marita. "There's no arguing with the mother goddess Herself."

"It's not Gaiva," Evita said. "Another deity tricked them using an illusion. How many Changers are here?"

"Including the ones patrolling the village?" Her forehead scrunched up. "No more than twenty of them. They seem to switch places a lot."

"Have you heard the name 'Master Drazer'?"

Marita blinked. "Might have. Who's that?"

"The person who's giving orders, I think. Not sure if he's human or not."

"Merciful Powers," Marita murmured. "I knew something wasn't right with those Changers even during their first visit here."

Was the illusion already at work? Evita's first encounter with Briony and Verne had been after they'd returned from a visit to Itzar to try to recruit her back into the fold, a decision that had never made much sense to her. Regardless, the current situation took precedence over their baffling behaviour in the past. "I'll do what I can to help."

"You can start by not getting caught," said Marita. "Are you sure you want to go out there alone?"

"I'll manage. Thank you for the help."

"Think nothing of it."

Grateful for the tavern owner's swift thinking in covering for her, Evita nudged the door open. A group of Changers clustered around the gate, to no surprise, so she headed for the fence to find a spot to climb over. More Changers patrolled the forest in pairs, as if on the lookout for her. *Gaiva's tits, they're everywhere.*

Without Chirp, she could theoretically use her cloak itself to fly, but she'd managed it only in moments of peril, not on command. Didn't this count as peril, though?

When the Changers' voices spiked in volume, she drew in a steadying breath and extended her arms to spread the cloak out to either side of her—and tried not to think about the likelihood of crashing into the canopy and alerting the entire village. *Help me fly. Please. Get me out of here.*

A breeze lifted her hair and the cloak along with her, which billowed out like wings as she glided into the air. The stone houses of the village shrank below her, and while her stomach turned at the drop, a deep sense of relief settled over her at the thought of leaving the Changers behind.

She had a momentary understanding of why the dragonet loved to fly for a brief instant before she hit the canopy and flipped over in midair, nearly falling out of her cloak in the process. Righting herself, she half climbed through the upper branches until she glimpsed the mountain path climbing up to the Sentinels' cave. Walking would take too long, so she'd have to take flight again and hope the Changers weren't patrolling the skies as well.

Her heart stuttered as she freed herself from the trees, but the cloak kept her buoyant. Taking in quick breaths, she turned her gaze towards the paths snaking through the mountains, scanning them for the crooked tower that formed the Sentinels' outpost.

Instead, she saw a net splayed above the canopy, and two figures caught within it like flies in a spiderweb.

Evita nearly fell out of the air. They were *Changers and ones she recognised.* Vekka and Izaura lay sprawled, arrows protruding from their backs and shoulders. Catching her balance, Evita flew closer to them, crouching awkwardly on a nearby branch. Izaura didn't stir, her eyes open but sightless, while Vekka lay on his front.

"Vekka," she hissed. "Vekka. Are you alive?"

He groaned into the net. "No. Go away."

"That's nice." She grimaced when he coughed, blood spraying the already crimson-soaked net. "Who did this to you?"

"We… disobeyed the Master."

Her mouth went dry. "Which Master?"

"*The* Master." He broke off in another coughing fit that shook the trees beneath him and put him in danger of falling. If his wounds didn't kill him first, that was.

"Not… Master Drazer?"

He flinched, prompting another tremor in the treetops. Evita caught her balance and swallowed hard. "Can I help?"

"Why would you want to do that?" More coughing followed.

"Because I used to be one of you." That wasn't it, though. The Changers could eat rocks as far as she was concerned, and Vekka had been worse than most... and yet. "Because even you don't deserve this."

"You're... a fool." His next coughing fit ended in a rattling noise that faded to silence.

Evita reeled, the branch creaking alarmingly beneath her feet. Vekka was dead, and if she stayed here, she might end up joining him.

She held out her arms and let the cloak carry her away, too stricken by the horrible sight to pay attention to the sheer drop. Instinct took over, or perhaps the cloak, and before she knew it, she'd crossed to the other side of the peaks and touched down beside the stone tower. Landing on shaky feet, she lifted the hood of her cloak and vomited over the cliff's edge.

Who was Master Drazer? Why did he kill his own novices in such an awful manner?

"By the Powers!" Aurel exclaimed from behind her. "I was all ready to stage a rescue mission."

"I told you that wasn't necessary." Grandma Carnelian's voice drifted in. "She found her way back, as I thought."

Evita wiped her mouth and turned around. "Where's Zelle?"

"She already left," Aurel answered. "So did Rien."

"Where?" A rush of foreboding hit her.

"Saudenne, of course," Aurel said. "To visit the Crown

Prince and warn him that the Changers are answering to the wrong deity."

She drew in a breath. "The Crown Prince? The Changers told me *he* was the one who sent their new Master with this so-called message from Gaiva."

Aurel groaned. "Oh, Powers."

6

Rien rode side by side with Zelle, each of them sitting on the feathery back of one of the majestic eagles they'd brought from Itzar. It was a somewhat conspicuous way to travel, but with the Changers watching the land as well as the sky, the risks were lower than hiring a carriage.

As a bonus, they covered ground much faster. Within minutes, the mountains shrank behind them, and the rest of Zeuten spread out beneath their eagles' wings. The quickest route would be to follow the spine of the Range, which was bordered by thick forests on either side, but that would take them directly over the Changers' base on the mountain closest to Saudenne.

Instead, they veered over the eastern forest until it gave way to a patchwork of fields and farms with towns and villages scattered throughout. Not too different from rural areas in Aestin, although he'd never viewed his home country from this high up. Zeuten's cities were primarily located on the eastern and southern coasts, while the western side of the country was more sparsely populated. He couldn't see Cathan from this angle, the small fishing town that they'd passed through on their way to the Isles of Itzar, but the entire northern part of Zeuten was an uninhabited mass of snowy peaks.

Zelle noticed him admiring the view and flew her eagle closer to his. "Zeuten has its charms, doesn't it? From up here, one can almost forget the utter madness down on the ground."

He had to agree. "I can see why the Changers spend so much time in the air."

Zelle's gaze went to the line of mountains on their right-hand side. "I doubt they expect us to go to the capital, but they're too close for my liking."

"There's nowhere to avoid them entirely, except possibly there." Rien gestured over his shoulder towards the northern part of the Range. "Might there be more Relics hidden up there, do you think?"

"If there are, you'd freeze to death trying to find them," Zelle said wryly. "Especially dressed as you are."

True. He'd worn his Aestinian garb—a peacock-blue cloak with gold buttons and navy buckled boots—to give the Crown Prince as good an impression of his nation as possible. Zelle had fewer options, with most of her clothes either at her shop in Saudenne or the Reader's house, so she'd worn a plain navy-blue dress with her hair in loose curls. The result was that she was notably shivering, and he wished he'd had the presence of mind to pick up a spare coat to loan her.

"The people of Itzar might be well-equipped to survive up there," he remarked. "Considering they swim in icy water for fun."

"That sea monster we saw near Itzar is nothing compared to the kind of beasts that are said to lurk in the northern parts of the Range," Zelle told him. "There's a reason the settlers took one glance at the mountains and set up camp in the foothills instead."

"Has nobody ever ventured north at all?" he asked curiously.

"Occasionally the frozen corpse of a tourist shows up in a river." Zelle grimaced. "The lands are touched by magic. More than the rest of the Range, if you can believe it."

"We have places like that in Aestin, too, but usually the damage was inflicted by humans."

The lands to the south of Aestin, for instance, were uninhabited as a result of past magical wars that had left large swathes of destruction carved into the earth. Locals sometimes called them the Scarred Lands, and Daimos had risked certain death when he'd ventured there—though it had undoubtedly paid off for him when he'd obtained Orzen's Relic. It wasn't impossible that he'd found a Relic of Invicten in similar circumstances.

Zelle exhaled. "As opposed to the nameless Shaper, I know."

He turned his gaze forward, to Zeuten's countryside unfolding below. From this angle, the towns and patches of trees resembled a child's toys that one might pick up and rearrange at will... which brought the image to mind of the nameless Shaper raising the continents from the sea.

Whatever Zelle might believe, recent events had only strengthened Rien's conviction that the deities' true powers were beyond their comprehension. The notion of them as agents of creation didn't seem implausible, given the brief glimpses they'd had of Gaiva's power in the Isles of Itzar and the way the Shaper's magic had manifested both independently and through Zelle's own hands.

He understood why she didn't want to believe herself to be a pawn of the deities. Rien himself had always prided himself on control over his own Relic and had always attributed any evils committed using magic to the Relics' wielders and not the Powers themselves. After all, the deities had handed mankind their own destinies when they'd departed this world—yet he couldn't deny that he'd seen proof with his own eyes that the deities did possess a will of their own, independent of how their Relics might be wielded.

A warning flash of crimson from the staff in his hand jarred his attention back to the present, and an arrow whipped past his face, grazing his ear. The sharp edge drew blood, and he shouted Zelle's name.

Changers.

Worse, the arrows were spelled, designed to find their targets, and the one that had grazed him reversed its path in mid-flight. Rien urged the eagle to slow down so that he could take aim, and a thorny vine shot from the end of his staff, latched onto the arrow, and squeezed tightly enough to snap it in two.

He twisted around in his seat, seeing no signs of their pursuers, but Zelle flew lower as a second arrow skimmed her shoulder. "Want to land?"

"No." He directed the vines to catch the arrow and break it clean in half. If they landed in Saudenne now, it was a safe bet that their pursuers would follow, and they'd be harder to track from the ground. "We need to draw them out first."

"Agreed." Zelle lifted her own staff, which lit up with blue light, but the Shaper's magic had a limited effect in the sky, and their enemies remained hidden underneath their cloaks.

Rien raised his staff. Thorny vines wrapped around the hilt at his command before lashing outward, but they struck nothing but empty air. He scanned the nearby clouds for any signs of movement, veering in the direction the arrows had come from. A flicker of light gave their pursuers away, where the sun glanced off the shimmering grey of their cloaks. *There they are.*

This time, the thorns hit their target. Blood sprayed into the air, and a choked cry sounded, followed by the sound of a body falling out of the sky. Zelle flew to his side, wielding her staff, but Rien's attack had already found the second assassin. A second cry echoed, a flicker of a panicked face appeared where the vines lifted the Changer's cloak—and then he tumbled out of sight.

The thorny vines withdrew into Rien's staff. "We'd better go before they send backup."

A momentary pang of guilt hit him—the Changers hadn't known they were being deceived by a false god, after all—but he refused to regret taking the lives of two people who would have happily done the same to him.

As they turned their path back towards the city, Zelle leaned closer to him and spoke in a hoarse voice. "We'll fly along the east coast. They won't dare shoot at us over the highest populated region of the country. We can fly over the sea, even, unless you'd prefer not to."

He blinked in surprise at her comment. While it was

true that he'd had several unpleasant near-drowning experiences in recent weeks, he knew that following the sea was the easiest way for them to lose any potential remaining pursuers. "Agreed. We can follow the coast, and if either of us sees anything suspicious, we'll fly inland at once."

"All right."

They continued southeast, passing over the eastern spear of the continent before veering along the long stretch of coastline to the capital. While this route extended their journey, the glittering ocean appeared undisturbed, with no signs that Daimos or one of his deities had caused another disturbance at sea.

Hoping it was a good sign, he urged the eagle to fly lower as they neared Saudenne. The capital of Zeuten was built upon a slope in the foothills of the Range, and the palace sat at the topmost point. Unfortunately, that meant their destination was also directly below the mountain that held the Changers' base.

Zelle leaned over the eagle, assessing the maze of rooftops fast approaching. "We can land near the eastern entrance. It's a bit of a walk, but that's better than drawing unwelcome attention."

"Good idea." He directed his eagle to follow Zelle's over the wide villas of what must be Zeuten's upper-class district. "Should I bow when I meet the Crown Prince, or do you do something different here?"

"Bowing will do," she replied. "You're a foreigner, so they won't expect you to know everything, though I'm guessing our manners are a lot less complicated than your own."

"I'll teach you when you come to visit." He'd spoken

without thinking—she was unlikely to be visiting Aestin as a tourist at any time soon, after all—and her mouth parted in surprise.

"My grandmother taught me a little," she said, "but I can't say I ever thought I might end up needing those lessons."

After landing on a gently sloping hill on the outskirts of Saudenne, they climbed down from their eagles and left them near the river that flowed underneath the bridge marking the eastern edge of the city.

Zelle drew in a steadying breath. "That's our way in. I should have landed somewhere with less mud, though."

Their clothes were rumpled from the flight, too, but the state of their attire was the least of the concerns that might arise from their arrival at the royal palace.

"I'm sure that mentioning a potential threat to the stability of the nation is bound to take their minds off a little mud," he told her. "Not that I've ever faced that dilemma before."

She managed a strained smile. "I suppose there's a first time for everything."

Upon reaching the wide stone bridge, they approached the iron gates marking the city's eastern entrance. A row of supply carts had halted in front of a pair of guards who were clad in uniforms with odd round hats, but plenty of foot traffic crossed the bridge without being stopped.

"It's the entrance to the royal district itself where we might have difficulty," Zelle told him in an undertone as they reached the other side of the gates. "Specifically me. Your clothes are more suited to meeting with royalty than mine."

He looked her over, finding his gaze inadvertently

drifting to her bare shoulders. "You look fine to me. Better than fine."

A flush spread across her nose, and she ducked her head. "They'll know I'm not from among the nobility, but this is the best outfit I have, so I have to hope my grandmother's name will do the rest."

Assuming the Changers haven't already been here and spread their lies. He shoved the thought aside, fervently hoping it was simple paranoia, and instead let himself imagine how Zelle would react to visiting his own capital city. She'd be intimidated, no doubt. Zelle plainly didn't feel comfortable among the upper class, but neither could he picture her fitting in among farmers or craftspeople either. The nature of the Sentinels was that they didn't quite belong, a notion he now understood far better than he would have in his former life.

The streets sloped upward the closer they grew to their destination and widened to accommodate carriages that could seat up to four people. Whenever one passed by, they had to step aside to avoid being sprayed by muddy water.

When they reached a second, smaller gate, Zelle halted at the sight of more red-and-black-clad guards. "Let's hope His Highness is in the mood for visitors."

As she approached, the nearest guard's gaze fell on her staff. "You're the Sentinel?"

"Ah—she's my grandmother," Zelle explained. "I'm here on her behalf. I also have a traveller with me from Aestin, the new head of the Astera family. Arien Astera wishes to come with me to speak to the Crown Prince, too, on matters concerning the safety of both our nations."

Upon recognising Rien's name, the man took a notable step back. "I cannot promise His Highness will be ready to meet you right away, but I will be sure to let him know."

He exchanged whispers with his fellow guard before flagging down a nearby carriage with crimson curtains masking the windows. To Zelle's evident surprise, the driver beckoned to them to climb into the carriage.

Zelle climbed in first, and as Rien settled down next to her on the plush seat, she spoke in a low voice. "I'm not sure how this will work, to be honest. The Crown Prince might want to speak to both of us together, but he's equally likely to ask to talk to me alone. It depends on his knowledge of the situation in Aestin and whether he believes that there's a threat from that direction."

Did that mean he might think *Rien* was a threat from Aestin? "I should wait outside."

"No, I think we should both be there," she said. "He knows who you are, after all. If anything, you're more likely to be believed than I am, considering your family status is far more respected than mine."

Her tone was more matter-of-fact than jealous or bitter. That was Zelle's practical streak showing, and while he knew she was out of her depth in this situation, he had little doubt that she'd do her best to explain their plight.

As for him? When the carriage rattled through the gates, the crimson curtains waving in the windows, he couldn't shake the sense of entering a cage.

———

The carriage rattled uphill, while Zelle positioned the staff between her knees to prevent it from tipping over sideways. Part of her wondered if it was the presence of the staff that had convinced the guards to agree to her request, but they couldn't possibly know of its true nature. The staff had been inside the palace before, for certain, yet it maintained a silence that did nothing to ease her apprehension.

Before the Changers had been created, the Sentinels had been more actively involved with the Crown, but there hadn't been a war or a large-scale conflict in centuries. No doubt that was partly why Daimos had easily been able to gain a foothold here, but she only hoped he hadn't laid his attention on the palace as well as the Changers.

When the carriage rounded a corner, the palace appeared on their right-hand side. Domed roofs topped the alabaster walls, lined with rows of tall windows that sat under arches decorated with latticework and polished wooden doors. The sharp outlines of the Range's peaks formed a striking backdrop to the palace and had the effect of making Zelle feel smaller than ever, especially compared to how high up she'd been while flying on the back of an eagle.

She glanced sideways at Rien, whose hands were folded on top of his staff. No doubt the royal palace looked unimpressive compared to what he was used to, but given its sheer size, she'd be in real trouble if they needed to make a hasty exit. Her heart jolted at every cobblestone they passed over on their way through the spike-topped gates.

"Will we definitely be meeting the Crown Prince?" he whispered to her. "Not his father?"

"The current King is indisposed." Why had he chosen *now* to start asking pertinent questions? "He's been in a fragile state for years, with his son poised to succeed him upon his death. The Crown Prince's name appears on all the royal correspondence, so he's the public face of the family."

The Crown Prince's advisors likely had more of a role in the actual decision-making. In a way, it wasn't unlike what Rien had told her of Aestin, in which the Emperor was the public figurehead but the Invokers made most of the important decisions themselves. It was anyone's guess as to whether his invitation to *visit* Aestin had been genuine, or at least not ill-informed given the current political situation, but she'd never even expected to meet the leader of her own country, let alone his.

A sensation of unreality washed over her as they climbed out of the carriage and ascended the wide stone stairs leading to a pair of mahogany doors. Rien looked more the part of an aristocrat than she did, and despite his unexpected praise, she still felt underdressed in her navy-blue dress and plain shoes.

More guards waited outside the doors, and Zelle's grip tightened on the staff, her hands slick with sweat beneath the gloves she'd worn to disguise the marks on her wrists. *What was I thinking?* Short of exposing her bond with the staff for the world to see, she'd brought no proof to back up a story that seemed more outlandish by the moment.

"Sentinel." A guard beckoned her through the doors and into a grand entrance hall. Dazed by the extravagance, Zelle found herself swept into a neighbouring corridor and then through another door. Colourful tapestries and gold-framed paintings lined the walls of the room on the other side, and Rien stopped to admire a towering painting of a battlefield.

"That must have been gifted to the royals from the Emperor of Aestin," Rien murmured into her ear. "There's an identical copy in his own palace."

If he was hoping to settle her nerves, he did not succeed, though part of her wondered how many of Rien's ancestors had walked these corridors as well. The guard continued to lead them through similar-looking rooms until she'd quite lost track of the way back, and then he held out a hand and brought them to a halt.

Through an open door ahead, he called out, "Your Highness, I have brought some unexpected visitors. The Sentinel Zelle Carnelian and Arien Astera of Aestin wish to speak with you."

Another voice answered: "Send them in."

The guard ushered them into a room dominated by a throne outlined in burnished gold and cushioned in vibrant crimson. On either side of the throne stood several glass cabinets that wouldn't have looked out of place in the Reader's house, containing valuable-looking weapons, jewels, and pieces of crockery. Gifts from past Sentinels, perhaps.

The man who sat upon the throne was rather plain, despite his clothing. He wore crimson and gold to match his throne, while his mousy-brown hair was cropped in a ridiculous style that made him resemble a crested eagle. Zelle jerked herself into a bow, as did Rien, and then she locked eyes with the Crown Prince of Zeuten. Her heart gave a stutter. *This is it.*

The Crown Prince gave them both a thin-lipped smile. "State your purpose here."

Zelle's throat went dry, but she swallowed down her apprehension. "Your Highness, it is an honour to meet you."

"The same from me," Rien said. "On behalf of Aestin and the Astera family, I thank you for your hospitality."

The Crown Prince's jaw tightened at his words. Then he turned towards Zelle. "Do you intend to explain why you brought a foreign criminal into my palace?"

7

Before the Crown Prince had finished speaking, several guards ran into the room. They wore thick crimson coats padded with armour and carried swords at their waists, and they formed a circle around Zelle and Rien, hemming them in place.

"Wait." Alarm flickered through Zelle. "You Highness, Rien—Arien—isn't here to harm anyone. We're here to warn you of a legitimate threat to the security of Zeuten."

"Is that so?" The Crown Prince tilted his head. "You admit to colluding with this criminal?"

"I—what?" Her manners fled, banished by the realisation that they'd been set up. "Rien isn't a criminal, and neither am I. Please, at least tell me what crimes he's meant to have committed."

"The murders of the entire Astera family, save for himself," said the Crown Prince, "and the theft of a valuable Relic from Zeuten's mountains."

His words struck Zelle like a heavy blow, and she swayed on the spot. "No... he didn't steal the Relic. I gave it to him." The words rushed quickly from her, while Rien's grip visibly tightened on his staff.

"Did you?" The Crown Prince gestured for the guards to move to either side, enabling her to see his face. He wore an expression of incredulity, which was a little better than his previous accusatory manner, so she pressed on.

"The Sentinels gave the Relic to Arien Astera as a reward for helping us to banish the rogue deity, Orzen. As to the rest, he certainly did not murder anyone. It was Orzen who slaughtered his family." At Daimos's command, but the specifics could wait until the guards gave them room to breathe.

"That is for Aestin's courts to decide and not ours, but the Sentinel was never the owner of that Relic," said the Crown Prince, "and it was not hers to give."

Zelle's breath caught. "With respect, your Majesty, the Sentinels' own ancestors brought that Relic across the ocean from Aestin a thousand years ago."

Arguing with the Crown Prince wasn't a wise idea, but the only reason he hadn't arrested them both was because she'd piqued his interest and kept him talking. She knew little of the man, but he had a reputation as someone who liked the sound of his own voice, and he especially liked being right.

"I disagree," he replied. "The Sentinels forfeited the right to claim any of the Relics in the mountains when they turned their backs on the Crown."

Powers above. "I thought the Sentinel and the Crown were allies."

"So did I." A hint of pensiveness entered his tone. "Until your grandmother took the side of a foreign criminal over her own nation."

It all came back to Rien again. "Who told you that Rien was a wanted criminal? If the news came from Aestin, there are many in his home country who have reason to spread lies in order to cause harm both to him and to Zeuten itself."

She had no idea if Daimos had genuinely convinced Aestin's authorities that Rien had murdered his own family, but who else would have had the resources to do so? Much less *wanted* to?

"I care nothing for the rivalries of the Aestinian Invokers," the Crown Prince said dismissively. "I am far more interested in why you came here to the palace, if not to hand yourselves in."

"We came here to request that the Changers cease their occupation of the town of Tavine." Zelle lifted her head, her heart thundering in her ears. "I can only assume you gave them the order yourself, but the villagers have done nothing to deserve their home being occupied by a group of trained assassins. Besides, my grandmother is ninety-five and recently suffered an injury. She's hardly capable of conspiring against the Crown."

Grandma herself would be furious at the very notion, but despite being in excellent health for her age, she was in no state to be hauled into the capital and put on trial. Moreover, if she did end up in custody, Zelle wouldn't be surprised if her grandmother clashed with her jailors and made the situation even worse for herself.

"Gifting Arien Astera a Relic that lawfully belongs to the Crown is an act of treason in itself, Zelle Carnelian. I would consider your own options carefully."

Zelle took in a measured breath. "I was not aware that

the Crown had a claim on any Relics, and neither was the Sentinel. In fact, none of us knew the Relic was present in the mountains at all until Rien and I stumbled upon it."

"Ignorance may be excused," he said—as if *he* hadn't been ignorant of those same Relics until recently—"but not treason. Your grandmother attacked the Changers who came to offer my invitation of a meeting, which gave me no choice but to assume the Sentinels are no longer allies of the Crown."

"My grandmother has spent the past week recovering from an injury," Zelle protested. "The Changers never mentioned following the orders of the Crown when we spoke to them. They claimed, in fact, to be following Gaiva Herself."

It was a gamble to mention the name of the deity, but why in the name of the Powers would the Crown Prince care what the occupants of an insignificant village in the shadow of the Range did? No, this had Daimos's name written all over it.

"But of course," he said. "Do we not all follow the guidance of our beloved creator goddess?"

Has he *seen Gaiva? Or some approximation of her?* Powers above, there was no doubt that Daimos had his claws in the palace somehow, but to what extent, she could only guess. "Yes, but… but the Changers, we believe, are compromised by a foreign entity."

"That is a serious accusation to make," said the Crown Prince. "Do you have proof of this claim?"

Unfortunately, Daimos had hidden his tracks, especially if the orders he'd given to the Changers had allegedly come from the Crown to begin with. True or not, that left her with a lot of speculation and no proof

"The Changers claimed to have received an emissary from the Great Power and creator goddess, Gaiva Herself," she began. "However, we know this is false, because I spoke to Gaiva myself in the Isles of Itzar less than a week ago, around the same time as the Changers received this supposed visitation. It's my belief that another deity tricked them."

"And which deity is this?" He asked the question in such a way that an indulgent adult might ask a child speaking of matters above their understanding.

The words died in her throat at the sense of futility at convincing someone who'd already made up his mind. She doubted the staff would deign to speak with him, but it might take nothing less than the word of the nameless Shaper to make him believe her.

He is not a Sentinel, the staff said sharply, almost startling her into dropping it. *He cannot hear me, and you'd do well not to tell him you can either.*

She tightened her grip on the staff's hilt. So be it, then.

"I believe the deity is Invicten, the god of illusions, acting at the command of Naxel Daimos, the man who formerly commanded Orzen and slaughtered almost the entire Astera family in cold blood. Clearly, he intends for Rien—Arien—to take the blame for his family's deaths."

Rien's jaw tightened, and the guards turned their attention on him, their hands twitching towards their weapons.

"According to my contact in Aestin, the only person seen leaving the scene of the crime was Arien Astera," said the Crown Prince. "However, I have no desire to debate. Your companion will be escorted to a holding cell before being sent directly to Aestin to stand trial, and you will stay here with me, Zelle Carnelian."

As he raised a hand, the guards moved in on Rien, drawing their swords.

"Wait—" She motioned towards him, but Rien's staff ignited in a crimson blaze that made the Crown Prince's throne look dim by comparison. Several vines shot outward, wrapping around the guards' ankles and yanking them off their feet.

Zelle watched with a sinking heart as Rien seized the chance to run from the room. The impulse to follow him briefly arose, but what good would it do? Either she'd be painted as a traitor to her country, and her entire family would become fugitives, or she'd be jailed herself.

Back on their feet, the guards ran in pursuit of Rien. He hadn't caused any of them serious injury, but the damage had been done. Shouts and footsteps echoed outside the room, signalling the arrival of reinforcements. Zelle risked a glance at the Crown Prince. He watched her, a tilt to his head that suggested he was curious as to whether she'd run too.

Powers above. Zelle had come here precisely to protect this fool of a prince from the very deity who'd seemingly bewitched him, and while his palace security wasn't lacking, he didn't seem to be afraid of her in the slightest. Nor the staff, which retained a faint blue glow around its edges but otherwise looked nonthreatening. She'd chosen to wear a pair of long gloves that came up to her elbows for a reason, however—and while nobody here should be aware of the staff's powers, exposing the marks snaking up and down her arms would invite questions she wouldn't be able to answer without risking the safety of everyone she knew.

If anyone tried to *take* the staff from her... Well, the results would have been equally chaotic if they'd attempted to force Rien to return the Relic he'd claimed. The current ruckus seemed tame in comparison, especially considering Zierne's penchant for mercilessly striking down his perceived foes. The guards' pounding footsteps remained in the background, suggesting Rien was doing a fair job at outrunning them, but even if he escaped the palace, was there any safe place to go?

The Crown Prince took a step towards her, wearing that same curious expression, as though she was another one of the trinkets lovingly preserved in the cabinets next to his throne. She didn't like it at all, but she'd chosen to stay and bargain for her own freedom.

Zelle cleared her throat. "I apologise for Rien—Arien's —behaviour. His... his Relic tends to overreact towards potential hostility."

"The Relic you gave him yourself?"

"He can't give it back even if he wanted to. Once an Invoker claims a Relic, then the bond is not so easily broken."

"I have no desire to discuss your companion." He gestured to the remaining guards flanking his throne. "Guards, leave us. I have many questions I would like to ask you alone, Zelle Carnelian, and I wish for you to answer me honestly."

<hr>

Rien sprinted down the wide corridor, cursing whoever had decided that every corner of the palace needed to be so uniform. The rooms all *looked* the same, from the tapestries to the carpets, and while he'd tried to take note of the route when they'd been brought in, it was considerably harder while running for his life.

When he came to the painting of a battlefield that reminded him of the identical one inside the Emperor's own palace, he knew he was close to the exit. The footsteps of his pursuers echoed behind him as he rounded a corner. *There.*

Sprinting through the wooden doors, he found two guards barring his way and more ahead at the foot of the stairs.

Zierne, don't kill any of them, he silently told the staff in his hand. We don't need to add murdering Zeutenian palace guards to my list of supposed crimes.

Zierne, for reasons unknown, obeyed. Crimson vines shot from the end of Rien's staff and dragged the guards out of his path without dealing any fatal wounds. When he reached the foot of the stairs, though, a new dilemma hit him. Hitching a ride in a carriage was out of the question, but the iron gates at the front of the palace were closed.

"Stop right there!" a guard shouted at him.

I can't stop now. He broke into a sprint and waved the staff in desperation. A flash of crimson light dazzled the guards, winning him time to reach the exit, and more thorny vines shot from the end of his staff to wrap around the gates. For several painful moments, he feared it wouldn't be enough, but the iron began to bend under the pressure of the magic-fuelled vines.

Shouts echoed at his back, but Rien broke into a sprint, urging the staff to force the gates open. The metal bent further with a grating screech, and he cleared the gap in a wild lunge, landing on the cobblestones on the other side.

With scarcely a moment to catch his breath, he broke into a run down the sloping hill away from the palace. The guards' panicked shouts echoed in pursuit, and for an instant, he was seized with the bizarre urge to turn back and apologise for the damage he'd caused to the palace gates. Zelle would have to clean up the mess he'd left behind, but he understood why she'd stayed. She had the staff, and she hadn't been accused of any crimes except helping *him*.

Therein lay his dilemma. Staying in Zeuten would only intensify the danger Zelle's family was in, but if Aestin's authorities believed he'd murdered his own family, nothing but misery would await him on the other side of the ocean. He and Zelle had left the eagles outside of the city gates, and he doubted the guards would let him pass without incident this time around, so his only other option was to aim for the docks.

As he neared the gates surrounding the royal district, more guards appeared in his line of vision. All were heavily armed, and it was only a matter of time before word reached them of the escaped fugitive from the palace. A well-dressed foreigner was an uncommon enough sight already, he was willing to bet.

Forcing himself to slow down, he spotted a blue-curtained carriage dropping off some passengers near one of the large mansion houses at the foot of the hill. Walking at a leisurely pace, he flagged the carriage down.

"Will you take me to the docks?" he asked the driver. "I'll pay."

The driver took in his foreign appearance, and his expression shuttered at the sight of the crimson staff in his hands. "No, that's not on my route."

"I thought all the passenger carriages stopped near the docks." He'd observed that much on his last visit here. "It shouldn't be too much trouble to take me there."

"Trouble? That's exactly what you look like."

Rien reached into his pocket and pulled out a handful of gold coins. "There won't be any trouble from me, but if you take me to the docks, then there'll be more of these."

Muttering something about ridiculous nobles under his breath, the man indicated for him to climb into the carriage, which he did. Rien's hands tensed on the staff when they passed through the gates, but the guards hadn't expected him to stow himself in a passenger carriage, and the curtains hid his face from sight. He'd never been so glad that Zeuten's nobles seemed to be in the habit of favouring privacy when they travelled—compared to Aestin, where most carriages had no roofs and many of the upper class revelled in the attention they drew as a result.

As they moved through the city, Rien inwardly cursed his own poor decision-making that had led him into this mess. If he hadn't decided to cut his last visit to Aestin short, Rien might have done any number of things that would have removed him from his current predicament. At the very least, he ought to have gone straight to the Emperor instead of immediately returning to Zeuten. He'd thought the authorities had seen the bodies of his family and sent out an alert for Daimos's arrest, but he'd little expected his enemy to conjure up such an outrageous lie.

No... Zeuten's authorities might have readily believed him a killer, but he found it hard to believe the same of those in Aestin, many of whom knew him in person.

The carriage halted, jolting him out of his reverie. They'd reached the docks, and Rien handed the driver the promised coins before removing his conspicuous bright-blue coat and bundling it under his arm along with the staff. His thin shirt was hardly appropriate for the cool weather, but at least it drew less attention while he surveyed the ships docked at the pier in search of a passenger vessel bound for Tauvice. Luck was with him for once, and he found one captained by an Aestinian man due to leave in half an hour.

The captain's brows rose when Rien pushed more gold coins into his hand as an incentive to hasten their departure. "I can't do that. My crew will mutiny if I force them to go back to work without a proper break."

"It's only thirty minutes." He tried to keep his tone calm, but in the background, there came the distinct sound of footsteps slapping against the wooden piers and sharp voices raised in anger.

"Is that the royal guards?" The captain lifted his head. "They're not after *you*, are they?'

Rien shook his head. "I have an emergency in Tauvice I need to handle. I'll pay whatever is necessary for the inconvenience."

The captain tutted. "I'll be out of business in a week if I get on the wrong side of Zeuten's royal guards. Who are you, anyway?"

"Reyes Martzel." He used the name of another of

Aestin's prominent Invoker families. "No doubt you've heard the name."

The captain did a double take at the sight of his staff. "Invoker or not, if you've made an enemy of the Crown, then it'll be on my head as well as yours."

The urge seized him to hide in Zelle's shop until the coast was clear, but for all he knew, the palace guards were watching her home too. The shouts drew closer, and Rien groped in the back of his mind for a convincing blend of truth and lie.

"They're under a spell and have mistaken me for someone else," he told the captain. "If you take me to Tauvice, I'll be able to speak to the Emperor directly and clear up the matter. If not, then there's a fair chance that the palace guards will order all the ships in the harbour to stay docked until they've managed to catch me, and I'm sure you'd rather leave early than be indefinitely detained."

"You're serious?" He eyed Rien's staff and apparently concluded that angering an Invoker with connections in the imperial palace was more trouble than it was worth. "Fine, get on board, and don't cause trouble with the other passengers, or else you'll have to swim home."

"Fair enough."

It was time to go home to Aestin... and face whatever he found on the other side.

8

While the guards retreated from the room, Zelle stood alone with the Crown Prince. Despite the splendour surrounding her on every side, the crushing sense of dread masked any sense of admiration, especially with the Crown Prince's silent scrutiny of her. She waited for him to speak, torn between the impulse to follow Rien and the knowledge that she'd only make things worse for herself if she did.

They need you alive, she told herself—but how did she know for sure? Daimos should never have been able to spread his influence this high up, and the suspicion that Zeuten's authorities were entirely under his grasp left a bitter taste in her mouth.

Finally, the Crown Prince spoke. "Our meeting has already been more eventful than I anticipated, but I confess that part of me thought I might have to order my guards to take you away too."

He'd spoken as if he'd done her a considerable favour, and while there was some truth in his claim, her intention had been to spare her family and herself from punishment, while convincing him to stop the Changers from occupying Tavine. Those two goals necessitated that she present herself as entirely harmless, even if it meant losing some dignity in the process.

Zelle had already bound herself to the nameless Shaper and walked away alive, so dealing with a spoilt prince ought to be simple by comparison. In theory. "What did you wish to discuss with me, Your Highness?"

Despite her fury over his treatment of Rien, she was genuinely curious as to how Daimos—if he indeed had visited the palace—had won over the Crown Prince.

"I would have asked for the return of the gift your grandmother gave away without permission, but I'd settle for an apology instead."

"In person?" Zelle fervently hoped not. "My grandmother has been injured recently, and when the Changers visited, her granddaughter had just been kidnapped by raiders from Itzar. She probably mistook their invitation for a threat. It certainly wouldn't be her first misunderstanding."

She had the mental image of the old Sentinel glaring at her with every word she spoke, but if Grandma refused to give ground even to save her own skin, Zelle would have to do it for her. She had little choice, because their impatience had already turned the Crown against them and made Rien a fugitive in two countries. Yes, the staff's magic might be able to help her escape the palace—but at the cost of condemning the rest of her family. Besides, she didn't want to declare war on her own country, for the Powers' sakes.

The Crown Prince studied her face. "I sympathise. My

own father has been ill for quite some time. However, the slight was keenly felt."

Zelle doubted it. He hadn't met her grandmother in years, and they'd made no efforts to communicate with each other in the interim. "My sister and I weren't in the country at the time, so we were unable to speak to her on the matter."

"Your grandmother's fragile state is no doubt to blame for her rash actions," he concluded. "Your sister... she is back in the country now?"

Evidently, he hadn't received a report from the Changers since before their return from Itzar.

When he found out that her sister had defied the Changers herself, he might be less inclined to give her the benefit of the doubt, but Aurel was in a better position to argue her case than Grandma was. If Zelle took care to avoid telling any outright lies, then she might stand a chance of achieving her aim of sparing the villagers at the very least.

"Yes, she is," Zelle answered. "Upon returning to Zeuten, we found the Changers occupying her home village of Tavine, and it's for that reason that I came here to speak with you."

He also didn't seem surprised by the "kidnapped by raiders from Itzar" part of her story, though for all she knew, he'd been aware of the situation in the Isles from the start. The Senior Changers had been there recently, and the Crown must have ordered that mission, though that little mattered now.

The Crown Prince's brows drew together. "I would have thought the villagers ought to be grateful for the Changers' defensive presence in their home."

"They're trapped in their own houses," said Zelle. "Maybe the Changers' intentions are good, but surely they have more pressing concerns than sending their senior members to intimidate farmers and craftspeople. Like Zeuten's security, for instance." She tried and failed to keep the impatient bite from her voice.

"I see." From his tone, she might have reported a minor inconvenience, not an entire village being held hostage by assassins. "Once I have confirmed that Arien Astera is no longer a threat, I will gladly order the Changers to withdraw. In the meantime, the Sentinel should present herself to the Changers at the first opportunity to mend the wrongs between them."

Unlikely, but for all they knew, the Changers would soon be distracted by a far bigger problem than a Sentinel who refused to respect them. "I will tell her myself. If we've finished discussing the Sentinel and the Changers, then I'll head back to the outpost right away."

"Not yet," he said. "In fact, I'm glad you were the one who came to see me and not your sister, Zelle."

"Why?" Her heart skipped a beat. "Your Majesty?"

"You interest me. For a multitude of reasons, chief of which is that staff you carry."

Zelle's blood chilled, and she found her hands clenching inside her gloves in case he'd glimpsed the glowing marks on her skin. The staff itself was, of course, impossible to hide. "Might ask why a Relic of the Sentinels interests you?"

"Why shouldn't it?" he queried. "I confess I've never taken an interest in magic before, but that staff has undeniably been at the centre of recent events, and I have some questions I would like to ask you."

"Such as…?"

"How did you come to be an ally of the nameless Shaper?"

Her blood froze, dread coursing through her veins. How in the name of the Powers did he know *that?* Daimos must have told him, but for what purposes, she could only guess.

"You want to ask how I knew?" he continued, cutting through her unvoiced reply. "The Changers informed me that you bound the deity known as Orzen into a Relic using the Shaper's magic."

That's not possible. He can't know. Evita hadn't told the Changers anything about the Shaper when she'd been interrogated, and the only other witnesses to Orzen's fate had been her and Rien. Daimos knew, though, and if *he'd* told the Crown Prince, he'd undoubtedly failed to mention his own responsibility for Orzen's rampage through Zeuten.

"You must not fear to speak," the Crown Prince added. "You'll receive no condemnation for your prior silence either. I understand you thought you were protecting your family. I simply wish to hear your perspective."

The words tangled in her throat. However reasonable he might sound, she couldn't speak freely to him when he might sentence her to death or take away her freedom with a word.

Zelle started with a piece of the truth. "I didn't think anyone would believe me."

"Yes." His mouth quirked. "It's quite a story. I almost didn't believe it myself."

His silence invited her to continue. "Orzen… he was a threat unlike any Zeuten has faced before. He infiltrated the Changers' ranks and had my grandmother kidnapped. That's how I came to pick up her staff."

"And it answered to you."

Literally, she might have replied, but she had no doubt his casual attitude would evaporate if she admitted she could sometimes hear the staff's voice in her *head.*

"Yes, it did."

He examined the staff for a moment. *Don't touch it,* she thought desperately. If he did so, and the staff retaliated, the blame would fall on Zelle whether she intended to cause him harm or not. Luckily, he returned his attention to her face without making a move. "How curious. Did you have experience with magic before?"

"Nothing like Orzen." An idea occurred to her. "He told us he was sent here to kill Rien—Arien—after slaughtering the rest of his family."

"I fear your friend may have misled you. All my sources have told me that Arien is a fugitive fleeing from justice."

"He told *me* that he was fleeing his family's murderer," she said. "Everything I have witnessed since I met him has confirmed his story."

"If you brought me proof, I would gladly believe you."

What kind of proof would surpass the lies Daimos had whispered in his ear? "Is my word not enough? You trusted whoever told you that I bound Orzen with the aid of the nameless Shaper, despite them not witnessing the events themselves, didn't you?"

"You're mistaken. The Changers did witness Orzen's defeat at your hands."

So it was the Changers, was it? Zelle tried to keep her polite smile in place. "If you mean the Senior Changers, it's my understanding that they were on a mission in Itzar at the time, and their Master was murdered by Orzen when he failed to capture Arien Astera. Otherwise, the only Changers in the mountains at the time were novices, who were fleeing Orzen's wrath and didn't see his fate."

Did the Crown Prince even know that Orzen had hired the Changers and then taken over their ranks? If he did, then the possibility of the same occurring again might have crossed his mind, but his expression remained distantly puzzled. "The Changers' reports were clear, so I'm inclined to believe they witnessed Orzen's defeat. I do not wish to cause strife, Zelle, but I would be very interested to hear your full account later."

"Later" didn't specify when... or where. "Does that mean I can leave?"

"Certainly," he said. "I'll call for a guard to escort you home. You live above a shop near the docks, don't you?"

How did he know that? "Yes, but I'm currently visiting my grandmother and sister in Tavine."

"Excellent." He smiled. "You can ask her to meet with the Changers and clear up their misunderstanding right away. I trust your sister hasn't done anything to offend them since her return?"

Powers above. He'd guessed, somehow, and she could only imagine the backlash if Aurel's infamous habit of speaking without thinking emerged during an audience with the Crown Prince.

"I wouldn't know," she lied. "My family has recently suffered a great deal of upheaval and would very much like to be left alone."

"And they will be, once the foreign intruder is apprehended."

Not likely. "We will have to disagree on the subject of Arien. I don't believe he's a danger to anyone here in Zeuten. That aside, am I truly allowed to go anywhere I choose?"

"Not alone," he clarified. "You're too vulnerable, despite that staff you carry. When I heard your shop was recently attacked by intruders, one of whom died at the scene, I knew that you were too unpredictable to leave unwatched."

Her hands clenched around the staff. "You told me I was free to leave. That strikes me as somewhat contradictory."

"It's a matter of public safety," he said. "Besides, the guards won't disturb you."

"They'll just follow me everywhere," she guessed. "And my family?"

"They'll stay undisturbed as long as you remain within the sight of my guards."

Bile burned the back of her throat. "What exactly do you want me to do, then?"

"I would like you to be my ambassador. It is time the Sentinels stepped back into the public eye as the face of Zeuten's defences against magical threats."

Her mouth fell open for a second before she closed it. Whatever she'd expected, being forced into a public-facing role had been far from her thoughts. "And do what, exactly?"

"And fulfil the duties inherent in the role of an ambassador," he said. "You can stay in the guest wing of the palace as an honoured guest for the duration. You'll want for nothing, and your family will be safe."

So that was what it would cost. Her sister and grandmother's safety in exchange for her freedom. The Crown Prince was a bully, no doubt, but it was Daimos who'd woven a spell over the entire palace. Would staying here enable her to unravel it?

"Do not look at me as if I am confining you to a prison cell," he added. "You'll be able to visit your family whenever you wish. I simply request that you take an escort with you for your own safety."

And to prevent her from escaping. Taking an ally of Daimos's with her into the Sanctum was out of the question, and she had no faith in the Crown Prince's promise to remove the Changers from Tavine and enable her family to return to the Readers' house. The urge arose to strike him on the head with the staff and make a run for it, but the impulse would only rebound upon herself and her family. The Crown Prince had already asked his guards to leave the two of them alone, suggesting he either didn't know what her staff was capable of, or was confident that she wouldn't use it against him. Whichever it was, he didn't believe her to be a threat.

She intended to prove him wrong... but not yet.

———

As more time passed and Rien and Zelle still didn't return, Evita took to pacing up and down the path outside the tower until Aurel called her inside.

"Do you think they might have been caught?" she asked. "Should we go after them?"

"They flew directly to the capital," the Sentinel growled from her armchair. "That means any enemies who found them will find you too. Besides, have you ever met royalty before?"

"No, but neither has Zelle, has she?" asked Evita.

"She hasn't, but she was at least educated on how to comport herself around the upper classes," Grandma Carnelian said. "I'd wager you were not."

Evita's face heated. "Well, I never *wanted* to meet the Crown Prince. If Orzen hadn't trampled my home and my family, then I might not have even left my village."

"Grandma, that's enough," said Aurel. "Zelle and Rien might need our help."

"Do you think the Changers caught them?" Evita's mouth went dry at the memory of Vekka and Izaura lying skewered in a net like freshly caught fish. "They have a new leader, and I think he's working with Daimos… but it was the palace that supposedly sent the order for the Changers to come after the Sentinel, so they might have ended up in trouble if they reached the capital too."

"Better for the Changers to catch them first," Grandma Carnelian commented. "The Crown Prince might be a feckless layabout by all accounts, but you'd have more luck breaking *into* the royal palace than getting out again. Built in wartime, that place was."

Evita's gaze dropped to the silvery folds of the cloak she wore, wondering if its abilities would enable her to slip past whatever security the palace had. Stealth had never been her strong point, however, and she'd got herself caught once that day already. "They might not have even got in. It can't be easy to get an audience with the Crown Prince."

"Who even know what he's playing at, sending orders to the Changers to capture Tavine," Aurel scoffed. "Why would he care about a small village in the mountains? And why is your cloak glowing, Evita?"

Evita lifted the cloak's silver-grey sleeve. "I don't know. When did that start?"

"When you came back from Tavine." Aurel's brow furrowed. "You were flying. How'd you figure out how to do that, anyway?"

"I..." *I didn't* was the honest answer.

Grandma Carnelian turned her cutting gaze onto Evita. "Does that cloak have any other special properties? Can't some of the Changers turn into birds or other beasts?"

"I never learned how," she admitted. "I was only a novice when I left, and I wouldn't have got to that level of training for years."

"Still useful," Aurel commented. "Would it work if I borrowed the cloak to have a snoop around the Changers' base?"

"Do you want to get yourself captured again?" the Sentinel enquired.

"No, I want to know if they have Zelle," Aurel corrected. "The Changers' base is easier to infiltrate than the royal palace, isn't it?"

"I suppose," Evita said grudgingly. For some reason, parting ways with her cloak bothered her more than the idea of letting Aurel fly on the dragonet. Loaning her cloak to anyone, even an ally, felt akin to leaving a beloved pet in the care of a stranger. "If you're sure Zelle is there, I'll go myself."

The thought was as appealing as climbing up to the highest peak in the Range in her underwear, but the new master could hardly be worse than Orzen. *Right?*

Aurel scowled. "No. You got caught last time because you sent the dragonet to save my neck instead of yours. I want to repay the favour."

"You're both being ridiculous." Grandma Carnelian leaned forward in her seat. "How do you hope to get Zelle and Rien away from the Changers without one or both of you getting captured in their place?"

"I know where Master Amery used to keep the letters from the Crown," Evita put in. "I don't know if their new leader is the same, but he'll be the one who has the proof. And... and if Zelle and Rien are prisoners, then I can sneak them past him using my cloak. It's risky, but most of the Senior Changers are in the forest, not at their base, so we won't get a better chance than this."

"Good point," said Aurel. "What about this supposed messenger from Gaiva, then?"

Evita's heart sank with dread. "That's their new master. Or so they claimed when they questioned me."

A calculating expression crossed Aurel's face. "I wonder if we can expose him as a fraud. Surely one miraculous appearance of the creator goddess shouldn't have been enough to convince every Changer that they had Her blessing."

"True." If their new leader had been sent to bring word of Gaiva's command, then exposing him as a fraud might turn the Changers against him. He couldn't spear them all with arrows at the same time, surely. "I wish we'd brought one of Gaiva's spare Relics back with us from Itzar. The *real* Gaiva, not the fake one."

"It's not a bad idea," said Aurel, "but Zelle claimed that Gaiva hasn't been able to communicate directly with anyone since the Relic shattered. If that's changed, we don't have time to take a detour to Itzar either way."

"Anything is better than barging into the Changers' base without a plan," said Grandma Carnelian.

"We have a plan," Aurel corrected. "Evita sneaks in and out, while I hide outside the camp and help Rien and Zelle get away."

"You're forgetting the part where your friend doesn't know how to *use* that cloak of hers."

Evita's hands curled protectively around the ends of her sleeves. "I do know. I just can't explain it in words."

"I wonder if this would help?" Aurel bounded across the room and rummaged in her pack before pulling out a book. "Here."

Evita dropped her cloak's sleeves. "Ah… I can't read."

"You can't *read?*" Grandma Carnelian raised both brows. "What did you spend your life doing, exactly?"

Heat seared her neck. "My family made a living by fishing and selling their produce at the markets in my village. They never learned to read either."

She'd had a little schooling as a child, but she'd been inattentive in her lessons and had preferred spending her free time swimming in the sea or walking in the woods. In those days, adventures had seemed a distant and appealing prospect, not a source of constant danger.

"The book is called *The Art of Changing*." Aurel held up the faded cover. "I assume the Changers used this manual to form the basis of their training."

Evita studied the faded red cover. "Why do you have it?"

"Thought it might come in handy." Aurel flipped open the book. "It might explain how to shift forms."

"I thought it required years of training." She studied the illustrations of flying figures as Aurel turned the pages. "Does it give any tips about the easiest way to access the cloak's magic at any time?"

"Synchrony," said Aurel. "Same as most Relics. Your desires have to align with the deity's wishes."

"I don't even know which deity its magic belongs to. If there is one." She still didn't entirely believe the cloak to be a Relic either. "I've never spoken directly to any gods, unless you count the Sentinels' cave."

"Few people actually hear their deities talk back," said Aurel. "Except Zelle, and the Shaper is an exception to pretty much every rule. Even the Invokers of Aestin have never heard a word from their gods, and most of the people in Itzar who claimed Gaiva's Relics didn't need to talk to Her either. Direct communication isn't a requirement."

"All right," she relented. "But I don't know how it applies to the cloak. I have to want the same as my Relic does? Is that all?"

Then why did it take most novices years to complete their training? Granted, they weren't usually allowed to *keep* their cloaks until they attained a certain level of competency, but she'd broken that trend when she'd kept the cloak instead of giving it back to the Master.

Synchrony. She might have failed her training as a Changer, but she might just have succeeded at something far more notable… claiming a Relic.

9

"Synchrony," Evita whispered, poised on the edge of a cliff. "Can you turn me into a bird?"

The dragonet chirped as if to question why she was having a conversation with the cloak, but she couldn't think of any other way to make her wishes known. Evita had picked a spot at the edge of the mountain path to practise, stretching her arms wide and keeping her gaze fixed on the horizon to avoid looking down.

"Synchrony." Evita flapped her arms, feeling more ridiculous than ever. "I can already fly. How hard can it be to become a bird?"

The wind caught her and flipped her head over heels, cloak and all. Panicked, she flailed her arms until she caught her balance, the cloak steadying her. Swooping upward, she touched down on the cliff's edge and tried again. Was her fear of the drop getting in her way, or was it simply that she didn't have enough training? Or *synchrony?* If the cloak wanted to fly, and she *didn't* want to fall, she understood where that might cause friction.

"I don't know whose magic you belong to," she whispered to the cloak, "but I want to work with you. Can you help me forget my fear?"

There had been times where her enjoyment of the soaring sensation of flight had overcome her terror, so it wasn't out of reach. Especially with magic at her command.

The cloak was a Relic. *Her* Relic.

Evita extended both arms again, a tingling sensation prickling her fingertips. *I can do this.*

The ground lifted out from under her feet, but this time, she let the cloak carry her upward instead of fighting or flailing. It helped to think of the cloak as a pair of wings, extensions of her own body, as *The Art of Changing* had described their connection without using the word "Relic."

Evita flew in circles until she was reasonably confident that unless a sudden storm hit her or someone crashed into her in midair, she should be able to get to her destination. Invigorated, she tried to coax the cloak into helping her become a bird again.

"Synchrony," she murmured, noticing that a shimmering silvery light had sparked along the surface of the cloak. She'd seen Zelle's and Rien's staffs glow occasionally, but she'd never given the matter much thought. Was it a kind of language Relics used to communicate with their owners? If so, then the cloak must be pleased with her progress. The dragonet, too, chirped encouragement at her as she flew. It might take a little more time before she mastered changing forms, but being able to fly would be enough to get her into the Changers' base.

Upon returning to the tower, she found Aurel waiting for her inside. "Ready to fly?"

"Surprisingly, yes," said Evita. "You take Chirp, and I'll fly with the cloak. I've been practising."

"Good," said Aurel. "I imagine the dragonet won't be able to get too close to the base. Is there anything else you need?"

Evita thought. "A lockpick. If the Master isn't in his office, then he'll have locked the door."

"I bet there's something in here." Aurel clattered around the room, while her grandmother glowered at her from her spot in the armchair. "Here."

Evita took the twisted strand of metal from Aurel and examined it. "What's this?"

"A homemade lockpick I made when I was a child. If it works on the Reader's house, it's bound to work on the Master's office too."

Grandma cleared her throat as though to remind them of her presence. "If you're committed to this ridiculous scheme, then at least consider that you might be going to the wrong place."

Evita frowned. "You don't think Rien and Zelle will be there?"

"If the Crown Prince is the one who sent the order, then the Changers will have sent them straight to the capital. I guarantee it."

"You might have mentioned that earlier." Mildly deflated, Evita turned to Aurel. "Still want to come?"

"Absolutely," said Aurel. "We can find out *why* the

Crown Prince wants Rien and Zelle, even if we don't find them ourselves."

Evita was less than certain they were making the right choice, but when Aurel strode out of the tower, she followed. Chirp waited outside, and Aurel wasted no time in climbing onto his back before giving Evita an expectant look. The dragonet wasn't pleased that she insisted on flying alone, but he respected her decision to use the opportunity to practise using the cloak. Besides, he was simply too big not to draw attention, and she didn't even have a spare cloak for Aurel, let alone a beast whose wings stretched wider than the tower's doorway.

The dragonet launched into flight, while Evita used the resulting air current to glide off the cliff's edge. Her path was slightly lopsided, but already her control had improved, and the dragonet was always there to encourage her with chirps and to help steady her whenever she lost her balance.

When they neared the Changers' base at the southern edge of the Range, Evita took the lead and directed Chirp to land behind a rocky outcropping. There, she briefly lowered her hood to speak to Aurel. "I'm going to fly into the camp. Wait for me here, and I'll come back to let you know if Rien and Zelle are anywhere in the base. If you hear any noise that suggests they caught me, leave at once."

Chirp shook his head, and Evita turned imploringly towards him. "I'll be fine. Even if I get caught, I can fly away without you endangering yourself."

I think. The memory of Vekka and Izaura's bodies suspended above the forest chose that moment to enter her mind again, and she swallowed hard.

Pulling up her hood, she spread her arms out and flew over the Changer's base until she spotted the squat shape of the Masters' building amid the caves and cliffs surrounding the novices' part of the Changers' base. Few people were outside, while it remained jarring not to see Master Amery striding across the cliffs and snapping at anyone who looked at him the wrong way. Now the Senior Changers were back, she would have expected them to reinstate order, yet they'd seemed content to send the best of their number to surround Tavine instead.

She saw no signs of the new Master, either, but that might be a good sign. Certainly, he wouldn't expect her to show up at the base so soon after their escape from the Changers in Tavine.

Evita entered the building, tensing at the creak of the wooden door, and then made her way to the office that had once belonged to Master Amery. The office was locked, suggesting its occupant wasn't in. Good. Reaching into her pocket, she pulled out Aurel's improvised lock-pick and jammed it inside the lock until she heard a satisfying click. Evita pushed the door inward as quietly as possible and crept into the office.

The small room had hardly changed in the weeks since she'd left the Changers, despite Master Amery's absence. With most of the Senior Changers' attention focused on guarding Tavine and finding the Sentinels, they'd neglected to focus on their own security, or maybe the new Master assumed nobody would have the audacity to trespass inside his office. The same worn wooden desk and chair sat in the centre, while a rickety set of shelves spilled out old scrolls and both spelled and regular arrows lined the weapons rack. Atop the desk lay a stack of official-looking letters on faded parchment.

Her inability to read might have been an impediment, but the most recent letters would be at the top of the stack, and the royal seal was easy enough to recognise. Three letters bore the crimson stamp of the royal palace, and she separated them carefully from the rest before stuffing them into her pocket.

Footsteps sounded outside, followed by a booming voice. "Who's there?"

Panic spiked. She'd left the door slightly ajar, which must have given her away, and while Evita didn't recognise the speaker's voice, the authoritative tone was hard to mistake. Was this Master Drazer?

When she didn't reply, a broad shoulder shunted the door wide open. The man that followed was taller and larger than the average Changer, his muscular frame filling the doorway. He didn't move like a typical Changer, either, with his shoes slapping against the wooden floor as he looked around the office with narrowed eyes.

"Show yourself," he said, "or I'll put an arrow through your eye."

Heart thumping, Evita held her breath. A commotion arose outside the building, several voices shouting, "Intruders!"

The Master twisted around to see the source of the noise, affording Evita with the chance to slip past him and out of the office. He snarled when she accidentally trod on his foot but she slid through his grip like soap and pelted out of the door. She'd been right in guessing he was slower than the average Changers, but what he lacked in reaction time he made up for in sheer volume.

"Intruder!" The shouting continued, picked up and echoed back and forth by more voices.

Outside the building, a flurry of novices emerged from the caves and swarmed down the mountain paths. A reptilian shadow passed overhead, and to Evita's horror, Aurel sat on the dragonet's back, throwing rocks at the Changers below. *What is she doing?*

"It's that rogue Changer!" someone shouted.

They'd mistaken Aurel for her, but Aurel never should have given herself away to begin with. Several arrows fired into the air, aimed at the dragonet. Chirp shrieked when one pierced his wing, and the pain hit Evita's heart too. His flight path turned lopsided. If she didn't divert their attention, he and Aurel were doomed.

Evita cleared her throat and shouted, "Over here!"

Heads turned in her direction. Evita stretched out her arms and urged her cloak to carry her into the air, narrowly avoiding several arrows in the process. The dragonet veered in her direction, seeing through her cloak, and a surge of recklessness seized her.

When she caught up to the dragonet, she trusted the cloak to keep her in flight as she reached into her pocket for the letters she'd taken from the office. "Aurel—take these."

"Evita, what are you—?" Aurel squinted at her, unable to see past the cloak, but she caught the papers when Evita shoved them into her hand. "What are these?"

"Proof," Evita said. "I'll distract them and follow you back to the outpost later. Go!"

Arrows shot towards them. The dragonet screeched,

and Evita spun wildly on the spot in a desperate attempt to get between the arrows and their target.

An arrow pierced the top of her cloak, sending her into a downward spiral. A second arrow joined the first, and her descent quickened. Below her feet, the broad shape of the new Master clambered over the rocks.

He wasn't a deity. He was human, like her. She must be able to thwart him.

A third arrow pierced her cloak, sending her tumbling out of the sky.

———

At the Crown Prince's command, an escort of guards swept Zelle out of the room, crowding her to the extent that she had to resist the urge to prod them with the staff to convince them to give her some space. Several twisting corridors later, they came to a room with polished floors and a gilt painting dominating the wall, showing a man with mousy-brown hair and a vaguely handsome face. The current King, she guessed, back when he'd been in his prime.

A lone guard stepped into her field of vision, masking the portrait from sight. His tawny complexion suggested he'd been born on the eastern spear of Zeuten, while he wore his straight dark hair long, similar to an Aestinian noble.

"It seems I have been placed in charge of you, Miss Carnelian," the guard said. "I am Jarven, and I will be escorting you around the palace to ensure that you don't become lost."

"How generous," she lied. "Whereabouts will I be staying, exactly?"

"In here." He pushed open a polished wooden door at the side of the portrait of the King, revealing yet another room with tapestried walls and gilt furnishings. "This is the guest suite. I trust you'll find it more than suitable for your needs."

Zelle's new quarters were bigger even than the downstairs of the Reader's house—though part of that might be the lack of any cabinets and shelves of old junk—and the bed alone wouldn't have fit into her old bedroom above the shop on the seafront. Even knowing the price that came with such rich accommodations didn't prevent her from staring at the plush carpets, the thick hand-woven tapestries, the mahogany furniture. Through another door lay a bathroom containing a large bathtub.

As the Crown Prince had said, she wouldn't want for anything... except her freedom.

Her gaze found the window on the opposite side of the bedroom, but it had been sealed with such a complicated-looking network of locks and mechanisms that she was at a loss to figure out how to open it.

As if sensing the direction of her thoughts, Jarven gave her a questioning look. "Is something wrong?"

"Suppose I was to get too warm during the night?" she asked. "Does that window open?"

"Would you like me to open it for you?"

Sensing a trick, she said, "You won't be in my room at night... will you?"

"Not at all." He gave a false laugh. "You can open the window yourself if you so desire. It's simpler than it looks."

Certain that he knew exactly what she was thinking, she crossed the room and attempted to find her way around the locks. Once she figured out the mechanism, she swiftly found that the window opened only the width of a finger or so.

Jarven smiled at her, and her insides curdled like spoiled milk. She glimpsed the unpleasantness beneath his veneer of politeness like she had the Crown Prince's, and it was anyone's guess as to how much of that was his regular personality and how much was due to the influence of Daimos's spell. The impulse struck her to hit him in the kneecaps with her staff to see if his mask slipped, but she didn't dare risk him trying to take it away from her and landing her in even deeper trouble.

"I see." She closed the window and turned her attention to the tall wardrobe and dresser opposite the bed. "Will I be able to bring my other possessions here? I don't have any other clothes with me except for what I'm wearing."

"You wish for us to send for your belongings from the Reader's house?"

"No—I don't live there." As long as she stayed in the palace, they'd promised to leave her family alone, but she wouldn't give them any excuses to find a loophole. "I keep most of my possessions in my shop on the seafront."

"I see," he said. "Give me the address, and I'll have anything you desire brought here."

"His Highness already knows the address." While she didn't relish the idea of the royal guards walking into her shop, they wouldn't find anything that would be of value or interest, and it was far better than them hassling her family.

As for the staff? Its notable lack of any barbed comments or sarcastic asides suggested the Shaper knew how dire their situation truly was.

"And how am I to spend my time?" she asked Jarven. "I'm not expected to stay confined to my rooms the entire time?"

"No, you may spend your time however you please… within reason." A slight smile curled his mouth, and the staff turned cold in her hands. A warning chill, like a precursor to a magical threat. Did he carry a Relic? Was there a reason the Crown Prince had assigned him to her and nobody else?

Powers above. He's Daimos's ally. He must be.

It took all Zelle's willpower to maintain a stoic expression. "Then may I be alone for a bit?"

"Of course." He gave a slight bow and withdrew from the room. Zelle waited for a short time and then nudged the door open a fraction. He'd taken up a position outside on the right-hand side of the door, so there was no way to leave the room without alerting his attention.

So be it, then. She pushed the door closed and sat down on the bed, hardly caring how comfortable the soft mattress felt compared to sleeping on a bumpy armchair as she had the previous night. She'd have given almost anything to be back at the outpost instead of in a palace, with a fire in the grate and Rien sitting beside her.

All she could do was trust that he'd got away—and judging by the guard's avoidance of the subject, they hadn't caught him yet. Might he have even escaped the city altogether? If he found his way back to the eagles, he might stand a chance, but if not, his only way out was across the ocean.

To Aestin, where Daimos might be waiting for him.

Her hands curled into fists. Knowing they'd be in the same dilemma if they'd gone to the Changers instead did nothing to quell her guilt for potentially sending him to his death and landing herself in an inescapable trap in the same instant.

If you're going to give up already, then you might as well drown yourself in the bathtub, the staff told her.

"I doubt you want to end up stuck in here without me," she murmured. "Even you can't give me the ability to walk through walls, can you?"

The palace was like a fortress on the inside, with guards at every corner and every door. But she'd find a way out.

Zelle wouldn't consent to being a prisoner.

urel paced in front of the tower, waiting for Evita's return. The dragonet circled above and made sad chirping noises, but otherwise obeyed Evita's request not to come back for her. Like the last time, the cloak would enable her to fly to safety.

Yet as the minutes trickled by, doubts crept into Aurel's mind. Zelle and Rien had run into trouble—she was certain of it—but if Evita didn't return soon, Aurel would have to go back into the tower with her grand-mother, and they would quite possibly murder one another by the day's end. Lifting her head, she called to the dragonet. "Give me those papers Evita stole."

Descending, Chirp lifted a claw, revealing several rather crumpled and official-looking papers. Aurel reached out a hand and took them, her gaze snagging on the Crown Prince's seal.

"What's that?" Grandma came out of the tower, leaning heavily on the new walking stick she'd procured. "Your friend's work?"

"She stole them from the Changers' new Master's office." Aurel turned over the letters and smoothed out the crumpled edges to reveal the curling handwriting sprawling across the pages.

"She can't read, can she?"

"She knew what she was looking for." Aurel showed her grandmother the letters that Evita had sacrificed her freedom to obtain. "They're from the Crown Prince."

"Recent too." Grandma indicated the date in the corner, which told Aurel that they'd been in Itzar when the Crown Prince had contacted the Changers.

Forcing her gaze to focus on the curling handwriting on the page, Aurel read the letter.

To Master Drazer,

Thank you for sending the information I requested. I will update my guards at once concerning the current location of the Sentinels, and once Zelle Carnelian returns to the capital, I will send out an emissary to find her. In the meantime, if you happen to run into her yourself, then I would be grateful if you sent her to meet with me. My advisors say that the palace is the best place for her to be.

"Powers above, they're looking for Zelle," she told her grandmother. "And she flew straight into their trap. The Crown Prince must have been thrilled."

She read on. *The criminal, Arien Astera, is believed to be travelling with her. I am anxious to see him brought into custody, as he is wanted for questioning in relation to several unpleasant murders in his home country of Aestin. You must be careful of him, as it has come to my attention that he has been gifted a dangerous and unknown Relic by none other than the Sentinels themselves.*

"Bullshit," growled Aurel. "They think *Rien* is a criminal?"

"I can read as well as you can," said Grandma.

"Then you know they're accusing us of helping him." Aurel's hands shook with rage. "That's why they took over Tavine. They think we were conspiring against the Crown by giving Rien the Relic he found himself."

The question was, who was whispering lies in the ear of the Crown Prince? If Daimos himself was in the palace, then Zelle and Rien had landed directly in his trap.

Aurel read the last part of the letter: *When he is caught, Arien Astera will be sent directly to his own country to face justice from the Emperor. In the meantime, I am glad for my advisors in this unusual and turbulent time.*

With Gaiva's Blessing, I hope we shall speak again.

Crown Prince Carlion.

She lifted her head. "I'm glad you never took me to meet the Crown Prince. He sounds like an obnoxious arse."

"He is," Grandma told her. "He also isn't the one you need to be worried about."

"Do *you* think Daimos is in the palace?" she asked. "Or these 'advisors' of the Crown Prince are his lackeys?"

"Most likely the latter," Grandma replied. "Resourceful though he might be, he can't be in several places at once."

"Then why is the Crown Prince so interested in Zelle?"

"Do you really need to ask that question?"

"Unless you know something I don't, yes." Aurel's and her grandmother's strong personalities were like flint to flame at the best of times, but the Sentinel's penchant for keeping secrets from her own grandchildren was downright maddening in situations like this.

"I have no doubt that word has spread across the country of Zelle's involvement in the defeat of Orzen," said Grandma. "Any strange magical events worthy of notice are difficult to keep quiet in a country with as few Relics as Zeuten has."

"The Crown Prince wouldn't know a Relic if it bashed him on the skull." Aurel might never have met him, but his reputation was clear enough. "He doesn't know what the staff is, right? Zelle didn't tell anyone."

"Daimos has likely worked it out," Grandma said. "Besides, the deities talk to one another."

"Did they tell you that themselves?" Aurel crumpled the letter in her hand and threw it across the room. "When you were in their realm?"

"They didn't need to. Let's see that other letter."

The second paper wasn't a letter, however, but a statement on the crimes of Arien Astera. Listed were the names of his supposed murder victims: *Volcan Astera, Torben Astera...*

Aurel's head snapped up in indignation. "They think he killed his own family? Did nobody else witness Daimos's massacre? Rien said he wasn't exactly subtle."

"Need I remind you that Daimos has the aid of the deity of illusions?" Grandma returned to her armchair. "He can rewrite reality according to his wishes, if the stories of that particular deity's prowess are true."

"What stories?" Aurel threw up her hands. "If you knew, why not tell us sooner?"

"Those stories." Grandma indicated the bookshelves at the back of the room. "The Great Powers might have lived a long time before anyone began to keep written records, but there are enough clues we can piece together to get a clear picture. What power exists in Invicten's Relics is based in trickery, whether through illusion or deception, and Daimos has not hesitated to use them to his advantage."

"I didn't know you'd read all those books." Admittedly, Aurel herself hadn't spent her childhood reading her way through every text in the Sanctum like her studious older sister had. Perhaps if she had, she wouldn't feel so lost— but even Zelle's extensive knowledge hadn't prevented her from being taken captive by the enemy.

Grandma scoffed. "It's been a long time, but I would have thought you might at least have some recollection of the abilities of the three Great Powers."

"I always thought Gaiva was the only one who mattered." The Shaper had been forgotten, including Her name, and Invicten—well, she didn't even know of anyone who sent prayers to the deity of illusion the way they did to Gaiva and Her many descendants. "You taught me that yourself. Besides, most people in Zeuten are ignorant of Relics in general. My knowing wouldn't have stopped Daimos from using Invicten's Relics against everyone else."

That had been a problem from the moment of Orzen's first attack, though. He'd brought a threat that nobody except the Sentinels was remotely equipped to deal with, and the Sentinels themselves had spent the past few centuries believing that they weren't intended to do anything but watch the Sanctum and keep the peace. Grandma, too, though she must know this situation was different than the norm. Zelle had been taken captive, and her nation's authorities had been put under the spell of a Great Power.

When Grandma didn't answer, Aurel walked over to her pack and pulled out her Book of Reading. It wasn't ideal, but the Book enabled her to Read objects, so if she applied it to the letters from the palace, she might get an insight into the goings-on in the palace itself.

"Don't be a fool," said the old Sentinel. "You won't learn your sister's location from that Book."

"Care to enlighten me, then?" Aurel lifted her head. "You've been to the palace in person, haven't you? You must remember the way around."

"That isn't the issue, Aurel, and you know it. The palace's security is unmatched."

"What do you want me to do, then?" Aurel challenged. "Leave her in there alone?"

"She isn't alone." Grandma's tone made the phrase sound more like a warning than a reassurance. "She has the staff. As long as Daimos remains ignorant of the truth of their bond, she holds at least one card."

"I don't follow." She could guess, though. Daimos might know the nameless Shaper's power was inside the staff, but he didn't know Zelle was entirely bonded to it as a true Relic.

In truth, Aurel had hardly had time to think on the matter herself, nor discuss the subject with her grandmother. Grandma herself had never been particularly attached to the staff despite her baffling refusal to give it to Aurel when she reached retirement age. When Zelle had swooped in and taken the staff for herself, Grandma had had no problem surrendering control, and while Aurel had briefly envied her sister for achieving what she herself had never been able to accomplish, wielding the staff seemed far more trouble than it was worth.

"Zelle knows the precariousness of her position," Grandma said. "She'll want to avoid giving away her reliance upon the staff, or else they might try to wrench it from her hands and doom themselves in the process."

Her heart gave a sickening lurch. "And if they try anyway?"

"Then Daimos will have succeeded at toppling the Crown without ever setting foot in the palace himself."

"No." Her sister might be inexperienced with magic, but she had a stubborn streak of her own. "I'll get her out of there first. But I need your help."

"You won't be convinced otherwise, I suppose." Grandma shook her head. "Fine. I'll tell you all I know."

———

I will return to Zeuten when I can, Rien told himself as the boat neared the docks of Aestin's capital, and the brightly painted buildings surrounding the harbour filled his vision. He had no way to disguise his identity, given that he'd left most of his belongings at the Sentinel's outpost, but there was no hiding his staff. Nor his godsmarks—the faded one from Astiva and the newer bright lines covering the backs of both his hands.

Rien handed the ship's captain a last handful of coins before walking down the pier. The smell of fresh fish and sea salt lingered in the air, while the distant sound of chatter and laughter from the market brought a rush of nostalgia tinged with wariness.

Who could he possibly ask to help him in a city that no longer felt like his home? Yes, Linas had generously taken him to his family's crypt during his last visit, but he wouldn't drag the old man out of hiding again. Their business together was done. He'd buried the dead and tidied his family's affairs to the best of his abilities, not realising that Daimos intended *him* to take the blame for their deaths.

In retrospect, it was an obvious move on Daimos's part. The Astera family's deaths had been public, true, but Rien had been the only surviving eyewitness save for Daimos himself. In his absence, all kinds of rumours might have sprung up.

As he neared the edges of the market, a faint crimson glow emanated from his staff. *What is it, Zierne?* The crimson sheen drew the attention of nearby shoppers, so he ducked into a side road.

It was then that he saw the figures tailing him, dressed in blue and gold. The Emperor's guards. Rien didn't slow his pace, though his godsmark tingled in warning, and the crimson glow brightened. After weighing the odds for a moment, he turned on the spot and found two imperial guards blocking his way back down the street.

"May I help you?"

"We seek Arien Astera," said a man with dark skin and close-shaven hair; most guards shaved their heads as a sign of dedication to their Emperor.

"I am he." Rien mustered the little patience he had, with difficulty. "As I'm sure you already know."

"His Excellency the Emperor has requested an audience with you," said a female guard. Like her companion, she'd shaved her head, which made her fine-boned features appear even sharper. "He has asked that we escort you to the Imperial Palace."

"Is there a particular reason His Imperial Majesty

wishes to speak to me?" He maintained a relaxed hold on the staff, though the warning crimson glow didn't dim. The temptation seized him to take the proffered chance to see the Emperor and explain the situation in person, but he couldn't ignore the risk of a repeat of his "meeting" with Zeuten's Crown Prince—except this time, instead of being put on a ship back home, he might find himself sentenced to death.

"There are some rather alarming rumours spreading throughout the capital of Zeuten that I was made aware of before my return," he went on. "I would prefer to know what His Excellency's viewpoint is before I put myself at His mercy."

"Mercy?" echoed the female guard. "You speak as if you expect to be detained."

"One such rumour claims that I murdered my family." He scanned their faces to assess whether they believed the same, but they retained the typical stoic expressions of imperial guards. "I have proof that I did not, but the authorities of Zeuten decreed that I would face a trial here in the capital. Is that true?"

"Certainly not," said the male guard. "Though if you speak of proof, then I would be curious to know what the royal guard of Zeuten considered unacceptable evidence."

They don't know. Daimos might have tricked the Crown Prince into believing that he was a criminal, but of course the authorities of Aestin would never have fallen for the same lie. They'd *seen* the carnage Daimos had left in place of the Astera family's home, and they'd also seen half the seafront blazing with fire as Daimos revelled in the new power he'd obtained.

If he'd boarded the ship home as intended, he'd likely

have been taken straight into Daimos's trap. As it was, perhaps he had a chance of salvaging this situation after all.

"This is my proof," he answered, pushing up his left sleeve to expose the new thorn-like marks on his hand and wrist, criss-crossing over the marks Astiva had left behind. "My Relic was stolen from me by my father's murderer. I carry another Relic that I was gifted as a replacement, but I still bear Astiva's mark."

The male guard peered at the markings, his eyes widening. Every Aestinian with at least a passing familiarity with magic knew what a broken godsmark meant. "I see why Zeuten's authorities wouldn't recognise... but who would spread such a rumour?"

"The same man who killed my family." His heart began to race, caution warring with hope. His father had been a good friend to the Emperor, but Rien had been the Astera family's youngest child, and so it was Torben who'd always been invited to accompany his father to their meetings.

"His Excellency would be most anxious to hear the story of your escape," said the female guard. "And how you came upon your new Relic. You did not step into the position at the head of your family as would have been expected, and as a result, there has been a considerable level of upheaval among the other families of Invokers."

Of course. He'd never truly considered the political fallout of his family's deaths in the wake of his own grief, but despite the tantalising notion of gaining the Emperor's support in his hunt for Daimos, if he'd learned anything from his recent dealings with the deities, it was that nothing came without a price.

"I must offer my apologies," said Rien. "I was unavoidably detained in Zeuten after I acquired my new Relic. However, my family's killer is at large, and it's my understanding that he might be here in Aestin. Is the Emperor searching for him?"

The male guard's expression flickered with puzzlement. "Not directly, but the Emperor was fond of your father and grieves his death greatly. For that reason, he has appointed a new security team to lead the search for the person responsible for your family's murders."

"Security." His mind flickered back to his last visit, in which Linas had informed him that the Trevain family had taken over as imperial security, a position they were vastly unqualified for. "Might I ask who leads this team?"

"Luvid Trevain," said the female guard. "It is he who will also be in charge of examining your new Relic and testing its readiness to serve the head of the Astera family."

Rien tensed. *So that's the price, is it?* "I thought the Trevain family's specialities were economics and trade, not imperial security. Moreover, I was under the impression that no single Invoker family was allowed to hold an elevated status over the others, according to the treaty established after the imperial revolution."

The male guard studied his face. "I can assure you that nobody has forgotten our history. It's a simple precaution for an unusual case such as yours, where you were presumed dead and then returned with an unknown Relic that might not fit within the constraints of the treaty itself."

"In what way?"

There wasn't a clause in that treaty that said every

major Invoker family had to keep the *same* Relic they'd started with, was there? Powers above, *Daimos's* ancestors had been in the original treaty, so not every aspect of its text was sacrosanct. Granted, Zierne's Relic had been removed from the country prior to the agreement between the original families of Invokers, but he had a suspicion that the new "rules" had been entirely Luvid Trevain's invention.

"I'm afraid I cannot say, but Luvid Trevain is well educated in such matters."

Powers above. This, he was sure, was how Daimos had infiltrated the capital. Rather than striking directly, he must have somehow gained influence over the Trevains, and if Rien entrusted them with his Relic, there was a good chance he'd never see it again.

"I must decline," he said. "I have already lost one Relic, and I am reluctant to part with another, especially with my family's killer at large."

"Clearly, recent events have distressed you." The male guard took a step forward, the concern in his voice masking a warning. "You must trust us, Arien."

Zierne reacted before Rien could hold back his Relic from striking, thorny vines unfurling from the staff and wrapping around the guards' ankles. When they hit the ground, he was already sprinting out of sight.

11

A palace was a strange place to be a prisoner.

Zelle's first day had passed in a bewildering blur of introductions to the various staff who'd been appointed to wait on her. She'd had a little time to settle into her rooms until a pair of guards had arrived with a suitcase of her own clothes they'd obtained from her shop in the seafront. Even knowing she'd made the request herself didn't make her any less repelled by the idea of them invading her home.

Nevertheless, none of her clothes were deemed suitable for that evening's dinner with the Crown Prince himself, with the result that she found herself walking down the corridor in a pair of shoes that pinched her feet and a dress adjusted to make it fit her short frame. Pins pricked her skin with every step as she walked behind Jarven, holding the edges of the lacy material off the ground to avoid tripping on the ends.

Jarven didn't say a word to her, though he'd barely left her presence all day, and she caught him looking at her occasionally as if wondering if he expected her to lose her temper and attack him. As tempting as it might have been, the risks were too high, and the Crown Prince was nearly as trapped as she was without even realising it. Until she found out how deep Daimos's influence ran and removed it, Zelle would do herself no favours by winding the noose tighter around her own neck.

They entered a sumptuous dining room, carpeted in blue and with a long table set out for two people. The staff must dine elsewhere—and so did the other members of the royal family—because the Crown Prince sat alone on one side of the mahogany table. Tapestries adorned the walls, while gilt furnishings reflected her own mismatched appearance back at her, down to the staff in her hand.

The Crown Prince gave her dress an approving look. "I like that much better than your other dress. If you put down that staff, you'd be quite lovely."

Anger seared the inside of her chest, while her hand burned with cold as if his comment had offended the staff as much as it'd irked her.

"Thank you," she said. "I am surprised you'd take the time to have dinner with me."

"Are you not a guest of mine?"

No, she thought. Rather than responding, she sat down in the chair opposite him, propping the staff carefully against the leg. Bowls of piping hot soup were placed in front of each of them, but she didn't pick up her spoon. Custom said the Crown Prince had to take the first bite, and her insides felt full of writhing snakes besides.

"Please don't look at me as if I were an Aestinian mountain viper," he said to her. "I do not intend to force you to bow before me like a commoner. I want to talk to you as an equal."

Her brows rose. "Equal? That is not my understanding of the relationship between the Crown and the Sentinels."

"You are more than a Sentinel, Zelle Carnelian," he said. "You are allied with one of the three Great Powers, and that gives you authority over anyone else who wields a Relic—let alone those who do not."

What? He couldn't be implying that she outranked *him*, not least because Zeuten didn't work like that. Aestin did, yes, but she was fairly certain he hadn't invited her here with the intention of letting her usurp him. Dizziness swept over her at the mere thought of being entrenched in royal life even more than she already was.

"I prefer not to think of it in that way." She'd also rather not admit how little she knew of her deity compared to most Invokers, but if he'd thought to appease her by telling her she was free to act as his equal, there must be a catch. "Nobody in Zeuten has ever allied with one of the Great Powers, to my knowledge, so there is not an established rule that I know of. I would prefer to act as though I were a regular guest."

"As you wish." He took a measured spoonful of soup and gestured for her to do the same. "This is good. All tested for poison, naturally."

Poison. Yet another worry to add to the list. She couldn't very well ask to be treated like a guest and then offend him, so she began to eat. It wasn't until they were finished with the soup course that he spoke again.

"The reason I wanted to talk to you should be obvious." He paused while a servant took their bowls away. "I want you to tell me how you became acquainted with the nameless Shaper."

Of course he did. He might have heard several versions of the story, true or not, but believing Rien to be a dangerous criminal had likely coloured his perceptions. While he'd agreed to leave her family alone in exchange for her cooperation, there had been no word of whether the palace guard had sent anyone to check up on Grandma or Aurel, and Zelle didn't trust them to hold to their promise. She'd have to be careful what she gave away.

"A few weeks ago, I went to visit my grandmother and found her missing, your Majesty," she began. "In the outpost, her staff was lying on the floor, abandoned. I took it for safekeeping, and shortly after, I found Rien outside the door, close to death from cold. I believed him to be a lost traveller, so I decided to take him to see my sister in Tavine. There, the deity known as Orzen attacked us, and we barely escaped with our lives."

Just the basic details would do. She didn't need to cover his temporary memory loss, nor the role the tales of Relics hidden in the mountains had played in his discoveries.

"Go on," encouraged the Crown Prince. "Who is Orzen? A child of Gaiva?"

"A descendent, I believe, your Majesty, like most of the other Powers," she replied. "He was sent across the sea from Aestin to kill Rien—Arien Astera. He also bewitched the Changers into assisting him, and they took my grandmother captive. When they found out Rien was staying with us, they offered a trade."

He raised a brow. "Your grandmother believed herself to be the Changers' captive, then?"

She ought to have guessed he'd take issue with that accusation, but she had no intention of admitting that her grandmother had not been captured at all but had ventured into the realm of the Powers of her own accord.

"We accepted the trade, so the Changers released my grandmother," she went on. "However, Orzen attacked again, forcing us to flee to the outpost. It was there that the nameless Shaper contacted me and told me how to bind Orzen into a new Relic. The Shaper also helped Rien find a new Relic to use against Orzen, and we successfully overcame him."

She'd hoped telling him that the Shaper had guided Zierne's Relic into Rien's hands might invite him to see the contradiction in the reports from his advisor. She risked a glance at the guard behind her, whose left hand had twitched a little closer to his weapon in an apparent unconscious movement.

"How fascinating," said the Crown Prince. "I thank you for your perspective."

The next course arrived, while Zelle mused on ways in which she might provoke him or Jarven into letting something useful slip. She hadn't the experience or patience for word games that Rien did, and simply existing in the same room as one of Daimos's allies made part of her want to cause a scene and shatter the glass on which everyone in the palace walked.

Instead, Zelle took a few tasteless bites of roasted beef before speaking again. "What do you know of the three Great Powers, your Majesty?"

"That's quite an odd question."

"Not necessarily. After all, you're in the presence of at least one of them."

Jarven's posture stiffened. With reluctance, Zelle tugged her gaze away from her guard before the Crown Prince saw, but he simply looked confused at her comment. "It's my understanding that a Relic contains a mere fragment of a deity's power. Is that not true?"

"Yes, your Majesty, but they say the Relics are the last remaining traces of the deities left in the human realm and are the closest we have to reaching them. Are you familiar with the stories of the three Great Powers?"

"You mean the children's stories, such as *Tales of the Three*?"

The familiar title brought a shiver to her arms. "That's one example, but no written texts mention the Great Powers being present in the world we live in. Since I have encountered two of them myself, I can only conclude that the deities are more involved in the human realm than any of us have been led to believe."

He put down his fork. "*Two* of the Great Powers? Are you saying that you have met another of the three, aside from the nameless Shaper?"

"Gaiva, your Majesty," she said. 'Her last Relic resides in the Isles of Itzar."

Another glance at Jarven rewarded her with a glimpse of the shimmer of light from beneath his sleeve. *His godsmark.* Further proof that he was human, not a deity, but that he undoubtedly carried a Relic of his own.

When she turned back to the Crown Prince, a glazed look had entered his eyes. "I have never been to Itzar myself. I'm told they have some outdated beliefs there."

"Outdated?" Her patience thinned. "Gaiva is real. I spoke to Her directly."

He picked up his fork as if she'd merely commented on the weather. "I have a question for you, Zelle."

"What is that, your Majesty?"

"I intend to hold an event at the end of this week for the noble houses of Zeuten," he told her. "I think it's appropriate to celebrate the return of the nameless Shaper with a special occasion."

Public appearances? Powers above, he had to be joking. And why had he changed the subject? Did he disbelieve her, or was there more to the glazed look in his eyes than simple ignorance? "Such as...?"

"A public event to introduce you as the new ally of the nameless Shaper. What do you think?"

Her mouth parted. "You wish for me to speak to the public?"

If he took her outside of the palace, she might have a chance to get away. She'd be a fool to pass up the opportunity.

"Yes," he said. "They can't wait to meet you, I'm sure."

"Then I'd be glad to accept."

He beamed, the expression not quite hiding the hazy glint in his eyes. "Excellent."

———

Rien turned the corner, leaving the guards in the dust—along with any hopes he might have had of getting the Emperor on his side rather than becoming a fugitive in two countries at once.

The odds had been against him from the start, but as

long as he refused to submit his staff to Luvid Trevain, then Rien would be viewed as untrustworthy whether they thought him a criminal or not, thanks to the laws his own ancestors had helped to create. He might have found the irony amusing if he hadn't been too busy running.

Rien veered into a side street, and a figure loomed in front of him. The staff reacted first, and the target ducked out of sight as Rien hastened to swing the Relic to the side so the vines would clash harmlessly against the wall. "Linas?"

The old man's leathery face peered from behind a door. "Come in here, quickly."

Rien hurried after him, more from the lack of any other options than a desire to hide. "Linas, what are you still doing in the city?"

"Didn't I tell *you* not to come back?" The old man firmly closed the door, plunging them into darkness. "What did you do to the guards?"

"They wanted me to surrender my Relic for an assessment." The staff continued to burn against his hand, as if Zierne sought another target to strike down, and its crimson glow illuminated the darkened room of what must be a safe house. "Why in Gaiva's name does Luvid Trevain have the authority to determine *my* status as an Invoker?"

"Powers above, Arien." Linas shook his head. "I don't deny Luvid Trevain is a crook, but the Astera family was believed to be dead, and someone had to take command of the guard who has the skills to deal with a dangerous Invoker."

"So this isn't Daimos's work?" He didn't try to keep the

scepticism out of his voice. "Luvid Trevain was promoted solely on his own merits, was he?"

Linas gave a low chuckle. "You sounded just like Volcan then."

Rien jerked back as if the old man had struck him. "It is an insult to his memory that the Trevains are allowed any authority at all, if they truly did ally with Daimos to save themselves."

"I don't disagree with you, boy," said Linas. "If Daimos put Luvid Trevain in his position, though, I have seen no proof of it."

The sound of hammering footsteps outside caused them to fall into a tense silence until the noise faded out. *I have to get out of here.* But where could he go? Hiding under the noses of Daimos's allies wasn't an option, but there was nothing for him outside of the capital either.

"If the Trevains are the ones in charge of the search, then Daimos could probably stride directly into the Imperial Palace without being challenged," Rien pointed out. "How am I to avoid capture?"

Linas muttered a curse under his breath. "I wish you'd sent word you were coming."

"I was expelled from Zeuten due to my alleged status as a criminal who'd been summoned to stand trial here in Aestin for murdering my own family," Rien told him. "They didn't give me the chance to send warning."

"I bet not." The old man heaved a sigh. "Why did you have to attack the imperial guards?"

"That was my Relic, not me." It sounded odd for an Invoker to speak of one's Relic as a separate entity, he knew, but he didn't have it in him to be anything but honest with one of his father's oldest friends. "I believe that Luvid Trevain would have found a way to deny me my former status regardless of whether or not I cooperated with the guards."

"You aren't wrong," said Linas. "If it is Daimos's doing, then I don't doubt he has eyes watching the other families too."

"What happened to the Martzels, then?" Rien referred to the third of the major Invoker families in Aestin.

"They fled south, out of the city, before Daimos could target them the way he did the others," Linas replied. "And if you want to last an hour without being arrested, then you'll have to join them."

12

Evita lay sprawled in an undignified heap, her cloak pinned by arrows, and looked up into the eyes of Master Drazer, the new head of the Changers. Her hood had fallen back, exposing her face.

"It's her," crowed one of the novices. "The fugitive."

"You." The large man grabbed the scruff of her neck, hauling her to her feet. "What did you take from my office?"

Evita gagged, unable to speak until he loosened his hold a little. "I don't have anything of yours. You're welcome to check."

All he'd find in her pockets was the lockpick that Aurel had given her, but she needed to get those spelled arrows out of her cloak if she wanted to make her escape.

The back of his hand slammed into her face, sending her pitching forward. "Then why were you in my office?"

Evita spat out blood from where she'd bitten the inside of her cheek, lies spinning through her thoughts as she struggled to pick out one that wouldn't result in her body being impaled with arrows to match her cloak. "I wanted to find out who told you to capture the Sentinel."

"You read my private correspondence, didn't you?"

"No. I can't read."

One of the novices laughed, and Master Drazer silenced him with a look. She thought of Vekka and Izaura and tasted bile in the back of her throat.

He picked her up by the scruff of her neck again. If he flung her off a cliff, there was a rather depressing chance that she'd fall to her death even wearing the cloak, thanks to the spelled arrows weighing her down.

"I… work for the Reader," she gasped out. "I wanted to stop the Senior Changers from trying to capture her grandmother."

"You work for the Reader," he repeated.

"Yes." She twisted her left hand around in an attempt to reach the nearest arrow sticking out of the hem of her cloak. "I'm her assistant."

Her hand closed around the arrow, and she gave a tug. Her grip broke when Master Drazer shook her like a sack of grain. "You broke into my office. You are also wearing a stolen cloak."

"It's not… stolen." She reached for the arrow again and managed to tug the tip loose, but the others were impossible for her to access unless he let go of her. "I was given it to use on a mission, but I wasn't asked to return it to the Changers."

He shook her again, unintentionally giving her the chance to snag another of the arrows in her fingertips. "I can see why Master Amery was keen to see you expelled from the Changers. Your attitude leaves much to be desired."

The arrow came free, along with a rush of recklessness. "Good job I'm not one of them, then."

Get me out of here. Fly. Please.

The next time he shook her, the cloak unfolded like wings. In a burst of triumph, she flew out of his grasp—but he caught her ankle first, giving her another shake that dislodged the last of the arrows.

"Interesting," he remarked, holding her upside down in front of him. "You're bonded to that cloak."

Her stomach lurched. How did he know? He might wear the uniform, but she was certain she'd never seen him among the Changers before today. His expression shifted, studying her in a manner that put her in mind of a bird of prey contemplating a cornered rodent.

"You're lucky." He released her ankle and then caught her arm, causing her to swing into an upright position. "Few are able to gain that level of skill without years of training. Were you still a Changer, you'd be qualified to join our senior ranks."

Was he serious? She'd turned down the same offer from Briony and Verne, but they at least hadn't tried to kill her prior to making their request. A murmur passed among the surrounding novices, and she coughed. "I declined... the offer."

"Yes, you did." He let go of her arm, causing her to land in a crouch in front of him. "I can see why the Senior Changers took an interest in you. If you join us, then I will teach you how to use the cloak to its full extent."

He's... asking me to join? She opened her mouth to ask if he'd lost his mind, but when his gaze bored into hers, her mind went fuzzy. Her legs swayed, as if she stood at the edge of a cliff, yet the ground underfoot remained steady despite the free-falling sensation in her mind. A strange orange glow infiltrated the corners of her vision, and her fear fled, to be replaced by a still calmness.

The cloak was a Relic. *Her* Relic. Why shouldn't she learn how to use it?

No, a voice whispered in the back of her mind, growing fainter. *No...*

"Come with me."

Her feet moved of their own accord, and the whisper in the back of her mind became entirely silent as she followed him towards the cave nearest to the building where the Masters made their home. *I always wondered what it looked like in there,* she thought, an odd turbulence battering at the edges of her mind. Yet when she probed further, she found nothing but blankness.

The Senior Changers' cave was considerably wider and more sheltered than the one she'd stayed in as a novice. Few people were inside, but that was to be expected, with the Senior Changers trading shifts guarding the village.

The village. Words came to mind, and she gave Master Drazer a querying look. "I met two Senior Changers at Tavine, the village..."

The image of two bodies pinned with arrows flitted into her mind, but the unpleasant picture vanished a moment later. So did the rest of her sentence, leaving a pleasant emptiness behind.

He studied her face. "Is something wrong?"

She shook her head. "No... I don't think so."

"You will be an asset to us," he said. "Your Relic will enable you to achieve feats that most ordinary people can never dream of. All we ask for in exchange is your loyalty and your service."

That sounded perfectly reasonable to Evita.

———

The next day in the palace passed in a blur of appointments. Zelle learned very quickly that most of the staff had been ordered to treat her like a real guest despite her being a prisoner without the bars. Only Jarven remained as a constant reminder of her precarious position, though mostly he stood in the corner like a piece of furniture. Zelle hoped to catch a glimpse of his Relic, but she'd had no luck so far. There were always other people around, from the seamstress to the various servants and other palace staff sent to wait on her during every waking hour.

Oddly, she hadn't seen the Crown Prince himself since that first evening's dinner. Perhaps she'd scared him off. Or Jarven hadn't wanted to give her the chance to drop hints about Daimos's treachery in front of him again. Jarven never let himself be alone with her, either—at least not until the second day after her arrival in the palace, when he came to escort her to the carriage that would take her to the Crown Prince's public reveal of his new ambassador. Afterwards, the two of them would return to the palace to welcome the guests to the private ball he intended to use to win goodwill with the nobility. Her only chance to escape would be during the public part of the event, or before, if she managed to get the upper hand on Jarven.

Don't do anything rash, the staff warned her.

I've been doing the exact opposite, she answered, having grown used to communicating silently with the staff over the past few days. *If I hadn't, I'd have stabbed Jarven in the eye with a fork during my first dinner with the Crown Prince.*

Instead of acting against her enemy, she'd been forced to spend the better part of a day trying on various outfits to find one suitable for the ball. It was a colossal waste of time and money, and she'd hated every moment of it.

When Jarven came to escort her to the carriage, however, he was accompanied by two more palace guards, neither of whom she was familiar with. Getting him alone would be trickier than she'd anticipated.

One would think he suspected you were plotting his death, the staff commented.

Ha, she replied. *No, murder is too conspicuous. I just wanted to expose his Relic.*

She was certain the staff was more than a match for him in a fight, but as long as he kept his weapon hidden, she didn't know how powerful he truly was. One misstep, and the staff would be ripped from her hands, and besides, what if he didn't carry his Relic on his person? Or if there was more than one in the palace? Igon, for instance, had been able to separate himself into five separate beings, each of whom carried a duplicate of the same Relic, and there was no telling what kind of powers the god of illusions would bestow upon someone.

Exactly. It won't be as simple as knocking him over the head and then running away.

I haven't a chance of outrunning anyone in this dress, you know. For the occasion, Zelle wore a dress that looked more like a cloud than a garment, puffy and white and floaty. It was mildly better than being stabbed with a thousand pins but not much.

Upon descending the stairs outside the palace, the guards ushered her towards a crimson-curtained carriage, in which the Crown Prince sat, resplendent in a dark red coat studded with gold buttons. His clothing was ostentatious but a touch more practical than Zelle's ridiculous dress.

She climbed into the carriage and sat beside him, and they rattled through the gates and out of the palace grounds. Her heart skipped a beat, but rather than heading downhill, the carriage remained within the royal district and took them on a winding route past the palace.

"What is it?" The Crown Prince studied her face. "You look disappointed."

"Where are we going, your Majesty?" she asked. "I thought you were going to address the public, not just the nobility."

"I am," he said. "However, my advisors told me that I would be better to give the address somewhere that attendees can be vetted so that nobody untoward would have the opportunity to sneak in. I'll be speaking at the Public Gardens instead."

Of course it wouldn't be that easy. "Should I have prepared a speech? Nobody has told me what I'm supposed to say."

"Oh, don't worry yourself," he said. "I'll do all the talking. I'm the one they're here to see."

The brief impulse hit her to push the Crown Prince out of the carriage and make it look like an accident, or simply to jump out herself and hope that she didn't break her ankles in the process. When they left the palace behind, however, people had already begun to fill the streets to watch the carriage, waving eagerly. Some held coloured banners, others blew whistles, and cheers filled the air in their wake.

The crowds grew denser the nearer they came to the Public Gardens. Mostly the nobility, but some commoners had dressed the part and entered the upper-class district to hear the Crown Prince speak. He was more popular than Zelle had realised, though she'd be the first to admit that she had no experience with how most regular people viewed Zeuten's royals. The patrons who visited her shop were typically more interested in history than the present, after all.

The Crown Prince rolled back the curtains to wave at everyone they passed, while Zelle sat stiffly beside him and tried not to roll her eyes. Whatever game he was playing, she wanted no part in it whatsoever. So few people noted her presence that she wondered if she might be able to hop out of the carriage and hide amid the crowd after all—but then the carriage came to a halt outside the Public Gardens, and she lost her chance.

In front of them, bright flowers filled beds arranged in rows between splashing fountains and carved hedges, and as soon as they climbed out of the carriage, they were surrounded by people waving banners. Guards formed a barrier between the Crown Prince and the crowd while they walked through the gardens to a raised platform. The audience filled the space in front of them, and a sense of unreality washed over Zelle, just like during her first arrival in the palace. While the Crown Prince ascended the platform with a wide grin, it was Jarven who gave

Zelle a firm shove in the small of her back, urging her to join him.

Jarven then addressed the crowd, his voice cutting through the clamour. "His Highness would speak."

Silence spilled into eager anticipation, and the sea of faces before Zelle swam like a mirage.

"It's an honour to be here and to speak to so many of you," the Crown Prince began. "This is my first visit to the public in quite some time, but I'm sure you'll find it worth the wait. There's someone I would very much like you to meet."

Zelle tensed, while cheers rose among the crowd, and the Crown Prince waited for them to peter out before continuing.

"This is Zelle Carnelian, the new wielder of the Relic of the nameless Shaper. Yes, you heard me correctly: one of the Great Powers has returned to this world."

More cheering. This time they were cheering *her* as much as the Crown Prince, and Zelle found her grip tightening on the staff. For once, it didn't venture a sarcastic comment, while the Crown Prince's next words silenced everyone.

"A great challenge is facing our nation," he told the crowd. "The nameless Shaper has returned to offer us aid against those who would threaten us."

A murmur travelled through the crowd. The impulse seized Zelle to take the stage for herself and reveal the true nature of those threats—but who would the public believe, their beloved royal, or a relative stranger of whom they knew nothing except what the Crown Prince had told them?

"Zeuten is under threat," he went on. "A great battle is

imminent against a nation much larger than our own, and Zelle Carnelian and the Shaper will be our defenders."

When he'd spoken to her of public appearances, he certainly hadn't mentioned fighting any wars. Who did he expect her to fight? Not Aestin, surely. A small nation like Zeuten was nothing in comparison. They'd be pulverised.

Powers above. He's not insinuating that we're going to war with Aestin, is he?

Wouldn't that be convenient for Daimos? The staff's response chilled her blood.

So did the smile on Jarven's face when she glanced in his direction. He knew *exactly* what the Crown Prince was planning and how it fed into Daimos's plans.

Reeling, Zelle looked out at the crowd... and saw her sister staring back at her.

Rien sat in the back of the curtained carriage, heading south of Aestin's capital. Linas had arranged the transport from his safe house, and then Rien had made his stealthy way to meet the driver, a trusted friend of both Linas and the Martzels. He'd been surprised to find himself faced with the rare sight of a carriage with a roof and curtains, Zeutenian-style, ready to take him to the neighbouring province where the Martzels had gone into hiding.

The experience of riding in a carriage in Aestin was noticeably smoother than in Zeuten, since the roads were of better quality, but he was grateful the curtains obscured his all-too-recognisable face. While he'd waited for the carriage to arrive, he'd had to conceal the staff under his coat and borrow a hat from Linas that was several sizes too big for him. He looked ridiculous, but at least he'd been inconspicuous enough to avoid attention. Yet he didn't fully relax when they left Aestin's capital behind, continuing to watch the countryside rolling past through a gap in the curtains in case of an ambush. Linas had reassured him that the carriage driver was known and trusted by the Martzel family, but that didn't completely reassure him that he was out of danger yet.

In the end, though, exhaustion won out. He'd barely slept on the voyage from Zeuten, part of him convinced he'd be woken in the dead of night by the sound of the door slamming open or the crash of the ship striking against a solid obstacle. Rien fell into a doze, waking to the setting sun painting orange stripes across the sky.

Shortly after, the carriage halted. Rien paid the driver, having to dig into his pockets for the right currency buried beneath the Zeutenian coin he'd become habituated to carrying everywhere, and walked down the winding country road to a large estate with whitewashed walls and arched windows. The grounds expanded to cover a stretch of nearby woodland, but Rien headed straight for the red-painted door.

The door opened before he reached it, and the leader of the Martzel family studied Rien from the doorway. Devan Martzel was around his father's age, with nut-brown skin and grey streaks in his long, dark-brown hair. An old injury caused him to walk with a limp, and he leaned heavily on the carved mahogany staff that also served as his Relic. His family wielded the Relics of Venzei, another of Astiva's siblings and one with a particular gift of mastery over the weather. For that reason, among others, the Martzels had been strong friends of the Astera family, and that had no doubt played a part in why they'd resisted siding with Daimos. The real question was, how much did old Martzel know of Rien's own situation?

"Devan Martzel." Rien bowed his head in the Aestinian

gesture of respect from one Invoker to another. "It's a pleasure to see you again."

"Arien Astera." Martzel repeated the motion. "Linas was right. You survived."

"I rather think my survival is the least of the rumours that are likely circulating in the capital."

"Yes… I've heard some of those too." Martzel hobbled backwards, leaning on his staff. "Come in."

A wide entrance hall with polished floors greeted him on the other side. Martzel led him through to a drawing room carpeted in burgundy and full of upholstered furniture.

Rien studied the worn bookshelves and cabinets. "You aren't alone here?"

"No, of course not," said Martzel. "Sanne's riding outside. Her husband stayed in the city, though he has plans to flee if anyone comes asking after her."

Martzel was a widower, while Sanne, his eldest daughter, had married a nobleman with no magical gift of his own. That didn't necessarily mean he was safe from being targeted by Daimos, however.

"Is Reyes not here?"

"He's supposed to be." Martzel pursed his lips. "He refused to listen to me, the fool."

That came as no surprise to Rien. Reyes had always had a rebellious streak, and as the younger sibling, Reyes wouldn't inherit his father's Relic upon his death. He'd also be expected to pass on his own Relic to an heir, and since Reyes preferred relationships with men, he and his long-term partner, Sarpe, would have to adopt from outside the family and run the risk of their Relic rejecting its wielder. Adoption wasn't unheard of among the lesser nobility, but the Martzel family's high renown meant that the subject had been the centre of a long debate, and Rien didn't blame Reyes for wanting to get away from all the attention.

Rien himself had been lucky, since Volcan had always supported his own children regardless of Torben's tendency to flirt with everything that moved and his inability to commit to a serious relationship or a plan for the future of his Relic. As for Rien, he'd had no plan either. He was unlikely to be able to envision his own future as long as he remained a fugitive, let alone who he might spend it with.

He'd left those hopes behind in a palace in Zeuten.

"You came here a while ago," he said to Martzel. "Not long after Daimos's attack."

Martzel grimaced at the sound of Daimos's name. "I would happily have offered you aid if I had been able to find you, but frankly, we thought you were dead."

"I expected that he'd go after the other major Invoker families next, so you were wise to leave. I barely escaped myself."

Martzel's gaze went to the staff in Rien's hand. "That Relic… it looks familiar."

"It's Zierne's Relic," he explained. "Astiva's brother. I found it in the home of the settlers in Zeuten."

Martzel's eyes widened. "Then it's true?"

"That I found a Relic in Zeuten?" he said. "Yes, but it seems His Excellency's advisors believe a new Relic isn't enough for me to qualify as head of my family. I was ordered to submit my Relic to none other than Luvid Trevain to be tested as worthy."

Martzel swore under his breath. "Luvid Trevain is the

worst of his sort—self-serving to the core. But you must tell me how such an event came about. To find a lost Relic of one of Gaiva's children is nothing short of a miracle."

"Don't get too excited," said Rien. "It's also the reason I'm a fugitive in Zeuten as well as here."

Rien told Martzel of his journey to find the Sentinels and his defeat of Orzen. He didn't mention the Shaper, though part of him wanted to—it wasn't his story to tell, and neither were the recent events in Itzar. Partway through, Sanne, Martzel's oldest daughter, entered the room. She had the same nut-brown skin and long, dark-brown hair as her father, her grey eyes serious and discerning. She wore riding clothes, and her boots were muddy and her hair windswept.

"That's a remarkable story," Martzel said when Rien had finished. "Yet not unsurprising, given the rumours about those mountains."

"I wish I could recall where I found out there might be Relics hidden there," Rien admitted. "My father's records were destroyed in the fire when Daimos burned the estate."

Not that they needed to know the reasons for his curiosity. Zierne was quiet now, but his reaction to the imperial guard proved his impulses to strike down his enemies were as active as ever.

Turning the subject back to his return to Aestin, Rien gave them a summary of Daimos's machinations in Zeuten, including the rumours he'd spread amid the royal palace.

Martzel's eyes widened. "He dared to accuse you of murdering the other Asteras?"

"He didn't try the same here, I notice," Rien added.

"Too many witnesses, I suppose… but when did the Trevains take his side?"

"That I don't know," growled Martzel. "I often talked with Volcan about the suspicious activities they were involved in, but I certainly never heard mention of Daimos's name."

"I was watching them too." Rien recalled that day with all too much clarity. "They were selling Relics at the market that appeared to be the genuine article. That was what my brother was looking into when Daimos—when he attacked us."

"I suppose the Trevains hastened to secure an alliance with Daimos at the first opportunity," Sanne remarked disdainfully. "No doubt to avoid the same fate."

"Some of the lesser families have joined with him too," said Martzel. "For their own protection. That's why it's been so damned hard to find allies."

"You're looking for them, though?" Despite himself, hope stirred within him. The Martzels were the only powerful family who'd managed to escape Daimos, evidently, but that was better than nobody at all. "I'd be happy to help if I knew where to start."

It remained to be seen whether any Invoker would believe the word of a fugitive, but he'd need help to expose whoever Daimos had sent to influence the imperial guard.

"We are," Martzel said, "but nobody with any influence has agreed to meet with us. They fear the consequences."

They're cowards, he wanted to say, but had he not fled for his own survival himself? Had he not betrayed the principles his father had instilled in him? He'd come to terms with his choice and put it to rest, and it would not do to condemn others for doing the same.

Martzel studied his face, perhaps discerning some of his inner thoughts. "We're doing our best with the limited resources we have available. Daimos, we believe, is not operating from the capital himself."

"But you think you might know where he is?" Tension ratcheted up his spine. If he found the man himself and slew him with his own hand, then he might not need to risk arrest at all.

"No, but I know where we can find out," Martzel said. "The house that belonged to Naxel Daimos's family prior to their exile."

"You have the address?" Sanne's brow furrowed. "It isn't abandoned?"

"I guarantee he would have returned there at least once," Martzel said. "After his return from exile."

"If he's operating from a stronghold here in Aestin, he'll have some proof in there," Rien concluded. "Have you been there yourself?"

Martzel barked a laugh. "This leg of mine makes navigating my own stairs difficult enough. I'm in no state to run from whatever security he's hired, Arien. You, however, might stand a chance."

Yes. This was precisely what he needed, despite Sanne's raised brows at her father's declaration.

"Alone?" she ventured. "Father, I wouldn't encourage Arien to risk his life and freedom."

"I'm risking both with every moment I spend in this country," Rien reminded them. "Daimos will not allow me to rest until I am dead or at his mercy. I've thwarted him too many times for him to leave me be."

"That seems excessive," Sanne commented. "Was the Daimos family always like this?"

"Driven to accomplish their goals?" Martzel's expression darkened. "Yes. In fact, it took the combined effort of three Invoker families to exile his predecessors."

"Including yours?" Rien asked, momentarily distracted by the reminder that he'd never gained conclusive answers on the exact circumstances of Daimos's parents' exile. "Alongside my father?"

Martzel's gaze turned downward. "Yes, I was there. I never would have believed we might face a similar threat again. We assumed that removing his Relic would prevent any member of the Daimos family from attaining enough power to challenge the Invokers or the Emperor."

So did my father. A rush of sorrow arose, along with fury at Daimos for denying him the chance to properly grieve with his family's close friends, but he knew that none of them would be safe until he ended Daimos's life.

"Daimos found a Relic belonging to the deity Orzen and managed to summon him, though," he said. "How?"

"A question we've been asking ourselves for weeks," said Martzel. "On that subject, how can he have obtained influence in Zeuten as well as Aestin?"

Rien had skirted around the subject of the Great Powers, reluctant to expose Zelle's secret, but with her in the Crown Prince's custody, it was only a matter of time before someone else revealed her bond with the nameless Shaper to the world. "He obtained the Relics of Invicten, the illusionist."

"Invicten?" Sanne exclaimed. "One of the three Great Powers?"

"According to the Sentinels of Zeuten," Rien said. "I

know he can't be wielding the Relics himself, since he already has…"

Astiva. The name stuck in his throat, bringing a rush of shame and anger at his ongoing weakness. He wondered if the pain would ever cease. Maybe when he killed Daimos and brought an end to his cruel games, his grief would be laid to rest.

Sanne swore under her breath. "He must be exposed. Using a Great Power's Relic to manipulate the Emperor is high treason."

"I know." Rien's hand clenched around his staff. "It's my understanding that the very nature of Invicten's magic is to manipulate the target into believing anything the Relic's wielder wants them to, regardless of their status or influence. The Crown Prince of Zeuten believes me to be a murderer and thief, and the Emperor is no doubt convinced I am unstable at best thanks to whoever is operating in his inner circle."

Compared to removing said person from the imperial palace without being arrested or killed, breaking into Daimos's house would be an easy feat.

"Then we must bring his schemes to a halt." Martzel took in a measured breath. "This is what I know of his family's property."

———

Aurel met Zelle's eyes across the crowd, shock reverberating through her at the sight of her sister standing atop a raised platform next to the Crown Prince of Zeuten. She almost hadn't recognised her; Zelle looked utterly unlike herself in a strange cloud-like dress and with her hair styled into layers of curls. Aurel hadn't seen her sister in formal dress since they were both children, and only the staff in her hand gave away her real identity. Despite the cheering crowd, she wasn't smiling. Unlike the prince, who grinned at his audience as though he was thrilled to be there, Zelle wore the expression of one resigned to her death. No surprise, given that despite her fine clothes, she'd been trapped in the palace for days. It didn't look as though she'd been ill-treated, at least, but Aurel's heart plummeted when the Crown Prince introduced Zelle as the wielder of the nameless Shaper.

Powers above, he knows. Zelle hadn't told him, had she? Maybe she'd been coerced into sharing the information, but this was too well put together to have been a last-minute plan. No, she was certain Daimos was the culprit, and he'd intended to make Zelle a public ally of the Crown so that her magic would be exposed to the world, and she'd become too recognisable to go back into hiding again.

Two days Aurel had spent creeping around the city, trying to find Zelle's location. Firstly, she'd gone to her shop and found the place deserted, learning nothing from the neighbours except that they'd seen the royal guards in the area recently. She'd already suspected that Zelle was being kept in the palace, but no ordinary people were allowed near, and exposing her status as the next Sentinel would only land Aurel in a cage as gilded as Zelle's.

A stroke of luck had hit when she'd learned of the first public appearance of the Crown Prince and his new ally. She'd have had a harder time sneaking into the royal district if not for the dragonet, but once she'd reached the crowds, it had been relatively easy to stay hidden while she made her way to the Public Gardens. Provided she didn't draw attention. While she might have tried to cause a diversion and smuggle Zelle over to Chirp's hiding place, half the palace's guards seemed to be here, while the size of the crowd would prove an impediment to a hasty escape.

"Zeuten is under threat." The Crown Prince's warning echoed throughout the gardens. "A great battle is imminent against a nation much larger than our own, and Zelle Carnelian and the Shaper will be our defenders."

Will she now? Zelle certainly didn't look as if he'd consulted her on the matter before throwing her onto the front lines of a war, but his comment cemented her certainty that this was Daimos's work. He wanted to *orchestrate a war between Zeuten and Aestin...* and if his claws had sunk as deep into Aestin's government as they had Zeuten's, he might just get his wish.

Aurel's gaze locked with Zelle's. Her sister shook her head, faintly, a reminder to stay hidden. Zelle couldn't possibly have agreed to be turned into a public symbol, put on display like a trinket in a cabinet—and to potentially be made a martyr as well.

Aurel refused to let her sister sacrifice herself. Enough was enough.

Applause from the crowd followed, and Zelle and the Crown Prince stepped off the stage. Aurel pushed her way forward, but guards surrounded the pair of them almost at once, herding them out of the gardens and into a waiting carriage.

"Gaiva's tits," she muttered under her breath.

The crowd cushioned her from sight as she squeezed out of the gardens, listening out for any clues as to their next destination. A brief span of eavesdropping on a group of well-dressed nobles told her there would be a ball at the palace following the announcement, and she had no doubt the prince planned to put Zelle on display there too.

Aurel wove through the crowd until she was certain no guards were nearby before hurrying to look for the dragonet. He'd hidden himself in a swathe of bushes at the far edge of the public park adjacent to the gardens, since it had been considerably difficult to find a suitable hiding place for a beast of that size in the nobles' area of the city.

As much as it amused Aurel to imagine the dragonet ambushing the Crown Prince's carriage and lifting Zelle out in his claws, the guards were armed with bows as well as swords. After her escape from the Changers, she'd had to help Chirp remove a spelled arrow from his wing that had caused him a great deal of pain, and while the wound had mostly healed, the dragonet had been skittish and reluctant to get too close to the imperial guards.

Crouching among the bushes, she whispered, "Thanks for doing this with me."

The dragonet chirped sadly. He'd been subdued since Evita's disappearance, but after a brief span of resistance, he'd been willing to help Aurel with her various trips back and forth from Saudenne to find her sister. Aurel had made the choice to help Zelle first, but she wished she hadn't needed to pick one over the other. Evita might be better equipped to escape the Changers than Zelle was to get out of the palace, but two days had passed with no signs of her return.

Now Aurel had a new dilemma on her hands. How in Gaiva's name was she supposed to sneak into a high-security event for nobles only and smuggle Zelle to the dragonet's hiding place? Her sister did at least know she was present in the city, which was a starting point, but she'd have to improvise from there.

Drawing in a deep breath, she addressed Chirp. "I'm going to need you to ambush one of those guards."

14

Zelle could hardly believe her sister had shown up at a public event in full view of the palace guards. Aurel hadn't even bothered with a disguise, though the sheer size of the crowd and the presence of the Crown Prince meant she'd gone unseen thus far. How had she sneaked into the royal district in the first place? Was Evita here? Questions circled around Zelle's thoughts as she rode in the carriage beside the Crown Prince. He waved at the crowd, beaming, while she bit her tongue and vowed to confront him later over his claims that she'd be willing to stride into battle at the head of an army to defend her nation.

Is it worse than attending a ball? the staff asked.

Her jaw twitched. *Do you want to go to war yourself? Do you think it will be anything other than disastrous for our country if we were to go head-to-head with Aestin's Invokers?*

The staff made no reply, while the Crown Prince continued to beam and wave at passersby.

Finally, the carriage rattled through the gates and

halted on the cobblestones at the foot of the stone staircase leading into the palace. Jarven waited for them, ready to lead her and the Crown Prince to the entrance hall and then through a gold-framed mahogany door into a vast ballroom. None of the guests had arrived yet, but two guards stood outside each exit, while servants set out delicacies upon tables at the edges of the large room.

The Crown Prince beckoned her to stand beside him beside the entrance to greet the guests when they showed up, while Jarven stood at a far enough distance away that nobody would realise he was watching their every move. Zelle's fingers twitched on the staff. The Crown Prince might have let her carry it, but the staff was as much of a prop as she was. She wasn't supposed to *use* her power... unless he was serious about sending her into battle.

The thought chilled her to the bone.

"You're cold," the Crown Prince observed, noticing her shiver. "Stand closer to me."

"I'd rather not, Your Majesty."

He chuckled under his breath. "Did you think the public might believe you and I are courting?"

The thought had crossed her mind. They were of a similar age and had shown up publicly in each other's company, which might have given a certain impression. Yet he repelled her, both in his attitude and in his willingness to submit to Daimos's commands, conscious or not.

"We have absolutely nothing in common," she said. "Besides, you just insinuated that you plan to send me to war on behalf of Zeuten. You can't court me if I'm dead."

He blinked. "You're certainly in a cheery mood, aren't you?"

"You didn't consult me first." Zelle kept her voice low

to avoid drawing too much attention from the servants or guards. "Sending someone into war at the head of an army isn't generally a decision you make without any input from the person in question."

"I never told them you would be sent into battle," he said. "What would give you that idea?"

"You said the country was under threat and that I and the nameless Shaper would be Zeuten's defenders."

"Is that not why the Shaper bonded with you?"

"To defend Zeuten, yes—not to ride into battle at the head of an army. I'm not trained as a soldier."

"Nobody suggested anything of the sort."

Some of Zelle's self-control slipped. "You told everyone Zeuten was about to go to war with a greater power than ours, unless that was purely an attempt to garner public approval and the reality is that you want me to be a symbol and not a fighter."

"So blunt." His gaze roved over the staff. "Do you think Aestin doesn't do the exact same with their Invokers? They *are* symbols of Aestin's might."

"The Invokers have more influence than the Emperor does," she corrected him. "Including over their own destinies."

"Is that what you want of me?" A mocking edge entered his voice. "You want me to let *you* rule?"

"I want you to consider that I had plans of my own, ones that didn't involve fighting your wars." A faint glow came to the staff, spreading to her hands beneath the thin gloves she'd worn precisely to avoid making a scene in this manner. *Powers preserve me from striking this fool of a prince down on the spot.*

"Did you?" Was he entirely oblivious to the danger of

provoking the nameless Shaper? "Did those plans involve Arien Astera? Would it bother you so much if he were to be the enemy you faced on the battlefield?"

"Rien." She almost laughed despite the spasm that tugged at her heart at the mention of his name. "You think he's going to start a war?"

"I think there's a possibility that we need to prepare for that scenario, yes."

Zelle shook her head, unable to believe that he'd convinced himself *Rien* was going to declare war on Zeuten. "I'd be surprised if a fugitive on the run from the law managed to raise an army."

He might, the staff ventured. *Or it might appear that way from here in Zeuten.*

That was the problem. Daimos was entirely responsible for the Crown Prince's beliefs on the situation in Aestin, and she had no way to determine the level of truthfulness in his claims as long as she remained inside the palace. After all, it was Zeuten's guards who'd been told to hunt Rien down and expel him from the country, and she hadn't heard of any actual Aestinians being involved in his capture. If he'd somehow escaped and reached Aestin, he might not be a fugitive there at all.

That was too hopeful a scenario to be accurate, so she firmly shoved the thought aside and returned her attention to the Crown Prince.

"If you object so strongly to going to war," he said delicately, "would you be willing to surrender the staff to another wielder?"

Her blood iced over. "That isn't possible."

"Isn't it?" His tone was lightly questioning. "Do explain."

"Bonding with a Relic isn't something that just anyone can do," she told him. "Besides, most Invokers could no sooner give up their magic than chop off their own limbs."

"If someone else were to take the staff from you, then?" A hint of eagerness to his voice raised the taste of bile in the back of her throat, especially when she spotted Jarven watching her and was certain he was able to hear their conversation.

"If someone were to take my staff?" She raised her voice a fraction, determined to set the matter straight. "Even if they killed me in the process, the staff might not choose another wielder. The Shaper is the one who makes the decision, in the end, and I imagine anyone who tried to take the staff by force would come to regret the decision."

"That is a pity," said the Crown Prince. "After all, if you were to give up your power and your bond with the Shaper, then you would be able to go back to your old life."

"Would I?" Her smile was less forced this time. "There's no telling whether the Shaper would willingly release me from Her service. The staff has always belonged to the Sentinels, after all."

His face reddened at the implied insult. "Then I might court you instead. It would make quite the story... and it would be doubly tragic if you were to then perish on the battlefield. In that situation, the Shaper would have to choose another partner, is that correct?"

The implied threat in his voice set her skin crawling. "If you sacrifice me, then you sacrifice your country," Zelle said tightly. "There's no alternative."

"I don't think you're being quite truthful, Zelle," he murmured. "Oh, look. Our guests are arriving."

Zelle turned away from him, disgusted beyond words, and saw the guards had opened the doors to the entrance hall. It was probably for the best that their argument had been cut short, but when she glanced over at Jarven, a faint orange glow outlined his hands. If he was using his magic, though, he wasn't using it on her.

He can try, but he'd regret it, the staff said. *I outrank every other Power in existence.*

I should never have talked you up so much, she returned.

The guests began to enter the ballroom, dressed in lace and velvet and silk and bedecked with jewels. The staff kept up a running commentary on each group of nobles that somewhat distracted her from the Crown Prince's frosty silence and Jarven's ominous presence behind her.

She looks like a fancy dessert tray, the staff remarked at one guest's ensemble, and Zelle bit the inside of her cheek to keep from laughing. She had a dim recollection of her and Aurel as children, forced to attend a similar event at some noble's country estate, when they'd escaped the adults' attention to sit in a tree and poke fun at the guests' clothing. She cast her mind around in an attempt to recall who the host had been and came sharply back to reality when none other than Aurel herself walked into the ballroom.

If she hadn't been thinking of her sister at that precise moment, Zelle might have missed the moment when Aurel entered among a contingent of guards, her bright hair clashing with the red of the uniform she wore. *Where did she get that?* The red-and-black uniform might have been a convincing disguise if not for her sister's complete inability to be subtle, and if Aurel came anywhere near Zelle or the Crown Prince, everyone in the entire room would notice.

Zelle needed to get her alone, but first she had to shake off her guards. She watched the constant stream of guests entering the ballroom for several moments before she cast a furtive glance around and spotted her sister standing stiffly against the back wall, completely out of alignment with the other guards.

"I wish to visit the bathroom," she told the Crown Prince.

"Take Jarven with you."

"I don't know where he is," she said, having genuinely lost sight of him somewhere behind the crowd of finely dressed nobles. "I'd prefer to take a female guard with me, besides."

Asking for Aurel herself would be too risky, given her shaky disguise, so she let the Crown Prince select another female guard to escort Zelle out of the ballroom and into the entrance hall. Zelle walked as swiftly as she could achieve in her impractical clothing, briefly glancing behind her to confirm that Jarven hadn't followed her out. Instead, she spotted Aurel making her entirely unsubtle way across the entrance hall.

Turning to her escort—a blond guard with a curving scar on her face that put her in mind of a rogue Invoker she'd met in the Isles of Itzar—she said, "I won't be long. I can find my own way back to the ballroom from here."

"Are you sure?"

"I'm perfectly safe. There are guards everywhere."

Like Aurel, for instance. Zelle kept her gaze turned pointedly away from her sister until her escort departed, at which point she frantically beckoned Aurel to follow her into an alcove.

"What are you *doing?*" Zelle hissed. "You're going to get arrested or worse."

Aurel adjusted the round hat she must have "borrowed" from another guard to sneak in. "I'm here to get you out, of course."

"Aurel, even if I managed to bypass the guards at the door, I can barely climb a staircase in this dress. I certainly can't run."

Aurel pursed her lips. "Is there anywhere in the palace where there aren't guards wandering around?"

"No, there is not," said Zelle. "What possessed you to come in disguised as a guard instead of one of the guests?"

"The guests all have invitations. Nobody looks twice at the guards."

"You aren't wrong, but—look, if I go missing, people are going to notice long before we find our way out."

"Not necessarily," said her sister. "The dragonet is hiding nearby. He helped me obtain this uniform."

Zelle groaned under her breath. Her sister had befriended the dragonet and asked him to steal a guard's uniform? Had she lost her mind? "Is Evita here too?"

"No." Aurel's mouth turned down at the corners. "That's why I had to come in this way instead of borrowing that handy cloak of hers."

"You shouldn't have," said Zelle. "Powers above, I barely shook off my personal guard. It's *him*, Aurel—Jarven is the one carrying the Relic."

Aurel's eyes widened. "He's been planted here by Daimos?"

"Don't speak too loudly."

"If anyone was listening to us talk, we'd know by now," said Aurel. "We have to find him and take the Relic, right? That'll stop the Crown Prince's plan to send you to war."

"It's not that simple." She had yet to even come close to exposing Jarven's Relic, and while he remained in the palace, so did Daimos's influence. "Besides, if I don't go back to the ballroom soon, the Crown Prince will get suspicious."

An intrigued glint appeared in her sister's eyes. "You two looked good together."

Zelle scowled. "The Crown Prince is an awful person, and even if he wasn't, I'm not here to find a match. I'm a prisoner. Or a soldier. Take your pick."

"You've made your point." An amused grin tugged at Aurel's mouth. "All right, I'll sneak up and stab your target in the back. What does he look like?"

"Aurel, he's carrying a Relic, for the Powers' sakes. Do you even have a weapon?"

Before Aurel could answer, footsteps crossed the entrance hall. Ducking farther into the corridor, Zelle grabbed her sister by an arm and pulled her out of sight behind a large vase.

"Where'd she go?" Jarven's voice came drifting from the entrance hall. "Is her guard not with her?"

Zelle's blood chilled. He'd noticed her absence, which meant she'd either have to allow herself to be escorted back to the ballroom or launch an attack and hope the staff was a match for that Relic of his.

"Her guard came back to the ballroom some time ago," someone replied to Jarven. "Want me to call for backup?"

"I'll handle this myself." The footsteps grew louder, heading their way.

"Go," Zelle hissed at Aurel. "If he sees you, you're dead. Find the dragonet and get out."

She didn't wait for a reply. While Aurel retreated down the corridor, Zelle darted out from behind the vase and walked out into full view of Jarven. "Is there a problem?"

Jarven's usually expressionless face twitched into a glare. "Were you trying to sneak out of the ball?"

"If you had to stand next to the Crown Prince all evening, you would, too." He hadn't seen Aurel. He thought she was acting alone... and better still, he'd left the other guards behind and come looking for her by himself. This was the best chance she'd have to expose him.

"You represent Zeuten now, Zelle," Jarven told her. "As the wielder of the nameless Shaper's Relic, it's your responsibility to support your monarch and your nation."

Her gaze dropped to his hand and to the faint golden glow emanating from his sleeve. "Does wielding a Relic of one of the three Great Powers come with an obligation to fight in a false war intended to bring ruin upon the nation?" she asked in casual tones. "Because if so, then I do wonder why he hasn't asked the same of you."

A flare of orange light rose from his palm and brought a rush of foreboding. She'd never seen how his magic worked in practise, and while he hadn't seen hers in action, either, he had more of an idea of her capabilities than the reverse. When he caught her looking, his brow twitched, indicating that he knew she was baiting him.

Zelle flashed him a smile. "Was that a 'no'? I'm surprised you're allowed to be alone with me."

"You overestimate your skills *and* your importance."

His lips barely moved, anger tightening his posture. "Do you truly wish to start a public incident? Would you risk the guests' safety by using the magic of the nameless Shaper?"

He'd guessed that she didn't want to risk causing unnecessary harm, but there was no telling what *he* would do if they came to blows. The glow around his palm deepened, and certainty hit her that he'd confronted her alone on purpose. He didn't intend her to walk away of her own free will.

"I know whose Relic you wield." Her grip tightened on the staff. "Whatever Daimos promised you must have been worth the risk of being executed for treason, am I right?"

Orange light filled her vision, and a hazy sensation swept through her mind. At once, the desire seized her to walk away, to follow Jarven back to the ballroom and the Crown Prince's side. What was she doing out here? Yes, the Crown Prince was unpleasant to be around, but she'd come here with a purpose. Namely, to protect her family.

"That's right," Jarven murmured. "Come with me, Zelle. I'll take you back where you belong."

Don't you dare move. The staff's voice cut through the haze in her mind, leaving her reeling. Had Invicten's magic caused her sudden change in mood? Zelle had assumed that holding the staff would make her impervious to his magical influence, but it seemed she'd been badly mistaken.

Zelle took a step after Jarven and then swung the staff at his kneecaps. He anticipated the move, dodging aside, and the staff struck the wall in his place. The dull thud left a visible dent in the wall, while Zelle's heart sank. If she used the Shaper's magic to its full extent, there was a high chance that she'd bring the roof crashing down on all their heads—but it was hard to ignore the surge of power spreading through her awareness, reaching into the very foundations of the palace.

Jarven gave her a pitying look. "I doubt you're capable of understanding, Zelle, but I made my choice for the good of the nation. Zeuten needs strong magicians to match Aestin. If we don't embrace our future, we'll become irrelevant."

"Daimos doesn't want there to be a future for any of us," Zelle responded. "Except himself."

An orange haze blurred her vision, and she swayed on the spot, the expansiveness of the Shaper's magic shrinking to a pinprick. This was how he'd manipulated everyone in the palace into believing his lies, and the allure of the thoughts whispering at the back of her mind was difficult to ignore. If she attacked, her family would be in greater danger than if she stayed here, if she submitted…

The staff's voice echoed in her mind. If you want this palace to stay upright, I'd suggest you resist his control.

Zelle's senses returned when Aurel leapt out and brought a vase down on Jarven's head with an almighty crash. He staggered, giving Zelle the chance to swing the staff at his kneecaps again, this time sweeping his legs out from underneath him.

Jarven climbed to his feet, seemingly unruffled by her strike. Orange light flowed from his palms, and Zelle knew that he was done holding back.

It was time for one Great Power to face off against another.

15

Evita's first day as a Senior Changer passed in a bewildering blur of training exercises and drills, meetings with the other Senior Changers and speeches from Master Drazer about doing their part to protect Zeuten from outside threats. She listened dutifully, eager to serve.

Being a Senior Changer was a major improvement over her days as a novice. Not only was she no longer spending all her time in the company of bullies, but the Senior Changers were allowed actual mattresses to sleep on in their cave, and their rations were much more palatable. She also had access to better weapons, including all the spelled arrows she could ever want. Occasionally, disturbing thoughts entered her mind, images of bodies pierced with arrows and of tumbling off a cliff to her death, but whenever Master Drazer looked into her eyes, the images disappeared.

On the second morning after she'd rejoined the Changers' ranks, the Master departed on a mission with several of the Senior Changers and didn't intend to return until nightfall. One of the other Senior Changers took over their training, but Evita's thoughts grew more anxious as the day went on. The images were more frequent, violent, and when one hit her in the middle of a training exercise, her arrow misfired, nearly spearing her fellow soldier through the arm.

"Gaiva's tits." The image of the Master dangling her over the edge of a cliff dominated her thoughts, bringing a bitter taste to her mouth.

The novice she'd almost struck stared blankly at her, as did everyone else. Evita dropped her gaze, flushing to her hairline. Until her exclamation, the silence of the training area had been uniform, and only now did it strike her as odd that everyone returned to the exercises they'd been assigned without so much as a word. The quietness blanketed her, both eerie and comforting, and the sense of discomfort lingered as she picked up her bow again.

Evita misfired two more arrows before the Senior Changer supervising the session ordered her to sit and watch instead. Perched on a rock, she watched arrows strike targets over and over, never missing. It wasn't natural. How had she not noticed before? Even without Master Drazer overlooking their training, he might as well have been guiding every move each of them made.

What has he done to us?

Ill at ease, Evita pushed off the rock and paced the outside of the training area, her cloak rustling around her. The silvery folds bore no marks from the arrow that had pierced them all over—an image that brought a sudden surge of horror. It wasn't merely an image but a memory.

And there were others. They arrived one after another,

with the precision of the arrows hitting their targets. Image after image, person after person. People she'd forgotten but shouldn't have.

Zelle. *Thud.* Rien. *Thud.* Aurel. *Thud.*

The last image brought the memory of the dragonet flying away, fleeing to safety after Evita had been knocked out of the sky. She'd expected to face death, but Master Drazer had promoted her instead... because she was bonded to her cloak. Her Relic.

Her steps returned her to the training ground, but she watched the other Changers in a new light, more certainty returning with every passing moment. They were all under the same spell as she, but she'd somehow shaken it off. When the Master came back... no, she had to get away before then, but how could she possibly evade attention? Every Changer was under his spell, and they were all within reach of the same arrows that had pierced her cloak during her capture.

She didn't dare run. Not yet.

The rest of the day passed in tense anticipation. Master Drazer was nowhere to be seen, but his Changers were everywhere, and none of the others seemed to have broken through the trance he'd put them in. When night fell, she thought she might seize her chance to escape, but as she waited in the cave for the others to fall asleep, a second group of Senior Changers entered in a rustle of silvery cloaks with the news that the Master had returned.

Wherever he'd been, he didn't show his face in the camp until the following afternoon, when he arrived to supervise their training session. The session took a predictably appalling turn for Evita, and after several near misses with her arrows, he beckoned her over to him. "Evita, I wish to speak with you in my office."

His words sent Evita's nerves climbing, and her heartbeat thundered as she followed him into the Masters' building, fighting the instinct to run for her life before he realised she'd broken his spell on her.

Master Drazer's office door closed behind them with a snap, and he spoke. "You have been selected for a mission this evening."

"I have?" She tried to keep her tone even, but his words echoed a different Master, and a spasm of fear shook her limbs.

"Yes," he said, not appearing to notice her reaction. "There are a number of tunnels and caves hidden within these mountains, both natural and otherwise. We have decided to eliminate any openings for our enemies to hide within the Range, so I have selected some of you to seal these tunnels so they can no longer be used."

"Tunnels?" The image of a lever moving to expose a cave in the cliff face burst into her mind. "You want us to close them off?"

"It shouldn't be too hard," he went on. "Briony will be leading the mission. Follow her instructions."

Briony. The name brought another flood of unpleasant memories. "Is she still in Tavine?"

He gave her a frown. "Did I tell you to ask questions?"

"No." *Gaiva's tits, I shouldn't have said anything. Her head pounded, the urge to dive into the orange light pooling in the Master's eyes warring with a desperate unwillingness to lose herself again.* Not when he intended to send her to sabotage the Sentinel's outpost, as if in preparation for the

Changers to launch an attack on Aurel and her grandmother.

"You had friends there, didn't you?" He studied her face, his expression suggesting that he'd suspected her sudden change in loyalties. She'd never been skilled at hiding her thoughts. "The order came directly from the Crown Prince himself. He and his advisors have decreed that the Sentinels are a danger to the Crown and that they must be removed by any means possible."

Her blood turned cold. So Daimos wanted them gone altogether, and he intended the Changers to carry out the deed. "The Sentinels? A danger to the Crown?"

Was he telling the truth? Zelle was supposed to be the Crown Prince's prisoner, and she'd thought he wanted her alive, not dead. He wouldn't have the nameless Shaper's wielder executed, surely.

Aurel, though? And her grandmother?

"The future Sentinel was once your employer, wasn't she?" Master Drazer asked. "Your friend?"

Evita didn't speak. Sweat trickled down the back of her neck, and the urge to grab one of the spelled arrows from a shelf and plunge it into his throat seized her like the current of a river.

"You have an unusual will to resist." Master Drazer's expression hardened. "That changes now."

Her cloak moved *its own accord*, tightening around her neck, and she choked as her breath was cut off. He hadn't laid a hand on her, and yet her own cloak—her own *Relic* was strangling her.

"How—" she gasped out.

Master Drazer gave her a grim smile. "The source of

my powers and yours is one and the same, Evita. Do not resist me again."

Dizziness swept through her. He couldn't possibly mean—?

It's true. The Relic that gave him his abilities owed its strength to the same deity whose magic filled her cloak, and the instrument that had saved her life countless times might now bring about her end.

The cloak's grip on her throat tightened, causing her vision to swim. The deity that served the enemy was embedded in the very fabric of her Relic. How could she hope to win now?

"Forget them," Master Drazer told her. "The next time you see the Sentinel, you will kill her."

The cloak released her, and as his magic washed over her vision, she felt her resolve crumble like a rock crushed in a storm.

———

Zelle and her former guard faced one another, the remains of the vase Aurel had shattered against his skull lying around their feet. Blood trickled down the side of Jarven's face, but he did not visibly acknowledge the pain. His hands glowed with an orange haze, and when she swung the staff at him, a wave of resistance stopped her mid-swing.

The overwhelming urge to put the staff down and surrender washed over her, until a sharp jolt of icy cold against her palms brought her back to her senses. The staff had countered his magic once again, but it wouldn't last. She needed to get hold of his Relic, or else he'd crush all her will to resist.

Behind Jarven, Aurel grabbed a shard of the broken vase and raised it over his head.

Shaking off the remnants of the spell, Zelle caught her sister's eye and shook her head, mouthing, "Not yet."

Quite apart from the fact that stabbing him to death would ruin any chance at a stealthy escape, he hadn't shown any signs of where his Relic might be hidden—or if there might be more than one. Upon noticing Aurel's presence at his back, Jarven turned his attention towards Zelle's sister and drew a dagger from a sheath at his side.

The instant he did so, Aurel swayed backwards, dropping the shard of broken vase. Orange light washed over her, and Zelle retreated, shards of broken vase crunching beneath her feet, while Aurel jerked forward like a puppet on strings. Towards the point of Jarven's knife.

"Let her go," she ordered Jarven. "This is between us."

"She shouldn't have come here."

Zelle swung the staff at him, aiming for his hands. He sidestepped, the edge of the staff catching his arm and knocking the dagger's aim off. The second strike disarmed him, but Aurel continued to sway on the spot, under his spell.

She swung again. This time, the staff hit him square in the chest. Jarven staggered, the breath knocked from his lungs, and Aurel stopped in her tracks, an expression of horror crossing her face. "You scumbag. Think you can use your power on me, do you?"

Causing him pain must have temporarily broken his spell over Aurel. Seizing her chance, Zelle drove the staff into his shins, causing him to stagger against the wall and lose his balance.

"The Relic." Zelle approached him, the nameless Shaper's magic urging her to stop holding back and unleash the entirety of the staff's might against him. "Give it to me, and I might consider leaving you alive."

"It's too late." He coughed out the words. "I gifted my Relic to the Crown Prince himself."

"You're lying." Zelle pointed the staff at his throat, a tremor travelling through the very walls of the palace. "Tell me the truth. How many Relics are there, and where did you put them?"

"Just the one, and I'm telling the truth." Another fit of coughing took him, and she wondered if she'd broken a rib or two when she'd hit him. "As for where it is, how else do you think I have maintained such a high level of influence over the Crown Prince?"

Powers above. He didn't mean to imply His Majesty was carrying a Relic of Invicten on his own person without knowing, did he? It was ingenious in a way; the Crown Prince had no gift for magic himself, but Jarven had the perfect way to exercise his influence over the Crown Prince's will whenever he desired.

An orange haze entered Jarven's vision, and Zelle turned malleable beneath his stare. He was right… Fighting back was a waste of time. Why fight with one another when they could join forces? Wouldn't it be so much easier to return to the ball and to tell the Crown Prince everything?

If you do that, I will beat you over the head, warned the staff.

"You can't do that." She accidentally voiced her reply to the staff aloud, but it would work for Jarven as well.

He pushed himself upright against the wall. "There's nothing I cannot do, Zelle. Even the nameless Shaper has limits."

The staff, however, had had enough. The Shaper's magic reverberated in her hands, and the staff burned ice-cold. When another wave of orange light entered Jarven's eyes, Zelle gave a final swing of the staff. The end struck him in the skull with a jarring thud, and the orange light faded as he crumpled, unmoving, into a heap.

Nearby, Aurel stared wide-eyed for a moment at Jarven's sprawling body. "Is he—?" She dropped to a crouch, felt for a pulse. "I think I'd have preferred my way."

"Too messy." Zelle's heart pounded in her throat. "It's only a matter of time before the other guards come looking for him. We've made too much noise."

"I'm sure he bewitched them." Aurel dropped his limp hand. "When he convinced them to leave him to confront us alone."

"True." Zelle swore under her breath. "I need to find the Crown Prince's Relic before the spell wears off, but I don't know where it is. How can I get him alone?"

"Seduce him?" Aurel suggested.

"He'd be less suspicious of me if I hit *him* in the shins with the staff." She paced around the guard's body, already regretting letting the staff take command of her actions. "He knows I'm not in the ballroom, and he'll be watching for my return."

There was nothing she desired less than to return to the ball after leaving a man dead at her feet, but if she wanted to find Invicten's Relic before the guards found the body and Jarven's spell wore off, she needed to move fast. Evita's cloak would have made it so much easier, but she'd have to wait until later to question her sister about why the former Changer hadn't come with her.

Aurel raised her head. "Need a diversion?"

"Absolutely not," Zelle said flatly. "If the sound of a vase shattering wasn't enough to alert anyone's notice, you'd have to dance naked in the ballroom. *Don't* get any ideas."

Aurel gave a pale smile that disappeared an instant later. "No, but don't forget I brought the dragonet."

"Where is he, exactly?" Zelle racked her thoughts for her little knowledge of the palace's layout. "I'd ask you to bring him to the nearest door, but there *is* no unguarded exit, and I might end up with half the palace guard on my tail when I get my hands on the Relic."

A thoughtful expression crossed Aurel's face. "I don't have to be the one to create the diversion. Should I bring our ride to the front doors?"

"The front doors..." Zelle trailed off. "I don't want to know what you're planning, do I?"

"Probably not, considering it involves serious damage to royal property."

"That might be less than the Shaper will unleash if I stay in here much longer." She sighed. "Go back to the dragonet, but for the Powers' sakes, don't let the guards see your face on the way out. And let me handle the Crown Prince."

"Got it," said Aurel. "How long should I give you?"

"Ten minutes." Waiting longer would increase the risk of Jarven's body being discovered, and it would take far too long to hide all the shards of broken vase. Instead, Zelle shoved Jarven into an alcove while she waited for Aurel to leave the palace. She then checked her reflection in the glass of a nearby window, fixing her hair so nobody would guess that she'd been in a fight.

Drawing in a deep breath, Zelle walked down the corridor and back to the entrance hall, coming to an abrupt halt when she spotted several guards gathering near the door to the ballroom. Had they noticed Jarven hadn't returned yet? Or had they realised there was an intruder among their number?

A moment later, Zelle caught sight of who the guards were talking to—a dishevelled and furious-looking woman dressed in nothing but her underclothes—who was saying, loudly, "I told you, I saw a dragon. It knocked me down, and this strange red-haired woman stole my clothes. I'm telling the truth."

Oh. She must have been the guard whose uniform her sister had stolen to sneak into the palace. Doubly glad that she'd sent Aurel fleeing in the opposite direction, Zelle walked towards them. "Excuse me, did you say you saw a dragon?"

"Yes, I did," said the underdressed guard in an indignant tone. "I know perfectly well how ridiculous it sounds, but it's the truth. Why?"

"Because I saw it, too. Over there." She pointed at the far side of the entrance hall, the opposite direction to where Aurel had gone. "Through a window. When I tried to get a closer look, it flew away, but it definitely looked like a dragon. Maybe it came down from the mountains."

"Powers above." One of the guards drew his sword. "Right, we'll take care of this."

Hoping the dragonet had hidden elsewhere in the palace grounds, Zelle hurried back into the ballroom. She found the Crown Prince standing amid a crowd of nobles who were listening avidly to whatever he was saying, and a jolt of disbelief hit her. Had he spent all this time basking in his admirers' attention without noticing half his guards were missing?

Zelle strode over to him, fixing an approximation of a smile on her face. "Your Majesty, may I talk to you alone?"

"Zelle." He beamed at her. "Where have you been?"

"I got lost." The sound of breaking glass sounded from the entrance hall, followed by a scream. "The guards are in an uproar, if you haven't noticed."

She *hoped* the noise was Aurel's diversion and not some new disaster, but as usual, her sister had acted too soon. Zelle hadn't laid eyes on Invicten's Relic yet, but she was starting to doubt that Jarven had planted it on the Crown Prince himself. That would involve placing a little too much faith in him not to accidentally leave it lying around or even lose it. No, it must be elsewhere in the palace... but where?

The Crown Prince took a step towards the door. "What in Gaiva's name is going on out there?"

"Someone claimed to have seen a dragon." Another crash sounded. Aurel's comment about causing damage to royal property had been all too accurate, and she fervently hoped they wouldn't have to pay for it later. "Outside the palace."

"A dragon?" He gave a strained laugh, the twitch in his jaw betraying his annoyance at having his ball interrupted. "Someone has had too much wine."

"Did you not hear that noise?" Powers above, she

couldn't afford to waste any more time. "I heard you had a Relic in the palace. Recently acquired."

He gave her a curious look. "Who told you that?"

The staff jerked forward in her hand as if of its own accord, brushing against the Crown Prince's arm. He gave a startled jump, but the staff said, *He isn't carrying it.*

"What?" She forgot not to voice her reply aloud, and the Crown Prince's brow crinkled in evident confusion.

"Are you quite well?" he asked.

"Yes… no, I need some air." This time she was careful to address the staff without speaking aloud. *Where else might it be?*

In one of those cabinets of his? the staff suggested. *They're next to his throne, so Jarven would still be able to exert influence on him.*

You'd better be right. Aurel's diversion was already in progress, but without the Relic, she'd leave the palace vulnerable to Daimos's influence again.

As yet another loud crash echoed from outside the ballroom, Zelle broke into a run. Pushing the doors open, she sprinted into the entrance hall and straight into a contingent of guards.

"I'm off to kill the dragon," she said breathlessly. "Get out of the way unless you want to be eaten."

She raised the staff, as if she intended to charge the dragon herself. Most of the guards wisely backed off, but one of them gave her a suspicious stare. "Where is Jarven?"

"Fighting the dragon himself, I expect."

Zelle veered around a corner, following the route of her initial visit to the palace. The only cabinets she'd seen had been in the throne room, but she'd quite forgotten the route. All she could do was keep walking, checking each door, and when she reached the large painting of a battlefield that Rien had recognised, she knew she was on the right track.

Upon reaching the throne room, Zelle hurried over to the cabinets, her gaze skimming the glass cases and their contents.

"Help me out here," she whispered to the staff.

There. The staff burned cold, pointing her towards an ornamental wooden knife. Zelle reached for the cabinet's door, but the complicated locks would take too long to undo. Footsteps pounded outside, and she heard the guards' voices shouts echoing nearby. Her escape hadn't gone unnoticed.

Zelle swung the staff, shattering the cabinet's front. Reaching in, she grabbed the Relic, her fingers curling around the knife's handle.

The footsteps halted. Zelle pulled the knife out of the cabinet, keeping a firm grip on the staff with her other hand as she turned around to find none other than the Crown Prince standing in the doorway.

His bemused gaze took in the destroyed cabinet and her wild appearance. "What are you doing?"

"You'll thank me for this later." She crossed the room, staff in one hand, Relic in the other. "Goodbye, your Majesty."

She pushed past him and out of the throne room before retracing her route to the entrance hall. Few guards were inside, but a mess of shattered glass filled the area where the front windows used to be. The doors lay wide open, and she hurried onto the stone stairs.

"Stop her!" shouted the Crown Prince.

Several guards moved in on Zelle, who ran down the stairs as fast as her impractical clothing would allow, her heart sinking when more guards clustered at the foot of the stairs.

Then a dragon-shaped shadow fell overhead, claws swiping left and right. The guards fell back, yelling, while Aurel reached out a hand towards her sister.

Zelle gladly let her sister seize her arm and pull her up onto the dragonet's back, wishing she had a pocket to store the Relic in. As she settled in front of Aurel, they took flight into the darkening sky, leaving the palace behind them.

16

Two days passed, during which Rien learned everything Martzel had to tell him about the Daimos family's home. He had little else to occupy his time with, save for dwelling on the chaos he'd left behind in the capital *and* in Zeuten, and so he applied himself to learning the layout of his enemy's estate.

"Where did you even get these?" he'd asked Martzel, indicating the pile of maps he'd found stacked on the table in the drawing room the day after his arrival. "I didn't know you'd visited Daimos's home."

"It's been years, but I have," Martzel responded. "The estate is where Daimos's family was initially apprehended. We removed anything dangerous, of course, including their Relics."

"I never asked," Rien said. "Whatever did you do with them? I assume the Relics aren't still in the country."

Martzel studied him for a moment. "Your father made the arrangements, I believe, and Mevicen's Relics were cast into the depths of the ocean near the Eastern Isles."

"I did wonder why he never tried to find them," Rien admitted. "Though I suppose he didn't own a Relic himself at the time of his exile, since he was only an infant."

"That is true." Martzel sighed. "If I have one regret, it's that we didn't take the child off their hands when we cast the Daimos family out. We judged it to be best for the boy to be raised away from the capital and the reminders of his parents' rash decisions, but I have to wonder…"

Rien himself had wondered, upon occasion, of the fates of Daimos's parents. He assumed they were dead and that Daimos had ventured upon his quest to find a Relic alone, but that was pure conjecture. Once separated from their Relics, his parents would have been in no shape to survive the harsh conditions of the Scarred Lands, marked by the magical wars that had once ravaged the continent.

"Daimos's parents must have told him that they were badly wronged and that our families turned against his for unjustified reasons," Rien suggested. "Without anyone to contradict their word, he'd have been inclined to believe them."

"Daimos's father was always jealous of the rest of us, especially our favour with the Emperor," Martzel said. "He thought that he deserved more than his fair share of the power, and in the end, he decided to challenge us directly. If he hadn't convinced the rest of his family to do the same, they might not have doomed their infant along with themselves."

"So you joined forces with the Trevains as well as my father in order to cast them out," Rien surmised. "I wonder what prompted Luvid Trevain to take his side this time, then."

"Fear, of course," he answered. "Last time, Daimos's family had the aid of one Relic, no more, and certainly not a Great Power. Maybe I was a coward to flee Tauvice myself, but I did not see an outcome of our conflict that would result in anything other than the loss of my own Relic."

"I could say the same of myself," Rien admitted. "For fleeing to Zeuten instead of confronting him here. I… lost my memories for a time, and I confess I'm not entirely certain on why I picked that particular Relic to search for."

"Zierne." Martzel's gaze dropped to the staff propped against the side of Rien's seat. "Yes… the lost sibling of Astiva."

"Did my father ever discuss the subject with you?" Rien asked. "That is—the settlers of Zeuten and the Relics they took with them to hide in the mountains?"

"I'm afraid not," he said. "We didn't discuss Zeuten, to my knowledge… but maybe you instinctively knew that it was the place Daimos was least likely to find you."

"I guessed wrong, in that case." He hadn't told Martzel that it was none other than the nameless Shaper who'd brought about Orzen's end and not Rien himself, but it was only a matter of time until he'd have to expose Zelle's secret. Especially if Daimos himself showed his face at his family's estate. "It might not matter, but I'd like to know more about the Relic I wield. We're not… entirely in synchrony."

Martzel gave him a considering look. "Don't forget

you had years to adjust to wielding your first Relic. Give it time."

His words were kind, more so than Rien felt he deserved, yet he couldn't shake the feeling that his uncertain alliance with Zierne was the product of more than a lack of experience. Especially given the books he'd read at the outpost, with their tales of how Zierne had so hated humanity that he'd gone to war with his own siblings. Telling Martzel *that* would only add a needless complication to an already-risky mission, so he held his tongue.

The morning they were due to visit Daimos's house, Rien came downstairs to find the front door ajar and Martzel speaking to a young man who had the same long, dark hair and nut-brown skin as the rest of his family. Rien hadn't set eyes on Reyes, the Martzels' youngest son, since they were children, but his mischievous smile and general air of excitement had evidently followed him into adulthood. While he must have been on the road through the night to have reached them at this hour in the morning, he was dressed as if he'd been invited to a societal function, wearing a waistcoat of peacock-blue brocade and a pair of polished black boots.

"You have a guest." Reyes spotted Rien approaching Martzel from behind. "You didn't mention him in your letters."

Martzel gave him a long-suffering look. "I assumed you never bothered to read my letters, or else you'd have taken my warnings seriously. As for our guest, I'd frankly prefer it if nobody was to know he was here."

"Arien Astera." Reyes's face broke out in a grin. "It's an honour to meet you."

"The same from me." A second man appeared behind

Reyes, who wore his hair in braids, a common style among Aestinians with heritage from the Eastern Isles. The rumpled state of his travelling clothes suggested that he'd slept in a carriage. "I'm Sarpe, Reyes's partner."

No wonder Martzel seemed so irritated. Not only had Reyes been ignoring his pleas to come into hiding, but now he'd brought someone else to their safe house on the very day they were due to break into Daimos's home. Whether the pair of them knew of the plan was debatable, given Reyes's absence so far, but he couldn't imagine Martzel giving him the details in a letter.

"Come in," Sanne said from behind her father. "It's good to see you, Reyes, but did you have to make us all worry that you'd been caught?"

"Sanne, it's lovely to see you too." Reyes sauntered into the house with a smile. "It also sounds like I got here just in time."

"Or the opposite." Martzel's tone implied he knew he was fighting a losing battle in trying to argue with his youngest son. "Please at least tell me you didn't tell anyone in the city you were coming here."

"What do you take me for?" Reyes strode after his father and they all crowded into the drawing room, where the various maps of Daimos's estate were strewn across the table. "What's all this?"

"Again, you'd know if you'd shown up a week ago." Martzel hobbled over to a chair and sank into it; his leg must be bothering him particularly badly today. "Arien, Sanne—the carriages are due to arrive in an hour. We haven't the time to get the newcomers up to speed first."

Reyes studied the maps. "You're going to break into

Daimos's house, which he may or may not currently occupy. Am I correct?"

"Yes, and I told you not to spread that information around," growled Martzel.

"I'm not a fool," said Reyes. "I didn't expect you to be so quick to risk blowing your cover, though now I see who your guest is, I understand why. Did my father talk you into breaking into Daimos's house, Arien?"

"I didn't need to be talked into it," Rien replied. "It's rather less risky than sneaking into the Emperor's palace to find who Daimos has feeding lies to the imperial guards, though that might be necessary as well."

Sarpe stifled a gasp, and even Reyes's amusement faded to concern. "You really think there's a spy?"

"He has Invicten's Relics," Sanne told her brother and his partner. "That's the part we were missing."

"Invicten?" Reyes's brows shot up. "Merciful Powers, no wonder he ensnared the Emperor so easily. I was starting to worry His Imperial Majesty was going senile."

"He's ensnared more than the Emperor," corrected Martzel. "I'd rather you took this seriously, Reyes. You're lucky not to have been targeted yourself, with all the time you spent in the capital."

"Some of us can't just drop everything and go into hiding." Reyes nodded to Sarpe. "We're here now and willing to help. Are you sure he'll have hidden those Relics at his country estate?"

"No," Rien said, "but we hope to find a clue pointing at his current location."

"What if he's there himself?" Sarpe looked less enthused at their plan than his partner did.

"Then we'll just kill Daimos and be done with it," Reyes said. "Has anyone suggested that yet?"

"Yes," said Rien, at the same time as Sanne said, "Father doesn't think he'll be at the house, and if he is… well, he wields Astiva's Relic."

Rien suppressed a flinch. He'd known intellectually that he'd have to face up to his former deity when he confronted Daimos, but his adversary had been out of reach for so long that he'd begun to forget that it wouldn't be Invicten's magic they had to fight against, but Astiva's.

Aware that the others' gazes had turned in his direction, Rien ventured to keep his expression calm. "That means Daimos doesn't wield Invicten's Relics himself. He gave them to others, including someone in the Emperor's circle as well as someone close to Zeuten's Crown Prince."

"The Crown Prince?" Reyes exclaimed. "How?"

"The details hardly matter." Martzel rubbed his temples. "He intends to stoke conflict between Zeuten and Aestin's governments, aided by Invicten's Relics. Why do you think I wanted you out of the capital?"

"We hardly knew it was *Invicten* he was working with," Reyes protested. "We assumed it was another child of Gaiva, not one of the Great Powers."

"There are no children of Gaiva who are unaccounted for," said Martzel. "None save for Daimos's family's original Relic, anyway, and we've seen no evidence that he's retrieved Mevicen's Relic from the ocean."

"Then where…" Reyes's gaze went to Rien's staff. "You found a new Relic."

"I did."

"You can catch up on the way to Daimos's house,"

growled Martzel. "Grab something to eat if you like, and then be ready to leave."

Sanne filled Reyes and Sarpe in on their plan, while Rien studied the maps one last time. If Daimos was at the estate, then he'd have to convince the others to wait outside.

He alone would confront Astiva.

Zelle and Aurel flew north on the dragonet's back without stopping to look at the chaos they'd left behind them. As the city gave way to a patchwork of fields, Zelle's tension gave way to discomfort, and the inconvenience of wearing nothing more than a flimsy dress while flying at night made itself known.

"Your teeth are chattering loudly enough to frighten the birds," Aurel said. "Come on, we'll land so I can give you my coat."

"It's fine." Her hands were numb, however, and if she wasn't careful, she might accidentally drop either the staff or the Relic she'd taken from the Crown Prince's cabinet.

"That dress is ridiculous," Aurel told her.

"Most of the other clothes they brought from my room at the shop are in the palace," Zelle said. "Changing my outfit wasn't a priority."

"They brought your *clothes*?"

"Just to prove they know where I live." She gave a brittle laugh. "You can't imagine how glad I am to see you."

"All right, we're landing before you freeze to death."

Aurel directed Chirp to fly downward to land in a

deserted field before giving Zelle her gloves and coat. Shrugging on the fur-lined coat, Zelle asked, "Where's Evita?"

Aurel's smile faded. "That's the bad news."

Zelle fastened the coat and switched her thin gloves for warmer ones as Aurel filled her in on their companion's second capture. No wonder Chirp seemed more subdued than usual. "The Crown *is* giving orders to the Changers?"

"Yes, telling them that Rien is a dangerous criminal." Aurel twisted in her seat as they took flight again. "Where is he, anyway? I'd have thought he'd have helped you escape."

Pain speared Zelle in the pit of her stomach. It was her turn to explain what her sister had missed during her time in the palace, and as she did, worry on Rien's part threatened to overwhelm her relief at finally being free of the Crown Prince and Jarven.

"The best-case scenario is that he's on the run," she told Aurel, "but if Daimos was able to trick the Crown Prince without even being in the country himself, I'd rather not think about what he might have done in Aestin."

"Then don't," said Aurel. "Think, I mean. You escaped that ghastly palace, which is enough of a miracle for one day."

"I don't know that I'd call it a miracle." The nameless Shaper had almost brought the place crashing down around them, although frankly, she wasn't sure it wouldn't have been an improvement. "I can only hope that His Highness develops a little sense without Jarven whispering lies in his ears. If we're lucky, he might tell the

Changers to leave Tavine and stop hassling the Sentinels, at the very least."

"Ah… that's another issue." Aurel paused for a moment. "I'm fairly sure the Crown Prince is the one who appointed the Changers' new leader. That's who caught Evita. Luckily, I doubt he's prepared to face the nameless Shaper."

"Powers." Zelle gripped the staff as the dragonet veered to the side when a particularly strong gust of wind swept over from the direction of the mountains. "Is sending me to kill the new leader of the Changers really your idea of 'lucky'?"

Aurel gave her a mock hurt look. "I *did* rescue you tonight, if you haven't already forgotten."

"I haven't." Exasperation warred with exhaustion, while it took all Zelle's remaining willpower to maintain a firm grip on her staff and Invicten's Relic. She needed to dispose of the latter as soon as they landed. "And neither will the Crown Prince. I'm probably the most wanted person across the entire capital now."

"So am I." Aurel laughed quietly. "I bet the rumours are glorious, especially the ones involving the dragonet."

"I hope that's what they focus on and not the fact that I murdered a guard." She looked down to avoid meeting her sister's eyes, although the land below was so dark that she could hardly distinguish between land and sea.

"He deserved it," Aurel said. "Aside from being Daimos's ally, he was a horrible person."

"So was the Crown Prince," said Zelle. "Sorry to disappoint you."

"I've decided I don't really care for royalty." Aurel laughed. "Besides, I bet you would have been too fixated on Rien to notice the Crown Prince even if he'd been a perfect gentleman."

Zelle suppressed a wince. Rien… There was no use dwelling on his fate, not when they were in a precarious enough situation of their own. Without Jarven influencing the guards, Daimos no longer had his ally feeding Zeuten's authorities false information, so they'd slowed him down, if nothing else. Yet she doubted he'd give up as easily as that.

Aurel was silent for a moment. "I'm sure he's fine, Zelle. He's too stubborn to let a little thing like a murder accusation stand in his way."

Zelle made a noncommittal noise and sought a change of subject. "Assuming Aestin *isn't* planning a war, then he might have got away. I honestly can't tell how much of what Daimos told the Crown Prince was the truth and how much was pure fabrication."

"I can't believe His Highness wanted you to go to war against Aestin," Aurel remarked. "That can't have been part of Daimos's plan. He must know he's no match for the nameless Shaper."

"It's not a matter of simple brute force, though," Zelle said. "Think of the backlash of a war against a nation like Aestin on Zeuten's economy. Our army is a fraction of Aestin's size, and even the Shaper can't fight a war on several fronts at once."

"I know that," said Aurel. "I'm lost on what he hopes to achieve with this, though. I thought his plan was centred on revenge against Rien and the other families."

"That was before we pissed him off," said Zelle. "He wants to drive us all to ruin and punish us for defying him, so sending both our nations into an unnecessary war would accomplish all his goals at once. If I were to die in the process and remove the nameless Shaper as a threat, so much the better."

"The Crown Prince wanted to keep you alive, didn't he?"

"Begrudgingly." Zelle shivered. "I did make it clear that if I were to give up the staff, then there was no guarantee it'd pick someone else as a replacement wielder. In fact, it wouldn't surprise me if the staff would sooner let Zeuten fall into ruin than let itself be manipulated into serving someone else."

She hadn't asked the nameless Shaper if She had planned for the possibility that Zelle would die before she'd completed her mission, and she'd decided on balance that she'd prefer not to know.

"Look, we're almost home." Aurel sat upright. "Grandma will be thrilled to learn I got you out in one piece."

The rugged outlines of the Range grew larger on their left-hand side, gleaming under the opaline sheen of the rising moon. As they drew closer, a dark blot became visible on their left, growing larger by the moment.

Zelle leaned forward. "Tell me that isn't what I think it is."

Powers above. The Changers were on the move, and they were heading for the Sentinels' outpost.

17

Evita flew alongside the other Changers, heading for the middle of the Range. Her cloak merged with the others on either side of her, forming a silvery mass, and she almost forgot she was a single person at all. Individual thoughts didn't matter, not when they all had the same mission to fulfil.

Once they'd reached the middle of the Range, the Changers split into several groups, each assigned to seal one of the passages hidden in the mountains. Evita's group descended over a crooked tower and landed in front of the sheer wall of a cliff face, searching for the entrance to a tunnel that was supposed to be hidden somewhere there. Upon discovering the lever that opened the cave, they began applying an adhesive that Master Drazer had given them.

Evita did the same, but seeing the passageway closed off filled her with a sudden sense of sickening dread. She grabbed the rock face for balance when a rush of dizziness swept over her, and an instant later, a gust of wind slammed into their group from behind.

The Changers stumbled, many of them knocked flat, but Evita's grip on the rocky wall spared her. Spinning on her heel, Evita looked up at the sky and saw a large reptilian shape hovering above the path. A woman with auburn hair jumped off the dragonet's back, followed by another who wore a bizarre ensemble: a windswept dress that resembled a cloud, together with a thick fur coat and gloves. It made such a peculiar image that Evita's instincts didn't kick in until the other Changers were back on their feet and reaching for their bows and arrows.

She did the same, an unconscious movement, yet alarm spiked when the woman dressed as a cloud raised a staff into the air, its edges glowing a vibrant blue. Her red-haired companion, meanwhile, reached into her pocket for a knife. Did they hope to defeat the entire group of Changers by themselves?

Arrows flew, curving towards the two women. Evita's heart leapt into her throat, but the first wave of arrows simply shattered against a rippling curtain of blue light. A tremor ran underneath their feet, as if the very mountain itself had woken to their presence, but the other Changers continued to move as they'd been instructed. Arrow after arrow arced from their bows, all of them missing their targets. Evita raised her own bow, and her gaze locked with the auburn-haired woman.

The next time you see the Sentinel, you will kill her.

Master Drazer's words echoed in her mind, and a certainty seized her that this was the woman she'd been ordered to kill. Her hands moved of their own accord, fitting an arrow to the bow.

"Evita." The woman recognised her, shock entering her tone. "What are you doing?"

The next time you see the Sentinel, you will kill her. Evita pointed the arrow directly at her target and drew back the bow.

The arrow buried itself in the woman's arm. She let out a startled cry, while her companion held up the staff, shock and anger crossing her face.

"Get off the mountain," she commanded, her voice clear, and an eerie glow the same colour as the staff entered her eyes. "Or I'll kill you all."

A chirping noise drew Evita's gaze away. The dragonet looked down at her, his expression downcast, but before she could put a name to the piercing sorrow filling her chest, the ground gave another violent heave underfoot.

The entire group of Changers slid downhill, vanishing off the mountainside and into darkness.

―――――

Aurel and Zelle slammed through the front door into the tower, reeling from the shock of the Changers' attack. Blood soaked Aurel's sleeve, while Zelle's thoughts flitted back and forth between worry for her sister and the concern that Evita might have fallen to her death along with the rest of the Changers. She'd been too late to stop the Shaper's attack, but she'd hardly expected to find Evita *helping* the Changers.

"Get her over here." Grandma appeared from the darkness, leaping out of her armchair. "Powers above, Zelle, what are you wearing?"

"It's nice to see you too." Zelle caught her sister's uninjured arm and steered her to the armchair before she collapsed. "The Changers did this."

"Evita *shot* me. Gaiva's tits, that hurts."

"It's going to get worse." Grandma gestured impatiently. "Lie down and don't move. I'll get the arrow out."

"I can hardly wait." Aurel spoke through clenched teeth. "Powers above, she's under a spell. Evita is."

"It has to be Invicten's magic." Zelle motioned forward when Aurel reached for the arrow with her uninjured hand. "Don't—don't pull the arrow out yourself. It'll make the bleeding worse."

"Right, I'll just lie here with it sticking out of my arm, then." Aurel groaned.

Zelle had no experience in dealing with serious injuries, and the nameless Shaper's magic would be no help in this situation. Grandma, though, fetched her pack and began pulling out bandages and jars of ointments, barking the occasional order at Zelle.

Once the arrow was out and Aurel's arm was bandaged, Zelle went in search of some warmer clothes. It was unlikely that she'd ever see the ones she'd left in the palace again, but losing a few clothes was a small price to pay for her freedom.

After she'd changed into her furs from Itzar in the guest room, she returned to the main room and found Aurel explaining their escape from the palace to Grandma.

"I'm glad you didn't completely mess it up," Grandma said to Aurel. "How many people are on your tail?"

"Nobody, unless the Changers have less sense than I thought." Since both armchairs were occupied, Zelle slumped in the window seat instead. "I knocked all of them off the mountain, but what possessed them to try to take on the nameless Shaper?"

"They didn't know you'd be here," Aurel guessed. "Since you're meant to be trapped in the palace."

"I suppose I am." Zelle gave a short laugh. "I was rescued from the clutches of a handsome prince at a ball by my sister and a dragon. It's like a reversal of one of those old stories."

Aurel's mouth twitched into a grin. "Speaking of stories, I can't wait to hear how the Crown Prince tries to justify the lengths to which you went to escape him."

"He'll have trouble discrediting me, since the entirety of Saudenne now knows I wield the power of the nameless Shaper," Zelle said, with some satisfaction. "No doubt the whole country will know by the end of the week."

"Why did he tell everyone?" Grandma asked. "It seems foolish of him to show his hand like that."

"To turn me into a target, I think." Zelle had wondered the same herself, though it was Daimos who'd made the decision to expose her, not the Crown Prince. "Also, with the truth out there, I had to choose to support the Crown Prince or else I'd look like a traitor to the nation. Especially with a supposed war with Aestin on the horizon."

Grandma scoffed. "As if that empty-headed prince knows a thing. If an actual war with the deities breaks out, he'll be the first to flee."

"You didn't hear his speech," said Zelle. "He's convinced there'll be a war with Aestin, and that Zeuten needs the nameless Shaper's help to win. It plays in Daimos's favour to pit both Zeuten and Aestin against one another, doesn't it?"

Grandma tutted. "This is a prime example of why the Sentinels never get involved in politics if we can help it."

"I think that ship has sailed." Aurel leaned forward in the armchair. "What do you want to do now?"

"You need to rest," ordered Grandma. "Zelle..."

"I need to get rid of this." Zelle held up the Relic she'd taken from the palace. "This is what enabled Jarven to put a spell on the Crown Prince. I've no doubt a similar Relic is in the hands of whoever is giving the Changers orders."

"He used it on Evita," Aurel concluded. "Scumbag. When I get to him—"

"You aren't going anywhere," Grandma interrupted. "And Zelle? Don't let the Shaper talk you into pursuing the Changers right away."

I'll be happy if the Shaper talks to me at all, she thought to herself. "I won't."

Once she'd put on her thick leather boots, Zelle headed for the upper floor of the Sanctum. While she worked the locks on the door, she spoke to the staff, aloud. "Would you have killed Evita if she hadn't fallen along with the others?"

The staff didn't answer. Zelle continued to undo the various padlocks, her thoughts spinning. She'd known what she was getting into by joining forces with the Shaper but not that she'd have to unleash the staff's deadly magic against an ally. If Evita had *died*—to the Shaper, it might be a worthy trade-off, but not to Zelle.

Upon entering the Sanctum proper, she spoke loudly and clearly. "I need to talk to the Shaper. I have a Relic to destroy."

The floor gave way beneath her feet, drawing her into the void of the Shaper's prison. Gripping the staff in one hand and the wooden knife in the other, she hovered within the fog, unsure of whether the Shaper had an actual physical body somewhere in here or if She existed solely in a form incomprehensible to the human senses. With a Great Power, it was anyone's guess.

What did you bring to me? The Shaper's voice echoed around her, reverberating as though inside a tunnel or cave.

Zelle held up the wooden knife. "Can you use this to speak directly to Invicten?"

No, the Shaper replied. *That Relic contains little more than a fragment of His power. It isn't conscious. More's the pity, for I have many words I might have shared with Him, and none of them pleasant ones.*

"Do you know if He *does* have a Relic that can talk directly to a person?" Daimos alone knew that, she supposed, but if the mere trace of Invicten's power could temporarily overwhelm the wielder of the nameless Shaper's staff, she didn't want to imagine what a stronger Relic might be able to do.

Need I remind you that my perception is regrettably limited? If such a Relic exists, then I haven't the faintest idea where it is.

"Just wondered," said Zelle. "Ah—it's not possible for Daimos to bind Invicten into a human form the way he did with Orzen and Igon, is it?"

You know as much as I do on the subject. I can say that it has never been done before, to my knowledge.

"We'll return to that one later, then," she relented. "Can you destroy this Relic? Or will it be like Igon, where all His Relics need to be in the same place for him to be defeated?"

No. Igon's Relics were tied to his human form. Invicten's are not.

"Good." She hoped that meant He didn't *have* a human form, because they had quite enough enemies to deal with already. "Then destroy it."

A flash of light enveloped the wooden knife, which burst into fragments in Zelle's hand. She opened her palm, scattering the remains into the void.

"Now I need to do the same for the one that has Evita under its spell," she said. "On that note, can you try *not to* harm my friends when you're unleashing your wrath upon my enemies?"

If your friends insist on fighting alongside those enemies, then they will have to deal with the consequences.

"She's under a spell, Shaper. She... oh, never mind. Is there truly no help you can offer me against Invicten?"

Is the aid of a Great Power not enough? Such ingratitude, Zelle Carnelian.

"I'm not ungrateful. I'm frustrated. My sister was shot, for the Powers' sakes."

Yes, and you want to defend the person responsible. I truly do not understand humans.

Maybe you and Daimos would be better suited. The thought slid through her mind before Zelle managed to quieten it, and a chill rose at the certainty that the Shaper had heard her.

Perhaps you need to reflect more deeply on what it means to be bound to a Great Power, the Shaper told her. *You committed to your choice, Zelle Carnelian.*

I know I did. She might not like the Shaper's way of thinking, but She was an immortal deity who'd been imprisoned underneath a mountain for thousands of years and had no friends to speak of. That was just one reason they were bound to have differences of opinion, but when it came to killing her friends, Zelle refused to concede.

The Shaper's voice was a chilling whisper in her ear. Then you'll have to undo the illusionist's spell before you're forced to make that choice.

———

Rien sat in the Martzels' carriage as they headed for Daimos's hideout. With only room for four people in the back of the curtained carriage, Martzel had opted to stay behind, while Rien and Sanne had done their best to give both Reyes and Sarpe all the necessary information. Regardless, Reyes insisted on bombarding them with questions on every detail of the plan throughout the journey, though it turned out that he'd been prepared for an assault on Daimos's estate and had even gone to the trouble of putting together a mechanical device that would make it easier to get through the gates without tripping any alarms.

"Why do you think I wanted to stay in the city?" Reyes responded to Sanne's incredulity that he'd managed to create such a complex device so quickly. "My workshop is there, along with all my experiments. Some of us need hobbies that don't involve making idle chatter with the Emperor's guards."

Sanne's jaw twitched. "If you'd ingratiated yourself better with the Emperor's inner circle, you might have more friends who aren't made of wood and metal. We might also have more allies, too."

Sarpe groaned. "If you're going to argue, keep the

noise down, can't you? Anyone within range can hear every word."

Rien agreed, though there were few people wandering the deserted country lanes. They rode for about two or three hours at a steady pace, the four of them comfortably seated in the spacious carriage. Reyes and Sarpe kept up a stream of chatter that annoyed Sanne into telling them to tone it down. Hearing the two siblings bicker reminded him of his own relationship with Torben in a way that made Rien's heart twist painfully. He offered no comment himself, keeping his attention on the road and checking for pursuers.

Eventually, the carriage halted near a high fence that surrounded a property around the same size as the Martzel's safe house. A spiked gate covered the front entrance, but otherwise, no obvious obstacles presented themselves.

"Here we are." Reyes gripped his Relic in eager anticipation. "No security guards, I see."

"Don't speak too soon," Rien warned. "We need to deal with the locks first."

"That's my job." Reyes climbed down from the carriage. "Give me five minutes."

Rien arched a brow at Sarpe. "Does he do this all the time?"

"Generally, he applies his skills to designing mechanical boats, not breaking into nobles' houses." Sarpe, unlike his partner, remained on edge as they waited for Reyes to send his odd mechanical toy to find any hidden traps outside the gates.

"How does it move without him giving it instructions?" Rien watched the device, which was shaped like a miniature dog with wheels, trundle up to the gates.

"He used a spelled arrow as a base," Sanne said in disapproving tones. "They're designed to seek out their target, so throwing an arrow at the gates would have had the same result."

"I think my hound is much more adorable than an arrow," Reyes commented. "Right, Sarpe?"

"Quiet," his partner said but with affectionate undertones. "We don't know who might be watching."

When no traps went off, Reyes hurried to the gates and worked open the locks. He then sent the hound to check for traps on the inside of the grounds, and when none appeared, Rien stepped into the lead.

A winding path cut through the overgrown garden to the front door, on which Reyes worked his homemade lock-breaking tool. While no signs of Daimos materialised, a crimson glow emanated from Rien's staff when the door swung inward.

What is it? He saw nothing out of the ordinary in the wide entrance hall. The polished floor and the mahogany banisters along the winding staircase were as ornate as the Martzels', albeit not as well-kept. Once again, Reyes employed his hound to test for traps, but despite the staff's warning glow, nothing materialised.

Rien and the others split into three directions according to their plan, checking each room for any signs of Daimos. The rest of the house had the same neglected air as the entrance hall, with the furniture gathering dust and the bookshelves empty. He did find several books lying on a table inside the drawing room, however, and a glance at the titles brought him to a stunned halt.

They were *his* books—or to be precise, his father's volumes on the Powers and their Relics. Daimos must have taken them from Rien's house prior to setting it ablaze. Rage rendered him speechless for an instant, but he snatched up the books and strode out into the entrance hall. Incensed, he didn't notice the thorns creeping over his hands until a blazing light drew his attention to the upper floor.

Clouds of fog swirled downstairs, forming humanoid shapes. Magical constructs. Good. Rien needed a target.

Dropping the books, he ran towards the wraiths and blasted them with crimson light, but his thorns made no impact on the constructs' semi-transparent forms.

"Hey!" Reyes ran out of a nearby room, brandishing his own staff. "Get out of here."

Reyes's staff glowed a purplish-red colour, and a clap of thunder sounded, the accompanying flash of lightning sending the wraiths into retreat. Sarpe and Sanne came running to back them up, the latter wielding a staff identical to her brother's. The Martzels tended to avoid using their ability to manipulate the weather indoors, but since none of them cared if they did any damage to Daimos's property, they didn't have to hold back.

Reyes and Sanne circled the wraiths, their identical staffs conjuring the illusion of blazing sunlight. As the wraiths hated bright lights, they recoiled, yet the strange glow continued to emanate from upstairs.

Rien moved to the staircase. "I think there might be more of them up there." *Or their summoner.*

"Go ahead." Reyes waved him off. "Sarpe, you should wait outside."

Trusting the others to handle the wraiths, Rien

climbed the stairs, intending to snuff out the source of the constructs. In the upper corridor, an open door led to an empty room, bare of all furniture—except for a squarish blocky shape in the air.

A doorway to the realm of the Powers.

Now, Rien understood why the house was relatively unguarded. Daimos didn't need to pay for security guards when the deities themselves were able to step in and out of the house as needed. No doubt that was where the constructs had come from, too, but walking into the deities' own realm would be too much of a risk. Zelle's grandmother had somehow survived the experience, but she was a Sentinel, and her family was allied to the name-less Shaper. As for Daimos, he hadn't gone in there himself... had he?

The staff burned against Rien's hands, and a similar glow ignited around the doorway. A human figure emerged, a man wearing a long cloak that looked like he'd pilfered it from Rien's own wardrobe. The man carried a crimson staff in his left hand, patterned with thorns.

Naxel Daimos.

18

Evita tumbled into the air alongside the other Changers, their cloaks merging with hers to form one entity. Around, the mountain continued to shake, great tremors that made her teeth rattle in her skull and gave the impression that the world itself was trying to throw her off the edge.

The nameless Shaper...

The strange words disappeared into a meaningless blur while the Changers' fall slowed, and as one, they caught their balance. The second group hadn't been so lucky, their bodies lying sprawled on the rocks below, but Evita's cloak had saved her.

My Relic...

Again, the words were whisked away as she flew along with the rest of her group, over the mountain and back towards the Changers' base. None of the others spoke a word until they landed on the ground near the Masters' building. The mass of silver cloaks dissolved into frightened, dishevelled faces, while Master Drazer came marching over to meet them.

"Finally," he snapped. "I was beginning to think you'd all fallen to your deaths."

"Some of us did," Evita blurted out. "There are dead Changers back there—"

"Quiet." Master Drazer cut through her words. "What did you do?"

"We were ambushed," ventured one of the other Changers. "By a dragon… and two women."

"I didn't tell you to fight the Sentinel, you fools," he growled. "Now look at the state of you."

"It wasn't the Sentinel who threw us off the mountain." Evita's mouth spoke without her mind's permission, and Master Drazer shot her a glare as piercing as an arrow.

"I thought I told you not to argue with me." A familiar amber glow entered his eyes, and her sharp fear began to retreat. "Your *friends* deserve to be taught a lesson."

My friends? Master Drazer didn't explain his strange words, instead addressing the surviving Changers. "All of you are to get ready for battle. Replace your weapons if you managed to lose them. I'll give you until the stroke of midnight to prepare. Then, we will destroy the Sentinels and any who fight alongside them."

Rien faced Daimos, who stood in the doorway to the other realm with Astiva's staff in his hand.

How long had he waited for this moment? He'd spent weeks ruminating on his family's killer and how he didn't deserve the mercy of a quick death, but in the flesh, Naxel Daimos didn't entirely fit with the image Rien held in his memory. Around Rien's height and somewhat slighter, Daimos had cut his dark-brown hair short as if to scorn the fashionable style, and his tawny skin was lightly pockmarked with old scars. He knew it was the same man, of course, but the last time he'd seen Daimos had been from the position of a man condemned to die.

This time, their positions would be reversed. Rien would see to it himself.

Daimos's mouth twisted in a scowl. "You're trespassing, Arien Astera."

Rien raised the staff, thorns wrapping around the end, and Daimos mimicked his movement. Crimson light suffused both weapons, but Rien felt no sense of familiarity from looking at the Relic that had once been his. Nor could he afford to spare a thought on the matter. Thorn-covered vines shot from the end of his staff, but Daimos dodged them smoothly, deflecting the vines with a swipe of his own staff. His movements didn't quite match Rien's memories of their initial fight. He was faster than before, notably so, but the last time, Daimos had taken Rien by surprise by using his own father's staff against him. They'd been equally matched, but Rien's shock and anger at his family's deaths had unbalanced him.

This time, something was different. Not just in Rien but in Daimos himself. He moved quicker, surer, but Rien didn't find it hard to predict his movements and counter them. He swung the staff, and the vines lashed at his opponent like whips, snagging his clothes and scratching his face. Daimos staggered back, but no blood spilled from the wounds, and not a mark remained when he lifted his head.

"You aren't him." The truth hit him. "Are you?"

The false Daimos gave him a smile. "Correct."

"Who are you?" Rien might have struck him again, but curiosity stayed his hand. Had Daimos known that Rien planned to break into his house? How had he opened a doorway to the realm of the Powers to begin with? "Are you a deity? Or a construct?"

The false Daimos rocked back on his heels. "Now, why do you think I'd answer your questions?"

"Because if you don't, I'll make you wish you'd stayed in your own realm. Where is the real Naxel Daimos?"

"Far too busy to deal with the likes of you." The imitation of Daimos lifted his staff, which transformed before Rien's eyes into a blazing spear.

"That doesn't say much for *your* value." Rien ducked underneath the spear and swung the staff at the false Daimos's skull. His strike missed, but the thorns trailing in its wake yanked the weapon from the false Daimos's hands. "Is this your Relic?"

"Give that back," warned the false Daimos.

"I don't think so." Rien reeled in the vines as he might a fishing line and took the spear in hand. "You *are* a deity. Who are you?"

"Nobody." The false Daimos made a lunge for the spear, but Rien held it above his head, out of the deity's reach.

"What did he offer you?"

"A body, what else?" He screamed when Rien's thorns lashed him like a whip, knocking him to the floor. The sound was so disarmingly *human* that it brought Rien up short, even as his Relic continued to wrap sharp vines around his target, intending to squeeze the life from him.

Wait. Zierne. Stop.

Rien focused his will on the crimson staff, forcing the vines to loosen their grip. The deity was Daimos's ally, yes, but he seemed younger, more fragile than both Orzen and Igon. He moaned, lifting his head to stare at Rien with frightened eyes.

When the vines loosened, he gave a lunge that Daimos himself would never be able to accomplish, his hand closing around the spear. In another swift movement, the false Daimos sprang through the doorway and into the realm of the Powers.

Rien swore, his foot on the threshold of the doorway before common sense caught up to him. Running thoughtlessly into the realm of the Powers was not a sensible decision, but it might be the only way to force a confrontation with the real Daimos.

Wishing he'd pressed Zelle's grandmother with more questions about her own time spent in the realm of the Powers, he tested the ground on the other side of the doorway with the sole of his foot. It felt solid enough, so Rien stepped through the doorway with both feet.

Daimos's house disappeared.

Zelle woke to the sound of rushing wings and a tremor underneath the tower that shook the furniture and rattled the cabinets.

They're back, the staff warned.

"The Changers." Jumping to her feet, she grabbed the

staff from where she'd propped it against the armchair that she'd slept in. Zelle had slept fully clothed, so she only needed to pull on her boots and coat.

Aurel appeared in the doorway of the guest room, her arm bandaged and her hair in disarray. "Shit. They're here again already?"

"Stay in here," Zelle told her. "The Shaper and I can handle this."

"You'd think they'd have learned from the last time," remarked Aurel. "I'll stop Grandma from going outside."

"Might want to watch out for constructs too." Zelle spotted a papery gremlin scuttling upstairs. "The Changers can't get into the tower as long as you don't open the door."

She heard her grandmother moving inside the other bedroom, but she'd have to trust Aurel to keep Grandma from recklessly confronting the Changers herself.

A flash of silver light from the direction of the window showed her the Changers descending in a mass of rippling cloaks and landing in front of the tower. Had they lost their minds? With Invicten's Relic potentially influencing their decisions, there was a chance that was true in a literal sense, but nothing in Zelle's recent encounter with the Shaper had filled her with confidence that She might spare anyone who didn't fight of their own free will.

As she ran out of the tower, Zelle looked for Evita among the crowd of silvery cloaks. She caught sight of her near the back, wearing the same glazed expression as the rest of them. If she separated Evita from the others, she might be able to stop the Shaper from harming her, but there were no guarantees. Arrows pointed towards Zelle, but she raised the staff and countered with a blast of the Shaper's power.

The impact knocked the cluster of Changers backwards, causing some to drop their weapons, but as long as they remained clustered together, it was impossible to attack the others without hitting Evita too.

Zelle lifted the staff in warning. "Back off. I know you're not in control of your own minds, but the nameless Shaper doesn't care, and there's only so much I can do to hold Her back."

The Changers continued to move as though obeying unheard commands, not acknowledging her words. Several arrows shot towards Zelle, who waved the staff with more force and sent a gust of wind ploughing into their formation. The Changers staggered back, the wall of silver rippling.

A sharp masculine voice shouted from behind them, "Don't stop, fools. Get back into line. That's an order."

That's him, the staff hissed in her ear. *He's the one in charge.*

As the Changers fumbled to find their feet, she caught sight of Evita among them, her eyes wide as if she'd heard Zelle's threat where the others hadn't. *Shaper, don't hit her. Aim for their leader instead.*

Would you rather she turned you into a pincushion? came its response.

Really, asking the Shaper to apply moderation was like asking a storm to be considerate or a landslide to stop in its tracks, but Evita didn't deserve to suffer the same fate as their leader. With one eye on the Changers, Zelle edged around their group, heading in the direction of the voice she'd heard.

The Changers' arrows followed her, but the staff deflected them without Zelle needing to consciously give orders. She glimpsed Evita, perilously close to the cliff's edge, but no recognition filled her gaze when they locked eyes. Dragging her gaze away, she reached the other side of their group. A broad-shouldered man, not part of the formation but nevertheless dressed in a Changer's silvery cloak, watched Zelle's approach without displaying any fear.

"You must be the wielder of the nameless Shaper's Relic," said the man. "Aren't you supposed to be at the royal palace?"

"Aren't *you* the one who created a fake vision of Gaiva to convince the Changers to obey your every command?" she returned. "And who sent false intelligence to the Crown Prince?"

"I don't think you realise who you're dealing with."

A familiar amber light shone from his hands, and an equally familiar sensation washed over her. The urge to surrender rose within her like a tide, but a sharp shock of cold against her palm brought her back to her senses. *No.* Zelle refused to let this man bring about her end, or Evita's, either—which meant staying in control of the staff. She raised it, intending to strike him down, but a choked noise stayed her hand.

Evita staggered away from the other Changers, her hands clawing at her neck, where her cloak—her own cloak—was strangling her, as if someone invisible had tightened the material around her neck. Orange light suffused the man's palms, brightening as Evita continued to choke. Since when could Invicten's magic turn a Changer's own Relic against them?

"Keep her out of this," Zelle warned. "This is between the two of us."

"She needed to be taught a lesson," the man growled. "There's a marked lack of discipline among the Changers. It's no wonder this country is rotten to the core."

"Is that why you became the head of the Changers?" Zelle drew on the Shaper's magic and reached downward to the ground beneath their feet

The staff thrummed in Zelle's hand, and it took all her willpower to keep hold of it as the nameless Shaper's anger reverberated through the mountain. Her opponent staggered as the ground lurched and heaved, hurling him sideways and scattering the Changers like fallen leaves. He came upright against the cliffside, blood streaking his face, orange light flooding his palms—

Zelle raised a hand, and the cliff *moved,* even as a wave of coercion slammed into her and made her sway on her feet. The sensation vanished as swiftly as it'd arrived, the nameless Shaper steadying Zelle's balance and directing all Her fury at the intruder. Rocks slid down, crashing around him, and a flicker of fear appeared in the man's eyes for the first time. Like Jarven, he was merely a human, albeit one who'd been lucky enough to win the favour of a Relic of a Great Power. He hadn't intended to end up facing down the nameless Shaper, and even if he had, Zelle doubted he'd truly known the futility of winning a fight in the deity's own domain.

More rocks slid down in a violent sheet, and with a sickening crunch, the mountain crushed the man and his Relic at the same instant. Zelle felt the moment his life was snuffed out and cringed. Swallowing bile, she took a couple of steadying breaths.

"That was excessive," she told the Shaper.

The staff did not deign to respond. Zelle took an unsteady step back, and a groan came from behind her.

Evita, who lay sprawled in a heap, lifted her head. "Zelle?"

"Are you all right?" Invicten's must have broken upon the man's death, but she looked disorientated, shaken. So did the other Changers, the ones lucky enough to have survived. "Come into the outpost."

"I can't." She squeezed her eyes shut. "The cloak… it's how he controlled us. Master Drazer's Relic has the same source as mine."

"If that's who you mean, then you won't need to worry."

Evita paled when she saw what was left of the Master. "Oh."

"Wait…" Zelle paused. "Are you saying that *Invicten's* magic is inside your cloaks?"

Oh, Powers. The cloak's magic was directly tied to Invicten? No wonder the Changers had fallen under Daimos's control so easily. This was a complication she hadn't foreseen.

Evita simply gaped at her without speaking.

"I've destroyed two of His Relics," Zelle told her. "The rest will have to wait until later."

19

Rien's first impression of the realm of the Powers was that it felt like standing inside a giant cloud. Its walls, floor, and ceiling alike were formed of a hazy grey fog, as substantial as the illusion of Daimos. It was as if an artist had sketched out the scenery and then erased their work, leaving only the bare traces behind. There was no sign of the deity who'd imitated Daimos, but the presence of the doorway explained how his foe had been effortlessly moving from one place to another without being detected.

The staff burned Rien's hand, a sharp chill that made the hairs rise on his arms. The outline of a vaguely bird-like shape appeared against the fog, and a booming voice spoke. "You're not welcome here."

"You're one of the Powers."

"And you're in our realm." The deep voice presumably belonged to a male deity, though he spoke in Aestinian without any traces of an accent.

"So is Naxel Daimos," Rien replied. "I'm guessing you've met."

The fog cleared a little, revealing a huge, towering grey bird. A second bird, jet black, flew down to join him, and their wings formed a barrier that prevented Rien from moving forward.

"Move aside," he warned, his heart racing. "I have no quarrel with you, but I won't hesitate to cut you down if you prevent me from reaching my target."

The second deity laughed in a high, feminine voice. "You cannot navigate our realm, Arien Astera, but you are welcome to try."

"What does that mean?" His heart hammered, his staff burning against his hand with the urge to strike them down. "Answer me."

At one time, he would never have dreamed of speaking to a deity in such a manner, but these two had allied with Daimos, and they were in his way.

"You think to give us orders, Arien Astera?" The raven-shaped deity laughed again. "Did you think you could step into the realm of the Powers without any understanding of how our magic works?"

The nebulous cloud-like ground warped beneath his feet, and Rien found himself surrounded by twisted, monstrous shapes. Constructs, cold and grasping, seizing Rien's arms even as he tried to swing his staff at them. More smothered him in a tide, and he heard the deities laughing as the cold press threatened to suffocate the breath from his lungs.

He lifted the staff, using its crimson glow to push the wall of constructs aside. Breaking into a sprint, he burst from the doorway, finding his feet back on the bare floorboards of Daimos's room. Gasping for breath, he waited a moment for the dizziness to abate before turning back to the doorway.

The two bird-shaped deities shadowed the entrance, their wings spread to block his view of their realm. They'd made no move to follow him into Daimos's house, however. Why? Had their master ordered them not to leave, or was there another reason?

"Not so confident now, are you, human?" The raven-shaped deity broke into mocking laughter.

Breathing hard, he waved the staff at them. "Why not fight me yourselves rather than relying on your constructs?"

The deity's laughs petered out. "You're in no position to taunt us, mortal. Why not come in here and find out what we're truly capable of?"

He frowned at that comment. Something in the phrasing made him pause. "You can't get out, can you?"

No response came from either of the deities, but a rush of inexplicable satisfaction fought past his lingering shock and breathlessness.

"That's why you need a human form," he went on. "Isn't it?"

No wonder the deities had withdrawn from the human world altogether. Most people had no

knowledge of how to summon them, and while that might not have always been true, how many would have dared take the risk the way Daimos had?

A crash sounded behind him, and the door bounced off its frame as two other people ran into the room. Rien spun on his heel, raising the staff, but it was only Reyes and Sanne.

"What—?" Reyes skidded to a halt on the bare floorboards, his eyes on the open doorway. "Is that what I think it is?"

"Yes, it is." Rien faced the doorway, but the bird-shaped shadows had withdrawn from sight. "The doorway's barred to everyone but Daimos and anyone he elects to gift with a human form, including a deity who just ran off to report our intrusion to his boss."

"You're joking." Reyes eyed the doorway. "All right, let's burn this place down and get out. Sarpe is already back at the carriage."

"Burning down the house won't destroy the doorway," said Rien, his breath quickening again. "Daimos is on the other side. I have to—"

"You want to wait for him here?" Reyes shook his head. "We barely got rid of the constructs downstairs. One nearly froze me from the inside out."

A shiver ran up Rien's arms at the reminder of the constructs that had swarmed over him in the realm of the Powers. Faced with a world entirely hostile to humans, Rien would be hard-pressed to chase Daimos down. He must have made some bargain with the deities for their protection if he'd survived in their realm for any length of time.

"Wait." Sanne paused. "You want to leave the doorway open?"

What choice did they have? "I only know one person who can actually close doorways, and she's a continent away."

"Who?" Reyes gave him a curious look. "You've been holding out on us, haven't you?"

Yes. He had, and he was starting to run out of excuses

for not exposing Zelle's secret. Especially with a new understanding of how, exactly, Daimos might have won over the deities he'd worked with.

"Otherwise, I've only ever seen doorways closed by the deity who actually opened them," Rien added. "I don't know who opened that one, but I can guess, and he won't be back without reinforcements. Are the constructs gone?"

"As far as I know." Reyes beckoned him out of the room, lowering his voice. "I still have my sniffer hound. Should I leave it as a present for Daimos?"

"If you do, he'll know we were here," Sanne warned.

"He already will." Rien's hands curled into fists. All he had to show for this trip was a stack of books that Daimos had stolen from Rien's own house—and the knowledge that deities were using Daimos's home as a gate through which to enter this world.

Reyes set up his mechanical hound to ambush the next person to enter the room containing the doorway to the realm of the Powers. On the way out of the house, Rien gathered up the books he'd taken and carried them with him. Sarpe waited for them in the carriage, all too happy to leave, and nobody spoke for the first part of the journey back.

This was something of a relief to Rien, but it wasn't long before the inevitable questions arrived. Reyes, who'd been shooting furtive glances in his direction for much of the journey, broke the silence. "What're the odds that Daimos already knows we paid him a visit?"

"High," said Sanne. "Those deities of his are reporting directly to him, and he can move swiftly from one place to another as long as he uses those doorways. Is he the one opening them?"

"No," said Rien. "Only another deity can—one with a human form, that is."

Rien had his doubts that Daimos would offer one to every deity who asked, but the prospect alone would be alluring to beings who'd been cut off from the human realm for Powers knew how many years. No wonder they'd flocked to his side.

"I didn't know it was possible," said Sanne. "That is, for anyone to give a deity access to a human form, let alone the ability to walk between realms."

"Maybe Daimos can't find any humans willing to work for him," Reyes suggested. "More's the pity."

"No… he has plenty of those too." Deities were unpredictable, and he couldn't imagine Orzen or Igon blending in among the staff of the imperial palace or in Zeuten's royal court. "He uses the deities as spies in places humans can't access, I'm guessing."

Reyes glanced at him again. "How is it that you're so comfortable with the realm of the Powers?"

"I'm not." Rien lowered his gaze from Reyes's curious stare. "I've never set foot in there before, but I know it's survivable for humans… in theory."

"And how would you know that?" Sarpe asked.

He weighed the odds then continued. "Because the Sentinel of Zeuten has been there herself."

His story took most of the rest of the journey. Rien's voice was hoarse by the end, especially as Reyes kept interrupting with questions about the Great Powers, the Sentinels, and everything in between.

"Don't spread any of that information around," Rien

warned them. "If you do, it's not me who'll suffer the worst consequences. Zelle… she's already a prisoner or a fugitive, so she won't thank me for bringing yet more enemies after her."

"Daimos has her in his sights?" Sanne, who'd listened with rapt attention throughout his explanation, spoke first. "The nameless Shaper… I can't imagine he'll want her walking around unchecked."

"Exactly." Rien sat back in his seat, exhaustion tugging at his limbs. "Regardless, we can't count on the Shaper's help if Daimos comes after us when he finds out we broke into his house."

His revelation had distracted everyone from wondering how many deities Daimos had following him, but the question remained in the back of his mind. Now that he'd seen their realm with his own eyes, he had to wonder why it was accessible for humans when the reverse didn't appear to be the case. According to the stories, the gods had once walked among humans, which suggested that some long-forgotten catastrophe had sealed the doors between realms, but he was more concerned with how Daimos had figured out how to get around that limitation.

When the carriage rolled to a halt, they found Martzel waiting on the doorstep of his house to hear about their narrow escape. Over a late meal in the dining room, Rien let the others give the details of their visit to Daimos's house, saving his energy for the inevitable moment when he had to tell Martzel about Zelle and the Shaper. He concentrated on not falling asleep in his plate instead of contributing, at least until Reyes startled him out of his reverie by saying his name.

"Arien went into their realm himself," Reyes told Martzel. "Because he has a death wish."

Martzel scrutinised Rien. "You went into the realm of the Powers?"

"It was unpleasant." He lowered his gaze. "I tried to chase down Daimos's ally, but he has others, ones who cannot leave their realm. None can unless they have a human form… Did you know?"

While the others surveyed him as though they expected him to repeat his tale of how he'd become acquainted with the nameless Shaper, he was more interested to know if anyone else was aware of the deities' major limitation.

"I guessed." Martzel's brows drew together. "The fact that it's been so long since any of the Powers have visited the human realm means it's a common enough theory among Invokers, but the deities withdrew from this world at a time when written records were sparse."

"Daimos can't be the first to have given a deity a human form, right?" Rien asked.

"Not the first but the first in a long while." Martzel heaved a sigh. "As for how he gained that knowledge, though…"

"You think he learned it in exile?" He must have, though Rien had never thought of the Scarred Lands as containing much aside from the damage left in the wake of those ancient wars. He found his attention drawn to the pile of books he'd retrieved from Daimos's house, which he'd stacked on the floor next to his chair. "I wonder if that's why he wanted my father's history books. Perhaps he intended to track more Relics that were lost after the founding of the initial Invoker families."

"He has quite enough Relics already," said Reyes. "The good news is that if he's in the realm of the Powers, he's not in *this* realm."

"Don't speak too soon," replied Martzel. "I have no doubt he'll find out what you did, and if he knows our location…"

"Then our cover is blown," concluded Sanne.

"Honestly, it was only a matter of time," Reyes said. "If you ask me, the only reason Daimos hasn't already come after us is because he doesn't know Arien is here."

Now he does. Guilt twisted inside Rien, but he pushed it down. "He still wants the other Invoker families dead or under his command. I'd say it's more that he's trying to be in too many places at once. Aestin, Zeuten, *and* the realm of the Powers. He's having to use intermediaries, who are less reliable, to deal with annoyances like us."

Was Daimos's ultimate goal to convince Aestin to declare war on Zeuten? That was what Zeuten's Crown Prince seemed to think, and if Daimos intended to involve the deities in that war, it would tie all three of his plans together into one catastrophic knot.

Rien would stop him first. He refused to let Daimos slip through his fingers a second time.

———

Naxel Daimos stepped out of the doorway, his feet touching down on the solid surface of the spare room in his house.

After the amount of time in recent days that he'd spent in the realm of the Powers, it was an adjustment to suddenly be in a room with actual boundaries and dimensions. In the deities' realm, nothing was solid or fixed, and the fluid nature of the Powers themselves didn't help with the confusion. They seemed to be confined to a single form once they took on a human body, but their choices were rather perplexing. Orzen, for instance, had taken on the form of a child who Daimos had run into in his flight from Arien Astera's estate. Igon had mimicked a wandering seafarer who now lay rotting at the bottom of the ocean, while Nahen had decided to imitate Daimos himself.

Daimos had been tempted to punish Nahen for the sheer audacity, but he'd refrained. He somewhat regretted that choice as his own face looked back at him, eyes wide with fear.

"He's gone," Nahen whispered. "Him and the others."

"What others?" Daimos snapped. "I thought I told you to kill them all."

"He has a new Relic," Nahen mumbled.

"I know he has a new Relic, you blundering fool," said Daimos. "You might at least have stopped him from walking through my doorway."

"He didn't get far," said Nahen. "The others stopped him."

Daimos shot a glare at the doorway behind him, where the birdlike forms of Kyren and Xeale watched from the shadows. "At least you did something right."

He must have missed the incursion by mere minutes, but the intruders hadn't stayed for long. They also hadn't caused any obvious damage, though young Arien must have known the futility of trying to destroy a doorway to the realm of the Powers.

"I'm sorry." Nahen's voice faltered. "I didn't know…"

Daimos glared at him. "I thought I could trust you with one task while I was away, but it seems I have to do everything myself."

The blasted Powers were hardly more reliable than the humans were. He'd been detained all morning listening to reports of his allies' failures in Zeuten the previous day. Not only had they let Zelle Carnelian escape the palace, but she'd destroyed the Relic and killed its wielder and then done the same to the man he'd put in charge of the Changers for good measure. That on top of Rien's transgression was the last straw. He stalked away from the open doorway, and something solid barrelled into his legs.

Nahen hurried up to him. "Sir!"

A sharp sting in his ankle made him curse, kicking out, and a metal contraption of some kind flew back into the wall. It looked like a cross between a model of a carriage and the sort of mechanised lockpick one might buy from a specialist in the capital—which appeared to have stabbed him in the leg.

"Deal with that, Nahen," he snapped. "Get it out of my house and have a think on how you'll avoid making the same mistakes again."

The sheer nerve of Arien Astera setting a trap for him in his own house. Daimos left the deity behind and made his way downstairs, reflecting that the youngest Astera had more resourceful allies than he'd anticipated. He'd need to do something about them, but between the situation in Zeuten and here, his resources were stretched thin. If he hadn't been delayed, he might have had time to finish off dear Arien himself.

His one consolation was that the Emperor would

make a decision soon, and Daimos had no doubt his allies would push His Imperial Majesty onto the correct path. Daimos himself intended to stay out of the war, for the most part, but he'd made a grave mistake in overlooking the power in Zelle Carnelian's hands. No longer.

Both she and Arien would perish, and he'd have the pleasure of watching their nations fall into ruin.

20

"They closed our tunnels?" Aurel said disbelievingly. "Bastards."

Behind Zelle, her sister and grandmother had exited the tower to observe the mess the Changers had left behind. They'd fled immediately upon the death of their leader, whose remains and Relic had vanished by the time Zelle returned to check on him.

She decided against asking the staff what had happened to his body.

The dragonet chirped, padded over to Evita's side, and let her stroke him on the nose. "I'm glad to have you back."

Aurel glowered at Evita. "You shot me."

Evita paled. "Gaiva's tits, I'm sorry."

"The spell is gone," Zelle told her sister. "It's all right."

Her gaze dropped. "It's in my cloak. Invicten's magic is still here."

"The man who controlled you is dead. You should be fine." *I think.* Zelle had seen Evita's own cloak almost strangle her. How could someone exert control over another person's Relic? Admittedly, she was far from an expert on the subject, and the Shaper would have warned her if Evita or her Relic was a potential threat to the Sanctum, right?

I can only sense magic, not its intent. The staff answered her implied question. *If another intruder arrives, however, I will alert you.*

That would have to do. Zelle turned to her sister and grandmother. "She's safe. Let her in."

Grandma hobbled into the tower first, followed by Aurel and then Zelle. Evita exchanged a few murmurs with the dragonet before darting through the door after Zelle.

"The Changers are dead?" asked Grandma.

"Not all of them," said Zelle. "The man who wielded Invicten's Relic is, though, so the Changers will no longer be coerced into obeying his orders."

Evita gave a shudder. "Where have you been? Were you really imprisoned in the palace?"

"More or less." Zelle returned to her armchair and sank into it, giving Evita a brief summary of her escape earlier that night. "Nobody can resist the spell of a Relic of Invicten, not even me."

"That shouldn't be possible," Aurel said. "You're bonded to the nameless Shaper."

Grandma made a noise that sounded halfway between approval and annoyance. "I expect your humanity alone was enough to make you susceptible to his control."

Was that a good thing? She'd have to think on that one later. "Grandma, did *you* know the Changers' Relics also contained the magic of Invicten?"

"No, of course I didn't," said Grandma. "The Changers? It isn't Gaiva they serve?"

"Apparently not, though it makes sense, now that we've seen the real Gaiva in Itzar." Zelle rubbed her temples. "How did nobody realise which deity they really belonged to?"

"Good question." Aurel raised a brow at Evita.

"Don't ask me," Evita said. "I didn't know, but Master Drazer did. I wonder who told *him*."

"Daimos," Zelle said. "He's been busy researching, I'd guess."

Evita cast another glance around the room. "Where's Rien?"

Once again, the simple question hit Zelle square in the chest. "Gone. The Crown Prince had him expelled to Aestin, and I can only hope Daimos wasn't waiting for him on the other side."

She and her family were reunited, and yet Rien's absence remained. In the palace, she hadn't let herself spend too much time thinking on his dilemma, but now...

"Anyway." Aurel spoke a touch too loudly. "We've saved two people from Daimos for one night, so that's enough of a victory for me. Want to go and set Tavine free while we're at it?"

"That... You know, that's not a terrible idea." Zelle wouldn't have minded a distraction from dealing with the aftermath of the battle. As soon as she closed her eyes, she knew she'd relive the man's death, when the Shaper had suppressed her human instincts entirely. Or she'd find her thoughts drifting to Rien and to words that she might never get to say. "Not until it's light, though."

Zelle's instincts told her that they might have won two

victories in the course of a single night, but Daimos wouldn't allow her a third.

———

Zelle, though exhausted, didn't sleep. The others had fallen silent long ago, with Grandma and Aurel inside the bedrooms and Evita sprawled and snoring in the window seat. In the end, it wasn't the Master's brutal end or even the ache in her chest when she thought of Rien that kept Zelle from resting but the staff. Its blue glow was incessant, and in the quietness, she heard it whispering to itself, unfamiliar words that nevertheless sounded unpleasant to Zelle's ears.

"Can you do that somewhere else?" she muttered.

Might I remind you that I don't have legs?

"All right." She sat upright. "I get the message."

After sliding on her boots, she took the staff and carried it upstairs, trying her best not to make too much noise and wake the others. Then she undid the locks on the doors to the Sanctum, shivering as a chill breeze swept through the upper corridor. The staff's whispers finally quietened when she entered the Sanctum.

"You're being unreasonable," she whispered. "I just escaped the royal palace and fought off two attacks from the Changers. I deserve a rest."

I might remind you that I did most of the work myself.

"I brought you here," Zelle hissed. "I flew all the way back to the Range with you, remember?"

You came here for your family, not for me.

"And you're a paragon of selflessness, are you?" She rubbed her tired eyes with her free hand. "You don't care for my well-being *or* my allies. You said so yourself. Besides, you were as much of a prisoner inside that palace as I was."

That may be, but you would do well to remember that you and I have an agreement.

"What do you want, then?" She studied the knotted wood as if to see through to the thoughts within. "What's bothering you?"

Invicten is not what I thought, answered the Shaper. *Neither are the Changers.*

"You didn't know the Changers were using Invicten's Relics?"

No. I should have guessed He would find a way to thwart me.

"You aren't making any sense," said Zelle. "Can you tell me the actual history between the three of you? The books gave a mythologised version of the story, but I need the facts."

Tales of the past are all we have left. Every story changes depending on the teller.

"As if you didn't *live* it yourself." Zelle heard a noise outside the door. "Now you've woken the others, too."

Zelle opened the door and found Grandma standing at the top of the stairs. "I thought I might find you up here."

"Sorry," she whispered. "I tried to be quiet, but the staff wouldn't let me sleep."

"Did it have a good reason?"

"Not really," admitted Zelle. "It's being cryptic and muttering to itself. Did it do that with you, too?"

"Occasionally," said Grandma. "I had to lock it up in the Sanctum once."

Zelle's mouth twitched into a smile. "I think finding

out the Changers wield the Relics of Invicten disturbed the Shaper, but I have no idea why that would matter."

"I assume the two of them disliked one another," said Grandma. "It seems to be a recurring theme with the Shaper."

"The Shaper won't tell me the details of their disagreement, which makes it difficult to come to any conclusions," said Zelle. "I don't know how the Changers have spent years using Invicten's Relics without realising, though. Much less right next to the Shaper's own domain."

"The Relics don't show any obvious signs of Invicten's magic," Grandma said. "They also aren't as potent as the ones carried by Daimos's allies."

"Being able to fly and transform into animals is useful in its own way," said Zelle. "But you're right... The Relics Daimos is using are different. Stronger."

How had he found them? Questions piled on top of questions, and yet the staff insisted on adding to the heap instead of decreasing her burden.

Grandma gave her a sideways look. "There's one place you might find guaranteed answers to any questions pertaining to the Great Powers."

"Where?" Zelle studied her face. "Not the realm of the Powers? No human can survive there. I know *you* did, but... do you think Invicten might be there? The real Invicten, not just a Relic?"

"I wouldn't know, but the deities are more knowledgeable on their history than one would expect of beings who have no written records."

Zelle lowered her gaze to the staff. "I can't go to their

realm without a doorway, though. Besides, the Shaper wants me to close the doors, not walk through them."

There's something else you can do, then, the staff put in. *Find Invicten's other Relics.*

"I would if I knew where they were."

"The staff means the Changers' Relics," Grandma put in. "Given the current state the Changers are in, I doubt they'd notice the theft."

Zelle hadn't known the staff had addressed her grandmother too. "You want me to steal from the Changers?"

I think they've earned it, don't you?

"All right," Zelle told the staff. "But only if you let me get some sleep first."

———

The next time Zelle woke was when Aurel came wandering into the main room of the Sanctum in search of breakfast, her bandaged arm encrusted with dried blood.

"Can't you at least clean up before we eat?" Zelle yawned, sitting upright in her armchair.

"You try doing everything one-handed," came her sister's bad-tempered reply.

By the time they'd scraped together a meal from their supplies, the general mood had improved somewhat. With Evita back and Zelle no longer trapped in the palace under the watch of the Crown Prince and Jarven—not to mention Daimos being down at least two allies—they might as well savour the victory while they could.

Their next step would be to take back the Reader's house.

"We need to go back to Tavine," Zelle said to the others. "We can drive the Changers off, if they haven't already moved back to their base when they found out their leader died."

"They might not know yet." Aurel chewed on a stale pastry. "If not, the Senior Changers will raise a huge fuss, but that's not our problem."

"I just hope Daimos didn't have a replacement waiting to take over," said Zelle. "The villagers have been through enough already."

Evita left the tower first with Zelle close behind her, greeting Chirp with a stroke on his scaly forehead. "Where'd the eagles go?"

"Good question." Zelle turned towards her sister, who'd exited the tower behind her. "Have you seen the eagles in the past few days?"

"You know… I never thought to look, but maybe they went home."

Evita gave the dragonet another stroke. "Might have. If so, then only two of us will be able to go to the village."

"Not necessarily," said Aurel. "Zelle and I will ride Chirp, and you can fly using your cloak."

Evita winced. "I really don't think that's good idea."

"Invicten's magic won't control you again." Zelle attempted a reassuring tone. "You can stay behind if you'd prefer, but Aurel—you *should* stay behind, considering you're injured."

"I lost the use of my arm, not my head." Aurel scowled and tried to mount the dragonet, but with one hand, she was unable to climb onto his back.

"You should be resting," Zelle insisted. "Not getting

into fights with Senior Changers. I'll go myself... What about you, Evita?"

"I'll stay behind." Evita nodded to Aurel. "I don't want to see the Changers again for a long time."

Neither did Zelle, whose memory of Master Drazer's unpleasant death was all too recent, but so was the staff's suggestion that she ought to go looking for Invicten's other Relics. Like the Changers' cloaks.

And they'll just let you walk in and take them? whispered a voice in the back of her head that didn't belong to the staff. Even without their leader, the Changers wouldn't take kindly to the intrusion, but Zelle would see what she found in the village before deciding how lenient to be towards them.

Zelle climbed onto Chirp's back. When he realised Evita wouldn't be coming with them, he whined and nudged her in the back with his snout.

"You'll be fine with Zelle," Evita told him firmly. "I've been with the Changers for days. I don't want to see them again for a while."

Chirp grumbled, but he gave in, taking off in a beat of his wings.

He and Zelle flew over the outpost towards the dark forest on the opposite side of the Range. From there, they circled downward and landed on the path that connected the village with the sloping mountain trail leading up to the Sentinels' cave.

"Wait for me here," she told Chirp, before hurrying away towards the village. While Zelle might have once been wary of beasts lurking in the woods, the idea of any predator making a dent in the staff was laughable.

Zelle circled the fence surrounding Tavine, noting the

absence of any Changers patrolling the outskirts. In fact, none stood outside the gates, either, while nobody stopped her from entering the village. Few people were around, maybe afraid to venture outside in case they ran into the Changers... but where had they disappeared to? Had they learned of the death of their leader and returned to their base?

Zelle made straight for the tavern and pushed open the door. Marita spun around from the table she was cleaning and gasped at the sight of her. "Zelle?"

"Marita." Zelle approached her, relieved to see a familiar face. "You're all right?"

"It *is* you. I thought they'd captured you."

"The Changers? Have they gone?"

"They left in the middle of the night," she said. "All of them. Someone came to the gates with an urgent update, and they called a meeting in their room that had me awake half the night with their whispering. When I came downstairs this morning, they were gone."

"Did they mention if they'd be coming back?"

"No, but they didn't tell me they were leaving either."

"Thanks anyway," said Zelle. "I'm going to tell Aurel and my grandmother the good news so they can come back to the Reader's house."

Marita beamed. "I'll be glad to see you all back."

"Me too." First, though, she needed to be certain the Changers had gone for good. Finding out who was giving them orders wasn't a bad idea, either, so Zelle briefly checked the Reader's house was undisturbed before leaving the village to reunite with the dragonet.

As they took flight, she found her gaze drifting towards

the southernmost peak of the Range. The notion of stealing the Changers' Relics had appealed to her last night, but landing in the middle of their camp and demanding their cloaks was bound to end in disaster. Despite the Changers' questionable choices, she'd have preferred not to let the Shaper's magic eliminate all the survivors.

Not least because they were supposed to be Zeuten's defenders, which was no doubt one of the reasons Daimos had intentionally targeted them from the outset. The staff might have got the better of the Changers with ease, but she'd seen for herself how effective their magic would have been against most other opponents. Even with the Shaper's magic set against her, Evita had still managed to hit Aurel.

Zelle didn't like to think what might have happened if she hadn't ended the fight when she had.

Below her, a flare of light caught her gaze, and she peered down at the rocky path. A patch of whiteness came into view, and her heart gave a stutter. It could only be a doorway to the realm of the Powers.

Where did that come from?

I imagine someone opened it, the staff replied.

"Meaning a deity," she muttered. "Let's have a look."

The dragonet flew lower at Zelle's command and landed on the path. There didn't appear to be anyone around, human or otherwise, but who'd opened the doorway to begin with? Zelle climbed off the dragonet's back, her fingers tightening around the staff in case something jumped out and attacked her.

Close the doors, the Shaper had told her, but last night's conversation with her grandmother had reminded her of the potential wealth of information within the deities' realm.

She's right, you know, the staff said, *but I'd be more concerned that someone might come* out *of the doorway.*

"There is that." She pointed the staff at the shimmering square of pure whiteness. Had any humans ever wandered into the realm of the Powers before her grandmother? It didn't strike her as the sort of thing one did casually, but Grandma had survived the experience. She'd never given Zelle the full story, but her claims that the deities had witnessed the very events that she wanted to know about were all too accurate.

Then again, so had the staff.

What are you doing? The question sounded petulant, as if the staff had picked up on her thoughts.

"Thinking about the reliability of deities," she said. "Or otherwise."

I rather think the same applies to humans, but leaving that doorway open will bring you nothing but trouble.

"Close it, then." The patch of whiteness smoothed over like stitches sinking into fabric, while Zelle tried to suppress the sinking suspicion that whoever had *opened* the doorway might have already got away. "I think my grandmother needs to know about this."

21

Rien moved as quietly as possible across the upper corridor, trying not to tread on any creaky floorboards and wake the others. The Martzel estate was old enough that such noises weren't unusual, but he'd prefer to leave without inviting any awkward questions.

Luck wasn't on his side, however. As he reached the stairs, a light from a nearby room drew his gaze to a lantern, held by Martzel, who stepped into view. "I thought you might try going after Daimos alone."

"And you thought you'd talk me out of it?" Rien guessed. "The deities went to report to him directly. If I can direct Daimos's attention away from your house, then I'll gladly do so."

"Foolish boy," Martzel said softly. "I know you think you're doing the right thing, but it'll only lead to more misfortune."

"Daimos knows we found his hideout by now," Rien argued. "He'll be furious."

"That doesn't mean you need to make it easier for him to find you," growled Martzel. "Especially alone."

"It's not that I don't appreciate the help." That was the worst part—he'd come here expecting enmity and found allies instead, ones who didn't seem to care that he'd abandoned his home country and claimed an unknown Relic from another nation. "I'm concerned that Daimos might be using the realm of the Powers as his base, and if he is, then my allies in Zeuten need to know as soon as possible."

"You mean Zelle Carnelian and the nameless Shaper."

Rien stared at him for a moment. "How—"

"How do I know?" Martzel finished his question for him. "Sanne told me in confidence. I assumed you intended to pick the right moment to tell me yourself, but I thought you should know."

An icy sensation grew in the pit of his stomach. "Did she think I might turn against you?"

"She's concerned, as we should all be." He beckoned to Rien. "Since you're already awake, you might as well come downstairs."

They made their way to the drawing room, where several candles illuminated the remnants of their maps of Daimos's house. Martzel sat in a chair and gestured for Rien to do the same, but he couldn't bring himself to relax. Had Sanne truly distrusted him, or were his own fears of bringing disaster upon the Martzel family colouring his perspective? Perhaps both, though Reyes had been right in that Daimos was bound to come looking for their safe house eventually.

"I wanted to tell you," Rien began. "Parts of the story weren't mine to share, but that's no excuse for hiding information from you. Especially concerning a Great Power."

"If the Shaper is entrapped within the mountains of Zeuten, then I can understand why you felt it wasn't directly relevant to our current dilemma, though it explains why you were able to find a new Relic in the mountains." Martzel's gaze dropped to Rien's staff, and he found his grip tightening in response. "The Shaper guided you."

"Not exactly." Was that the case, though? Zelle's claim that none of the myths were true in a literal sense had put into question the stories he'd grown up with, including those concerning his own family and their long-standing alliance with Astiva… but while he had no recollection of his father ever telling him that the Great Powers had ever truly existed, the Shaper's magic *did* permeate the entire mountain. "The Sentinels themselves were unable to find the Relic before I did, and it was their own ancestors who concealed it there. The deities… They are sometimes hard to comprehend and none more so than the Great Powers."

"Yes… there is that," Martzel mused. "Are you sure you want to go back to Zeuten, though? If Daimos is indeed travelling using the realm of the Powers, then it's unlikely that he will escape your allies' notice."

He had a point, but Rien was less than enthused at the notion of waiting for Daimos to find the safe house either. "No, but there's also the deities he's gifted with human forms. Zeuten wasn't prepared for the last one, and even now…" He trailed off, not wanting to betray Zelle by exposing her country's vulnerability to a magical assault from Daimos and his allies.

"I see." Martzel studied him for a moment. "I have to

admit, I've always found it fascinating how readily most Zeutenians have adapted to life without magic. Sometimes I wonder what might have become of us if we'd done the same."

"How can you think that?" The brief time that Rien had lived without his Relic had been pure agony, and the scars etched into the back of his left hand were the least of the damage he'd suffered as a result.

"I don't mean to imply I intend to give up my staff," Martzel amended. "Merely that we have believed ourselves to have dominion over magic for so long that we grew complacent and forgot how little we know about the deities themselves."

"I'm not convinced Daimos knows them that well either," Rien said. "He's offering them their wishes—access to the human realm—but he can't possibly believe his plan will result in anything but chaos and anarchy."

"I believe *that* is his plan," Martzel said. "It was evident in his choice of allies from the start. Orzen must have had an extraordinarily strong will to have done the damage he did."

"You mean… when Daimos killed my family." Rien lowered his gaze. "You're right. Orzen had no human form when Daimos launched his initial attack, as far as I know."

"No, but he was present as more than a Relic."

Rien frowned, unsure what the older man was implying. He'd assumed that Daimos had given Orzen his human form specifically to send him in pursuit of Rien himself, but he'd initially been confined to a Relic, hadn't he?

Then it hit him. "You think the actual *deity* was speaking to Daimos? From his own realm?"

"That is precisely what I believe, Arien."

Then the doorway must have already been open. Daimos had made actual contact with the gods, long before he'd enacted revenge on Rien's family, and he'd chosen to forge a partnership with a deity whose destructive nature was precisely what he needed.

"How could he have achieved it?" he murmured. "He had no magic in exile, nothing to guide him."

"He was lucky to find a deity who happened to be looking for an ally," said Martzel. "I don't doubt the Scarred Lands are teeming with Relics that were abandoned by the families who formed the original alliance of Invokers after the new Aestinian Empire was established. Orzen was one of them, certainly."

"You've been reading up on the subject too?" The books Rien had taken back from Daimos's house might contain similar information, but he wondered what had driven Martzel to fixate on a deity who'd already been subdued. *Orzen was the start of all this. I suppose.*

"Yes, I have," Martzel replied. "I suspect that Orzen was able to speak to Daimos through the Relic itself and teach him to open a door to their realm."

"Merciful Powers," Rien murmured. "And he might do the same for any others? Is that what you mean?"

"Only if he has a Relic belonging to the deity in question," he said. "The ritual for binding a deity into a human body is complex, and the actual deity must play a part themselves. Not all deities would deign to form an alliance with a human, and despite its nebulous nature, their realm is as vast as ours."

"It's not as simple as standing on the edge of a doorway and calling their name." A chill arose at the memory of their realm, of the constructs suffocating the breath from him. "He had other deities protecting him in their realm. No doubt he promised them access to the human realm in exchange."

If he used their Relics. Strange to contemplate. To most Invokers, Relics were tools, first and foremost. While they worked best when the owner's wishes and the Relic's were in alignment, the actual deity was never involved in that agreement.

But Daimos hadn't just used Orzen's Relic to kill Rien's family. He'd used the deity himself as a confidant, an advisor, and Orzen had always maintained his own will, independent of his Relic.

What did that say of Rien's own Relic? Was Zierne himself fighting Rien's control, or was it simply that he and the Relic were out of alignment? The Relic itself shouldn't have been able to strike without Rien's conscious command, should it?

Martzel indicated a stack of books on the nearby table. "I should return to bed. If you can't sleep, feel free to read any of those."

"Is there a book on other Relics like Orzen's?" he found himself asking. "Relics with an unusually strong influence on their wielders, that is?"

Martzel's brow furrowed. "No... not that I'm aware of. Is there a reason? You think Daimos has another?"

"No." He had Astiva... and while Rien had become close enough to his own Relic to experience it as an extension of his own will, he'd never heard the god's own voice speak in his mind, or felt the Relic stir with wishes of its own. "No, it's mine."

Martzel's gaze dropped to the staff. "Yours?"

"The staff... It acts as if it has a will of its own." He struggled for the words. "I read a text in Zeuten that claimed Zierne once went to war with his siblings due to his jealousy of humans. There have been times when my Relic has attacked innocents or even struck my own allies, and I was only able to gain its allegiance when I made it clear that I don't expect it to be like my former Relic—like Astiva. But I'm not sure I want to be allied to the deity in those stories either."

The words felt like sacrilege, as if he were betraying the very heart of what it meant to be an Invoker. Part of him wondered if his father's old friend might throw him out of the house, as irrational as it might seem.

Concern lined Martzel's face. "No Relic should be able to act outside of your control, Arien. Not even one that was initially resistant. That's how Daimos was able to seize..."

"Astiva." Speaking the name brought less pain than usual, buried under his sudden rush of panic. If even Martzel was willing to admit something might have gone wrong between him and Zierne, then what did that say for his chances against Daimos? "I need another Relic to beat him. A Relic of equal strength. That's why I claimed this one."

The Relic had forged a bond with him based on his need for vengeance, and they worked best when their goals were in synchrony... which would serve him well in his clash with Daimos, but afterwards? What then?

"I understand." Martzel rose to his feet. "It's been a very long time since I claimed a Relic myself, and I cannot speak to the specifics of losing one and gaining another. As for the stories of the gods themselves... if you want to know the history, then like I said, the books ought to be able to help you."

Was it Rien's imagination, or had he spooked the old Invoker? Surely not. Martzel did not scare easily, after all.

"I will," Rien replied. "Thank you."

Yet as Martzel departed, so too did one of Rien's hopes of finding someone who understood the truth of his struggle with his Relic. Someone aside from Zelle, that is.

He hadn't been thrown out... but part of him wondered if he shouldn't have left anyway.

———

The Relics belonging to the children of Gaiva reside with the major families of Invokers in Aestin.

"I already know that," Rien muttered to the volume of Aestinian history that lay open on the table in front of him.

"Talking to yourself?" Reyes blew out one of the candles, and Rien began to protest before realising the light streaming through the curtains into the drawing room was more than sufficient for him to read by. "Dad said you've been sitting there all night."

"Couldn't sleep."

"So you thought you'd refresh your mind on our recent history?"

"Not so recent." Rien lifted his gaze from the textbook.

He'd started with the intention of reading stories of the children of Gaiva, but Martzel's claim that the deities' own behaviour did not affect what wielders did with their Relics had nagged at him. Unfortunately, none of the history books from either his family's own collection or Martzel's contained so much as a single mention of Zierne's Relic.

He'd read one tale of the first Sentinels' voyage to Zeuten, but it hadn't mentioned what they'd taken with them, save for the voice of Gaiva Herself guiding their path. He knew that to be untrue based on Zelle's own accounts, but the story itself had been written several hundred years after the fact and had been heavily modified. Who was to say where the truth lay?

"Looks as dry as the Scarred Lands," Reyes remarked, eyeing the textbook. "What are you trying to find, anyway?"

"The history of the Sentinels and the Invokers of Aestin," said Rien. "Particularly how the Relic of Zierne came to be in Zeuten."

"Why do you want to know that?"

"To get to know my new deity."

Reyes gave him an odd look. "Did you do the same with Astiva?"

"Astiva's Relics have been in my family for a thousand years," Rien reminded him. "Zierne's has never been held by anyone before me, as far as I'm aware, since it spent a thousand years buried in a mountain."

"I forgot that part." A thoughtful expression crossed Reyes's face. "If there are more Relics hidden in there, that'd be one way for us to gain an edge."

"Don't you even think about it," Rien warned him. "The nameless Shaper wouldn't allow it. Nobody has ever been near the hidden Relics without ending up lost or worse."

"You got lucky, then," said Reyes. "Why does it matter where your Relic came from?"

Because we're not in full synchrony. Because the staff acts independently of me sometimes... and I can't afford to mess up when I fight and kill Daimos.

Yet it wasn't his revenge on Daimos that would suffer if he lost control of the staff at a critical moment, and he hadn't found anything in the textbooks hinting at a Relic gaining dominance over its wielder either.

He *had* found a vague reference implying that the Relics abandoned in the Scarred Lands after the wars prior to modern Aestin's founding had been deemed too dangerous to allow into the newly formed nation, but nothing referencing Relics being removed from the continent altogether. The notion of certain Relics being designated as "dangerous" reminded him of Martzel's comments concerning Orzen the previous night.

What had Orzen done to earn that fate? He gathered that it had to do with the Invokers' wars prior to Aestin's founding, though the wars themselves were not a subject he was particularly expert in. Everyone knew the original Aestinian Empire had been ruled by a King and not an Emperor, with no Invokers to keep him in check. As a result, his conquests had grown more and more outrageous, as had his abuse of the Invokers under his rule. The Invokers' rebellion and subsequent foundation of modern Aestin were common knowledge, too, but nobody knew how many Relics had survived from those days. Those battles had been fought upon lands already scarred by ancient wars between deities and humans, of which there were no remaining records to speak of at all.

When Reyes opened the blinds, causing brightness to spill across the room, Rien put the book aside and rubbed his temples.

"You know," Reyes said, "if Daimos shows up here, those textbooks won't be any help. Unless you planned to throw one at him."

Rien got to his feet, stretching his cramped legs. He'd quite lost track of time, and he hadn't intended to get so wrapped up in his research that he'd overlooked the more immediate threat. "I'm aware, Reyes."

Reyes tilted his head to one side. "Is it that Zelle who convinced you the answers were inside a book?"

Rien gave him a startled look. "What would give you that idea?"

"You mentioned she lived in a giant library."

So he had. "Yes, but it's also controlled by the Shaper. We might as well be walking in the dark."

Reyes retreated from the room. "If you want to come into the light, then breakfast is ready."

"Noted."

When Rien joined Reyes in the dining room, he found Sarpe and Sanne already there. They'd barely sat down when Martzel came hobbling into the dining room. "We have a problem."

"What is it?" Rien's mind instantly jumped to Daimos. *He found out we were in his house. He must be furious.*

"We received a communication from the Emperor himself. He has declared all the Invokers in the country must present themselves in the capital tomorrow for a briefing."

A rush of foreboding seized Rien. "A briefing on what?"

"In these situations, there's usually only one answer," said Martzel. "He means to send us to war."

22

While she waited for Zelle to return, Evita read *The Art of Changing*. Or rather, listened to Aurel read from the book, which was an entertaining experience if nothing else. Ignoring her grandmother's orders to rest her injured arm, Aurel insisted on striding around demonstrating the book's instructions on how the Master Changers attained synchrony with their cloaks. Evita had guessed most of it herself, but she was happy to bask in the freedom of being back in control of her own thoughts after the nightmare of the past few days.

"The book definitely doesn't mention Invicten?" Evita asked.

"No, it doesn't," said Aurel. "But Gaiva's name only comes up twice, too, and not connected to the cloaks. I'm not sure the writers of this book actually knew they were Relics at all."

"Master Drazer did." That didn't mean the others had

known, of course. She'd have to ask the Senior Changers... which wasn't an appealing idea.

"We already knew that," interjected Grandma Carnelian. "The question is, how many are there, and where are the others?"

At that moment, the tower's door opened, and Zelle entered the room. Her fur-lined coat suited her a lot better than that bizarre dress she'd been wearing the previous day, but she also wore a grim expression on her face.

"What's the bad news?" asked Aurel.

"It's mostly good news," Zelle replied. "The Changers have vacated Tavine, presumably to head back to their base. Marita was thrilled to tell me the news."

"Good." Aurel put down the textbook. "We can finally go home."

"But?" Grandma's eyes narrowed. "What else happened?"

Zelle drew in a breath. "I found an open doorway to the realm of the Powers. I didn't see any deities walking around, but there's no telling if any got out."

"I didn't see any deities in the Changers' base," Evita ventured. "Granted, my memory is a little hazy."

Being under Invicten's spell had been a strange duality of forgetting and remembering, and it'd be a long time before she trusted her own judgement again. As for the cloak...

"It wouldn't surprise me if that Master of yours was secretly chatting to the deities through that doorway without anyone knowing, but that's the least of what might have escaped." Zelle addressed her grandmother next. "I thought you'd want to know. I did close it."

"I see." Grandma Carnelian pursed her lips. "As long as there isn't another... I thought you were going to the Changers' base."

"I might need backup. Someone who knows the way around."

She didn't mean Evita, did she? If she expected Evita to jump at the chance to visit the Changers' camp again... frankly, Evita would rather dive into the Perilous Sea, sea monsters and all.

"Why?" she asked when all eyes turned towards her. "What do you hope to find there, except for a lot of traumatised and angry Changers?"

"The nameless Shaper wants me to find out how Invicten's Relics ended up so close to the Shaper's domain," Zelle explained. "And get rid of them if necessary."

Evita's brows shot up. "You mean the cloaks?"

"Exactly," said Zelle. "I understand why you don't want to go back, but the Changers are weakened, and so is Daimos's hold over them. This might be the only opening we have."

Unfortunately, Evita had to agree. And the longer she put off reclaiming her cloak, the more she'd come to dread the inevitable moment when she had to trust it to keep her in flight again.

"All right, I'm coming," Evita relented. "But if the Senior Changers attack us, and Daimos *isn't* there, I'd rather the Shaper didn't kill every one of them."

"Neither would I, if I can avoid it." Zelle gave her staff a pointed look as if daring the nameless Shaper to disagree. "We should go before it gets dark, though."

They'd lost part of the day to recuperating, so Evita

reluctantly agreed. She opted against using the cloak, though, instead climbing onto Chirp's back to join Zelle. The dragonet chirped in delight when she took her seat.

"I'm surprised you still want to fly with me," she murmured. "After… after Invicten."

The dragonet hummed, vibrating beneath her, as if to reassure her he didn't hold it against her. That helped her nerves somewhat.

"Ready?" Zelle asked from behind her.

Evita shuddered. "I hated being under that awful man's control, but at least his Relic got rid of my fear of heights for a while. Yes, I'm ready."

Chirp took off in a beat of his wings, and they flew over the peaks, angling south towards the Changers' base.

"How do the Changers go about selecting a new Master after one dies or retires?" asked Zelle after they'd been flying for several minutes.

"I'm not sure on the specifics," said Evita. "Usually, they pick someone from among the Senior Changers, but they made an exception with Master Drazer. They don't have many senior assassins left by now."

"Typical." Zelle was silent for a moment before speaking again. "They struck me as incompetent from the start, but they must have once been good enough at their jobs to acquire the reputation they have."

"I think they were, once." Some of the passages Aurel had read her from *Art of Changing* had implied their fighting skills had once rivalled Aestin's lesser Invokers. "They were originally established by one of our past monarchs. That's why their base is at the edge of the Range nearest to Saudenne."

"Makes sense." Zelle leaned forward on the dragonet's back. "Here we are."

They flew downward and landed on a path just out of sight of the Changers' camp. Even from high up, it was clear to Evita that there weren't many people about. Her nerves spiked, as she was unable to tell if that was a good sign or a bad one.

"I'll go alone," she told Zelle, hopping off the dragonet's back. "You keep your distance, and I'll find someone willing to talk."

Evita hadn't worn her cloak. A mistake, maybe, but at least she was secure in the knowledge that her own garment wouldn't try to strangle her. As she neared the caves, she saw a few novices scattered around, but no Senior Changers were in sight.

A group of novices emerged from the cave, some carrying packs and rolled-up bedding. When she recognised a familiar face, she took a decisive step forward and tailed their group. When Ruben fell behind, she quickened her pace and grabbed his arm.

"Evita?" He jumped in alarm. "What... I thought you were dead."

"I survived." She assumed he didn't know about her change of loyalties, since he wasn't highly ranked enough to have been sent on the disastrous mission to sabotage the Sentinels' tunnels or the attack on the outpost, and they'd once been friendly enough for her to be reasonably confident he wouldn't turn her in. "Why is everyone leaving the caves?"

"We've been ordered to leave," he said. "The instructions came straight from the capital, and the Senior

Changers have split into two groups. I'm supposed to be with the ones heading to the palace."

"The palace," she repeated. "And—the second group?"

"Somewhere to the west. Are you interrogating me?" His expression showed a mixture of confusion and hurt, with a hefty dose of wariness. "I thought you were one of us again."

"No." Powers above, she hadn't meant to put him on edge. She hesitated, torn between explaining and leaving him to separate truth from lie himself. "Master Drazer was bewitching the Senior Changers using a Relic, and he caught me in the same spell."

"Shit." Ruben's eyes widened. "Is that why they were acting so… weird?"

"Did you not think anything was strange?" asked Evita. "The spell broke when Master Drazer died, but there was something similar affecting the Crown Prince the last I heard. I wouldn't trust any orders coming from the palace."

He blinked in bafflement. "What, you think I should desert, like you? Why?"

"If I were you, I'd go to Saudenne and find somewhere to lie low for a while."

His eyes narrowed in suspicion. "What are you plotting?"

"Me? Nothing." He meant her allies, though, she was sure. She also didn't know why she was warning him, except that if not for the vastly different paths they'd ended up on, they might have ended up being friends. "Good luck."

She left him on the path and made for the building that housed Master Drazer's abandoned office. Evita had

had the presence of mind to put the handy lockpick Aurel had given her in her pocket, so she ought to be able to get in. Before she reached the building, the dragonet swooped down to land, and Zelle hopped off his back.

"You're lucky the Senior Changers aren't here," Evita remarked. "Did you know?"

"I had a suspicion when I saw how empty this place is." Zelle motioned towards the building. "I'm not sure they'll have left any of their Relics behind if they're vacating the base."

"Worth a look," Evita replied. "I'm going to check the Master's office, but I might need your help to read any letters I find from the Crown Prince."

"All right." Zelle let Evita lead the way into the building, where she made quick work of the lock on the office door.

A single letter lay on the desk, which Evita passed to Zelle. "Is that what we're looking for?"

"I'd say it is."

"Good." Evita ducked out of the office and made her way down the corridor, eyes open for any other intruders. None came, but the door to the storeroom where the Changers' cloaks were kept lay ajar. Not a single shimmering silver cloak remained hanging on its hooks. "Oh no."

Zelle caught up to her, half her attention on the letter in her hand. "What is it?"

"They took every one of the cloaks."

"Powers, really?" Zelle's forehead scrunched up. "That can't be good news. And neither is this letter. Two groups of Senior Changers were sent to different locations. One went to the palace to prepare for war… and the other went to the Isles of Itzar."

"Itzar. Why Itzar?"

Wait. If they'd gone to Itzar, it could only be for one reason. *Gaiva.*

Daimos must have sent them after Gaiva's Relics.

———

"You aren't thinking of going?" Rien asked Martzel and the others. "Daimos wants us all in the same place for a reason. Who are we even supposed to be going to war against?"

He could guess, but he'd thought the Emperor was more intelligent than Zeuten's Crown Prince. Granted, that didn't necessarily matter with a Relic of Invicten influencing his decisions.

"That, I don't know," growled Martzel. "It wouldn't surprise me if Daimos manufactured a nonexistent enemy for us to face. However, it seems to me that we either have to walk into his trap or wait for him to come to us."

"What if he intends to kill any Invokers who openly refuse to join this false war of his?" Rien himself knew that showing his face in Tauvice would mean certain arrest, and he wouldn't willingly walk into Daimos's trap in front of an audience who thought he was a murderer or a thief.

I should have left last night after all.

"That would be a dire waste," said Martzel. "The Emperor's message does imply that any Invokers who refuse to answer the call will be stripped of their status and otherwise suffer heavy consequences, but nothing like that."

"I don't count as an official Invoker in the Emperor's eyes any longer, not as long as I refuse to submit my Relic for testing," Rien reminded him. "Whichever choice I make, I'm likely to end up being arrested at the very least."

"The rest of us, though?" Reyes's expression showed mingled defiance and anticipation. "We already have his attention. If he wants us in the capital, then I'm all too happy to see if he's not too much of a coward to show his face in person this time."

"It's not cowardice so much as practicality," Rien said. "Daimos murdered my family in such a public manner that he can't erase the aftermath. Even Invicten's Relics can't blot out the memory from everyone in the capital, so he's backed himself into a corner."

"That hasn't stopped him from yanking the Emperor around like a puppet on strings," said Sanne dispassionately. "If you ask me, we pushed him into this when we invaded his house."

"No... he must have had this plan in the works for a while," Rien said. "He already convinced Zeuten's Crown Prince there was going to be a war with Aestin, so it stands to reason that he was working on something similar here. Regardless, I'd rather we went into this with our eyes open."

"Agreed," Reyes decided. "I'm going. Sarpe, you should stay here."

"You don't expect me to let you go alone?" Sarpe reached for his hand. "No, I'll stay in the capital but keep my distance... unless you get into trouble, that is."

"As will I," said Martzel. "He's looking for young and strong Invokers to fight his war, not the likes of me."

Sanne shook her head. "No… I don't like the idea of getting on the bad side of the Emperor, but it's not really him giving the orders, and fighting an illegal war for Daimos is out of the question."

"I know," Rien said. "I understand. But if he's planning to get every Invoker in the country involved in his war, legal or not, then he must have a contingency plan to deal with anyone who refuses to answer his offer."

An uneasy silence followed. The Martzels knew that Daimos theoretically ought to have just as much reason to target them as he had Rien's family—not to mention the Trevains, who'd thought it would be safer to capitulate than to risk being targeted, too—but he didn't doubt that they'd find themselves facing Daimos soon, whether they answered his summons or not.

Reyes looked down. "You know… I'm not keen on the idea of delivering ourselves into his hands after all. Especially if we're outnumbered by Invokers who answered his call willingly."

"If there's anyone he expects *not* to show up, it's me," Rien pointed out. "If Daimos is calling all the Invokers to the capital, then he'll likely be there himself, but he won't be out in the open. We don't have to go into the palace, but if we keep an eye on the situation from a distance, we might be able to track him down."

"We can hide in plain view," Martzel agreed. "Reyes, Sanne… choose whatever suits you best."

The two siblings exchanged indecisive glances, and Rien could understand why. The others might not be able to get away with hiding, not when they *were* on the list of official Invokers and liable to be subject to the Emperor's orders. Yet if the alternative was being stripped of their status as Rien had been, did they really have a choice in the matter?

The sound of a door slamming open had them all on their feet in an instant, and a gust of freezing wind swept in when they ran into the entrance hall. Several wraiths had drifted into the house, spindly creatures that appeared to be formed of the fog that trailed along with them.

"Arien Astera." A chilling voice raised the hairs on the back of Rien's neck. "You stole something that wasn't yours."

"The books?" he guessed. "They were no more Daimos's than mine. Get out."

Rien's staff ignited in crimson as he swung it at the wraiths, while Sarpe hurried into the drawing room and came out brandishing a candle. The wraiths shrank away from the brightness, into the path of Sanne's Relic. Lightning flashed at the end of her staff, mingling with Reyes's, while Martzel opened the front door wide enough to allow the sunlight to reach the wraiths from behind.

The wraiths flowed together, merging into one form, which pointed a spindly finger at Rien. "There's nowhere you can hide, Arien Astera."

"Then by all means tell your master we're coming for him."

Without another word, the wraith flew backwards and out of the open door, vanishing on the wind.

"I think that sends a clear message," Rien said. "Daimos didn't trust us to show up at the palace, so he gave us an incentive."

"Some choice," scoffed Reyes. "Either we walk into his trap or wait here to be attacked again."

"Next time he might send one of his deities," Rien replied. "I think I'll take my chances in the capital."

"Agreed." Sarpe nodded.

Now they'd come to an agreement, they hastened to get the carriage ready while keeping an eye out to make sure Daimos didn't send any more unwelcome surprises. Or doorways into the realm of the Powers, which would be impossible to close for anyone but Daimos himself.

Or Zelle. If she were here, she'd have already got rid of the doorway in Daimos's house, which was no doubt one of the reasons he'd seen to it that the pair of them had been separated from one another.

She'd also have shaken her head in exasperation when she learned he was going back to the capital of Aestin after his narrow escape from the imperial guards, but he wouldn't be going there alone. With the horses saddled and the driver ready, the five of them climbed into the carriage and prepared to face whatever trap Daimos had left for them.

23

For the second night in a row, Zelle found her rest disturbed by the nameless Shaper. The staff's vibrant glow infiltrated her sight and pried her eyes open, and its incessant muttering in the background made it impossible to turn off her thoughts.

"What is it this time?" she whispered to the staff. "The Relics have gone, I told you. The Changers took all the cloaks when they left."

Something isn't right.

"Yes, you're keeping me awake." Zelle rubbed her eyes. "Either tell me what I can do for you or let me sleep."

I am a deity whose power is beyond your comprehension. I would appreciate it if you were to show me the bare minimum of respect.

"No need to be difficult." She quietened her voice when Evita stirred in the window seat. "You don't respect *my* time, either, but if it's that urgent, then tell me what you want me to do."

The Changers have been meddling with the passages in the mountains, the staff said. *Near the Sentinel's cave.*

"You might have told me earlier." Zelle sat upright, squinting at the glowing staff. "I can't walk all the way over there in the middle of the night. You'll have to help."

Naturally.

Fighting a groan, Zelle swung her legs over the armchair and went looking for her clothes. Once she'd put on her thickest coat and boots, she picked up the staff and exited the tower through the front door. Going upstairs to the Sanctum would run the risk of waking her grandmother as she had the previous night, and besides, she wanted to talk to the staff alone.

After closing the tower door behind her, Zelle addressed the staff. "Please don't throw me off a cliff this time."

As if I would do such a thing.

Zelle rolled her eyes and walked the short distance downhill to the cliff that concealed the hidden passageway in the mountain. Instead of opening the tunnel, however, the lever jammed in her hand. "What—?"

I knew it, the staff said. *Get rid of that.*

Zelle studied the lever and then reached for the Shaper's magic. It came in a trickle then a flood, her awareness heightening until the very rocks stirred beneath her feet. A simple shifting of energy broke through whatever had jammed the lever, and the tunnel opened before her.

The passageway didn't appear to have suffered any lasting damage from the Changers' meddling, but she made sure to check for hidden traps before she stepped inside. Lanterns hung on the walls on either side of the path, illuminating the way downhill, but as soon as the entrance closed behind her, a grating noise rang in her ears as a piece of the wall peeled back to reveal an opening.

Zelle peered warily into the newly created tunnel, unable to see in the pitch-darkness, and the staff made an impatient noise in her ear. *Hurry up.*

"Stop jabbering in my ear, and I will."

Zelle stepped through the passage and emerged into the grey light of dawn. Blinking at the sudden brightness, she recognised her location as somewhere on the other side of the mountain, near the Sentinels' cave. The path sloped downward, littered with rocks, while mist shrouded the peaks.

Shivering, she descended the rest of the way to the cave and found the lever jammed. The Changers had blocked the cave's entrance too.

"How did it take you this long to notice?" The staff's magic removed the barrier with one wave of her hand, revealing the entryway to the Sentinel's cave. "Don't your senses cover the entire mountain?"

No.

The short answer made her frown. "You're in an odd mood tonight."

There are many questions I would like answers to. Perhaps the cave will be able to shed some light on them.

"You want to ask yourself a question?"

It's not that simple. The staff's tone was defensive, as if it felt she was mocking it.

"Is it to do with the reasons you can't tell me anything of the history between yourself and Invicten?" She entered the cave, partly to get out of the cold, partly to approach the shimmering *presence of the Sentinel's rock.* Even in near darkness, its obsidian surface retained a luminosity that drew the eye.

It has been a long time since those days. The rock carries those memories, not I.

"You forgot, but the rock remembers?" Weren't the staff and the rock supposed to be the same?

Can you perfectly recall your childhood?

"I'm pretty sure I'd remember something as significant as my own siblings' location."

Humans, grouched the staff. *I doubt you'd say the same after a few thousand years had passed.*

"Since I won't live that long, then we won't get to find out, will we?"

Listen to me. The staff's tone became more serious. *This rock has been touched by every past Sentinel who has ever stood in your place. If anywhere holds the answers as to how Invicten's Relics fell into the hands of the Changers, it's here.*

True. The Sentinels' cave might be able to reveal how the Changers had come to wield Invicten's Relics without being aware of their source… but would that help them to beat Daimos?

She halted in front of the rock. "Does it matter how the Changers got those Relics? I'm curious to know, yes, but we have more pertinent matters to deal with."

You don't think it's relevant to our dilemma that my sibling has managed to thwart me even so many years after my imprisonment?

"You're still fixated on your old rivalry? What *did* happen between you?" Without waiting for an answer, she pressed her hand against the rock. "What happened to cause a rift between the three Great Powers?"

Light flared outward from the rock, and Zelle's vision

tunnelled as she was propelled forward into the void that preceded a vision. Except this time, she kept falling, tumbling downward until she came to a halt inside what appeared to be a large chamber or hall. Fog blurred her surroundings, but she could make out the vague shapes of ruined pillars and crumbling walls beyond the haze.

"What is this place?" She'd been somewhere similar in a previous vision the Sentinels' cave had shown her, and despite the fog, it wasn't the same as the void she visited when she spoke directly to the Shaper.

An echo. The voice sounded like the staff, yet it came from all around her, reverberating from the walls of the chamber.

"An echo of what? A real place?"

There is nothing left of our realm but echoes.

"The realm of the Powers. That's where we are. But... I mean, the deities are alive in there, aren't they?"

In a manner of speaking.

That didn't make a great deal of sense to Zelle, either, but there was a melancholy note to the Shaper's voice that she hadn't heard before. The deities might be everlasting, but if their entire realm was in ruins, then it was no wonder they craved access to the human world.

"I want to understand," she said. "Is that why you brought me here—to show me what happened to you and the other Great Powers?"

The Shaper didn't answer for a long moment. Then a distant voice arose, speaking words she couldn't understand. Gradually, it grew louder, until it took on the cadence of the nameless Shaper.

"At one time, the Great Powers walked among humans."

The voice sounded like someone reading a story, but she couldn't have pinned down the speaker's location if she'd tried. Yet the voice's owner was unmistakeable, despite being more resonant and distant than whenever the Shaper or the staff spoke directly in Zelle's ear.

"Time passed, and the Great Powers departed, save for one," the Shaper went on. "Gaiva, ever attached to humanity, spent so much time living among them that she forsook the realm of the Powers altogether. In the end, Invicten grew jealous and bitter that his lover had abandoned him, and he decided to enact a plan to draw her home. They had had five children, all of whom ruled over portions of the realm of the Powers and were equally respected. Thanks to Invicten's meddling, they turned against one another and became enemies."

Images appeared in the fog, showing flashes of light, crumbling pillars, the chaos of a battle playing itself out before her eyes. Winged shapes dove at one another, clawing, stabbing, beating and brawling. *Are those... the children of Gaiva?*

"Invicten's plan worked," said the Shaper. "Gaiva returned to the realm of the Powers and was furious to see her own children warring like mere mortals. Invicten tried to persuade her stay by offering to lift the spell on their children if she agreed not to spend any more time with humans. She agreed, but when Invicten learned she was pregnant with the child of a human herself, he flew into a rage again."

The images of the fighting faded out, to be replaced with the outline of a large chamber. Not the ruin of before but majestic and flooded with vibrant light, with living flowers growing up its pillars and its roofs open to reveal a pure-white sky.

Within gathered a number of figures who appeared human from her first glance, but some had wings, while others had horns or tails or other features she couldn't put a name to. None wore a stitch of clothing, but since most were too inhuman to resemble regular people, it would have felt odd to see them clothed.

"Gaiva gave birth to several children," the Shaper went on, "and Invicten gleefully exiled these half mortals to the human realm."

The image of a field bordered by mountains filled Zelle's vision. Not somewhere she recognised but undoubtedly a part of the human realm. The same humanoid figures as before reappeared, looking around in evident confusion. Some conversed in words she didn't understand, while others approached a group of ragged individuals who were markedly separate from the newcomers. The group had none of the deities' animalistic features, and they were dressed in simple clothing where the deities wore none. *Humans.*

"Yet he made a fatal error," said the Shaper, "because these lesser deities taught the humans how to trap pieces of the deities' magic within objects in order to carry their power in their own hands. And soon enough, the children wanted to return to the land of their ancestors."

A doorway appeared behind the humanoid figures, towering as high as the mountains, and revealing the Powers' chamber on the other side. Fascination and dread gripped Zelle in equal measures.

"Gaiva was happy to welcome her half-human children home, but Invicten once again refused," said the

Shaper. "When His back was turned, She smuggled the lesser deities into their realm herself and made a home for them without Invicten's knowledge."

The large chamber filled Zelle's sight, replacing the field and mountains. The same humanoid figures filled the space, some holding objects that could have only come from the human realm, such as metal tools and pottery, and others even wearing human clothing. Zelle's dread intensified, but she could no more have intervened in the vision than she could drag her attention away. She was trapped, held captive by the Shaper's voice.

"When he learned the truth, Invicten forced the half humans to confess to having shared their magic with mortals," said the voice. "This was unacceptable to him, and he declared war, seeking to eliminate the lesser deities from both realms altogether."

The chamber turned dark, and the deities shed all human trappings altogether, shifting forms into fearsome beasts. Pillars crumbled in the wake of their clashes, and bodies lay bleeding on the ground. Worse, a window into the human realm displayed a similar sight in the fields on the other side, the grass stained red with blood.

"The deities kept fighting even as the realm of the Powers was reduced entirely to ruin," said the Shaper. "The realm of humanity would have suffered the same fate... if the nameless Shaper had not intervened."

The window grew to dominate her vision, the mountainous backdrop marred by bolts of magic and swords clashing against one another. Some fighters appeared to be human, but others resembled the winged or horned beings from the realm of the Powers. Gods and mortals, fighting alongside one another... and wreaking devastation. The deities might be half-mortal themselves, but they crushed their enemies with power only magic could bestow. Images flickered before her eyes—tidal waves that consumed whole coastal settlements, earthquakes that ripped the ground apart, hurricanes that tore forests up by their roots...

When the flood of images settled on the fields again, Zelle glimpsed surviving humans huddled in terrified groups while the deities fought on.

The voice spoke yet again. "Unlike gods, humans are not eternal. They would not have time to fix their mistakes if none survived, and so the Shaper brought an end to the war by closing the doors between the realms and making it impossible for any deity to enter the human world without the aid of a mortal."

A swathe of blinding white light cut through the battlefield, engulfing humans and deities alike. When it faded, only the humans remained. Some clutched weapons, others held objects of metal and stone that could only be Relics—and despite the ruins at their feet, the turbulent forces of nature had quietened.

"The other Great Powers, furious at being thwarted, turned on their sister."

The human realm faded away, to be replaced by the ruined chamber that the vision had started in. Zelle stifled a gasp; she'd been swept up in the vision so intensely that she'd almost forgotten her own location, and while she felt nothing of her physical body, even her emotions had been muted, her mind caught up in the horror of the Shaper's vision.

"They combined their magic and bound the Shaper's living consciousness within Her own mountain." The voice spoke dispassionately, as if the events did not concern the Shaper's own history and Her own terrible fate. "As the other two Great Powers had already been gravely wounded in the battle, this feat took the last of their strength. They perished shortly after, while the Shaper was left alone, never to enter the realm of the deities again."

Zelle's mouth moved, perhaps to offer an apology, but no words came out. Besides, what could she possibly say?

The voice quietened, turning melancholic. "She even lost Her name, and was forgotten by all, including those She once trusted. And here we remain."

As the voice faded, so did the chamber. The glowing rock peeled away from her hand, and Zelle took a step back into the silent cave.

One final whisper found her ears. "With the arrival of the first Sentinels, the Shaper found Her way to consciousness again and gifted them with the staff. That alone will save us all."

Zelle found her voice. "Is that… true?"

I assume it is. This time, the voice came from the staff, not the rock or the cave.

"What do you mean, 'assume'?" Zelle tilted her head. "You closed the doors between realms yourself, didn't you?"

Yes, it appears that I did.

The uncertainty in the staff's phrasing made her frown despite the lingering shock of the images she'd seen. It didn't entirely surprise her that the Shaper had closed the doors to keep the Powers from waging war on one another and destroying this realm as well as their own and had paid the price with Her freedom. Had the rock somehow preserved the memory of the experience to show to the Sentinels? If so, why did the staff not appear to remember? Or was it simply pretending? She had her doubts the latter was the case, given the serious nature of the vision the cave had shown her, but the staff ought to remember how it had fallen into the Sentinels' hands at the very least.

You wanted to understand our history. Now you do.

Zelle's brow furrowed. "Was that really you, though?"

More questions? You're dissatisfied even now?

"That wasn't what I said." The staff had never behaved like an ordinary Relic, but it was conscious. Unlike the Book of Reading, it had a will of its own, even while bound to Zelle. She had an inkling most Relics did not retain the memories of the deities to whom they owed their power either, but what was consciousness but a collection of memories and thoughts?

That question is the domain of my brother, not me.

"Invicten." She'd forgotten He was the deity of consciousness as well as illusion and trickery. Yet even His Relics hadn't spoken to Zelle, hadn't exerted control over their wielders. Now she'd seen the deities themselves on the battlefield through the Shaper's vision, there was a marked difference between the way the gods fought and the way humans wielded their power through Relics.

There is a reason He is known as the god of trickery.

"Yes, and Daimos seems to have an unlimited supply of His Relics." A reminder that the quandary of the tangled natures of the staff, the rock, and the nameless Shaper was not the pertinent issue at hand. "Including the ones in the hands of the Changers, who the Crown Prince has summoned to the capital, possibly to send them to war with Aestin."

She hoped she was wrong, but if the Crown Prince had had every intention of sending Zelle onto the battlefield, then it wasn't impossible that he intended to do the same with the Changers instead. She had no desire to be his martyr, but staying in hiding and relying on the protection of the Shaper's magic while the rest of her country fell apart was not an appealing strategy either.

Besides, Daimos had almost broken the mountain's defences once before. He might try to do so again.

Precisely, the staff said. *In fact, I can almost guarantee he will. The question is... if Zeuten and Aestin do go to war, whose side will you fight on?*

"What do you mean, she's gone?" Aurel blinked at her grandmother, who sat calmly in her armchair as if her granddaughter hadn't disappeared and put their plans to travel to Itzar on hold.

Grandma, Aurel gathered, hadn't actually spoken to Zelle before she'd left, but if the Shaper was involved, it was anyone's guess as to when she'd come back.

"She did the same the previous night," said Grandma. "That staff of hers dragged her up to the Sanctum to give her a lecture."

"Honestly." Aurel tutted. "What are we going to do now, then?"

Her arm felt much better; her injury was healing nicely, but she had no intention of staying in the tower regardless. Not with the Changers on their way to the capital and more of them heading to speak to the people of Itzar. To attack or recruit them? That, she couldn't say.

"The Changers took all their spare cloaks," Evita commented. "Most likely to the palace, not the Isles. The letter wasn't clear on their reasons, was it?"

"No, unfortunately." Aurel had read every word of the letter that Zelle and Evita had brought back from the Changers' base at least twice. "I'd like to know what mischief they're up to in Itzar, but the palace has got to be where the action is."

"It's also a trap." Evita turned the piece of stale pastry she was eating over in her hands. "Don't you think we should help? In Itzar, I mean?"

"I'm not all that keen to help the people who kidnapped me." That was only half true, since they'd been almost friendly with the villagers of Dacher before they'd left. The islanders didn't deserve to be hassled by the Changers, but who'd be left to help Zeuten if she and Evita went to the Isles instead?

"Most of the villagers didn't have anything to do with that," Evita reminded her. "Though Zelle is the only one of us who spoke directly to Gaiva, so Her followers might not listen to the rest of us if we try to warn them that the Changers are bad news."

"Typical," said Aurel. "I'm surprised there were enough Changers left to go to two places at once, though splitting their forces gives us a bit of an edge. Personally, I'd take the islanders over the royal palace, but… oh, Powers. I bet that's where the eagles disappeared to."

"Of course." Evita dropped her pastry. "But… that was more than a day ago. We didn't check *when* the Senior Changers left Tavine, did we?"

"No," said Aurel. "But the date on the letter suggests it was sent *before* Zelle killed Daimos's helper."

"Master Drazer." Evita's hands clenched. "He must have already given the orders, and the Senior Changers decided to follow them even after his death."

Which meant there was a strong chance those orders came straight from Daimos himself. The notion of going back to Itzar didn't appeal to Aurel in the slightest. The group who called themselves Gaiva's Blades had been responsible for kidnapping her, but the Blessed who'd once had direct contact with Gaiva had hardly been trustworthy either. By the end of their visit, she and the others had gained their allegiance, but Aurel hadn't been sorry to leave them behind.

"Daimos isn't taking any chances," she said. "He wants the people who wield Gaiva's Relics on his side or taken out."

"This isn't even their first visit," said Evita. "The Senior Changers met the Blessed before, though I don't think they were able to come to an agreement."

"I hope the rogues drive them away, then," Aurel said. "I think the people of Itzar will be more open to persuasion to help us than the Crown Prince, but that isn't saying much."

"Assuming the Changers weren't sent to kill them and take Gaiva's Relics for themselves."

That, unfortunately, was always a possibility. "I'm not staying here. Grandma, where will you go? Back to the village?"

"I intend to," the Sentinel replied, "but I will wait for Zelle to return before I do. And both of you had better be certain of your choice before you leave."

"Some choice," Aurel said. "The palace is a dead end,

but Itzar might easily end up being the same. We won't know until we get there."

She was certain that Daimos's influence hadn't relinquished its grip on the Changers yet, and if they went after Gaiva's Relics, then it could only end in disaster.

Evita drew in a breath. "I know it's ridiculous, but I'm going to Itzar."

"Are you sure?" Aurel hadn't expected Evita to make that choice, not least because of her fear of heights and the recent unpleasant aftermath of being controlled by Invicten's magic. The twinge in her sore arm reminded Aurel of her own narrow escape, but if anything, that only made her more determined to stop Daimos from ensnaring anyone else.

"I don't trust the Changers not to start a fight with them," Evita said. "I also don't think the Crown Prince is likely to listen to a word I say."

"Same with me, considering I broke all his windows." Aurel cracked a grin. "It *is* ridiculous, but I'm coming with you."

With Chirp's help, they ought to be able to make the return trip within a day, two at most.

"At least it'll be quicker than our journey to find you," said Evita, when Aurel pointed this out. "We had to go through Saudenne and find a boat willing to take us all the way north."

"If it's any consolation, flying blindfolded on a giant eagle wasn't much fun either."

"At least you couldn't see the drop." Evita shuddered. "Though I think I'd take that over the giant sea monster that attacked us in the Perilous Sea."

"We'll avoid that route, then."

After they'd packed what was left of their rations, Evita and Aurel left the tower and walked to meet the dragonet, who was chewing the corpse of a rodent he must have caught while hunting. Evita stroked the side of his long reptilian head and made their request for a lift across the sea to Itzar, to which the dragonet reacted with an enthusiastic chirp.

"What's the quickest way?" Evita asked. "Last time we flew over Saudenne, but we don't need to make a supply run, do we?"

"Better avoid Saudenne," Aurel said firmly. "I know that route well, since we had to fly back and forth several times to figure out how to get Zelle out of the palace, but the Changers are too close."

Evita dropped her gaze. "You mean… you flew past the Changers' base while I was there?"

Aurel's mouth parted. Did Evita think Aurel had abandoned her to them? She'd thought Evita wouldn't have any trouble making her escape, but she'd never guessed that her own cloak might have ended up turning against her. "It took longer than I planned to get Zelle out of the palace. In the end, I had to sneak into an official function dressed as a guard."

Evita lifted her head. "You fooled the palace guards?"

"Oh, no, I did a terrible job," said Aurel. "Zelle covered for me, though, and the dragonet helped by breaking a few windows. Your cloak would have made it a lot easier."

Evita, she noticed belatedly, hadn't worn the cloak at all since her return from the Changers. Was she afraid Invicten's magic might take control of her again? Or worse, try to kill her?

"It might be better that you didn't have it," Evita said.

"You said you fought another wielder of Invicten's Relics?"

"We did," said Aurel. "Zelle killed him too. She's become quite the warrior."

Evita flinched. "It wasn't her who killed the Changers, though. It was the nameless Shaper."

Aurel wasn't entirely certain that was true. Her sister seemed different than before, though her ordeal in the palace couldn't have helped either. Then again, Evita hadn't been her usual self since coming back to her senses. It struck Aurel that travelling alone with someone who'd recently tried to kill her wasn't the most sensible idea she'd had, but this might be a chance to rebuild trust between them after she'd left Evita to her fate with the Changers.

"You should put the cloak on before we get on the dragonet," said Aurel. "If the worst happens, and we fly into a trap, you have another way out."

"Don't tempt the Powers," Evita muttered. "I know I should wear it, but it tried to *strangle* me. And what if one of the Changers in Itzar has another of Invicten's more powerful Relics?"

"It's a risk we'll have to take," said Aurel. "Gaiva and Her followers will help us out, I'm sure."

Evita didn't look convinced, but she did as Aurel suggested and put the cloak on before they climbed onto Chirp's back.

In one bound, they took flight, the dragonet's strong wings carrying them over the mountains and towards the Isles of Itzar.

Rien and the others travelled all day, their carriage stopping every few hours for the horses to rest, and they spent the night in a remote village outside the capital. They were the only Invokers staying at the inn they'd chosen, and while the owners didn't treat them any differently than any other travellers, their use of false names and the care they took to keep their Relics hidden wouldn't prevent them from being tracked by Daimos's allies.

None of their group slept much, including Rien, who was certain the other guests at the inn had noticed their whispered conversations and secretiveness and drawn their own conclusions. Everyone had heard about the Emperor's orders, after all. No more foes showed up, however, though it was anyone's guess as to what kind of a state they'd find the house in when they went back.

If they went back.

The following morning, their carriage entered the capital of Aestin. While several roads led to the imperial district of Tauvice, they chose an indirect route and stopped near the area where Rien had met Linas before travelling to the Martzels' home. Sarpe volunteered to gather information from near the palace, since he wouldn't be recognised, while the rest of them waited in the dusty downstairs room of Linas's safe house.

The old man himself did not look surprised to see Rien again. "I knew you'd be back as soon as His Imperial Majesty put out the call for Invokers to come to the city," he said. "Are you sure you want to do this, though? You know what you stand to lose if they take your Relic."

"I'm not going to the palace... not with the others, anyway." He and Martzel had discussed their options and had decided that the two of them would be the least likely to be missed among the gathering Invokers. Daimos would never expect Rien to show his face in front of the Emperor, and Martzel was on paper as retired. "There's too many people in there who want me dead, like the Trevains, and whoever else Daimos has coerced over to his side."

"He'll have even more by the end of the day, at this rate," Linas said darkly. "Nobody will defy the Emperor's orders unless they want to be accused of treason."

"Or unless the Emperor changes his mind," Rien added. "Daimos doesn't need to use the powers of persuasion if he has the magic of Invicten doing the talking for him, but if we break the illusion, he'll lose his grip on everyone. We might not have time to find proof that this war of his is built on a false premise, but we can slow him down."

"I hope you're right," Martzel said. "Damn leg... I don't

like the idea of sending either of my children into the palace. How do I know you'll come out again?"

He directed the question at Reyes, who shrugged. "This isn't the kind of request you say no to. Also, if things go sideways, I want to be there."

When Sarpe returned from gathering information, he closed the door firmly behind him and wiped his brow. "I was sure I was being followed at one point, but the guards are mostly flagging down any Invokers they see in order to give them directions to the palace."

"How generous of them," Reyes commented. "What's the news?"

"The Emperor is going to give his public address in the upper courtyard," he replied. "That's not an easy place to sneak into... unless you can fly, anyway."

"Typical." Yet unsurprising, given that his own ancestors had helped design the palace in the first place. If he'd been able to bring the dragonet, or the Changers' cloak—even one of those giant eagles would have been an asset. As it stood, he wouldn't be able to get past imperial security using his Relic alone without leaving a trail of chaos behind him. At least their current dilemma seemed to have erased the tension he'd unintentionally caused between himself and Martzel when he'd mentioned his misgivings concerning his deity the other night.

"The northern entrance has the fewest guards," said Martzel. "If we take them out, we can get in that way."

"I'd rather not have to kill anyone if I don't have to," said Rien. "If nothing else, it won't make it any easier to win our way back into the Emperor's good graces."

"That ship has sailed, I think," growled Martzel. "If

Daimos is determined to ruin us all, then we might as well cause as much trouble for him as possible."

"I'll drink to that." Sarpe knocked back a glass of the dusty liquor Linas had dug out of the back of a cabinet. "For courage."

Rien didn't drink anything himself. He needed his wits to be about him, and he had an inkling that Martzel had a plan that he had not shared with the others. Rien was starting to understand where Reyes had come by his scheming tendencies, despite the two otherwise having little in common. Reyes himself would have to enter the palace through the front door along with the other Invokers. Since everyone would be searched upon entry, he wouldn't be able to bring any of his mechanical contraptions with him, so he'd left them with his father.

Drawing in a deep breath, Reyes pushed to his feet. "Ready to go?"

Sanne nodded. "Let's get this done."

Martzel embraced his children, one at a time, while Rien averted his gaze and wondered what *his* father would think of all this. Knowing him, he wouldn't have waited for a summons before marching into the Imperial Palace to demand an explanation, which was likely among the reasons Daimos had chosen to kill the Astera family first.

Sarpe embraced Reyes after his father let go of him. "Be careful."

"Always am."

After the two siblings had departed for the imperial palace, Martzel beckoned to Rien. "We'll go in the carriage."

"You don't think someone might recognise a carriage that belongs to your family?"

Martzel gave him a grim smile. "That's the intention."

If Martzel were anyone but his father's oldest friend, Rien might have had reservations about following a plan he knew little about. As it was, he said goodbye to Linas and Sarpe and walked the short distance to the carriage. He could only assume Martzel had already filled the driver in on his plan, but he had to admit it wasn't a bad way to get into the imperial district without anyone seeing Rien's face. The curtains also gave them the chance to watch the other bright carriages rolling back and forth along the smooth roads, and for Martzel to take note of which other Invoker families were in attendance.

When they reached the Imperial Palace itself, an impressive construction of smooth marble mined from the southern mountains bordering the Scarred Lands, they departed from the path to the front gates and followed a circling route around the palace itself. With windows of stained glass and elegant buttresses decorated with colourful banners, the imperial palace was rather less fortress-like than Zeuten's, despite being more likely to face invasion or war. The Emperor didn't need sturdy walls or barriers when he had an army of Invokers, after all.

While the bronze front gates lay wide open, the other entrances were barred by armoured imperial guards, while archers stood on the rooftops armed with spelled arrows. The latter were deadlier than the former, since spelled arrows were designed to guarantee to hit any target who had no magical protection of their own. Rien's staff would easily deflect their arrows, but the real danger was in the bell tower in the courtyard. If one of the archers atop the tower rang the bell, it would signal to every Invoker in the Imperial Palace that they were under attack.

His one advantage was that nobody was expecting him to arrive, and all their attention was focused on the front of the palace alone. The carriage rolled towards the northernmost gate, where Martzel gestured at the driver to bring them to a halt.

When they stopped, Martzel lifted his staff and climbed out of the carriage. "Stay there until I say otherwise."

"Right." Rien obeyed, more out of curiosity than anything else, and watched Martzel hobble towards the gates.

The two guards outside had already noticed their arrival, and both came running over to waylay Martzel.

"You can't park your carriage there," one of them said.

"How else am I supposed to avoid walking for half a league to get to the doors?" Martzel growled, exaggerating his limp. "Besides, if I'm to answer His Imperial Majesty's summoning in decent time, then I need to park somewhere that isn't swimming in self-important youngsters."

The guard remained impassive. "Rules are rules."

Rien stayed back, his face hidden behind the curtain, and surreptitiously checked to make sure no archers were facing their direction.

"I was told *all* Invokers were commanded to come here, so I wanted to honour that promise despite my limitations." Martzel drew himself upright. "If His Imperial Majesty doesn't respect that, then I will take my leave."

"There's no need for that... Devan Martzel, right? Come with us. We'll take you into the palace."

Rien nudged the curtain aside, and Martzel waited until their backs were turned before giving Rien the faintest nod. Moving to the door, he addressed his staff silently. *Don't stab them, just incapacitate them.*

Zierne's Relic, he hoped, would see the need to avoid drawing too much attention. Hopping out of the carriage, he sent a flurry of thorny vines at the guards, yanking both men off their feet and into the shadow of the carriage. Rien and Martzel then blindfolded and gagged them before binding their hands and feet and instructing the carriage driver to drop them off at a far enough distance from the palace that they wouldn't come barging in.

With the way clear, the two of them had a clear route into the palace. Once they were through the gates, Martzel hobbled up the stone steps to the back door and pushed it open with his staff, revealing the corridor that ran directly behind the courtyard. Rien was glad he knew this palace more thoroughly than the one in Zeuten's capital, though he'd never had to sneak around in the shadows like this before.

More guards stood between the marble pillars circling the courtyard, but there was an array of statues and fountains to hide behind as they made their stealthy way forward. The other Invokers had already begun to fill the remaining space, and while Martzel drew the nearby guards' attention by claiming he was lost, Rien slipped behind a marble statue and angled himself in such a position that made it appear to anyone who glanced in his direction that he'd arrived alongside the other Invokers.

Since everyone in the courtyard was armed, and most Relics took the form of weapons, he looked as if he belonged... as long as nobody looked too closely at the staff.

The tricky part would be spotting Daimos's allies among the statuary. They must be present, including whoever carried Invicten's Relic, but if Rien got too close to anyone who'd met him in person, he'd lose his anonymity. He let his gaze skim the gathering Invokers. They were all dressed well, but an air of wariness and anticipation crackled throughout the courtyard like a well-tended fire. Snatches of conversation reached him.

"Something about a war—"

"We're not under attack, surely—"

"The Emperor..."

All conversation faded when the Emperor ascended the white marble steps in the centre of the courtyard, in front of a large statue of a long-extinct winged beast that put Rien in mind of the dragonet. On either side of him stood his advisors, dressed in white and gold, and at the foot of the steps, a row of Invokers assembled. This would usually be the spot in which the three heads of the leading Invoker families would stand with their Relics, but the Emperor had made some notable changes. The staffs in the hands of each of the favoured Invokers were identical, made of a dark wood that had been dyed a deep navy blue, and their wielders wore embroidered coats decorated with flags bearing a blue-and-gold design that resembled the flag once flown by the monarchs of the old Aestinian Empire. They also looked very pleased with themselves.

The Trevains. Anger shot through him at the sight of

them, especially Luvid, whose smirk transformed his otherwise handsome features into a mask of unpleasantness. At one time he'd been a friend of both Devan Martzel and Volcan Astera, and yet he hadn't hesitated to turn his back on them to save his own skin. The Trevains had chosen the coward's way out, and in the process, they'd left Rien's family to die.

Did one of *them* have Invicten's Relic? No—the Trevains already had their own Relics, and as tempting as it was to make them pay for betraying the Astera family, his main target lay elsewhere.

"Welcome." The Emperor's voice echoed throughout the courtyard. "Thank you all for answering my summons. As I'm sure you're aware, it takes a grave emergency for an imperial decree to be sent out to all the country's Invokers, and I regret to say that we have reached that point."

The silence rippled with tension. Only the Trevains appeared unconcerned at the Emperor's pronouncement.

"There is a threat from outside our nation," he went on. "They mean to bring war to us the likes of which we haven't seen since the days of the old Aestinian Empire, before the Invoker families who currently serve us laid down their arms and joined forces to protect our great nation rather than warring with one another."

My family was devoted to our nation, and Daimos killed them. Rien's hands curled into fists, and it took all his willpower not to proclaim that the Emperor was answering to a group of traitors and being misled by someone who would happily have seen them all dead and himself placed on the throne instead.

The crowd listened with rapt attention. Some even

looked enthusiastic at the idea of going to war, and Luvid Trevain's face was positively radiant. Rien's hands clenched and unclenched as the Emperor moved on to the next part of his speech.

"There is one land Aestin has never conquered, and it is in that land that a great danger has been allowed to fester," he said. "The country has been warped by the touch of the deity we call the nameless Shaper. Beasts roam the mountains and seas, and while there are some humans who live there, they are ignorant of what else sleeps beneath their feet."

Rien's breath caught in his chest. *It can't be possible. How could he—*

"The country of Zeuten is the last remaining stronghold of the Great Power called the nameless Shaper," said the Emperor. "Until recently, the Shaper was in a deep slumber, but now She has awakened. And the deity wants one thing… total domination."

What? Rien waited, holding his breath, for someone to demand to know why he was levelling such accusations at a nation that had never done Aestin any harm—and that he had no proof of any word he said. Except nobody did. Challenging the Emperor was unheard of, and besides, there was one notable truth in his words… the nameless Shaper *had* awakened. Everyone in Zeuten doubtless knew it now too.

"They have weapons the likes of which we cannot comprehend," said the Emperor. "The Shaper has the power to tear every one of us to pieces and rip our country apart. This I know, but I also know that we are prepared to meet their challenge… but only if every one of us in this room is willing to take a stand against them."

Against Zeuten. Against Zelle, who might still be trapped with the Crown Prince, unable to escape. The sudden urge hit him to find a way to get a message to her, but how?

Don't be a fool, he told himself. His priority, rather, should be finding the person who wielded Invicten's Relic and exposing their deception. They weren't working their magic upon the entire audience, just the Emperor and his closest advisors. The rest took his word as truth, except the handful who knew better, but when the illusion broke, so too would their fervour for war.

Rien returned his attention to the audience, his gaze travelling along the row of the Emperor's allies, but his attention snapped back to the front when none other than Martzel cleared his throat loudly. "Your Excellency, might I offer my opinion?"

"Devan Martzel," said the Emperor. "I was beginning to wonder if you were going to ignore my invitations to come the palace indefinitely."

Martzel hobbled to the front of the courtyard. Luvid Trevain stepped out of the way, his lip curling, while Martzel turned to face the audience with no fear in his expression.

"I have been away from the city for the sake of my health," said Martzel. "I'm not as strong as I used to be, but I assumed that your summons concerned a terrible foe, not a nation which hasn't a tenth of our military resources and has always been an ally to Aestin in the past. For a thousand years, in fact, the last time I counted."

A murmur ran through the courtyard, but it was hard for Rien to tell whether the response sounded favourable or not. Martzel's recent absence would work against him, but he belonged to a highly respected family, and unlike Rien, he wasn't facing potential criminal charges.

"Unless Zeuten has secretly been training Invokers for the past thousand years, we significantly surpass their magical resources too," Martzel added. "If they *have* been training Invokers, then it doesn't reflect well on Aestin's own spy networks that we have only become aware of that development in the past month."

"They stole from us," Luvid Trevain said, in tones that rang through the courtyard like a bell. "The original settlers of Zeuten stole Relics straight from the imperial palace and smuggled them out of the country. They even doctored the historical records to hide the truth from us."

Rien's heart missed a beat. Did he mean the Sentinels? Had he convinced the Emperor that the *Sentinels* had conspired against Aestin all those years ago?

"Our ancestors were betrayed," Trevain added. "By our own fellow Invokers… and that isn't the only betrayal."

"Do tell." Martzel sounded unimpressed. "If destroying a smaller nation based on a supposed thousand-year-old grudge is what it means to be a proud Invoker these days, then I want no part in it."

"That is enough," said the Emperor. "You are respected among your fellow Invokers, Martzel, but you must know that this is not your battle to fight. Do not argue with your allies."

"Allies." Martzel gave Luvid Trevain a contemptuous look. "Do I see you wearing our old flag, Luvid? I though Aestin outlawed those when our predecessors put the monarchy to the axe."

Trevain flushed. "It is a symbol, no more, a reward I was granted for my services. My family has been a great asset to the Emperor in this troubling time, especially compared to other Invoker families with the same pedigree but less honour."

Meaning me. He didn't know Rien was here, did he? Or was his accusation directed at Martzel alone?

"Don't speak to me of honour," growled Martzel. "Your own ancestor stood on this very ground to swear allegiance to the first Emperor along with his fellow representatives, yet I can see you courting favour based on gold and not on love of your country. You only care for what you can personally gain from this war and not the lives that will be lost if you have your wish."

Trevain's flush deepened. "The threat is real, and you would do well to remember what *your* ancestor promised. We will stand together. All of us."

"Not all." Martzel addressed the crowd. "Some of the Invokers who made those promises were killed by their own treachery. Others fell from grace. And others—the group you might know as the Sentinels—departed the nation to establish their own in direct allegiance with ours. If they supposedly doctored our *own* historical records, then I imagine they'd have had difficulty doing so from the other side of the ocean, don't you?"

"Lies," Trevain spat. "They stole Relics from us, with the aid of the nameless Shaper."

Another murmur arose among the crowd. Most of the Invokers in the courtyard wouldn't know that the Sentinels of Zeuten had ever been close to their own predecessors, but the Trevains' claims that they'd taken Relics with them across the ocean were unfortunately true. The proof lay in his own hands, but he also had no doubt that Trevain was twisting the truth to his own ends.

The Sentinels hadn't *stolen* from the others, at least not with malicious intent. Perhaps they'd even predicted a time when someone like Daimos would try to take more than their fair share of power and had, in fact, been intending to prevent a scenario exactly like this one, in which one man tried to gain supremacy over all other Invokers.

Before anyone could speak, the sound of a bell ringing reverberated through the air. For a heart-stopping moment, Rien thought he'd been found out... Then he spotted a cloud descending from the sky, formed of overlapping wings and claws. Magical constructs, warping into monstrous shapes.

"Zeuten is attacking!" someone shouted. "It's already started!"

It's not them. It's Daimos. He did this.

And if Rien didn't stop him, a war wouldn't be necessary to bring down anyone who might challenge Daimos's supremacy. The Invokers would do it to themselves instead.

25

The dragonet flew west of the Range, over the forest surrounding Tavine to the sea beyond. Soon, a vast blue expanse stretched in all directions, though fog masked the path north, where the Isles lay. Evita squinted, trying to make out their route, but she might as well have been flying in the darkness. At least they didn't have to row right through the fog this time, but the visibility level wasn't much better from the air.

A sudden dark blur appeared ahead of them, several winged shapes forming amid the haze.

"Shit," said Evita. "Aurel, hang on tight."

Aurel swore and scrambled to duck out of sight, hampered by her injured arm. It was too late to change their route, though; their adversaries moved much faster than they did. Several pairs of wings beat, and a bright blue light pierced through the gloom. Then came an eagle's cry. Coupled with the unmistakeable light of Gaiva's Relic, Evita knew who they were.

"It's Gaiva's Blades," Evita breathed. "They're safe."

Aurel grunted. "They don't look that friendly to me."

The fearsome sight of the warriors on their eagles with bone daggers in their hands and icy blue magic at their fingertips was certainly intimidating, but Evita was glad not to have run into the Changers instead. Even when the eagles circled the pair of them, their riders assessing the threat.

"It's the Sentinels," one of the riders said in accented Zeutenian. "Nobody else I know rides a dragonet."

"Kolt, isn't it?" Aurel eyed the man, who was younger than most of the others and had a friendly tilt to his otherwise rugged features. "Zelle couldn't make it, but we're here to help you drive off the Changers. If you want us to."

"The Changers." Kolt's mouth turned down at the corners. "They're not bothering us, if that's what you mean."

"They didn't go back to see the Blessed, did they?" Evita asked.

"Yes, they did." A female warrior with a scar on her face who Evita recalled was named Del looked them over. "Are you with them?"

"Definitely not," said Evita firmly. "We need to talk to you, though. It's important."

Some of the islanders looked less than convinced, including Del, but Kolt nodded. "Of course. You are always welcome here."

The group of eagles turned around as one, allowing Chirp to fly alongside them. Following their lead made it a lot easier to navigate their way through the fog, but Aurel made no attempts at friendly conversation. Evita didn't blame her for her wariness, since Aurel had been less than thrilled at being mistaken for Zelle and kidnapped before being thrown into a battle with an angry deity, but it seemed that Evita would have to do the talking instead.

"Did the Changers mention why they were here?" she asked Kolt.

"No, they didn't, but I gather that it was urgent," he replied. "We aren't welcome among the Blessed, however, which makes it difficult for us to know what concerns them."

Aurel lifted her head. "They still haven't forgiven you?"

"No," Kolt replied. "They've been immersed in debates concerning how to train the new wielders of Gaiva's Relics since your departure, but they are less keen to allow our return."

That didn't bode well for their mission, either, but at least it didn't sound like they'd readily let the Changers sway them into joining Daimos's war.

"We'd like to talk to them, if possible," said Evita. "The Changers... We think they're under the mistaken belief that Zeuten is on the brink of being attacked, and they want to recruit anyone with magic to fight on their behalf."

"Do they now?" Kolt remarked. "That isn't likely to be successful for them. The Blessed may have begun to open their minds to the notion of using their magic in defence of Itzar, but that does not mean they would do the same for another nation."

The fog cleared, and the village of Dacher appeared before them, its stone houses heaped upon the cliffs of the largest island in Itzar. To her surprise, the eagles didn't bypass the village but instead landed on the neighbouring island, connected to Dacher by a rickety wooden bridge. Several wooden huts had been constructed on the island that hadn't been there during their previous visit, while similar huts occupied the other small islands to the north and east.

"You've been busy since we last saw you," Evita remarked as the dragonet landed beside the eagles on the beach of the smaller island.

"The villagers wanted us to move closer to their homes to teach them how to use their Relics," explained Kolt. "We were glad to oblige. Our eagles make it easy to carry supplies and many of the villagers were willing to assist us in building our new settlement."

When they dismounted the dragonet, a man emerged from one of the huts, around forty years old with pale eyes and hair. Gatt, their former guide, and the man who'd initially made a bargain with Igon to protect his fellow villagers.

Evita tensed. "You let him come to live on your island?"

"Some of the villagers are not entirely pleased with his choices." Kolt spoke with a touch of disdain in his voice. "Neither are we, but he showed great courage when he helped bring about Igon's end. He also wields a Relic of his own now, so we have agreed to train him. Unlike the Blessed, we see forgiveness as a necessary step towards healing."

Aurel tilted her head as if considering his words, but she didn't speak.

Upon seeing them, Gatt raised a hand in greeting, and Evita glimpsed the shimmer of a godsmark on his palm. "You're back."

"We are," said Evita. "I'm surprised you stayed."

Gatt looked slightly embarrassed. "This is my home. Despite my past actions, I desire to protect my fellow islanders."

"As do we all," said Kolt. "Regardless of our turbulent history, I hope we can work together… and with you too."

Aurel made a sceptical noise. "That's a nice way to say you kidnapped me and then captured my sister in my place."

Evita cleared her throat. "You should know why we came back. This time, we have bigger problems on our hands than a single deity."

Gatt's brows rose. "A *single* deity? There are more of them?"

A lot more, potentially. She thought over everything that had occurred since they'd left the Isles and began with Daimos and his involvement in Igon's Relics ending up in the Isles.

When she told them of Invicten's Relics and the spell they'd woven over the Crown Prince, Kolt exclaimed in shock. "The Great Power?"

"Unfortunately, yes," said Evita. "Since Zelle has the allegiance of the nameless Shaper, he went to find the others."

"Including ours," Del growled. "Correct? That's why the Changers are here?"

"Yes—sort of," amended Evita. "I'm not sure if he means to recruit you or threaten you, but the Changers believe they're following orders from the Crown Prince, not Daimos, so they might not react well if the Blessed turn them down."

"The Changers didn't stop to speak to the rest of us,"

Kolt said. "Tamacha and the others do have access to what's left of Gaiva's main Relic, of course."

"I bet that's what he wants," Aurel said. "Scumbag."

Kolt gestured to his fellow islanders, some of whom mounted their eagles again. "If that's the case, then we'll have to chase them off."

Evita hastened to climb onto the dragonet's back, as did Aurel. Then they took to the skies, bypassing Dacher and soaring over its neighbouring settlements. Beyond were smaller islands of various sizes, the majority little more than rock and sand—and blue crystals. Relics, fragments of the giant piece of Gaiva that Zelle had helped to shatter into fragments.

No wonder Daimos hadn't been able to resist coming back.

They slowed when they came upon a group of individuals dressed in moon-white robes who stood on a beach on an island that had formerly been uninhabited. The Blessed must have moved to a new home after their own island had been mostly destroyed in the fight with Igon, but their reluctance to meet with visitors apparently didn't extend to the Changers. Two familiar Senior Changers stood talking to them, and the Blessed appeared to be listening intently.

Would the former defectors be able to talk sense into them? Evita had barely exchanged a few words with the Blessed, and Aurel hadn't even met them before. It had been Zelle that had held their interest. They should have brought her with them instead, but it was too late for regrets.

As they landed, Verne and Briony turned around, their cloaks billowing and fury in their eyes.

———

The courtyard of the Imperial Palace erupted into chaos as the cloud of beasts descended upon the gathering crowd. A winged shape landed in front of Rien, and he sent it reeling in a flash of crimson light. At least his Relic was sufficient to drive off Daimos's constructs, but the real danger came in the fog that accompanied their descent, preventing any of the Invokers from effectively seeing their surroundings and meaning their attacks were as likely to hit their fellow Invokers as not.

No doubt that was the entire point. It seemed that Daimos had decided to goad the Invokers into open war with Zeuten through faking an attack that would have the added bonus of turning them against one another as well. While close to every Invoker in the country was present in this very courtyard, the Emperor and his guards had no magic, and it came as no surprise to Rien to see that they'd disappeared from sight. The Emperor would have been taken to safety, but the constructs could only be coming from a doorway into the realm of the Powers.

If the person responsible for opening the doorway was hiding elsewhere in the palace, then Rien needed to get out of the courtyard. Another winged beast descended from above, and he lifted the staff, blasting crimson thorns at it. The brightness repelled the construct, but more took its place. He needed to cut off the source before anyone got badly hurt. Some of the Invokers already bore cuts and bruises, though they were likely to be the result of misfiring attacks from their own allies or being knocked over by the crowd.

Swearing under his breath, Rien edged around the

courtyard, moving from one pillar to another and wondering where the Trevains had disappeared to. *They must know who'd caused this and would no doubt be hiding away from the battle.* As for the Emperor—his guards would have a hard time arresting Rien while there was a life-or-death conflict engulfing the palace.

Ducking through one of the doors out of the courtyard, he emerged into a corridor that was surprisingly free of any constructs. The doorway must have been opened near the courtyard—even above it—to preserve the impression of the constructs having descended from the sky, sent by an outside enemy. He fought off the occasional stray construct as he made his way north, until he entered an empty corridor where a handsome fifty-something man dressed in an embroidered coat bearing a blue-and gold flag waited, a vibrant blue staff in his hands.

"Arien Astera," said Luvid Trevain. "I should have known you'd find a way to sneak in."

"I was invited." Rien's hand twitched on his staff. "Besides, I intend to find the cause of this farce of an attack and eliminate it."

"Those are bold words from a convicted murderer and a dead man."

"I was not convicted of anything," Rien told him. "As for the 'dead' part, that's debatable, but I don't have the time for a discussion on the subject."

Luvid Trevain gave a short laugh. "You've developed a sense of humour in your absence, haven't you? I heard tell of your exploits... and your new Relic, of course."

"What are *you* sneaking around the palace for?" Rien lost his last thread of patience. "Never mind. If you aren't going to tell me who's responsible for this, then get out of the way and let me find them myself."

Crimson light covered the marks on his hands, illuminating the staff. Luvid Trevain lifted his own staff, which he must have recently dyed blue to match his ridiculous outfit. "I am His Imperial Majesty's head of security. Did you think I'd let a criminal like you anywhere near him?"

"I never said I was going near the Emperor." Fighting one of the most powerful Invokers in the nation had not been part of his plan, not when he had a war to stop, but Trevain seemed determined to goad him into open conflict. "I simply have no desire to speak to *you*."

Does he mean the Relic is close to the Emperor? Or was he simply feigning concern for his Emperor as part of his act? Rien didn't know, but neither did he have any patience for games. There were no constructs in this deserted corridor. The two were alone.

"My family has been close to the Emperor for a thousand years," said Trevain. "He trusts me considerably more than he trusts you, since you so cruelly turned your back on your country at its time of need."

Rien arched a brow. "I thought I was a murderer and a criminal. Daimos really needs to choose one lie and stick with it."

The name hung in the air between them, unacknowledged, but Trevain's brow tightened. He knew the thin line they walked and that while the Emperor believed him an ally, Daimos was still a criminal in the public eye.

"I've heard rumours that you're losing your grip on reality," Trevain said softly. "Pity but understandable in the wake of such a tragic loss as yours."

His words sank into Rien's chest like the point of a

dagger. "How long have you been planning to get close to the Emperor? To replace my father in his sphere of influence?"

Before his family's deaths? Undoubtedly, but despite knowing that the Trevains had leapt at the chance to join Daimos's side, he hadn't thought that they might have formed their allegiance *before* then.

Trevain said nothing, but Rien's hands clenched. "Why were you selling those Relics in the market? Was that on *his* orders too?"

Trevain didn't need to answer for him to know the truth. He'd been involved with Daimos long before the Astera family had met their ends. Trevain had known Daimos had survived and that he'd come back to the city.

He'd helped him kill Rien's family.

A roaring noise in his ears drowned even the sound of the fighting from the courtyard, and the staff jerked in his hand. Thorns lashed at Trevain, who blocked the attack with the edge of his own staff. "The Emperor will thank me when I bring you into custody."

The blue staff emitted a purplish glow, and a torrent of wind hit Rien, causing him to slam into a pillar. The air flew from his lungs, but he launched forward again, more thorns rising to bite at Trevain. His opponent deflected each of his attacks, but he was near twice Rien's age and moved less fluidly, his staff decorated for show rather than for speed. And while Trevain's skill and experience might outrank Rien's, the effectiveness of a Relic always came from how closely intertwined one's desires and impulses were with the deity whose magic resided within. He'd always known that Zierne possessed a violent streak, and for once, his anger and Zierne's were in synchrony. Trevain was undoubtedly tied closely to Lauvet, his own deity, but he'd expected to find Rien a broken man without any of his old drive.

He was wrong. In a burst of rage, Rien's thorns raked across Trevain's face, leaving bloody scratches behind. Staff collided with staff, and while a powerful roar of wind threatened to rip the Relic from his grip, the vines wrapped around Rien's own hands, the thorns not breaking his skin but tightening his hold on the staff and keeping Lauvet's powerful magic from ripping it away.

Rien's next strike sent Trevain crashing to the floor, the thorns dragging his enemy's staff out of his reach. Trevain's eyes widened as he looked up at Rien, and then his mouth twisted in an inexplicable smirk. "To die at the hands of *that* Relic would be a bitter irony, I confess, dear Arien."

His words brought Rien to a halt despite the staff's anger burning against his hands. "What's that supposed to mean?"

"You must know. Look at your Relic."

He glanced down briefly and saw the thorns creeping towards Trevain independently of his own conscious command. Despite himself, Rien jerked back sharply, *demanding* the staff cease its attack.

Trevain gave a laugh, and Rien abruptly recalled his earlier words, addressed to the waiting audience of Invokers. Namely, that the Sentinels had smuggled certain Relics out of the country to keep them from being used by anyone in Aestin.

Did Trevain know the truth? Or had the whole thing been a lie concocted by Daimos, if not by Trevain himself?

Powers above, he didn't have time to second-guess his

own Relic when he had a war to win. Frustration and anger vibrated in his hands, but he forced the vines to wrap around Trevain's feet and bind them together without striking a killing blow. Trevain smiled at him all the while, as if they'd shared a private joke.

Rien snarled through his teeth. "Lying to the Emperor is high treason, you know. Even you won't escape the consequences."

"I disagree," Trevain. "In my experience, any lie can become truth if enough people believe it."

"Doubtless the aid of a deity of illusion helps with that." Without letting Trevain speak another word, he forced the vines to cover his enemy's mouth to keep him from shouting and giving himself away.

Rien hurried down the corridor, hoping he wouldn't come to regret leaving Trevain alive. Veering to the side, he made for the route to the Emperor's own quarters. Two guards stood outside the heavy wooden door, but neither appeared to be armed with Relics. Rien listened out, hearing nobody else nearby, before approaching them.

"I'm not here to harm the Emperor." Rien spoke quickly. "I need to speak to him. That attack out in the courtyard isn't Zeuten's work. We can find the real source but only if you believe me."

"You," said one of the guards, a stocky man with shaved hair. "You're Arien Astera. Are you responsible for this?"

"No, but I came to warn His Imperial Majesty." Rien ignored the warning thrum beneath the surface of his staff, willing it not to strike the guards down without his permission. "He's been betrayed from someone within the palace itself, and—"

"I'll deal with this one," offered the second guard, a broad man with longer hair than was typical of the Emperor's personal guards. "Perhaps a visit to the dungeon is in order."

Not a chance. Crimson light spread to both of his hands, and a faint orange glow drew Rien's eyes to the long-haired guard's hand.

A godsmark. He's the wielder.

This man held Invicten's Relic, but his companion didn't appear to have noticed the imminent danger. Rather, his attention was on Rien instead.

Rien drew in a breath. "Someone in here has betrayed the Emperor. I can prove it."

"You have a warrant on your head for attacking the imperial guards and causing a public disturbance," said the long-haired guard. "And now another for breaking into the imperial palace. To say nothing of your alleged exploits in Zeuten..."

Vines shot from both of Rien's hands, yanking the two guards off their feet. The stocky man went down hard, while the Relic's wielder recovered first, an amber glow sparking in his fingertips. "To think your family once had a reputation for integrity, Arien Astera."

"We both know I committed no crimes other than being on the wrong side of Daimos's grudge," said Rien. "You, I'm guessing he paid off with that Relic of yours."

Kicking the vines away from his ankles, the long-haired guard climbed to his feet and reached for Rien's staff. "Give that here."

Rien's reply died on his tongue as the overwhelming

urge to surrender rose within him. The crimson light of his staff faded, while the amber light around the guard's hands brightened. The other guard, back on his feet, wore a glazed expression that mirrored how Rien himself felt. A voice whispered in the back of his mind, telling him to hand over his staff and accept his fate.

"You're incorrect," the long-haired guard added. "I simply desired to protect His Imperial Majesty. It's not a matter of picking sides but survival."

Survival. Rien had survived through so much turmoil himself, and he was *tired*. Why shouldn't he hand over the staff and let the Trevains take it?

Trevain.

A burst of rage extinguished the spell gripping him, erupting in a flash of crimson light, and he swung the staff at the guard's face. The long-haired man crumpled, bleeding from his mouth, and Rien struck him again.

The second guard let out a choked noise, reaching for his sword, and his evident shock drew Rien out of his fury. He hadn't come here to kill the Emperor's guards but to bring an end to Daimos's scheme. Ignoring the burning hate emanating from the staff in his hand, he crouched beside the twitching form of the long-haired guard. "Give me your Relic."

The man didn't reply. Rien reached out and checked his pockets, a familiar orange light catching his eye. The Relic resembled a round, polished stone, unremarkable save for its faint amber sheen.

"What in Gaiva's name are you doing?" demanded the other guard.

"Destroying this." Rien held up the stone to reveal the faint glow around its edges. "Did you know your fellow guard was an Invoker, casting a spell on the Emperor?"

Vines shot from his staff and wrapped around the stone. The guard exclaimed, but a cracking noise sounded, and the stone shattered beneath the thorns. He released the Relic's remains—and it was at that moment that he realised that the door to the Emperor's quarters had opened.

His Imperial Majesty himself stared at Rien through the open door as the Relic crumbled at his feet.

26

Zelle's return to the outpost brought her unexpected news.

"Aurel and Evita went to Itzar?" she asked Grandma. "Why?"

"To find Gaiva's allies before Invicten gets to them first." Sitting in her armchair, Grandma looked entirely too relaxed at the prospect of their allies being scattered once again. "We expected that you'd be gone for a while."

"You didn't even know where I was."

"I guessed," replied the old Sentinel. "Based on our conversation about the realm of the Powers."

"You thought I went *there?*" Zelle said disbelievingly. "I went to the Sentinels' cave. I can't go into the realm of the Powers without a doorway, can I?"

"Ask that staff of yours."

Zelle's spine stiffened. "You don't mean to say the *staff* can open doorways?"

"I've long suspected it can," Grandma said. "The nameless Shaper is the only known deity who can close doorways, so it stands to reason that the reverse is true."

"But—" She cut herself off then addressed the staff. "Does that mean you could have found Grandma the whole time when she was missing?"

No. She might have been anywhere in the realm of the Powers. I may be able to open doorways, but I cannot control what you might find on the other side.

"I don't believe this." She lifted the staff into the air, as though looking at it on eye level would make it more likely to listen to her. "I could have at least *tried* to find her if I'd known I had a route to her location at my fingertips the whole time."

Would you have wanted to give Orzen any more chances to escape? He did enough damage with his own doorways without you creating more.

Grandma cleared her throat. "That's done, Zelle. It's over."

Zelle shot her a frown. "You left the staff behind because you thought it'd draw too much attention, but if you'd taken it, you'd have been able to open a way back."

Grandma hadn't necessarily known that at the time… but the staff certainly had.

There's no need to sound so accusatory. I hardly expected my wielder to walk into the realm of the Powers of her own accord.

"Still." Drained, she lowered the staff and rested it against the second armchair, sinking into the seat next to her grandmother. "Grandma, I saw a vision in the Sentinels' cave that showed me how the Shaper ended up imprisoned… and why the other Great Powers hate one another."

"Tell me everything."

Zelle did so. When she'd finished relating the vision, her grandmother studied her face for a long moment. "So it was the Shaper who closed the doors between realms."

"Apparently so," said Zelle. "It makes a kind of sense, but She isn't the only deity who can open doorways. Orzen and Igon did too…"

"They had human bodies," said Grandma. "Is that the condition?"

Correct, the staff replied.

Zelle dropped her gaze to the staff. "You mean to say that any deity with a human body can open doorways anywhere they like?"

You speak as if they are in abundance. They are not.

"The other deities can't get out at all." She rose to her feet and began to pace up and down the room. "That explains why Orzen was so willing to work with Daimos. Igon too."

And, maybe, Invicten Himself, if it was even possible for Daimos to offer a human body to a Great Power.

Not in the same way, no, the staff told her.

Grandma lifted her head. "What isn't the same, exactly?"

"I wondered if a Great Power could be bound to a human form," said Zelle. "No, apparently, so at least Invicten doesn't have the ability to walk in this realm."

That does not make him any less of a threat. Especially since his Relics have been close to my prison for centuries without being detected.

"The Changers." She paced the room again. "They've gone to the capital, except the ones who went to Itzar… I hope they *don't* plan to recruit the islanders to fight in Daimos's war."

Tamacha wouldn't say yes, surely, but a large number of the islanders held Relics now, and there was no telling what the Changers might do to persuade them to join Daimos's side.

You cannot do anything to stop them now.

"I *can* stop Daimos." Zelle looked down at the staff. "Provided you help me, that is."

Naturally.

She caught Grandma watching her, her expression difficult to read. For some reason, her warning from a few days ago came back to Zelle. Words could lie, and the Shaper certainly had Her own motives. How could she know that everything that she'd seen in the vision had been the truth? The odd disjunction between the staff's claims to have lost its memory and the way the Shaper had given her an insight into the past nagged at the back of her mind but without any conclusions to be drawn.

All the same, if she distrusted her own deity, then how was she supposed to ensure victory over Daimos?

To that question, the staff gave no answer.

The two Senior Changers faced the newcomers, their attention focusing on Evita and Aurel. At least they appeared to be the only Changers present, but if Daimos had managed to work his influence upon the Blessed, then Evita and the others would have little hope of getting through to them.

"What are you doing here?" demanded Briony.

"I could ask you the same question," said Evita. "I thought you were supposed to be guarding the village of Tavine in case any terrifying farmers or craftsmen decided to mount an attack on you."

Verne's jaw tensed. "Did you truly come all the way here to mock us?"

"No, we came to tell them not to listen to you." Aurel gestured to the robed figures gathering on the beach.

One stepped to the front, who Evita recognised as Tamacha, leader of the Blessed. She wore the same moon-white robes as the others, a headdress sat atop her white hair, and her face was lined with the beginnings of age. "I would like to ask you to take your arguments elsewhere, if you wouldn't mind. We have had quite enough of outside interference."

Ouch. Evita imagined that she and the others were not dealing well with the aftermath of their island sinking into the ocean and their prized Relic being reduced to rubble, despite the shattering of Gaiva's rock being the reason for their survival.

"Why did they say they came here?" Aurel addressed the leader of the Blessed. "Did they claim to have seen your deity in person? Because it's a lie."

"Blasphemy," hissed Briony. "Gaiva has directly requested that we ask for the aid of the people of Itzar."

"It's not Gaiva," said Evita. "Gaiva—or what is left of Her—is here in the Isles of Itzar, not in Zeuten. They're here to recruit you to fight in an illegal war."

"We want no part in your wars," Tamacha said firmly.

"She is lying," Briony insisted. "The Crown Prince of Zeuten has requested your help against a dangerous foe.

You're free to decline, but I cannot promise you that our enemies will not find their way here regardless."

"In fact, we can almost guarantee they will," added Verne. "Aestin, it seems, is back to their conquering ways."

"It isn't Aestin," said Evita. "He's setting you up."

"Enough," Verne growled. "This one betrayed us, twice over. She even assisted in the death of our leader."

"Is that true?" Tamacha finally looked at Evita, who flushed.

Oh, Powers. "Their leader was acting under the influence of Invicten, and he manipulated *me* into fighting against my own allies. I came here to stop them from doing the same to you."

"Lies and slander," Briony said. "The fact remains, Blessed, that we need your help. As does Gaiva Herself."

"I'm afraid I simply cannot spare anyone," she answered. "We have enough problems of our own to deal with. However, some might feel differently. I would invite you to ask the other people of the Isles for their own perspectives."

Evita might have said it was an improvement on the Blessed ruling the Isles from within their caves and refusing to let anyone else claim any authority, but the last thing they needed was the Changers inflicting their lies upon the villagers. Especially those who'd recently claimed Relics.

"We accept your choice," said Verne. "I will convey your response to the Crown Prince of Zeuten."

"And we will take our leave." Briony then glared at Evita, as if she was entirely to blame for their refusal, or perhaps as if daring her to stop them from going after the villagers next.

When she and Verne took flight, cloaks spreading into the form of wings, the eagle-riding defectors rose to surround them, preventing them from flying south of the island towards the settlements. Heart racing, Evita urged the dragonet to join them and addressed the Changers from the air. "I won't allow you to spread your lies among the Isles. Leave the villagers in peace."

"And if you want to know if any of *us* will fight for you, the answer is no," Kolt called from the back of his own eagle.

"Exactly," Aurel called, shooting Evita a triumphant grin. "You're outnumbered, Changers. Go home."

Briony and Verne hesitated for a moment as if debating the odds of winning against a group of angry warriors wielding magic and bone knives from the backs of giant eagles. Evidently deciding that they'd come off worse, the pair of them flew upward and soared away on their cloak-made wings.

The eagles withdrew, but the Blessed continued to look up at the newcomers with expressions of intense distrust, including Evita.

Tamacha drew in a breath. "I don't know why your nation insists upon bothering us, but I would appreciate it if you left us in peace."

"We will, but—can I explain first?" asked Evita. "Zelle might be in danger."

"Zelle?" Tamacha's gaze sharpened. "She is still allied to the nameless Shaper, isn't she?"

"She is," confirmed Evita. "But our enemy, Daimos, has also allied himself with a Great Power, Invicten. He's infiltrated the governments of both Zeuten and Aestin and taken over the Changers with the intent of starting a war between both nations."

"Come with us," Kolt offered. "We'd be willing to discuss the subject further with you."

Tamacha turned towards him. "You would go to war on behalf of another nation, rather than the villagers that you betrayed your own deity in order to protect?"

"Not at all," said Kolt. "We simply wish to hear them out."

Tamacha plainly didn't want to talk to the former defectors any more than she had to, though there was more resentment in her manner than outright anger. She watched with a thin-lipped expression as the former rogues took flight, leading the way south across the Isles.

"Not a wasted trip after all, then." Aurel shot a mischievous grin in Kolt's direction. "I knew Tamacha would say no, but I suppose at least Daimos himself didn't come with them."

He didn't need to. Their Relics belonged to Invicten, and whether they willingly took his side or not, his influence would never be far away from them.

And you? a voice whispered in the back of Evita's mind. *What about you? You kept the cloak, didn't you?*

She had no answer. She hadn't felt so much as a twinge from the cloak since she'd put it back on, but she was a long way from trusting it to catch her mid-flight as she had before. If they'd had to fight with the Changers, she might have found herself in serious trouble.

Chirp and the eagles landed on the beach near the newly constructed settlements, where they found Gatt sitting on a rock waiting for their return.

"You spoke to the Blessed?" he asked.

"A little," Evita replied. "The Changers left when Tamacha made it clear she wasn't interested in sending warriors to help in their fight."

His brows shot up. "They wanted to recruit us to fight for Zeuten?"

"They're under the impression that Aestin intends to conquer the Isles," she said. "It's not true, of course, but we had to drive them away from trying to recruit the villagers as well."

"Scumbags," Del said. "They made a mistake if they thought Tamacha would be easy to persuade—and us too."

Their tones suggested they had no intention of getting involved in the war, but had she really expected them to volunteer to risk their own lives on behalf of Zeuten? Even to help Zelle, without whom the Isles might be at the bottom of the ocean?

"Zelle is convinced that Daimos wants all three Great Powers involved in this war," said Aurel. "And she might not be wrong either."

"Did you plan to fly back to Zeuten right away?" asked Kolt. "Because there's a storm coming, looks like."

Evita would have to take his word for it on that, since the islands were permanently wreathed in mist that made it otherwise hard to tell the weather conditions. Since it got dark early and fast here, however, they'd be hard-pressed to reach the mainland again before nightfall.

"We would be willing to let you spend the night in our village," Kolt offered. "I can't promise it'll be comfortable, but it's better than flying through a storm."

Evita thought for a moment. She was reasonably sure the Changers wouldn't come back to attack them during the night, and they'd have another chance to persuade the former defectors to offer them aid. "We'd be glad to accept, right, Aurel?"

"All right." Aurel gave Kolt an assessing look. "If those huts of yours flood, then I hope the villagers don't mind us staying at the tavern."

"It won't flood," he said, looking amused. "Besides, we have ways to keep ourselves entertained out here. I heard there's a card game you're quite the expert in."

"That's Evita, not me." A smile stole onto Aurel's mouth. "Tell you what, we'll teach you how to play."

27

With Evita and Aurel yet to return, Zelle hoped for a night free of unwelcome surprises, but it was not to be. The staff woke her in the early hours by turning ice-cold and jolting against the warm she'd draped over it in her sleep. Rubbing her wrist with her fingertips to get some sensation back into it, she whispered, "What was that for?"

You should really check on the weather.

Zelle's blood chilled, and she ran to the window. Fog pressed against the glass, making it impossible for her to see what was on the other side.

"Where did that come from?" She couldn't see any wraiths or anything similar in the fog, *but it was* thick enough to resemble a solid wall, preventing her from seeing past the tower. If Evita and Aurel came back, they'd have considerable trouble finding their way to the outpost without risking the dragonet colliding with the tower.

This must be Daimos's work, but Zelle saw no signs of him or anyone else, including the cause of the strange fog.

You know where it came from.

"The realm of the Powers?" Was there another doorway somewhere out there? If there was, she hadn't a hope of pinpointing its location from here, but there was no telling what else might come out of it if she didn't close the doorway herself.

"What?" Grandma emerged from her room, leaning on her walking stick. "What is it this time?"

Zelle indicated the window. "See that fog? The staff thinks it's from the realm of the Powers."

Grandma looked up sharply. "To find out, you'll have to walk into it. Are you sure you want that?"

"No." She dropped her gaze to the staff. "You can close a doorway without being able to see it, right?"

You already know the answer to that question.

The answer was yes, though it left her with the dilemma of catching the person who'd *opened* the doorway. Zelle returned her attention to the thick mass of fog. The notion of walking into it wasn't appealing, but the staff must be more than a match for whoever had cast the spell. "Can you sense the person who did this? Human or deity?"

No, the staff replied.

"Then they aren't here." She felt Grandma's stare boring into her back. "They might be hiding in the realm of the Powers... and as you decided to tell me yesterday, you *can* open a doorway there yourself. Have any Sentinels ever done it before?"

They lacked the imagination. It's your choice, but certainly the quickest way to find the culprit is to seek them out at the source. They can't have gone far.

Zelle thought it over. "If I can close a doorway as easily

as opening one, it might be worth the risk."

Grandma sucked in a breath. "Don't do it in the Sanctum, for the Powers' sakes."

"I wasn't planning to." Zelle turned her back on the window, gripping the staff in her hand. "In fact, I won't do it inside the outpost at all."

Grandma watched without speaking while Zelle put on her thick coat and shoes. Picking up the staff, she made for the door out of the tower.

The fog was even worse on the outside, where a thick haze of grey smothered the peaks and masked the cliffs from view. She walked a short distance before halting within sight of the tower to avoid getting lost before she even set foot in the realm of the deities. "How do I do this? Wait, I don't have to leave you behind, do I?"

You can take me with you, but it will draw attention. Not the pleasant sort either.

"I'll have to risk it." The staff was closely bound to her now, and without it, how could she possibly navigate her way through an unfamiliar realm that was hostile to all humans? "Right. Open a doorway."

A rush of potent energy travelled through Zelle's body, and the marks on her wrists ignited like the flame of a lit torch. A tingling ran to her fingertips, while the staff's bright glow pierced the fog. Zelle's awareness spread throughout the mountain around her, encompassing the lands the Shaper could bend to Her will... and then her reach went beyond, to a place no human could touch.

Focusing on the staff's glow, Zelle reached out towards that nebulous place, and a whitish patch formed in the air. A doorway to the realm of the Powers.

The flood of energy dissipated, leaving her drained but

exhilarated. Now she understood why no Sentinels had ever figured out how to do this. She could never have achieved such a feat without the new bond with the Shaper she'd formed in the Isles of Itzar, which had given her access to a dimension beyond her ordinary senses.

Taking a step forward, Zelle peered through the doorway. The air must be breathable in there, but the world on the other side was as indistinct as the fog spreading across the mountain.

"Here we go." She put her right foot through the doorway, testing the ground. She couldn't actually *see* what she was standing on, but her foot didn't dip or sink, so she had to assume it was solid enough for her to walk on.

With wary steps, she crossed the threshold and emerged into a mass of grey that wasn't unlike the fog she'd left on the other side. It fit with the vision the Sentinels' cave had shown her, but why hadn't she asked Grandma to draw a map first?

There's no need for maps in this place, the staff informed her.

"What happens if I get hungry or thirsty?" she asked. "I don't have enough supplies for longer than a day or two."

That won't be a problem. You will be free of all earthly concerns here.

Come to think of it, she didn't feel hot or cold either. Strange and more of an absence of feeling than anything else. She couldn't imagine *living* in a place like this.

"Was it always like this?" she whispered.

Yes, and no. The scenery used to be more appealing.

Through the fog, she glimpsed outlines that might have been walls, pillars, or other formations reduced to crumbling ruin. Whatever damage had been done here had turned the entire realm into something resembling a vision like the one she'd seen in the Sentinels' cave—except this was no vision. One thing was clear to Zelle: spending too much time in this oblivion would be enough to drive her to madness. Was this how it felt for the nameless Shaper to be eternally imprisoned in the mountain?

You are correct. It would drive you to madness.

She sometimes forgot the staff could read her thoughts when she hadn't intended to share them, though it was difficult for her *not* to wonder how it must feel for the Shaper's Relic to look upon the ruins of a realm She would never be able to set foot in again.

Don't feel sorry for me. I won't stand for that.

"Sorry you don't like what you find in my head," she muttered back. "If you didn't read my mind, it wouldn't be an issue. Anyway, why is nobody else around?"

Was the person responsible for casting a spell on the mountains somewhere here? Might they be able to hear her? It belatedly occurred to Zelle that the Shaper had been imprisoned by the other beings within this very realm, who might not take kindly to the staff's presence. She'd been willing to take the risk rather than leave her only advantage behind, but now...

As if in response to her thoughts, the staff turned cold in her hands, the first sensation she'd felt since her arrival in the realm of the Powers. *We aren't alone. Someone else is here.*

———

Breathing heavily, Rien straightened upright. The body of the long-haired guard lay twitching on his back next to the shattered remains of his Relic, while both the Emperor and the other guard stared at Rien.

"Arien Astera." The Emperor's fine clothes were dishevelled, his usually impeccable sheet of black hair in disarray. "What have you done?"

Heart thumping, Rien bowed at the waist, a gesture one gave to a superior, rather than using the typical gesture an Invoker used when addressing someone who was technically their equal. "Your Excellency, I apologise for arriving in the palace in this manner. This man was using a Relic to cast a spell upon you and everyone else in your inner circle."

The second guard looked at Rien with open distrust. "This is madness. You attacked us without provocation."

"Did you know he was an Invoker?" Rien indicated the shards of broken rock. "You can examine the remains of his Relic for yourself if you like, but you must know that the attack in the courtyard is not Zeuten's doing."

The Emperor turned to the second guard. "Remove that rock and take it to be examined."

"I cannot leave you alone with him, Your Imperial Majesty."

Rien gave him a sharp look. "I'm not here to harm the Emperor. If I was, I wouldn't have gone to the trouble of attending the announcement with the other Invokers and risking discovery."

Two more guards ran into view, grim and hard-faced. One of them stopped short at the sight of him. "Arien Astera."

"Your Imperial Majesty." The other guard ignored Rien and addressed the Emperor. "Those creatures have ceased their attack. I believe the Invokers have neutralised the threat."

Daimos must have called them off. He knew Rien had intervened. With his spies able to walk in and out of the realm of the Powers anywhere in the world, it was no surprise. Evidently his attack had been intended to raise a sense of alarm, not start the actual war... yet.

The real battle was coming. Of that he had no doubt.

Rien indicated the shattered remains of the Relic and its unconscious wielder. "This man brought a Relic of Invicten into the palace and used it to cast a spell on the Emperor and his advisors, on the orders of Naxel Daimos. He intended to provoke a false war with Zeuten."

"Daimos?" echoed one of the guards.

The Emperor studied the unconscious guard and then lifted his gaze to the others. "I want answers. Where is Luvid Trevain? He's supposed to be protecting me, but I've heard nothing from him since the battle."

"He betrayed you too." If the guards hadn't already stumbled upon him tied up in the corridor where Rien had left him, then Trevain must have managed to free himself and run off to warn Daimos. "He told me himself that he helped Daimos enter the capital when he came after my family."

"What proof do you have of this?" asked one of the newcomers, who Rien belatedly recognised as the man who'd tried to convince him to come to the Imperial Palace a few days prior and surrender his Relic to Trevain. "Your word doesn't negate the centuries of loyalty that the Trevains have given the Emperor."

"Yet it seems you were ready to believe the worst of *me." The words escaped* before he could think better of them. "I apologise for entering the palace in this manner, but I would strongly advise you to track down and question Luvid Trevain before he escapes."

"You're in no position to give anyone orders, Astera," said the guard. "Your Imperial Majesty, should I take him to the dungeon for the time being?"

"Yes, I think that's the best course of action."

"Wait." Rien hadn't expected to win them over right away, but the crimson burn of his staff urged him to knock the guards aside and make a run for it. "I'll come with you, but I hope you'll consider that the next attack might come from within your own walls and not from Zeuten at all."

Without acknowledging his warning, the guards herded him down the corridor until they came to a staircase leading to the palace's lowest level. The dungeon was typically designated for political prisoners or people who had too much money and influence to be locked in a provincial jail. For a prison, it wasn't unpleasant, with each cell the size of an expensive suite and equipped with facilities most noblemen would envy. Yet a prison was the same no matter how fine the conditions, and when they brought Rien to an empty cell, one of the guards reached for his staff. "We'll have to take your Relic."

Rien's shoulders tensed. "I would rather not be parted from my Relic when we might be attacked again at any moment."

"Nevertheless." The guard's hand closed around the staff. "We need the weapon. Emperor's orders."

A primal surge of panic rose within him, turning to alarm when the staff erupted with sharp thorns in the guard's hands. The man cried out in pain and dropped the

Relic, while the other guards all but shoved Rien through the door into his cell.

"Wait." He reached for the door, but a sharp pain shot up his wrist from his godsmark, causing him to flinch.

The door slammed. Rien heard the guards arguing with one another over who had to pick up the staff next, but his own pain drew his focus from their shouts. His godsmark pulsed bright crimson, as though the Relic itself was incensed at being manhandled.

"You shouldn't have attacked them, Zierne." He walked to the hard-backed chair on one side of his cell and sat down, doing his best to ignore the throbbing pain in his hand. "Be patient. It's obvious to anyone who looks at that broken Relic that I was telling the truth."

As far as prisons went, the palace was positively luxurious, but that didn't make him feel any better about being confined here while Luvid Trevain walked free. As for the man whose Relic he'd destroyed, his own confession would have to wait until the aftermath of the fight with the constructs had been cleared up. Even if he was found guilty, it wouldn't happen soon enough for Rien's liking. After all, Daimos had already made his move, and the Trevains had been working for him long before he'd shown up in the city in person.

My father knew they were up to no good, he thought. Their business dealings at the market, selling Relics to the public... and yet that had been the least of his crimes. *He invited Daimos to the city. He sold out my family.*

"I should have killed him," he said to the empty room.

As his anger rose, his godsmark gave another painful throb. Being separated from his Relic wasn't the same as having it claimed by another, but the absence bothered him like an itch that he couldn't scratch, stirring an echo of the pain in his other godsmark too. How many people had the misfortune to lose more than one Relic in a lifetime? Would Zierne's Relic ever forgive him for this? Granted, he'd been having misgivings concerning his Relic's impulses for a while now, and Trevain's taunting hadn't helped—but he needed his Relic's cooperation to stand a chance of beating Daimos.

If he ever got out of this cell. The pain in his hand made it hard to think, but if Zierne had decided Rien had betrayed him, then he didn't know what he'd do. He hoped the Martzels had escaped unscathed at least, but it looked as if he might end up watching the start of the war from behind bars instead of the battlefield.

If Rien hadn't come to the palace—if he'd gone back to Zeuten to warn Zelle instead—he might have been able to do more. In fact, part of him wished he'd never left Zeuten in the first place. Even if he managed to convince the Emperor to abandon his notions of a war with Zeuten in the absence of Invicten's influence on the palace, that wouldn't stop Daimos from continuing his manipulations on the other side of the ocean.

No... when he got out of this cell, the only place for him to go was directly to Zeuten. He'd go and help Zelle rid her country of Daimos's influence and bring the war to a halt, with or without the Emperor's blessing.

Minutes passed in silence, and the pain in his hand faded to a dull throb. Rien had concocted and discarded a number of plans before the sounds of a commotion reached his ears from somewhere above. He rose to his feet, guessing that less than an hour had passed since his imprisonment. Was the palace under attack again? If so, he'd be in trouble without his Relic, but his worry was reserved for his allies, not himself. *I have to get out of here.*

The sound of hurried but uneven footsteps echoed down the corridor, and relief flooded Rien when Devan Martzel's face appeared on the other side of his cell door.

"There you are," Martzel said. "We'd better get you out of there."

"What's going on up there?" he asked.

Martzel drew in a breath. "Nothing good. The docks are under attack... and this time, the threat appears to have come directly from Zeuten."

———

Aurel and Evita left Itzar early the following morning. As Kolt had promised, the hut did not flood overnight despite the rain battering the islands. In fact, not only did its sturdy walls keep the rain out, but they retained enough warmth that she'd been content to talk and play cards with the others for hours. Having time to rest her healing injury hadn't hurt, either, and Aurel found herself in a good mood as she chatted to Kolt over a breakfast of fried fish. Not her preferred fare, but she'd developed quite the rapport with her former kidnapper.

"If you have need of our help, then I would gladly accompany you to Zeuten." Kolt watched her and Evita settle onto Chirp's back, ready to fly home. "That said, not all my fellow islanders would agree, and I imagine our small number wouldn't be enough to compensate for an army."

"We'd be grateful for any help we can get," said Evita. "I don't know if there's any quick way for us to contact you… or the reverse, either, given the length of the journey."

Gatt looked up from his boat, which he was preparing for another journey across the Perilous Sea. "I take frequent trips to Cathan and other places on Zeuten's coast. Should word reach my ear that you have need of us, I will inform the others at once."

"We'd appreciate the help," said Aurel, lifting a hand to wave goodbye to the warriors. "Thanks for the hospitality."

In one beat of Chirp's wings, they took flight. The mist had lingered, but the storm appeared to be over, though she didn't envy Gatt having to cross the ocean in that fragile-looking boat of his.

During their flight back to the mainland, Evita didn't talk much. Aurel knew she was worried that they'd stayed too long and that the majority of the Changers had gone to the capital instead. Or perhaps she wished they'd convinced the former defectors to come with them directly to Zeuten. That had been a long shot from the start, but she had to admit that she'd hoped they might return to Zelle with more than a vague promise of help.

When they neared the coast, Aurel glimpsed a haze of fog gathering around the mountain's peak. "Oh, Powers. Don't tell me the storm has moved here."

"Looks like fog to me, not rain," Evita said. "We'd better slow down. Right, Chirp?"

They flew lower once they reached the edge of the coast, but the fog persisted, and even the forest at the foot of the peaks was smothered in grey.

"There's some kind of spell at work," Aurel said. "Bloody Powers. What did we miss this time?"

Evita didn't answer. They drew closer to the Range, as far as Aurel could judge from the wavering outlines of the peaks, but the grey mass below was dense enough that they might have been hovering over the ocean and not the forest.

"Where's the tower?" asked Evita.

"Good question." Aurel craned her neck. "I hope Zelle and Grandma aren't outside in this."

So low was the visibility that she didn't notice the two Changers until the dragonet almost flew into them. Evita yelped, grabbing Chirp's neck for balance, while Aurel recognised Briony and Verne, who flew with their cloaks spread out around them.

"Watch where you're going," she told them. "Where're you off to in such a hurry?"

"We've been called to the capital." Briony threw the words over her shoulder without slowing down. "Aestin has declared war on us."

"It isn't Aestin," Evita insisted. "Whoever called you is lying."

"We received a summons directly from the palace," Verne said. "You may have thwarted our efforts to gain allies, but we will honour the Crown's orders."

"You can't even see where you're going." Aurel leaned forward over the dragonet's back, but the two Changers had already disappeared into the fog. "We need to find Zelle."

"Agreed." Evita directed Chirp to fly towards the hazy peaks, hunting for the tower-like form of the Sentinels' outpost.

Aestin has declared war. Or Daimos has. Powers above. How can this be possible?

When the tower loomed out of the fog ahead of them, the dragonet veered sideways, barely avoiding a collision, and Aurel lost her one-handed grip on his back.

Then she was falling, tumbling over and over in the air. Chirp and Evita vanished from sight as Aurel fell, caught in a haze of breathless terror—until the sharp edges of branches slowed her fall.

As she came to a bewildered halt, she hung there, suspended in a nest of branches. They hadn't been that close to the forest, had they? The fog made it impossible to see much of her surroundings, but she did appear to be in a tree.

The dragonet was nowhere to be seen, and Aurel wasn't one to hang in midair and wait to be rescued, so she one-handedly began to climb down. The descent took less time than she'd expected, and her arm gave her no pain, which struck her as odd. Yet when she touched the ground, she forgot her questions. The shape of a building appeared from the gloom, a large stone house surrounded by a fence.

The Reader's house.

It had to be a trick, or a construct, a creation of the fog. Aurel moved as if in a trance, reaching for the door, which opened.

"Good, you're home," said Grandma.

The old Sentinel sat on the sofa as though she'd been waiting for Aurel to come home. A peculiar sense of unreality washed over her, though Grandma appeared as solid as Aurel herself. Like the house.

"I thought you were at the outpost," she said. "It isn't safe for you to go outside in this weather."

"You have the staff," said Grandma. "You can't be scared of a little fog."

She glanced down at her hand and found that she did indeed hold the nameless Shaper's staff, which cast a familiar blue glow across her palm. That wasn't right. "Where's—?"

"There you are," interrupted a voice. Evita walked into view, wearing an apron and carrying a cloth.

Aurel's mouth parted. A thousand questions arose, but she found herself voicing the most mundane. "What are you wearing?"

"I thought you wanted me to clean the cabinets."

I what? More to the point, why did *Aurel* have the staff? What had happened to…?

"Grandma," said Aurel, slowly. "Where is Zelle?"

"Zelle died," she said. "Don't you remember? She died, and you inherited the magic of the nameless Shaper yourself."

Mouth agape, Aurel backed against the front door and tripped over the edge. Instead of hitting the ground, she plummeted downward until she knew no more.

28

Zelle turned on the spot, scanning the emptiness of the realm of the Powers. "Is anyone there?"

No response came. If she moved any farther, she risked losing sight of the doorway. Assuming the Shaper had spoken the truth, if she ended up stuck in here, at least she wouldn't starve to death, but that didn't mean the deities couldn't harm her. She remained a vulnerable human despite the staff in her hands.

The sound of wings beating came from above, and a blurred shape descended next to Zelle. She took a step back from the new arrival, who was the height of a person but resembled a large grey dove. The dove addressed her in a booming voice, but Zelle didn't understand the words. What language was he speaking? It sounded… familiar.

Wait. "Are you speaking Aestinian?"

"Another trespasser?" The dove switched to Zelle's own language, startling her, though it shouldn't have been surprising that the deities could speak both. They might be cut off from the human realm, but they weren't entirely separated.

"Why do these humans keep coming in here?" A second large bird, this one resembling a man-sized raven, landed on Zelle's other side. "They must know they aren't welcome."

Her mouth parted. "Do humans frequently make a habit of walking into your realm?"

"She's making fun of us, this one is," said the raven-shaped deity, whose voice sounded more high-pitched than the dove's, suggesting to Zelle that she was female, and the other deity was male. "We should kill her."

"I'm really not a fan of that idea, to be honest." They weren't working for Daimos, were they? If so, then he hadn't given them access to human forms the way he had to Orzen and Igon, but that didn't mean they could do no harm to her. She was on their home territory, after all, but she wasn't unprotected. Zelle raised the staff, and the flash of blue light caused both birds to launch into flight again.

"What is that?" shouted the dove. "Get it out of here!"

Zelle lowered the staff. "I have no quarrel with you, but I *am* allied with the nameless Shaper. Now, tell me who you're working for."

"The Shaper!" the raven howled. "Go away! Go!"

The birds flew at her, their beating wings pushing her backwards, but Zelle stood her ground.

"You're working for Naxel Daimos, aren't you?" she asked. "Does that mean he's in Zeuten?"

"Get out, human."

Zelle braced the staff on the ground to prevent them

from pushing her any farther back. "Look, neither of you can outdo the nameless Shaper, so give it up."

They must be the least of the lesser deities, but if Daimos had hired them, then they had to know who'd caused the fog to surround the mountains. In response, the two birds landed with their wings spread outward so that they appeared even bigger than beforehand.

"Leave," the dove said again.

"Only when one of you tells me who cast a spell on Zeuten's mountains."

"Mountains?" The raven put on a wistful tone. "Oh, I miss those."

"So do I." The dove sighed. "It's been so long. I can hardly wait to walk under the stars once again."

"You won't get that chance if I kill you both first." Zelle lifted the staff, calling on the Shaper's magic to brighten its glow. "I'm not leaving this realm until I get some answers. Tell me who you are."

"They call me Xeale," said the dove. "This is Kyren. Who are *you?*"

"Zelle Carnelian," she replied. "You asked, 'Why do these humans keep coming in here?' Does that mean you met my grandmother?"

"The trickster?" Kyren shrieked, a horrible noise that made Zelle want to cover her ears. "I will never forget her betrayal. She tricked us into betraying Orzen and then let him torture us without coming to our aid."

It was them. They opposed Orzen at Grandma's request—and he punished them for it. "So you're working for Daimos now? Wait, is he here?"

"Not at the present moment."

That meant he *had* been in the realm of the Powers—

and recently. "He's using the realm of the Powers to move around, isn't he? But you can't leave yourselves."

"Tragic." Kyren sniffed. "The human means to mock our plight."

Xeale gasped. "So hurtful."

"I'm not mocking you," said Zelle. "I only found out recently that you can't get out of here. Daimos is offering you a way out, isn't he? That's why you're helping him."

Don't sympathise with the likes of them, the staff reprimanded her. *You have a job to do.*

"The human doesn't understand," said Xeale. "We have been here longer than you've been alive."

"I understand more than Daimos does, I guarantee it," Zelle told them. "He wants to drive two nations into war."

"Should we care?" Xeale asked. "They're only humans."

Annoyance flared within her. "That is a prime example of why inviting you into the human world is a bad idea, if you have no value for lives that aren't your own."

They seemed to fear the staff, though. If Daimos wasn't here, then she could do worse than press his allies into telling her whereabouts he'd hidden the source of the spell on the mountains.

"Mockery." Kyren sniffed again. "Humans kill each other all the time. Even your grandmother turned her back on us."

"She can no more come here than you can set foot in the human realm," Zelle said. "Unlike you, we have the limitations of age and injury. She didn't intend for Orzen to torture you." It would give too much away if she admitted how long it'd taken her and her grandmother to figure out that they could use the staff to open a doorway at all, though that was more the Shaper's fault than anyone else's.

"Humans lie," said Xeale. "Why should we believe a word you say?"

"You can believe whatever you like," Zelle said, "but I'm not leaving until you tell me where the Relic causing the fog in the mountains is located. You must have been watching even if you didn't hide it yourself."

"No, our job is to find the Relics, not—" Kyren was cut off when Xeale's wing clipped her in the face.

"Don't tell her anything," Xeale said.

Zelle's grip tightened on the staff. "Your job was to *find* Relics? Which Relics, exactly? Invicten's?"

Kyren yelped when Xeale's wing hit her again. "Nothing, nothing! Not telling."

"How can you find Relics when you can't leave this realm?" The answer hit her before the question had finished leaving her mouth. Invicten's Relics must have come from *here*. From the realm of the Powers.

I should have known, the staff whispered in her ear.

"Enough questions," Xeale said. "You're trying to trick us, just like your grandmother."

"Are you really loyal to Daimos?" Zelle had her doubts, given her experience with the lesser Powers so far, and if her grandmother had once managed to coax the pair of them into helping her, then perhaps she might do the same herself. "What if I can make you a better offer than he can?"

"Only if you offer us access to your realm," Kyren said. "Nothing less."

Given the deities' callous remarks earlier, that struck her as unwise. Even if she'd known how to use whatever spell Daimos had cast to give certain deities access to a human form, was it wise to extend that offer to a pair of deities whose attitude towards humans was decidedly murky? No, she wouldn't take the risk.

A twinge in her hand drew her gaze down to the staff. Its blue glow had dimmed, sputtering out like a candle being extinguished.

What's wrong with you? she asked the staff.

No response came, but the deities spread their wings wide, casting menacing shadows over her.

"Was that a 'no'?" Xeale beat his wings, causing a gust of wind that drove Zelle backwards. "Then get out."

Zelle might have fought back, but arguing any further was futile, and the absence of the staff's usual blue glow brought a worried twinge to her chest. Considering the Shaper's magic was all that was holding the doorway open, getting out of here seemed the wisest course of action.

Her visit had brought her at least one answer: Invicten's Relics must have been left behind after the doors between realms had been closed. Daimos had likely been the first human who'd found them in a thousand years or more, though she couldn't begin to imagine how he'd figured out their location.

Retreating through the doorway, Zelle emerged back on the mountain path outside the tower. The fog had thickened in the short time she'd been gone, and the staff's glow was barely visible at all.

That's not a good sign.

———

Evita shouted aloud when Aurel tumbled off the dragonet's back into the thick fog. They'd been close to the path—she'd thought—but it would be a painful landing. She urged Chirp to fly lower, but the only source of light was the faint silver shimmer from her cloak. In fact, it appeared to be brighter than usual, a realisation that brought more dread than relief.

If the fog was a result of Invicten's magic, then might she be in danger of falling under another spell? She needed to find Aurel and get out of here. Squinting, she caught sight of an indistinct form that she at first thought might be the tower before it resolved into a group of hovering figures. Changers, cloaks billowing around them, many familiar faces among them. *I thought they were dead.*

"Evita," one of them said. "You're back."

"You had us worried," said another.

"I... did?" Her gaze passed over the Changers, pausing on Vekka and Izaura. *How is this possible?* Hadn't she found them dead in a net on top of the forest canopy, speared with arrows?

"Yes, Evita," said Vekka. "You're our leader, aren't you? We'd be lost without you."

As Evita watched, mute with disbelief, the Changers began to cheer. Chanting her name. She shuddered, a visceral dread gripping her like the claws of a large beast.

Then she made the mistake of looking down.

Chirp was no longer there. Evita was floating in the air, supported by nothing but her cloak, at the head of the chanting Changers.

"Stop!" She squeezed her eyes shut and lowered her

arms. Her cloak released her, and she tumbled out of the sky.

Chirp screeched, his claw catching her leg, and the remnants of the scene scattered like falling leaves. Gasping, Evita hung upside down, the world reeling below her and not a single Changer within sight.

None of it had been real. The fog had created an illusion that had come close to making her fall to her death. With Chirp's help, she scrambled back onto his back and clung tightly to his neck. He was real and solid enough to counter some of her dread, but it took a great effort for her to risk lifting her head again.

The fog shifted a little, revealing a dim view of the mountain paths. The peaks remained engulfed in grey, but far more alarming was the sight of a wall of fog, rolling southward as though propelled by an invisible force.

In fact, she was certain the fog was heading directly for Saudenne. Evita couldn't begin to make sense of her own vision, but a mass illusion spell falling over the capital could only end in disaster.

Where had the images she'd seen come from? Her own thoughts and memories, she assumed, but not her desires. Evita had seen herself become respected, the Changers' leader— but she'd never been devoted to the Changers' cause and had never truly wanted to rise in their ranks.

If simple confusion had been the intent, though, then the spell had succeeded. Had Aurel been shown a similar vision, assuming she'd survived the fall?

As for the people of the city... the timing couldn't be coincidental. This must be Daimos's final gambit. He'd intended for the people of Saudenne to be engulfed in utter confusion at the very moment when their supposed war with Aestin was intended to kick off.

And if Aestin truly did intend to attack Zeuten, her allies would be faced with a war they couldn't possibly win.

———

"So much for that idea." Back outside the tower, Zelle pointed the staff at the doorway. "Close the door."

The staff took longer to close the doorway than the last one, and several tense moments passed before the light winked out and revealed the lingering fog on the other side. Had Invicten's magic somehow sapped some of the Shaper's power? It couldn't be possible, especially not on Her own territory.

You're incorrect.

"That's not reassuring at all." Zelle held out the staff in an attempt to illuminate the fog, but the thick greyness remained impenetrable. "Does this spell go beyond the mountains? Is the rest of Zeuten affected, too?"

There is a high chance that it is, yes.

Throat dry, Zelle turned back towards the tower. "If a Relic is causing the fog, you must be able to sense it."

Not if it isn't within my domain.

"It isn't?" She'd have to take the staff's word for it on that, because she couldn't *see* any of the Shaper's domain beyond the door of the tower. Glimpsing her grandmother's blurred face on the other side of the tower window, she nudged the door open and darted inside before the fog crept in.

Grandma hadn't budged from her spot in the armchair. "Well?"

Zelle drew in a breath. "One or more of Invicten's Relics is causing the fog, but Daimos's deity assistants don't know where it's hidden. Or they won't tell me."

"And does the Shaper know?" Grandma didn't sound surprised to hear that Daimos had deities assisting him. Zelle might have mentioned the deities in question had had personal experience with the Sentinel, but that conversation would have to wait until a less urgent moment.

"The staff claims it's not in Her domain." Maybe a Changer was flying around carrying the Relic, or it had been hidden in one of the valleys. "The dragonet isn't likely to be able to find the tower in this fog, so I can't search from the sky. I need the Sanctum's help."

Zelle climbed to the upper floor and began undoing the locks on the door, swiftly losing patience. "There's got to be a more efficient way to get in."

The staff didn't reply. She hoped it was conserving its energy and not too weak to communicate, a possibility she'd never thought she'd ever need to consider. Sweat gathered on her palms as Zelle continued to tug at the locks until the outer door came open. She did the same to the inner door, too, and once inside the Sanctum, she broke into a sprint.

Zelle came a breathless halt next to the room containing the book that listed every title in the Sanctum. After a brief pause to catch her breath, she walked up to the pedestal, letting the giant pages of the book fill the edges of her vision.

"Tell me how to get rid of the fog outside," she gasped out. "Please."

You know how, the staff whispered in her ear. *Find and destroy the Relic responsible.*

"I can't do that if I can't see anything." If the Shaper couldn't detect the Relic's location, then her own limited human senses were unlikely to make much headway. "Is there a spell that might help me?"

No ordinary spell will work on that fog. It's a creation of the deity of illusions, after all, and the fog is as much inside your mind as outside of it.

"Then what use are you?" Her temper broke, inching towards despair. "What else am I supposed to do?"

She should have guessed something like this would happen when Jarven at the palace had used his Relic to manipulate her mind, and even the aid of the nameless Shaper hadn't made her completely immune. Yet how could the illusionist's magic have infiltrated the Shaper's own territory? Great Power or not?

There is only one way to best a Great Power: with the aid of another.

"I already have your help." Provisionally, at least.

Not entirely.

"What's that supposed to mean?" She frowned at the staff. "You and I are bound. I wear the godsmark. Isn't that enough?"

There is a way to be more fully bound to a Great Power, but it would require a sacrifice on your part.

"Sacrifice?" The word brought chills to her arms, and a sense of peculiar dread unconnected to the notion of Invicten's magic getting the better of the nameless Shaper.

We would need to merge into one. You would have to let me use your body as if it was my own.

"That's... That is a big sacrifice." The Shaper wanted her to allow Her to walk in this realm through *Zelle? She hadn't known it was even possible to share one's body with a deity, let alone a Great Power.* "Can it be reversed?"

It has never been done before, so I have no idea.

"Powers above." That the Shaper admitted ignorance wasn't a good sign. "What will happen if I refuse and go back to looking for the source of the fog?"

It will spread even farther. I'd be surprised if it hadn't already reached the capital.

"Saudenne?" she exclaimed. "Merciful Powers. I thought Daimos intended to start a war, not... whatever this is."

If Aestin attacked while the capital was gripped by the illusionist's spell, the people of Zeuten would never see it coming. They'd be at an even worse disadvantage than they already were.

A flood of foreboding seized Zelle, and she dragged her attention away from the pedestal. In the corridor behind her, fog seeped through the gaps in the walls and into the Sanctum, threads reaching for the bookshelves like the tentacles of some great beast.

"Shaper, keep it out."

I can't. The staff's voice was quiet.

"Grandma." She broke into a fast stride, and the fog thickened as she walked, brushing against her skin like ghostly fingers.

Rounding a corner, she came to an abrupt halt. Her sister lay sprawled on the stone floor, blood seeping from several wounds in her chest. She was dead.

Zelle looked numbly at Aurel's body for a long moment. Variations of *it's a trick* spun through her mind, but her sister's body certainly appeared to be solid, and her eyes were closed, as if she was sleeping.

"Aurel," she murmured. "Staff, tell me this isn't real."

The staff made no response. Aurel didn't budge, either, and while her wounds continued to drip blood onto the flagstones, there was no sign of their cause. No. She couldn't be real… but how could the Shaper have been silenced by a mere illusion?

"Shaper," she said loudly. "You have another Great Power attacking you right this instant. Inside your Sanctum, no less. What do you plan to do?"

Without waiting for another reply that never came, Zelle wrenched her gaze away from Aurel and continued onward. The fog had already grown thick enough to mask the corridor around her, and it brought little comfort when she turned back and saw that Aurel had vanished too.

As she jogged around a corner, Zelle tripped on a gap between two stones, her knees striking the hard floor.

"Powers above!" Wondering if she'd broken both kneecaps, she bit the inside of her cheek and pushed upright. The throbbing pain in her knees at least reassured her she was awake and not caught in an elaborate trick of the illusionist's, at least, and the fog receded when she reached the door.

With careful hands, Zelle opened the door and slipped into the short corridor between the inner and outer doors of the Sanctum. The fog had yet to get that far, but it was only a matter of time before it did. After slamming the door behind her, she redid all the locks and then did the same for the outer door too. Her knees protested when she descended the stairs into the downstairs room of the tower, where Grandma stood at the window, watching the fog pressing against the glass.

"Grandma." The image of Aurel's body lying on the floor pushed into her mind's eye again, and she faltered. "Are you definitely real?"

"What kind of question is that?"

Zelle's shoulders slumped with momentary relief. She hobbled to the armchair and sank into it, wincing at another throb of pain in her knees. "I saw Aurel, dead on the ground, but she wasn't real. The fog…"

"It's in the Sanctum." Grandma's tone was grim. "That means it's already too late."

Zelle squeezed her eyes shut. "Then he's got his wish. Daimos has."

How far did the illusion stretch? All the way to Aestin? Jarven had already convinced the palace that Aestin was plotting against them, and if this illusion backed up his claims, then Zeuten would be drawn into war before she knew it. Especially if he'd woven a similar spell over the imperial palace in Aestin.

"I hope you aren't giving up," said Grandma.

Zelle lifted her chin, eyes opening again. "You said it was too late, didn't you?"

"Then why did you go to the Sanctum at all?" Grandma challenged her. "I thought you planned to ask the Shaper for advice."

Zelle grimaced. "The staff gave me one suggestion, but you won't like it."

"Go on."

"The Shaper wants us to merge into one being." She

spoke without meeting her grandmother's eyes. "I'd have to give my body over to Her in order to fight Invicten's illusions."

A moment passed before her grandmother replied. "You know not to trust the gods, especially that one."

"I know." Was the Shaper telling the complete truth? That she couldn't be sure of, but the danger from Invicten's spell was clear enough, and she'd already forged one unbreakable bond between herself and the Shaper. Zelle held up her arm to examine the swirling marks. "I don't think we have many other options, to tell you the truth."

"You're right," Grandma said. "But it's your choice, Zelle."

If she gambled on the Shaper and lost, humanity might pay the price. A Great Power given access to a human body—*her* body, in fact—would have consequences. They might lose the war regardless, or she might find herself utterly subsumed by the nameless Shaper's will.

Then again, could it be worse than Daimos using Invicten's Relics to drive two nations into war against one another? It took one Great Power to beat another, after all.

"What about Gaiva?" she asked aloud.

She is nowhere within reach.

"The others went to Itzar," she said. "They might have requested her help."

But she knew the odds were low of Gaiva opting to interact with Aurel or Evita. She hadn't been thrilled to speak to the Shaper, unsurprising given their contentious history, and Zelle couldn't see Her agreeing to an alliance with Her sibling.

Give up on the notion of Gaiva showing Herself, Zelle, the staff told her.

"Even if Invicten tries to destroy humanity? Wasn't it Gaiva who created humans and wanted to protect us?"

Gaiva is not coming. I am all you have.

The staff was right, unfortunately. The Shaper was their only hope.

She drew in a breath and spoke to the staff. "If I wanted to do as you suggested, where should I start?"

Go back into the Sanctum.

———

Rien watched Martzel manipulate the locks on his cell door before opening it to let him out. "Where are the guards?"

"Distracted or subdued. It isn't important."

"I need my staff," he said. "I can't leave it behind."

"We'll find it." Martzel turned away from the cells. "Otherwise, don't stop for anything."

He hobbled ahead of Rien, who hurried past the neighbouring cells, most of which were unoccupied. The sound of muffled footsteps sounded from upstairs, but Martzel gave them no acknowledgement.

Upon reaching a room at the end of the row of cells, Martzel produced another key he must have swiped from the guard and opened it to reveal a number of shelves containing the confiscated weapons taken from prisoners. Rien's staff lay on a table, easy to recognise by the thorns protruding from its wooden edges. Crimson droplets scattered on the floor and table, confirming the Relic had put up a fight against the guards who'd taken it from him.

Anger didn't mean loyalty, though. Rien hesitated for a heartbeat—long enough for Martzel to give him an impatient nod—before he picked it up. He'd been braced to feel the sharp prick of thorns, but it didn't come. Zierne's Relic's anger hadn't dimmed—its crimson glow and the occasional spasm of pain in his godsmark were proof of that—but they were still bound together.

"What's going on out there?" He joined Martzel at the door, and they left the room behind them. "What do you mean, the city's under attack? From where?"

"The sea," Martzel replied. "The Emperor put out a call for all warships to mobilise, and the Invokers are heading for the port."

"Merciful Powers." It wasn't genuinely an attack from Zeuten, was it? No, it could easily be the work of Daimos's allies, but given Daimos's own influence in Zeuten itself, nothing was certain.

Rien and Martzel climbed the stairs to the upper level. Since most of the guards were too busy following orders to grab weapons and mobilise to head to the seafront, they were able to dodge patrols with relative ease and make their way to the exit.

At the palace's rear entrance, they found their carriage waiting on the other side of the gates, with Reyes and Sanne peering through the curtains.

"There you are." Reyes reached out to help his father climb into the carriage, and when he was seated, Rien joined him.

"How'd you get away?" Rien asked the others as the carriage began to move. "Weren't you in the middle of it all?"

"We left the palace when His Imperial Majesty ordered

us to," explained Reyes. "Not long after, a report came in from the seafront of attacks on the port towns and another fleet approaching the capital."

"Which fleet, exactly?" Rien asked. "Does Zeuten even *have* any warships?"

"I wouldn't know," said Reyes. "Powers above, did you really get into a fight with the Emperor?"

"No, I exposed the traitor in his guard and broke his Relic," he explained. "No thanks to Luvid Trevain. I thought I had him subdued, but he must have slipped out of the palace."

Martzel swore. "I'm sure he had other allies in there."

"*I'm* sure it was his family who let Daimos into the city in the first place," Rien added. "That's how they were primed to take advantage of Daimos's takeover. They betrayed my family to spare themselves."

"I haven't seen him," Sanne said. "Scumbag. We'll get him."

The carriage rattled through the streets, having to dodge a fair bit of foot traffic coming from the direction of the harbour. The Emperor's guards must have warned the public to leave, as the market stalls were in disarray, some abandoned, others knocked over by fleeing customers hurrying away from the docks.

A thought hit Rien like a lightning bolt. "The Trevains ran a stall at the market."

"Huh?" Reyes studied his face.

"They were selling Relics," said Rien. "Luvid never said if that was part of their plan, but I wonder…"

"Speculate later." Martzel peered out through a gap in the curtains. "We're almost there."

"Don't go to the seafront," Sanne told the driver. "We'll get out here and walk the rest of the way."

"Coming?" Reyes beckoned to Rien. "Sarpe will kill me for this, by the way. I didn't drop by Linas's place in case someone from the palace followed me."

They leapt out of the carriage and ran towards the docks. Ahead of them lay the glistening expanse of the ocean, dotted with boats—and marred with what appeared to be a wall of fog creeping from the direction of Zeuten. Several ships were visible within, but he couldn't make out who they belonged to. They didn't fly Zeuten's flags, at least, but the Emperor seemed to have taken this threat as seriously as a real declaration of war. Groups of Invokers from the palace gathered on the seafront, holding staffs and other Relics in their hands. Others had boarded the Emperor's ships, no doubt intending to pursue their adversaries. Around the harbour, the fog was thick enough that he could only recognise the Emperor's ships thanks to the bright-blue flags on each mast.

To find the source of the spell—if it was indeed a spell—Rien would have to find a boat of his own... but one mistake might see him cast into a watery grave.

Rien reached the seafront, slowing his pace. At the very front of the ships facing the harbour, one vessel stood out, larger than the others. A lone figure stood out on the deck, and even from here, a piercing mixture of pain and anger hit him in the core. He knew exactly who the man was, and the crimson staff in his left hand confirmed his guess.

Naxel Daimos.

29

Zelle's heart pounded in her ears as she worked at the locks on the inner door to the Sanctum for the second time. Her instincts urged her to stay far away from the creeping fog, but if she stayed downstairs, it was only a matter of time before it reached her and her grandmother anyway.

In the time she'd been gone, the fog had advanced even farther into the Sanctum. When she opened the door, a dense layer of whiteness covered the shelves, obscuring the rows of leather-bound volumes. If she couldn't dispel the fog, the only path forward was directly through. The staff's light didn't make a dent in the fog, but by extending it in front of her, she'd at least be able to avoid colliding with the walls. Her knees throbbed faintly from her earlier fall, but she ignored the pain and pushed on.

Movement stirred in her peripheral vision. Before she could help herself, her head turned, and her mouth went dry. A body lay sprawled on the floor, dead. A man.

Rien.

Keep walking, the staff told her. *He can't possibly be here, can he? He's in Aestin.*

No. He couldn't be here. There was no logical reason for him to be in the Sanctum, and that knowledge dragged her attention away. Keeping her gaze on the blue glow of the staff, she walked on.

Aurel's body was next to appear, sprawled on her back with her sightless eyes fixed on the ceiling. Her body lay in a different spot to the last time, designed to block Zelle's path so she had no choice but to look at her sister's corpse.

"You'll have to try harder, Invicten," Zelle muttered.

She pressed onward through the fog-wreathed corridors until she once again stood on the brink of the room containing the pedestal. Even there, the chill of the fog penetrated her to the bone. Her knees protested when she shuffled over to the pedestal and leaned over the book. "Maybe I should look up a healing spell first."

There isn't one.

"Great." She addressed the book in front of her. "How... How do I merge myself with the nameless Shaper?"

There is no book in here that can tell you how to do that.

The staff's words made her jerk back from the pedestal. "Then what was the point in all this?"

You need to enter my prison in order to perform the binding.

"Binding." Her head snapped up. "It's like a Relic. You want *me* to be the Relic."

Yes and no. Very few Relics are conscious, as you know well.

"Gaiva's rock is—was," she corrected herself. "And the staff too."

Exactly.

"But the rock and the staff weren't already conscious before they became Relics," said Zelle. "Does that mean your consciousness will replace mine?"

Not entirely, but I will have access to both your body and mind. I would call it an equal partnership, but between a human and a Great Power, there is no such thing as equal.

"At least you're being honest with me." Zelle's hands clenched. "I won't let you take over my body and mind, Shaper."

You have no choice. I have power you do not, and you have access to a physical form. I would call it a fair exchange.

The truth sank into Zelle like the point of a blade. The Shaper had needed her help from the start for this very reason. Her imprisonment limited Her ability to move around and interact with the world, and the staff came with its own limitations. Ultimately, a Great Power's consciousness was too strong to be contained within a regular Relic, and instead, a living human would have to give themselves up as a host.

The fog drew closer, wrapping around the pedestal. An unpleasant thought entered Zelle's mind. If she was vulnerable to the illusionist's spell despite her bond with the Shaper, what would happen if the Shaper grew too weak to bring her back to her senses?

I already told you, said the staff. *Invicten desires nothing more than to destroy humanity. He has always envied you for taking Gaiva away from Him, and He will never forgive you for allying with me.*

Another horrible possibility struck her. If the fog kept creeping through the Sanctum, would it eventually reach the Shaper's prison? What would happen then? The Shaper's imprisoned form was trapped, unable to flee or strike back in Her own defence... except through Zelle.

Exactly.

Heart beating wildly, she drew in a breath. "I'll do it."

The book filled her vision, drawing her into blank whiteness until she found herself hovering in the void of the Shaper's prison. At least the fog didn't appear to have reached this far, but the hazy whiteness of her surroundings would make it difficult to tell. How much damage could the Sanctum take before the Shaper withdrew and left Zelle to die?

Will you bind yourself fully to me? asked the Shaper.

"I will. Tell me what to do."

The staff jerked in her hand. A blue glow suffused its wooden edges, spreading to the marks on Zelle's hands and wrists until her eyes screwed up against the glare.

A sense of openness tugged at her mind, similar to when she used the Shaper's magic to sense the world around her and feel the connections beyond the reach of her physical senses. This time, however, it didn't stop, the sense of openness expanding until she could sense the very roots of the mountains below.

With this newfound expansion came the profound realisation that she was no longer alone in her head. A consciousness lurked at the edges of hers, like a mountain towering over a small hill, one she couldn't look directly at without surrendering her sanity.

With a gasp, she staggered backwards, away from the pedestal. The Shaper's prison had faded as if she'd never left the room at all, but everything had changed now Zelle was sharing her body and mind with another person, another being who was fundamentally *not* human. She clutched her head with one hand, reeling with dizziness at the sudden expansion of her awareness. The Sanctum itself felt understandable in a way it never had before, as if she could shift the very stones beneath her feet if she so desired.

Yet the Sanctum was only one small part of her newfound awareness, which extended from one end of the Range to the other, encompassing every rock and strand of grass. Even the living things, which weren't creations of the Shaper's magic, were within her perception. Including... *Evita. Aurel.* She sensed them both—closer than she'd expected, on the path outside the tower.

They're alive, she thought, and it came with a rush of relief that the thought *was* hers, despite another being now sharing her mind.

If you want them to stay that way, then get rid of that fog. The staff's voice didn't *sound* any different, despite coming from directly inside her head, but its tone hit her with more urgency than she'd expected, as if its feelings— the Shaper's feelings—were bleeding into her own.

Zelle reached outward with her senses in the hopes of finding the Relic responsible for causing the fog, but the sheer vastness of her new awareness made it difficult to figure out where to direct her focus.

A tendril of fog snaked past her face, away from the pedestal. Wait. The fog was in retreat, seeping out of the Sanctum and through the cracks in the walls through which it had entered.

"I didn't even do anything," she murmured. "Is that me?"

We are stronger together, the Shaper whispered in her mind.

Yes, they might be, but at what price? Had she lost part of herself in accepting the Shaper's offer? How much control did the Shaper have over her actions?

You haven't lost anything, only gained more than you can ever imagine.

"We'll see," she said aloud. "The fog's still outside… and I don't know where to look for the Relic."

Like I said, Invicten's Relic isn't in the mountains. At least, not within reach of my senses.

Zelle stepped away from the pedestal. Even the pain in her knees had faded as the fog retreated from the Sanctum, and the absence of grisly visions of dead family members was a welcome improvement.

"Let's go back down to Grandma," she said. "I'm sure she's waiting to yell at me."

Zelle's grandmother did not yell at her. Instead, she sighed. "Really, Zelle. You had to volunteer to share your mind with a god, didn't you?"

"It wasn't exactly optional," she said. "It takes one Great Power to beat another."

"I have no doubt that's true, Zelle, but sharing your *mind* with one of them isn't the same as wielding their Relic."

"I'd worked that much out for myself." Zelle paced the room, uncertain if she felt restless or exhausted, but knowing she could do little from inside the outpost. She caught sight of her reflection in the window glass. The marks on her arms had brightened a little, but as far as outside appearances went, little had changed. That might have been the most disturbing part, and it made her want to avoid her own eyes. Instead, she turned back to her grandmother. "Are you going to stay here? The fog isn't inside the Sanctum any longer, but I can't guarantee it'll stay that way."

"I won't be any safer on the ground," she said. "I came here intending to use the outpost as my base."

"All right," said Zelle, doubtfully. "I wouldn't advise you to go walking outside. The weather's terrible."

Her grandmother didn't seem amused at her attempt to lighten the mood. Zelle ought to be able to figure out the general direction the fog came from and pinpoint the Relic using the Shaper's magic, but it might be easier to do so without the overwhelming presence of the Sanctum above her head.

"Let me do the work," the Shaper said.

It took several moments for Zelle to realise *she'd* been the one who'd spoken aloud.

"Don't start using my mouth to talk," she told the other presence in her mind. "People will think I'm unhinged."

Admittedly, that kind of confusion was to be expected when one had an extra person sharing one's body and mind. Nobody who spoke to her would be able to tell who was replying.

I think it's too late to worry about that. Or should that be "we think"?

"Stop that." Zelle pressed a hand to her forehead. "I'd like to keep at least *some* of my sanity, thanks."

Still, she obeyed the Shaper's suggestion and reached out with her newly honed senses, allowing her awareness to move wherever it was prompted. The fog had already begun its retreat from her current location, but it was moving southward, towards the Changers' base—and towards the capital.

Aurel opened her eyes, finding herself lying on the mountain path. Her wounded arm throbbed, but she was otherwise unhurt. Not a trace of the trees nor the Reader's house was to be seen, nor the staff… which had been in her *hand* the last time she'd been aware.

Where had that vison come from? Was the fog to blame? She had no other explanation, but in the time that she'd been unconscious, the view of the peaks had begun to clear.

Trails of grey drifted south, and a winged shape appeared in the haze an instant before the dragonet landed beside her.

"Aurel!" Evita leaned over Chirp's side. "You're alive."

"I am." Aurel decided against mentioning the role Evita had played in the bizarre vision she'd seen. "Where'd this fog come from?"

"I was hoping you knew." Evita looked up and down the mountain path. "We must be close to the tower. We need Zelle's help to destroy the Relic responsible."

"You think it's Invicten's work?" Aurel let Evita help her climb back onto the dragonet's back, but before they took off, a tremor ran through the ground beneath them. Aurel dug her fingers into Chirp's scales to keep from tumbling off his back. "That was Zelle, right?"

"I think so," Evita replied. "I *hope* so. Let's find her."

They flew up the path, the fog continuing to drift south. When Aurel twisted to look behind her, she was alarmed to see it creeping downward across the Range and towards the coastline.

"It's heading for Saudenne," Evita told her. "Someone ought to warn the palace guard, if they haven't already."

"You want to go and warn the Crown Prince?" Aurel said incredulously. "Are you out of your mind? Weren't the Changers meant to be going there?"

"Yes." Evita's shoulders slumped with visible relief when the tower came into view. "Zelle."

"Thank the Powers." Aurel leaned forward on Chirp's back to wave at her sister, who closed the tower door behind her.

"Good, you're back." Zelle's eyes were wide, her hair dishevelled, the knees of her trousers torn where she must have fallen on hard stone.

"We are." Evita loosened her grip when Chirp landed. "I take it you know that fog was caused by Invicten's magic?"

Zelle inclined her head. "It even got into the Sanctum, but I managed to drive it out."

"It got *where?*" Aurel studied her sister, trying to pinpoint what was different about her appearance. The wild, half-crazed look in her eyes wasn't characteristic of Zelle, nor was the restless energy in the way she paced on the spot. "How did you get rid of it?"

"Ah… I had to do something risky."

"Like what?" asked Evita.

Zelle's gaze dropped. "The Shaper and I… we merged together. Part of Her consciousness now lives inside my body and mind. It was the only way."

Aurel sat rigidly on the dragonet's back. *She did what?*

"Oh." Evita's voice was quiet, stunned. "Ah—can you get rid of the fog around the capital?"

"Only if I find the Relic causing it... but we can't fit three people on the dragonet."

Aurel opened her mouth to offer to stay behind—though she'd sooner have cut off her own hand—but Evita hopped off Chirp's back first. "I'll fly using the cloak."

"Are you sure?" Aurel asked her, surprised.

"No." Evita ran her fingers over the sleeves of her cloak. "We need to get off this mountain, though, and it's the quickest way."

"Agreed." Zelle climbed onto the dragonet to join Aurel, who tried not to think about the fact that she was about to fly with the nameless Shaper.

Evita stretched out her arms like wings and took a few shaky steps towards the cliff's edge, muttering to herself. "Synchrony... avoid the fog. Please."

The dragonet made chirping noises of encouragement. Aurel's breath caught when Evita tumbled off the edge of the cliff, but the cloak caught her as she fell, and then she flew like a gull on the breeze. Chirp then launched into flight, too, and Aurel and her sister held on as the mountain path shrank below them.

"I thought you were in Itzar," Zelle said to Aurel.

"We were, until this morning," she replied. "We went to ambush the Senior Changers. The Blessed turned down their offer anyway, but we stopped them from trying to recruit the villagers."

"Bet that stung."

"They weren't happy," said Aurel, with some satisfaction. "It doesn't mean we're out of trouble yet, considering we ran into the Changers again on our way back, and they were heading for the capital. They think the Crown Prince called them in to go to war with Aestin."

Zelle swore under her breath. "Or someone did."

Daimos.

With the fog lifting, they could see the rolling countryside beneath them as they flew. Zelle went oddly quiet, or maybe it wasn't that odd, if she had an extra person sharing her body. Aurel hadn't known it was even possible for a person to become a vessel for a deity.

After a long stretch of silence, Zelle shifted, pointing ahead of them. "Is it just me, or is something approaching the shore?"

Aurel squinted past the wall of fog smothering the distant houses of Saudenne. Between patches of fog, she glimpsed ships and boats, docked and abandoned. No surprise, given the fog creeping down the mountains and inching up the coast... but out at sea, a patch of darkness rippled across the water.

"I think it might be Daimos's forces," Zelle said. "I can sense... people. Though it might be an illusion."

"You can *sense* them?"

Fog surrounded the entire southern peak of the Range, forcing them to fly around and approach the city from the side instead of the north. As they flew lower, an arrow whipped past Aurel's ear.

Zelle lifted her head. "I think we have company."

30

Rien faced Daimos across the expanse of sea, taking in the blurred but unmistakable sight of the man who'd ripped his old life away. The crimson staff glowing in his hands brought a familiar ache to Rien's chest, and his left hand throbbed.

"I need to get out there," he said to Reyes. "On a boat. Any boat."

Daimos was goading him with his presence here, he was sure, but Rien counted at least ten other vessels approaching the harbour. How had Daimos recruited so many people? Or were they all illusory creations of Invicten's magic? He'd have to get closer to find out, and most of the harbour's other ships had either moved out of the way or were being boarded by the Emperor's soldiers.

Sanne swore under her breath. "Where'd Daimos get that ship? Did he steal it from us?"

Rien squinted across the water at Daimos's vessel. "Probably, yes. I have to get over there."

"Do you have a boat hidden somewhere?" Sanne made an exasperated noise when Rien ran down the seafront, Reyes hurrying behind him. The Emperor's soldiers would no doubt raise a fuss if he sneaked onto one of their boats, but short of growing wings, he was out of any other options.

"Hang on." Reyes halted in his tracks. "Is it just me, or are those boats facing away from us?"

"They are." Even Daimos's vessel was moving in the opposite direction, despite his own gaze remaining fixed on Rien. "Powers above. I bet they're going to Zeuten."

Sanne came to a breathless halt. "What would give you that idea?"

"I think Daimos intends to make Zeuten think his army has been sent directly by Aestin, and when the Emperor's forces catch up with them, Zeuten's army will assume they're both on the same side. It's a war of his own design."

Rien would be wasting his time trying to convince anyone here that that Zeuten wasn't to blame. To most of the Emperor's forces, he was a murderer at worst, a coward at best, and there was little he could do to mitigate the damage to his reputation in time to stop Daimos from reaching Zeuten—and Zelle.

Rien tracked Daimos's ship with his eyes as he marched down the seafront towards one of the Emperor's war vessels.

"Arien, do you not remember that you were recently in the Emperor's jail?" Reyes called after him. "You can't show your face in front of his soldiers if you don't want to end up back where you started."

"Then can't you distract them?" He backed into the

shadow of a warehouse, wishing he wasn't so damned recognisable, until Reyes overtook him.

"Fine." Reyes marched towards the boats and called to the nearest group of soldiers, "Where do the Invokers sign up?"

"You're too late to join them," answered a young soldier with a shaved head. "The Trevains are already leaving."

"The Trevains." Rien forgot about his intention to stay hidden, moving forward to scan the boats leaving the harbour. Sure enough, a large vessel moved in Daimos's wake, and even from a distance, the glow of Relics upon the deck was unmistakeable. "*They're* leading the charge?"

The soldier pointed his rifle at Rien. "You—you should be in the Emperor's custody. Did you help him escape?" He addressed the last question to Reyes.

"We aren't your enemies," Reyes answered. "That man is."

He pointed at the retreating shape of Daimos's boat, recognisable only by the bright crimson glow emanating from the deck.

A cry cut through the soldier's reply. "Help!"

The soldiers' attention turned towards the noise, as did Reyes and Rien. A woman past, frantically pointing out to sea. "My son is out there. He took my son!"

"Took him?" Rien echoed. "Who?"

"Mine too." An elderly man came over to join her, wheezing, and halted in front of the stupefied soldiers. "He was on one of those boats."

"Which boats?" Not the blue-flagged Emperor's vessels, most of which hadn't left the docks yet. "Not Daimos's fleet?"

"Who?" The woman's eyes bulged when she spotted Rien's staff. "He had a staff like that. The man who took them."

"Daimos." Rien glanced at the Emperor's soldiers to be sure they were listening to every word. "What did he do?"

"He came to our doorstep," the elderly man said. "My son walked straight out the door, didn't even say goodbye. I saw a whole group of them walking towards those boats…"

Oh, Powers. Had Daimos recruited Tauvice's citizens to fight for him? Evidently he had, and the noise had drawn the attention of other nearby citizens. Several others approached the soldiers, calling out their own stories and pleas for help.

"Powers above," Reyes murmured. "I think my dad has been busy."

Sure enough, Martzel hobbled along behind the group of newcomers, an expression of satisfaction on his face. Reyes let out an exclamation of surprise when Sarpe emerged from behind his father and hurried over to embrace him.

"What are you doing?" Reyes said. "You can't be here."

"I might say the same to you," Sarpe said. "We had to do something to help you."

The two of them must have been talking to the locals and had figured out where Daimos had recruited his army from, but how had they mobilised everyone so fast? Martzel had been too busy going back and forth from the palace, he'd thought—but the sight of another familiar figure near the back answered that question. *Linas.*

The soldiers were soon surrounded, and several disembarked their ship to ask questions of the new arrivals on the pier.

"You said your son went on one of those boats?" a soldier asked the elderly man. *"Did he give any reasons?"*

"No." The man faltered. "Well... he's been talking about training as an Invoker for weeks. We have no gift for magic in the family ourselves, but he bought this Relic from the market..."

Rien didn't hear the rest. Two words rang in his mind: *Relic. The market.*

Luvid Trevain's face flashed before his eyes, and he turned sharply towards the speaker. "What kind of magic did this Relic offer him?"

"I... I couldn't say," replied the old man, his brow scrunching up. "He was acting strangely when he brought it home, now that I think about it."

Invicten. This man's son had purchased a Relic from the market, and it had somehow bewitched him into joining Daimos.

"It wasn't Luvid Trevain who sold him that Relic, by any chance?" Rien lifted his gaze to the soldiers and pointed at the retreating boats with his staff. "Listen to these people's stories. Their loved ones are on their way to a war they're unprepared for, under a bewitchment caused by Daimos and his allies. He's counting on you being willing to sacrifice your own people."

"It's true!" the first woman who'd arrived at the pier shouted out. "My son went with them. He's never been on a boat before."

"It's those Relics!" exclaimed a middle-aged noble. "Those Invokers bewitched them all. My son is innocent!"

The rest of the crowd moved towards the soldiers, shouting their own grievances, and Rien caught sight of Martzel beckoning him over. He made his way through the crowd of panicking locals and found Sanne standing beside her father.

"There's a boat over there, unmanned," Martzel told him. "If you move fast, you can catch up to those Trevain scum."

"Good," said Rien. "You're not coming with me."

"I am." Reyes broke away from his embrace with Sarpe, who gave him an exasperated look.

"I'm guessing I can't talk you out of this one?"

"Definitely not," said Reyes. "Rien needs someone who knows their way around a boat. I want to see that Luvid Trevain sink into the ocean myself."

"Thank you for this," Rien said to Martzel and Linas. "I won't forget it."

Leaving the soldiers occupied by the shouting locals, Rien made his way to the boat that Martzel had pointed out, which bobbed against the shore.

Reyes hurried to keep pace with him. "Have you ever sailed before?"

"Some years ago," Rien answered. "We'll have to move fast to catch up to the others."

He jumped off the pier into the small wooden boat, which rocked underfoot. Hardly a match for a war vessel, but he'd once fought off a sea monster in the Isles of Itzar from a mere rowing boat, so he'd faced worse odds.

He just had to ignore the sound of his heart pounding and the warning pain in his hand that reminded him that Zierne's Relic hadn't yet forgiven him for letting the guards take his staff away.

Reyes untethered the boat, and they drifted outward into the harbour. The wind caught their sails almost at once, but the Invokers had a head start, and with the thick fog gathering over the water, they'd be lucky not to crash into another boat. Their smaller vessel would have a speed advantage over the heavier ships equipped for war, though, so they kept moving forward, watching for any signs of the Trevains.

They'd been sailing for several minutes when Reyes exclaimed, "There they are!"

The large vessel they'd seen leaving the harbour appeared ahead of them. Rien watched the ship from behind, readying himself to jump.

"What are you doing?" Reyes asked.

Rien glanced at him. "I'm going to swim over to them. If we get any closer, we'll run the risk of them spotting us first."

Reyes cursed. "Right, of course you are."

Before he had the chance to second-guess himself, Rien dove into the water. The water was freezing cold, while the staff in his hand and his heavy cloak were impediments, but determination pushed him onward as he swam to the other vessel.

Holding on tightly to his staff with one hand, he clambered upward and onto the deck. Several people exclaimed when they saw his dripping-wet appearance, but he ignored them and reached over the edge with his free hand to pull Reyes out of the water.

"Hello, there," Reyes told the bewildered Invokers on the deck. "I think we're commandeering this ship."

Zelle sat atop the dragonet behind her sister and concentrated on ignoring the other presence lurking in her mind. The second arrow that skimmed past them was rather more difficult to overlook, however.

"Someone shot at us!" yelped Aurel.

"I know, but we can't stop." Zelle held on tightly to Chirp's back, looking around for any signs of their pursuers. "Where did Evita go?"

They'd lost sight of her cloak amid the thickening fog near the Changers' peak, but a faint shimmering silver light told her their enemies were close. Zelle used the staff to deflect another arrow, following it to its source. As she'd expected, several Changers hovered in flight, bows and arrows at the ready.

"Get out of the way." She held up the staff in warning. "I'm not your enemy. In fact, if you think we're going to war with Aestin, then I thought I was supposed to be on your side."

"Hey!" Evita spoke from within the fog, her cloak billowing around her. "Stop shooting at us."

"You," said one of the Changers. "You betrayed us."

"I really didn't." Evita yelped when another arrow skimmed past her. "Don't you have a battle to fight?"

"She's right," one of the Changers said. "It's not worth wasting our energy on the likes of them. Aestin will be here soon."

"No, they won't," Zelle muttered, but she didn't push the issue. Instead, she urged the dragonet to fly lower, dropping out of the Changers' line of sight.

Evita caught up to them, emerging from the grey, and Zelle was impressed at how well she kept her balance despite the fog sweeping around them and towards the city. Peaked roofs stood out amid the grey, while the expanse of the ocean glittered beyond. Dark shapes were visible against the blue. Boats? No, they were too large, surely.

"Fuck," Aurel said quietly. "Look at that."

Zelle squinted, following her sister's gaze, and her mouth went dry. They *were* boats but massive war vessels the likes of which she'd only seen in books about Aestin's military prowess. From this high up, she couldn't see how many there were, but they doubtless outnumbered Zeuten's own paltry forces.

"I suppose it's too much to hope that they're all an illusion?" Zelle gave a brittle laugh. "Do *they* have the Relic, I wonder? If so, then prying it out of the enemy's hands is going to be tricky."

"Or impossible." Evita flew alongside them, her head peeking out from under her hood and her eyes wide with shock. "That might not be Aestin's actual army, but the Changers and the Crown Prince will think it is."

"I know." Zelle was silent for a moment, thinking hard. "I can't sense the Relic from up here. The Shaper's magic is more effective on the ground."

"Where is it, then?" Aurel twisted in her seat, gesturing at the grey haze sweeping over the city. "If the fog's coming from the Relic, then it's in at least three places at once."

"There's more than one." Given that Zelle had already destroyed two, then it shouldn't be a surprise that Daimos had been prepared. "It shouldn't be an issue, but I need to be on the ground to find them."

Chirp flew lower, over the city, following Zelle's directions. When they neared the docks, Aurel gave her a questioning look. "You want to land there?"

"I should be able to sense the Relic even if it's out at

sea." The Shaper's magic didn't work as effectively from the air, but she'd manipulated the sea's currents in Itzar when she'd held a fraction of the Shaper's power in her hands. Even if Daimos had stashed the Relics away from the shore, finding them wouldn't be any trouble. "I'll be all right."

As for everyone else? That depended on whether she destroyed the Relics before Daimos's warships reached the shore... and whether the rest of humanity could weather the storm of the nameless Shaper being active in their realm once again.

They landed, and Zelle climbed off Chirp's back. She raised the staff, and the Shaper answered her call, Her consciousness sweeping in.

Find those Relics. Destroy them.

When Zelle was on the ground, Evita landed beside her, visibly relieved to no longer be airborne. Aurel, meanwhile, remained sitting on the dragonet's back. "Where now?"

"Someone ought to warn the palace," she said. "Tell them Zelle is here to help."

"Are you sure they won't start firing arrows at us again?" Aurel glanced at her sister, who faced the seafront with her hand clenched around her staff. "If they target Zelle when the Shaper's in control, I doubt that'd end well for them."

Evita inclined her head. "If she's sharing her mind with a deity, she might not even notice them."

That didn't strike Aurel as a cause for celebration. "I

suppose we'll have to hope that she still retains some will of her own."

Zelle was alone on the seafront, though the absence of any royal guards was notable. Did they even know an army of ships was fast approaching their shores?

Evita climbed up to join Aurel on the dragonet's back. "Chirp, fly us to the palace."

"Hang on a moment," Aurel said. "Are you sure that's a wise idea?"

"We have to warn them," said Evita. "The Changers as well as the Crown Prince."

"That hasn't worked out so well for us in the past. Also, did I mention I broke the Crown Prince's windows?"

"I attacked the Changers' leader," Evita reminded her. "We have to move. If we stay down here, that fog might start throwing illusions at us again."

Aurel hadn't known that Evita had seen anything in the fog like she had, but now wasn't the time to ask for the details. "Fair point."

Even in the sky, it was hard to avoid the encroaching grey mass sweeping throughout the streets. Chirp made disgruntled noises when they flew uphill and over the upper-class district towards the palace.

Before they reached the gates, however, shouts rang out from below. A contingent of royal guards marched downhill, all armed with swords and bows, while some even carried Aestinian rifles. All of which pointed in their direction.

"Hold on." Aurel suspected no amount of feigned innocence would erase the guards' memories of her last visit to the palace, but it was too late to run. Those arrows could put a hole through the dragonet's wing even from a distance. Not to mention the bullets. "We're not here to fight you. We're here with a warning."

"We don't need a warning from you," said one of the guards. "You brought death upon us yourself the last time you came here."

He had a point, and it drove home why she'd thought warning the palace was a bad idea. Before anyone could move, however, none other than the Crown Prince himself jumped out of a nearby carriage. He wasn't dressed for battle, though he'd forsaken his more ostentatious clothing in favour of a thick coat and boots. He took in the sight of Aurel, sitting on the dragonet's back, with an incredulous stare. "Is Zelle Carnelian with you?"

"My sister's helping to stop the cause of that creepy fog," Aurel told him. "You might not have noticed, but someone called Naxel Daimos is using the Relics of Invicten to provoke a war between Aestin and Zeuten."

"Preposterous," the Crown Prince spluttered. "You're lying. Last time you were in my palace, your sister killed my guard and stole from me, yet you dare to show your face here? You even have the nerve to bring that beast after the damage you caused to my palace?"

"I know we didn't exactly conduct ourselves in an appropriate manner, but we were running on limited time," Aurel said. "Your guard had you under Invicten's spell, and Zelle had to destroy his Relic. Are the Changers here?"

"The Changers are the ones who brought us the warning that a fleet is coming from Aestin to declare war on us," said the Crown Prince "That strikes me as more important than your ridiculous stories."

Aurel's stomach lurched. "Listen, do you really think

Zeuten can win a fight with a nation as huge and magically strong as Aestin?"

"It's that or surrender, and I don't intend to." The Crown Prince retreated into his carriage. "I won't let you waste any more of my time."

It wasn't exactly a blessing, but at least the guards didn't shoot at them when the dragonet took flight. Most likely they didn't want to waste their bullets or arrows, but it'd take a while for them to march to the seafront, and Aurel could already see the outlines of war vessels on the horizon. *They looked too real to be an illusion, and if the speed by which they were approaching the coast was anything to go by, they'd reach shore within minutes.*

We're too late.

31

The ship Rien and Reyes had boarded did indeed contain Luvid Trevain, as well as several other bewitched Invokers and other citizens of Tauvice. The latter did little but watch with expressions of detached curiosity, as if Daimos's orders hadn't covered unexpected incursions. *Powers above, he even got at the other Invokers.*

Trevain himself confronted Rien and Reyes on the deck. "Get off this ship, or I'll throw you overboard myself."

"I don't think so," Reyes lifted his staff. "Did you tell the Emperor you're planning on sacrificing his Invokers in a fake war?"

Rien did likewise. "You don't have the right to kidnap citizens of Aestin to fight your wars, especially ones who have no experience with magic."

"They came here voluntarily," Trevain replied.

"And I suppose they took those Relics of their own accord?" Rien went on. "Without being coerced?"

A smirk flitted across his face. "I'm surprised it took you this long to work it out."

"You're scum." Rien's hand clenched on his staff. "Get off this ship. If you swim fast, you might be lucky enough to reach my boat before it's out of reach."

"Absolutely not," Trevain said. "You might have got the best of me once before, young Astera, but—"

Rien struck him across the face with his staff, knocking him backwards. Reyes's second blow caught him in the chin, sending him toppling backwards into the sea.

"He'll be all right," Reyes said to the onlooking crowd on the deck. "Unfortunately."

Trevain deserved worse, but Rien needed to focus on Daimos and let the Emperor deal with Trevain. Leaving him to swim to the boat they'd left behind, he turned to the bewildered citizens.

"You." Rien addressed a young man who looked to be barely out of his teens. "What did he tell you to do?"

"Take our Relics to Zeuten." A haze clouded the young man's eyes, as if he was listening to orders Rien couldn't hear. "As fast as possible."

"They're causing this creepy fog, right?" Reyes took a step forward. "Tell you what, we can take them off your hands."

"Wait," Rien said in an undertone. "They still outnumber us, and we can't harm innocent people."

"True." Reyes swore. "Wait... where's the harbour gone?"

Rien looked back, eyes widening. The ship was moving at a speed that hadn't been obvious until now, and so was the entire fleet. Given the size of some of their vessels, it didn't seem natural. "There's magic at work."

He couldn't tell where it was coming from, either, but the entire fleet moved at the same high speed. None of the others seemed to notice the creeping grey fog slithering between the vessels. Unlike Trevain, the other people on the boat hadn't gone into this knowing exactly *why* they were being drawn into battle. Or with whom. Separating every one of them from the Relics they carried would be tricky, if not impossible, but the notion of drowning them all in the sea was repellent. He doubted Daimos would care, but unlike his enemy, Rien refused to take a group of innocent people hostage to get to his foe.

Turning to Reyes, he said, "I have to get to Daimos before he reaches the shore."

The curving coastline of Zeuten was already visible in the distance. Alarm flickered inside him, and he scanned the nearby vessels until his gaze snagged on a ship that had fallen behind the others. Daimos's, slowing its pace, as if inviting him to draw closer. A familiar crimson glow brought a spasm of pain to Rien's chest.

"Want to borrow a bow and arrows to knock him into the water?" asked Reyes.

Rien shook his head. "He has Astiva's staff and possibly more of Invicten's Relics too. I'd rather destroy them than risk them sinking to the bottom of the ocean where they can find their way into the enemy's hands again."

"If you're sure." Reyes glared at Daimos's vessel, which was relatively small compared to the others and wasn't equipped with weapons. He hadn't used any magic since his brief span in jail, and Zierne's Relic might not be keen to obey him, but he'd have to hope their shared thirst for vengeance overrode the Relic's annoyance at its wielder.

The crimson glow brightened on the deck of the ship they approached, and his left hand began throbbing as if he'd thrust it into an open flame. He gritted his teeth, but his chest spasmed with every motion that brought them closer to the staff in Daimos's hand. The man himself didn't look surprised that Rien had managed to catch up to him. Unlike his imitator, he didn't wear a copy of Rien's own clothing but an Aestinian-style dark-blue coat and buckled boots. His hair was in the long style of a noble, and a familiar set of crimson lines shone on his left hand.

The mark of Astiva.

Pain shot up Rien's left hand and wrist, causing his grip to tremble on the staff. A smile tilted the edge of Daimos's mouth, as though he was conscious of the effect his Relic had had on its former wielder.

That alone proved this was the real Daimos. Not a double.

Reyes sucked in a breath. "Ready?"

"Yes." Rien's knuckles tightened on his staff. "I'm going to kill him."

Energy rushed through his veins, along with a flood of righteous fury that all but took away the lingering pain in his left hand. Crimson light flared up his own staff, and his new godsmarks ignited. Two of Gaiva's siblings were about to meet face-to-face, or as close as possible in this realm—and Zierne's reaction was pure, breath-taking rage.

"Isn't this a nice little reunion." Daimos held up his free hand to gesture towards the glazed-eyed civilians gathering on the deck of his ship.

"Leave them out of this." Rien raised his voice, projecting it across the water. "This is between the two of us. It always has been, despite your decision to turn a simple revenge scheme into a bid to destroy several nations."

"This was never simple." As he spoke, the civilians lifted their weapons, pointing rifles and swords directly at Rien. "Besides, every member of my army chose to be here. They leapt at the chance to buy those Relics and win a chance at glory. Why wouldn't they, when you and your kind have hoarded the supremacy of magic for a thousand years?"

"Your family held the same status until your father tried to steal our Relics and was justly banished for it." Rien knew that Daimos couldn't have had an easy life in exile, but he'd gone far beyond simple revenge in his machinations. "Release them, and we'll settle this between ourselves, Daimos. I've earned that."

"Our last fight didn't end in your favour, but I'll grant you the honour of a more dignified death this time around." Daimos lifted his hand, and the bespelled civilians lowered their weapons, while a crimson light circled his staff. "I admit that I intended to destroy your Relic rather than claiming it, but it does rather suit me, doesn't it?"

Anger tightened a hard fist over his chest. "Not in the slightest."

"Oh, don't be so dour. You have a replacement, don't you?" His gaze dropped to Rien's staff and the thorns wrapping around the edges. "A remarkable likeness. One might forget that the two were sworn enemies."

The deities. Not the Relics. The two were not the same,

and he'd do well to remember that. Daimos was trying to unbalance him, to gain an edge before their weapons clashed.

"Did you miss him?" Daimos asked softly. "Astiva?"

The name caused an echo of pain to travel up Rien's left hand. The boat rocked underfoot, and he glimpsed Zeuten's coastline drawing closer. If Daimos survived to reach shore, he'd seek out Zelle. Rien had to bring an end to him first.

Even if it meant destroying the last remnant of Astiva along with Daimos.

Daimos raised Astiva's staff, thorns wrapping around the hilt, and Rien mirrored his movement.

This is where it ends.

While the soldiers marched in formation towards the seafront, Aurel held on tight to the dragonet's back as they flew ahead of them.

Evita leaned over Chirp's back. "Look—there she is."

The vibrant blue glow of Zelle's staff stood out even amid the grey, and the dragonet veered towards the docks. Zelle stood completely still, oblivious to the sound of the assembling soldiers in the background, her eyes closed and her expression intent as if she was listening to a voice none of the others could hear.

"You haven't found the Relics yet?"

Zelle's eyes flew open, and the sheer power in her gaze knocked Aurel backwards. A faint blueness had crept into her sister's eyes, but the difference went beyond the hint of colour. Her sister's eyes belonged to someone else entirely, someone not of this world.

"No." Zelle at least *sounded* like herself when she answered. "No, they aren't on the shore. I think they must be out there."

She pointed across the sea, where the rippling fog closed in on them and where the warships would soon be visible from the ground as well as the sea.

"Gaiva's tits," said Evita. "You can't move the entire ocean, can you?"

"I can try," offered Zelle.

"Definitely *not*," *Aurel said firmly.* "You don't want to flood half of Saudenne, do you?"

Zelle didn't look like she cared either way, which was alarming if nothing else, but the sound of a thousand heavy boots marching drew closer. Despite her warning, there was a worrying chance that they'd assume Zelle to be an enemy and strike first—and there was no telling what the nameless Shaper would do to them in retaliation.

"We can help." Evita looked to Aurel for confirmation. "We might be able to see where the fog is coming from if we fly high enough, right?"

Zelle paid them no attention. Short of asking the dragonet to grab her and drag her to safety, they wouldn't have a hope of removing her from the army's sights, but Zeuter's forces were moving on foot, which gave them a little time.

"The Relic must be close to the shore for its illusion to have reached all the way to the Range," Aurel said. "Chirp, can you fly higher?"

Evita repeated her command, and the dragonet

obeyed. Aurel scanned the harbour, where few vessels remained docked, and her gaze snagged on a ship that had been abandoned near the western edge of the city. Or more specifically, the blue Aestinian flag at its mast.

"Does that look suspicious to you?" she murmured to Evita. "Why would anyone abandon their ship next to a city that's about to be under attack?"

An Aestinian vessel wasn't an unusual sight, by any means, but her suspicions grew when they flew closer. Grey fog pressed against the edges of the harbour, swirling in eddies above water and land alike, yet it didn't seem to touch the ship at all.

"Let's look closer." Evita clung to the dragonet's back as he flew lower, angling towards the exposed wooden deck of the vessel.

Nobody appeared to be aboard, but a faint shimmer caught her eye from somewhere on the deck. Aurel leaned over the dragonet's side until her fingertips brushed the wooden deck. Her eyes might have been playing tricks on her, but she'd been sure she'd seen—

A strong hand closed around her injured arm, yanking her off the dragonet's back. She landed hard on the deck, and a voice growled in her ear. "You shouldn't be here."

Aurel squirmed free of his grip and found herself looking up at a man dressed in a well-made red coat and carrying a crimson staff. Wincing at the pain in her injured arm, she took in the man's dark skin and long hair. "You're Aestinian..."

He gave her a firm shove with the staff, and she stumbled across the deck, her feet catching on the edge of an open trapdoor. Evita shouted her name from above, but the same shimmer as before caught Aurel's gaze from the darkness below the open trapdoor. Was the Relic some-where in there? How had this man—this *Invoker*—managed to get into Saudenne's harbour without being spotted? Yes, the fog hid him from view, but the crimson glow from his staff was as bright as a star.

He swung the staff at her, and Aurel threw herself flat on the ship's deck. Recognition hit her at the sight of the crimson thorns wrapping around the staff, despite her certainty that she'd never seen this man before in her life. "You're Naxel Daimos, aren't you?"

He displayed no surprise that she knew his name. Instead, he swung the staff again, causing her to roll side-ways and straight through the open trapdoor.

Aurel tumbled downward into the darkness, squeezing her eyes shut. An instant later, she landed on a surface that felt softer than it ought to.

For a moment, she lay sprawled on her back breath-less. Then she opened her eyes and bit back a scream. Two figures leaned over her, each the size of a person—but that was where the similarities ended. They resem-bled giant birds, one grey and one black.

"Why," said one of the birds, in fluent Zeutenian, "do you humans insist on trespassing in here?"

"Trespassing?" She pushed into a sitting position, a sense of unreality making her head spin. Her surround-ings were foggy, indistinct, and the two man-sized birds were the only living creatures in sight. "You're... not an illusion, are you?"

The large raven-like bird peered at her and spoke in a higher, more feminine voice than the other. "Humans are strange creatures."

'Speak for yourself." Aurel's arm throbbed, which

proved to her that she wasn't trapped in another illusion… and which left only one explanation. "You're… not human, though."

"Well observed," said the dove, whose voice sounded vaguely masculine, but that was pure conjecture on her part. "This one's a little slow, isn't she?"

"I was on a ship a moment ago," she protested. "This place…"

She must have fallen through a doorway into the realm of the Powers. It explained why hitting the ground had barely jarred her injured arm, because nothing here appeared to be entirely solid, formed of a cloud-like substance with nothing to break up the monotony except her two bizarre companions. Deities, undoubtedly, but since when did the deities *talk* to humans? A light drew her gaze upward, and she made out the squarish shape of the doorway above.

Aurel put on a smile. "I don't either of you would like to help me fly out?"

The raven made a derisive noise. "Not a chance, human."

The patch of light shifted as the man who'd shoved her through the doorway leaned over the edge to peer down at her. "You won't be able to cause any more trouble from in there."

"I beg to differ." Did he not know who she was? Maybe he didn't. She didn't carry a visible Relic, unlike Zelle, but she couldn't help feeling a little insulted.

"We'll see." He moved out of sight of the doorway—which vanished, leaving nothing but the blurred surroundings of the realm of the Powers behind.

"What…?" Aurel stared up at the place where the

doorway had been. "How did he do that? I thought humans couldn't close doorways… or most humans can't, anyway."

Her companions didn't say a word, but dread slid down her spine. Daimos had trapped her in the realm of the Powers with two deities who might kill her at any moment. They might have already tried if she hadn't taken them by surprise.

When she reached into the pocket of her coat, her fingers brushed against the Book of Reading. It was of little use as a weapon, but she had no other ideas as to how to find a way out. Heart racing, Aurel pulled the book out of her pocket. At once, both deities took flight in a cloud of feathers, landing close enough to make her flinch.

"What Relic is that?" demanded the dove-shaped deity. "Get it out of here."

"I can't get out." Did that mean they didn't plan to kill her after all? "I'm intending to find out how to rectify that, so if you don't mind, back off."

"What is that book?" the raven-shaped deity asked. "What are you?"

Aurel gave them a bewildered look. "I'm a Sentinel… or I was supposed to be, anyway."

"Not another one," the dove-shaped deity groaned.

"Another one?" How could the deities know who the Sentinel was? Unless…

"Do you mean Zelle was here?" she asked. "Or—my grandmother?"

Wait. Hadn't her grandmother made an alliance with a pair of deities to oppose Orzen? She couldn't imagine it'd worked out in their favour, but it proved they were willing to negotiate with humans, didn't it?

When neither replied, she voiced a more pertinent question. "You know that man, Daimos. You're not working for him, are you? Is that why you're here?"

"What does it matter to you?" said the dove-shaped deity. "He has offered us what we desire."

"Meaning what?" Daimos hadn't behaved the way she'd expected at all. Why had he left her to die here in the realm of the Powers rather than killing her himself? Hadn't he brutally murdered Rien's family? "Daimos is a known liar. The other deities he's worked with can attest to that."

The raven-shaped deity made an affronted noise. "He gave Orzen access to the human realm by gifting him with a human body of his own."

"And sent him to his death," corrected Aurel. "Same with Igon. Really, you should be grateful he hasn't given *you* access to the human realm yet, because if he had, you'd be rotting in the dirt."

"Careful what you say, Sentinel." The dove-shaped deity's voice dropped to a growl.

"Maybe I can offer you a better deal," she ventured. "Daimos is entirely self-interested, and he's got at least two of your kin killed already."

As Aurel had learned the hard way, the deities had little concept of loyalty to anyone. Maybe that included Daimos, whatever promises he'd made them. She had nothing else to bargain with.

"Your sister already refused to offer us access to the human realm," said the raven-shaped deity. "Why should we believe you're any different?"

"That isn't something either of us can offer, and unlike Daimos, I won't lie." Aurel lifted the Book of Reading. "I can use my Relic to find out any piece of information, anything you might want to know. If you help me get out of here, that is. What do you say?"

The dove-shaped deity scoffed, but the other deity shuffled closer to her. "I'm listening."

32

Daimos held Astiva's staff high and sent a blast of thorny vines towards Rien. Astiva's magic, which had served him for most of his life, came at him with the force of a storm.

Zierne's magic answered in kind. Thorns clashed against thorns, vines tangling, dragging their owners closer together. While Daimos was using Astiva's power to its full extent, Zierne's anger and Rien's combined to blot out the pain in his hand and chest.

Daimos hadn't seen Rien in a long time. He knew nothing of what Rien had faced since he'd been ripped apart from his deity. *This time I will win.*

Their boats veered towards one another, and Reyes shouted, grabbing the rail for balance. Rien gripped his staff tightly, refusing to give ground, but the sea drew their vessels closer together until the tangled vines threatened to cast their occupants down into the ocean.

Keeping the staff in a firm hold, Rien readied himself to

jump. When the ship bumped against the side of Daimos's vessel, he climbed atop the railing and flung himself over the gap, his feet slamming down on the deck. Daimos stumbled, and Rien pressed his advantage, their weapons clashing with the added sharpness of thorns. Rien hardly noticed the blood trickling from his hands when his vines locked around Daimos's wrist, trying to break his grip on his staff.

"You want your Relic back, do you?" Daimos spat out as their staffs wrenched apart, scattering thorns onto the deck. "I wonder if your new deity knows?"

He's just talking, he told himself. Nothing more.

"And you?" he returned. "Is there anything you desire, except to reduce the world to ruins to spite everyone who wronged you?"

"The world has been brought to ruin before." Daimos managed to land a hit that sliced open the back of Rien's hand. "But like the Invokers who founded Aestin, I will build a new world of my own in the ashes."

He's lost his mind. Rien blocked Daimos from landing a hit on his skull, the trailing thorns biting into his exposed hands. "The Invokers who survived those battles wanted to build a better world. You want nothing but your own self-satisfaction."

"How do you know what those Invokers wanted?" Daimos raised his staff to catch Rien's next blow. "The deities alone survive to tell the truth of our history, and they have given me a clarity I could never have found in any record written by humans."

"They can lie, too, you know." Another jarring crash of staff on staff locked both their weapons together in a tangle of thorns. "Even you aren't immune to their manipulation, despite all the effort you made to win them over to your side."

A smile flickered on Daimos's face. "I confess I wondered if I might stumble upon a true child of Gaiva in their realm, but it seems only the lesser deities remain."

"Why would you want to meet Astiva?" Thorns bit into thorns, as Astiva and Zierne's magic fought for dominance. "Or was it Mevicen you sought?"

"Neither." Daimos's thorns gained the upper hand, but Rien's pushed them back before they sliced through his sleeves. "After you slew Orzen, I thought it would be appropriate to find one of his kin... or to be more accurate, a *distant* relation."

If Daimos intended to distract him, Rien had no intention of taking the bait. "Stop talking."

Daimos laughed. "That Relic of yours... After the damage it caused in the wars, it's no wonder that the first Sentinels wanted it out of Aestin. And yet it doesn't hold a candle to the real deity."

"You wanted Zierne?" Rien broke away from Daimos, trailing thorns, and struck him viciously across the face. "You thought he would fight for you?"

"Zierne fights for nobody but himself." Daimos spat out blood. "No human has ever been able to dominate his Relic."

That doesn't matter. We both want you dead. A crimson glow emanated from Rien's staff, and a surge of anger pulsed in his veins as thorns lashed at him, drawing blood through the fabric of his coat.

Daimos was bleeding, too, but like Rien, he paid no heed to the pain. Unlike Rien, however, his left hand wasn't ablaze in white-hot agony, as if the open wound of

Astiva's godsmark was unable to bear being so close to his old Relic.

Or was it Zierne's mark causing him pain, not Astiva's?

Unbalanced, he staggered, Daimos's vines pushing him against the railings at the edge of the deck. Thorns dug into his throat, tightening, and Daimos bared his teeth. "Ready to die at the hands of your former deity?"

"Astiva isn't here." It was Daimos alone who intended to deal the killing blow, and as the thick vines tightened around his neck, Rien refused to blink, refused to look away. The pain in his wrist intensified, and Daimos's face swam before his eyes.

For an instant, his enemy disappeared. In his place stood a blurred figure, human-shaped with large wings, like the statues at his family's crypt and at the gates of the old estate before Daimos had trampled it to the ground...

Astiva?

It must be a trick, a desperate illusion conjured by his own mind, but the blazing pain in his left hand overtook the sharp edges of thorns piercing his throat. Astiva's thorns.

"No." He whispered the word, not knowing whom he addressed. "I won't allow this."

Daimos fell back, eyes widening, as the vines released Rien. He regained his balance, gasping for breath, but the thorns had scraped the skin of his neck without slicing open his throat. His left hand was a torrent of pain, but his right hand maintained a solid grip on his staff when he swung it at Daimos.

The boat rocked beneath them, his attack missed, and cannon fire roared in the background. Daimos spat out a curse, his gaze dropping to his staff in disbelief. Rien ought to have pressed his advantage, but more cannons fired, snapping his attention northward. *Powers above.*

Their army had reached Zeuten, far faster than should have been possible, and through the grey fog gathering around the coast, Rien could see lines of soldiers gathered in formation. Surely not enough to face an army of Invokers—but Zeuten also had the Changers. Silvery-grey forms flew over the ships, firing arrows at Daimos's fleet.

This is wrong. Most of the people on Aestin's ships were civilians, bewitched into fighting for Daimos, but Zeuten hadn't been spared either. Rien's mouth went dry when he saw the impact of the first round of cannons on the seafront. Zelle's shop was somewhere in there, he knew, but she wasn't there. She couldn't be.

Their ship lurched sideways, causing Daimos to fall against Rien. His back hit the railing, whirling darkness beckoned below, and he and Daimos both tumbled into the abyss together.

Evita watched in horror as the doorway vanished, while the man who'd left Aurel to die turned on her. "Who *are* you?"

"Excuse me?" She was fairly sure she knew who *he* was. "You're Daimos, aren't you?"

Why had he had a doorway into the realm of the Powers open on his ship? Why was he here and not in Aestin? She had too many questions, but her chief concern was getting Aurel back into this realm before whatever lived on the other side of that doorway slaughtered her.

Instead of answering, he raised his weapon—a crimson staff patterned with thorns—and advanced on her.

Daimos failed to notice the dragonet behind him until Chirp leapt, claws tearing at his fine clothes. The dragonet positioned himself in front of Evita with his fangs bared and his sharp claws at the ready.

"Thanks," she breathed. "I owe you."

Daimos looked between her and the dragonet and then spat out a curse in a language Evita didn't know. A patch of whiteness opened at his back—a doorway—and as he leapt in, Aurel's voice shouted Evita's name from the other side.

An instant later, the doorway began to flicker at the edges.

"Aurel!" Evita moved towards the doorway, but Chirp got there first. He reached in and seized Aurel in a claw, snatching her out of the doorway as it winked out of existence.

Aurel swayed when Chirp put her down on the ship's deck, staring wide-eyed at Evita. "I... thank you. That was a close one."

"He escaped into the realm of the Powers." Evita stared at the patch of air that now showed nothing but sea-drenched wooden planks. "That *was* the realm of the Powers, right?"

"Yes." Aurel braced her hands on her knees, breathing hard. "I owe you, Chirp."

"I said the same." Evita stroked the dragonet's nose, relief sweeping over her. "I'm guessing Daimos has never seen a dragonet before."

"That was really him?" Aurel shook her head. "Powers above, at least we didn't have to fight him ourselves."

"Where's that Relic?" Evita moved towards the trapdoor. "You saw it, too, right?"

"Yeah." Aurel grunted, clutching her injured arm. "I didn't expect there to be a doorway down there."

Chirp dove at the trapdoor, startling them both into jumping back. His claws tore right though the wooden deck, exposing splintered wooden boards, and a glittering light snagged Evita's eye.

The dragonet stuck his head into the newly enlarged trapdoor and emerged with a small, amber-coloured stone between his teeth. He spat it onto the deck, where it clattered to a halt at Evita's feet. "Thank you, Chirp."

Aurel reached for the stone. "I'm not sure anyone but Zelle can destroy this, but it's a start."

"There's more than one," Evita recalled Zelle's words. "Pity we can't use one to track the others."

"You know, I might be able to." Aurel turned the amber-coloured stone over in her hand. "When I used my Reading ability on one of Gaiva's Relics in Itzar, I caught glimpses of the others. It's worth a shot."

"You can do that?" Would it work on Relics that didn't appear to have a wielder? Unless Daimos had claimed them, that is, but he already had that crimson staff, and she'd thought nobody could wield more than one Relic at a time.

"I can." Aurel pulled the Book of Reading out of her pocket and laid its blank pages open on the deck. Tightening her hand over the amber-coloured stone, she stared at the pages for a few long moments. Whatever she saw wasn't visible to Evita but for the Reader's eyes alone.

Aurel lifted her gaze. "Do you want the good news or the bad news?"

"Good," Evita responded. "How bad is the bad news, though?"

Aurel grimaced. "The good news is that I know the Relics' locations. The bad news is that there are more of them than I thought, and they're all on boats or ships. You'd think he knew Zelle would be able to detect them on land."

"Did Daimos spread them around himself?" It must have taken ages, and it was a wonder he'd never been caught.

"His deities did," Aurel said. "The two I saw in the realm of the Powers are his personal helpers, it sounds like."

"You… You saw two deities?"

"Yeah, but they weren't what I expected." Aurel returned the Book of Reading to her pocket and reached up to climb onto Chirp's back again. "I think we should ask Zelle to destroy this one first, in case it tries to unleash some trickery on us."

Evita clambered up behind her. "Good idea. Besides, last we saw, Zelle was standing directly in the path of an army."

"I'd be more concerned for the army, to be honest." Aurel was quiet as they took flight again. "She… She didn't look like my sister. I don't know what that Shaper did to her."

"Neither do I." Evita had no words of reassurance to offer her, but all thoughts of Zelle fled her mind when they spotted several large shapes soaring through the sky from the west towards Saudenne. Huge, feathered beasts, whose riders carried glowing shards of blue-white stone and weapons of bone.

Itzar had sent reinforcements after all.

"That can't be possible," murmured Aurel. "Powers above, they *did* come to help us."

"We'd better catch them up." Evita coaxed the dragonet to pick up speed, wondering how they'd known Aestin's threat was imminent. Maybe they'd guessed, or even seen some of Invicten's creeping fog with their own eyes.

Kolt spotted them, slowing down his eagle's pace. "Nice to see you again."

"What are you all doing here?" She counted at least ten eagles carrying riders armed and ready for war.

"A surprising number of people didn't want Aestin to attack the Isles."

A grin spread across Aurel's face. "I knew you wouldn't let us down."

"Wait, you're not going straight to the seafront, are you?" Evita asked. "The soldiers might mistake you for enemies if you don't warn them first."

"They'd be fools not to accept our help." Kolt flew into the lead of the group of eagles, while Evita and Aurel kept a close eye on the docks. The soldiers had reached the seafront by now and had spread out in formation, and Evita urged the dragonet to overtake the eagles before the soldiers caught sight of the approaching forces from Itzar.

To no surprise, panic erupted among the soldiers when they spotted the newcomers, but Aurel leaned forward and called to them, "Calm down! The people of Itzar are here to help Zeuten."

"Where's your sister?" Evita didn't see Zelle, but she ought to have had the sense to get out of the way of the army. She *hoped* so, anyway, because Zelle hadn't exactly seemed aware of her surroundings the last time they'd seen her. Or concerned that she might be perceived as a foe either.

"I don't know," Aurel said. "I—*shit.*"

A row of archers near the back pointed their arrows directly at the newcomers. A soldier who appeared to be at the head of their group bellowed, "Who are you? State your purpose here."

"We're from the Isles of Itzar." Kolt didn't appear to be at all concerned about the number of weapons pointed in his direction. "We are ambassadors here on behalf of Gaiva Herself, and we must offer our apologies for our hasty arrival. We didn't have time to announce ourselves in advance, but Aurel here told us you have need of our help."

The guards lowered their weapons, possibly more out of a reluctance to be torn to pieces by giant eagles than the desire to respect the ambassadors.

"They can fight from the sky," Aurel told them. "With the Changers, if they'll allow it. Where are they?"

Evita twisted in her seat, her eyes on the sky. "I wouldn't count on them fighting as your allies. They've been forced to switch sides at least three times without even knowing, and I don't trust the enemy not to mess with them again."

A tremendous booming noise sounded. The dragonet launched higher into the air with a startled cry, while the soldiers' formation scattered. Smoke billowed out from the docks, and Evita's heart leapt into her throat.

Several boats were already bearing down on the shore —and judging by the cannon one of them had fired at

Zeuten's docks, they were no creation of magic. Daimos was here.

"Bloody Powers!" Aurel shouted. "Fly higher. We don't want to get hit by one of those."

Chirp obeyed, wings pumping, and they took in the sight of the approaching army from Aestin. It didn't look like an organised force, more of a collection of vessels ranging from fully stocked naval ships flying Aestin's flags to smaller boats that might have been borrowed or stolen from merchant sailors. On the deck of each boat stood several individuals, and while Evita couldn't see their faces from this height, the amber glow streaming from each deck shone vibrantly even from the sky.

Everyone on the boats carried Invicten's Relics.

Zelle paced down the street near the seafront, impatience mingling with the dread and the knowledge that the army would arrive at any moment. Both armies, in fact. If Aestin's forces held Invicten's Relics, she'd have to wait for them to draw closer to the shore in order to destroy them.

In the background, she heard the pounding footsteps of Zeuten's soldiers assembling, but with her enhanced senses, it was easy for her to avoid their locations and pick a route through the otherwise deserted streets. The members of the public who lived near the seafront had retreated inside and with good reason.

A deafening boom hit her ears. Even the Shaper's presence didn't stop her from stumbling, hitting the ground on her already-abused knees. Wincing, she clambered upright and stared at the smoke billowing out from the docks she'd left behind mere moments ago. Aestin's army had reached the shore.

Zelle turned back and ran directly into the smoke, holding her breath to avoid choking. The pain in her knees didn't bother her; the Shaper's presence in her mind masked out all unnecessary distractions and focused her attention on her goal.

"Zelle!" Aurel shouted from the dragonet's back, holding a glowing stone in one hand. "You're all right. Thank all the Powers."

"Is that Invicten's Relic?" Zelle reached out to take the stone from her.

"One of them," Aurel said. "We'll get the rest. You can't stay this close to the sea with Aestin's ships firing cannons everywhere."

"We can't." Evita blurted the words out. "Zelle... the Relics are on Aestin's ships. With the army."

"Of course they are." Neither she nor the Shaper was particularly surprised to learn that Daimos had remained several steps ahead of them. "We'll just have to sink them."

"Look." Aurel pointed up at the sky. "They can help us."

Zelle raised her head, seeing several large birds flying over the harbour and recognising the icy blue glow of Gaiva's Relics. "Did Itzar send reinforcements?"

"I think they made the choice on their own," Evita said. "Good timing, given the size of Aestin's army."

"I wouldn't call it an army." Aurel's tone sounded conflicted. "Half the people on the ships aren't armed, except with those Relics."

"That counts as being armed." Zelle lifted the stone

and clenched her fingers. The Shaper's magic flared, shattering the Relic into pieces.

"Powers above." Evita's eyes widened at the fragments scattering onto the pier like dust. "Can you do the same to the others?"

Aurel made an indistinct noise. "I'd say yes, and that's not what worries me. Those people out there..."

Zelle squinted at the harbour, where Zeuten's forces had assembled. The cannons had left a trail of smoke in their wake, and it didn't help that the thick fog had yet to dissipate. "We have to put an end to this."

Another cannon fired. Aurel winced, grabbing the dragonet's side with her uninjured hand. "This can't be... I really thought Rien would stop them."

His name brought a jolt of pain to Zelle's chest that almost made her forget the other consciousness bound to hers, waiting to take control. "If he was coming, he'd already be here."

Zelle wouldn't give up on Rien that easily, knowing his single-minded pursuit of revenge on Daimos would keep pushing him onward, but the Shaper was less convinced, and it was the Shaper who urged her to keep moving towards the harbour.

I can't fight them all at once, she thought.

You can if you let me take control, whispered the Shaper. *Stop holding me back. I can destroy those Relics and end this war.*

Yet another cannon fired, and several screams rose from the harbour. The Shaper's presence rose within her, reaching outward beyond the shores of Zeuten. Towards the ships approaching, readying themselves to attack again.

Zelle felt for the connections holding the world together and pushed back the waves. The great expanse of the sea heaved, carrying the ships away from Zeuten's shores, driving Daimos's army back.

When she let go, the waves returned with a brutal crash that drenched the harbour and sprayed her with salt water. Zelle felt nothing, and neither did she hear the screaming.

The Shaper saw to that.

33

Rien surfaced, tasting salt water in his mouth and feeling the sting of a thousand cuts on his hands and face. Someone shouted his name from nearby. *Reyes.*

Blinking the sting of salt from his eyes, he tilted his head and saw Reyes leaning over the edge of the boat alongside him. Somehow, he'd kept hold of his staff, helped by the vines wrapping around his left hand and wrist, but his foe and Astiva's staff were nowhere in sight.

He took Reyes's hand and let him help him climb up before collapsing on the deck, coughing up water. "Thanks. Daimos… Where is he?"

"Hope he drowned," said Reyes dispassionately. "We need to get out of this fog."

Rien lifted his head, assessing his surroundings. Fog pressed against the boat and circled the fleet, but it didn't quite hide the edge of Zeuten's harbour ahead of them. They were even closer than before. He'd give it five minutes before they reached the shore, and with other boats hemming them in, they'd be hard-pressed to escape. Especially as the other occupants of their own ship had gathered on the deck, blank-eyed, still in the grip of Invicten's magic.

Before Rien could begin to consider how to deal with their Relics without harming the wielders, the ship lurched sideways, tossed upon waves which turned from calm to turbulent in the blink of an eye. He and Reyes both grabbed the railing as the sea itself drew backwards, retreating from the shore.

A wave of water crashed over his head, but he managed to keep his grip on the railing. "What in the name of the Powers—"

The Powers. Only a deity could be responsible, but he knew of only two Powers with the ability to control the waves. One was Igon, bound and imprisoned over in Itzar. The other's Relics had been cast to the bottom of the ocean upon the Daimos family's exile. Daimos hadn't somehow found Mevicen's missing Relics after all, had he?

The ocean's grip released them, propelling the fleet forward in an uncontrollable surge. It took all his effort to keep his footing as their ship lurched closer to the shore... towards a lone figure with a staff in her hand, outlined in blue light.

Zelle.

Her expression was completely blank. She moved her hands, and the waves broke apart at her command. He'd seen her using the Shaper's magic before but not like this and not with the lives of countless people in her hands. If the fleet sank along with their Relics, it might break

Invicten's spell, but most of the people aboard were civilians. They didn't deserve to die.

"Zelle!" he shouted, but she didn't hear him. He was too far away, and besides, he had the sinking feeling she couldn't hear anything at all, and that it was the Shaper's magic that guided her hands. Even if she'd been driven to the brink of desperation, she wouldn't have risked unleashing the ocean's might upon her own side as well as Aestin's, would she?

A glint of crimson caught his eye from the edge of the pier. Was that Astiva's staff? *Yes. There it is.*

"We need to get to the shore," he murmured.

"Why?" Reyes said. "I'm not going near that... Invoker. Is that what she is? Or a deity? I didn't think Zeuten even *had* Invokers—"

"It's Zelle." Rien cut through him. "I don't know what's wrong with her, but if you can see her, too, she can't be an illusion. I can talk to her. I might be able to stop—"

"If you have a death wish." Reyes gripped the railings when the ship lurched to the side again. "Wait. Zelle... is that the *nameless Shaper's* magic?"

"Yes." Rien swore when he spotted a dripping wet figure pulling himself out of the water and onto the pier. Snatching up Astiva's staff, Daimos cast a wild glance around and then ran, while Rien's hands clenched over the railings. "We have to move faster."

"Tell that to the captain, not me." Reyes swore under his breath. "I already pulled you out of the water once—and if that Zelle uses her magic again, you might drown."

"That's a risk I'll have to take."

He launched himself over the railing. Once again, icy water drenched him from head to toe, while the staff remained locked to his hand by the vines twisting around his wrists. He swam one-handed, his gaze on the pier, and a familiar bright light shone from farther along the seafront. *A doorway.*

Rien bumped against solid wood and pulled himself out of the water. Pushing a handful of sopping hair out of his eyes with his free hand, he looked for Daimos and spotted a crimson-cloaked figure hurrying along the seafront and towards the open doorway.

With a curse, Rien broke into a sprint—but too late. Daimos and the doorway vanished in the same instant.

———

Aurel looked down at Zelle from the dragonet's back, dread sinking its teeth into her. Any hopes that what her sister had done to the ships had been an accident faded when Zelle raised her hands again, driving the waves forward until they crashed upon Zeuten's seafront. Sea spray drenched the piers, including Zelle herself, but she didn't appear to notice.

When her sister joined forces with the Shaper, she'd changed. Aurel had seen it right away, but this—controlling the waters of Saudenne's harbour without a care for the damage she caused—wasn't anything like Zelle at all. Boats crashed into one another in a splintering of wood, and the fog made it even harder for anyone who fell into the water to find their way to dry land.

If the Shaper had taken total control, Zelle might not be consciously aware of what she was doing, and while the people aboard the ships had seemingly chosen to fight for Daimos, what if that wasn't the case? He'd bewitched innocent people into fighting for him before, after all. What if they had hostages, or the Emperor himself had accompanied the army? Zelle hardly seemed to care for her *own* side, as her waves swept all the way up the pier, dragging several of Zeuten's soldiers into the sea.

"We need to stop her," Aurel murmured. "Zelle!"

"What is she doing?" Evita shielded her face against the residual spray from the waves. "She's not... She's not herself."

"No. I think..." Aurel faltered. "I don't think she's the one in control, and the Shaper doesn't care who dies as long as She destroys Invicten's Relics."

Chirp shrieked when another spray of seawater hit them, while the tide lashed forward and back and threw the ships around like leaves tossed in a storm. Without warning, Evita leaned over the dragonet's back, her cloak billowing behind her.

"Wait," Aurel said. "Evita—what are you doing?"

"Stopping her." Before Aurel could protest, Evita had descended into the fog, her cloak spreading out like wings as she flew straight at Zelle.

"Powers above, Evita!" Aurel exclaimed.

Chirp let out a panicked noise and flew in pursuit, and Aurel glimpsed the bright flare of a doorway on the water-slick pier. Had the deities come to join in the battle too? That was all they needed. Though most of the deities couldn't get out of their own realm, including the two she'd talked to.

They'd made a bargain, in fact, and while they might prove as treacherous as any of the Powers, the deities surely didn't want the nameless Shaper to wreak destruction on the world any more than Aurel did. It wasn't her best idea, but Aurel wasn't going to be able to do much good from up in the air.

"Drop me off by that doorway and make sure Zelle doesn't kill Evita," she told Chirp. "I'll be all right."

The dragonet made a disgruntled noise that turned to a panicked chirp when another wave hit the shore. Dodging the waves, they flew lower, and Aurel jumped off Chirp's back and landed on the pier.

Another wave surged over the wooden planks, causing her to stumble. She reached the doorway and leapt through, scarcely catching her balance before a man crashed into her, causing them both to fall into a bedraggled heap on the cloud-like ground. The blurred outlines of two familiar bird-shaped deities appeared on either side of her, as if they hadn't moved since her last visit.

"Hello, there." She rolled free of the man who'd landed on her and found herself nose to nose with none other than Naxel Daimos himself. "I should have guessed I'd find you fleeing the battlefield."

"You *again?*" Daimos pointed his staff at her. "Who *are* you?"

"Aurel Carnelian," she replied. "The Sentinel. You might have asked my name earlier before you tried to strike me down."

"You came back in here of your own accord. You're a fool." He pointed his staff at her—which must be Rien's original Relic, though it looked similar enough to Aurel's eyes that she might have mistaken it for Rien's new staff if she wasn't close enough to see that he wielded the staff in one hand and not two. "You shouldn't be here."

"I've heard that a lot," said Aurel. "This is the realm of

the Powers, so you shouldn't be here either. You're as human as I am."

The raven-shaped deity shrieked with laughter, but before Aurel could ask what she found so amusing, the dove-shaped deity clipped her in the face with his wing. "Your *sister* isn't human! She's the nameless Shaper!"

"The nameless Shaper!" The raven-shaped deity's shriek drew Aurel's gaze to a window in the air that showed Zeuten's seafront. On the other side of the doorway was a clear view of the turbulent ocean and her sister standing alone on the pier, facing down Aestin's army.

Not alone. Zeuten's soldiers—drenched to the skin and having long-since abandoned their formation—moved forward to the seafront. They must know that it was risky for anyone to go near Zelle in her current state, surely, but their oddly glazed expressions showed no concern for the waves breaking on the shore, propelled by the nameless Shaper's power.

"Powers above," Aurel said, half to herself. "Are they under Invicten's spell too?"

She'd thought Zelle had been intending to destroy Invicten's Relics, but her attention was on the sea, not on the soldiers gathering at her back.

"That is your sister," said Daimos from behind her. "The nameless Shaper."

"My sister is *not* the nameless Shaper." Aurel's skin prickled. "Is she the one you were running away from?"

Daimos's eyes narrowed. "I should quieten you myself."

"You can try." In truth, Aurel didn't have the energy for a battle with an Invoker and not just because Rien would be incensed if she deprived him of his revenge. "Was this your plan? You provoked the nameless Shaper, so it looks to me as though you got exactly what you deserved."

From what Rien had said, Daimos hadn't spared any attention for Zeuten at all until Zelle had thwarted his goal of killing the last of the Asteras. She doubted he'd ever seen the Shaper up close except through the eyes of his intermediaries, and he hadn't a clue what he'd unleashed upon the world.

Aurel dragged her gaze away from the window in the air and faced the raven-shaped deity, who'd moved closer to her.

"We made an agreement, didn't we?" She nodded to the deity. "I haven't forgotten."

"Kyren," Daimos snapped. "Don't you even think about listening to that human."

"Too late," said Aurel. "You ought to know better than to trust the gods. Kyren, is it? Do you want to complete our bargain?"

"Bargain?" Daimos echoed. "Haven't you learned from your sister's fate?"

"You aren't winning this, Daimos." She gestured in the direction of the window showing Zeuten's seafront. "I know you promised to give the deities access to the human realm, but I can prove why that isn't possible."

"Tell me," Kyren burst out. "You promised to let me know where my Relic is."

"I did," Aurel said, "and I have your answers."

"How dare you—?" Daimos was cut off when both deities brushed past him, bearing down on Aurel instead.

She drew in a breath. "The truth is, I'm sorry to say,

that your Relic was destroyed. Yours, too… Xeale, was it? Sorry to be the bearer of bad news."

Both deities howled and shrieked, causing her to cover her ears to block out the sound. Even Daimos staggered back, his free hand clutching his forehead.

"She lies!" screeched Kyren.

"I have no reason to deceive you." Aurel reached into her pocket and pulled out the Book of Reading—and the two feathers she'd hidden between the pages. "I used my Reading ability on feathers belonging to both of you. If there'd been any Relics left in the human realm, I would have found them, but there was nothing. Sorry."

Daimos stared openly at her, heedless of his companions' distress. "What did you say?"

"They asked me to track the location of their Relics, and I did," she replied. "Your promises mean nothing. You can't give them access to the human realm without their Relics, can you?"

"You can locate a Relic?" Daimos's expression was as dazed as the soldiers assembling on the other side of the doorway. "Belonging to any deity?"

"What does it matter to you? You're human."

"No, he isn't," Kyren whimpered. "You have the wrong person."

"You aren't…" She trailed off. She'd thought there was something odd about the man, not least the fact that he hadn't killed her immediately upon laying eyes on her. "But you look just like him…"

"No," said the false Daimos. "My real name is Nahen. Can you find *my* Relics? I have one, but there might be others."

Aurel gave the deity who wore Daimos's face a blank

stare. "I'm not doing this for every deity I run into. Not without any reward."

"Why not?" His expression hardened. "You need our help to get back home, don't you?"

Oh. Now it made sense that Daimos seemed to have gained the ability to open doorways. No human could move between realms without outside help, unlike a deity with a human form... but where was the *real* Daimos? With his army, most likely, but it shouldn't have surprised her that one of the deities who served him had chosen to wear his face.

"I need an actual physical object to Read," she replied. "Besides, you attacked my allies and unleashed Invicten's Relics in the human world. I'm not doing anything for you unless you stop fighting for the real Daimos."

"Your sister is the one who is causing the most damage," the false Daimos said. "She let the nameless Shaper take control of her body."

"To stop Invicten's illusions," Aurel corrected. "She'll call the Shaper off as soon as she's destroyed His Relics."

"Wrong," said the false Daimos. "The Shaper will not release Her grip on the mortal so easily. Besides, it was the nameless Shaper who was responsible for barring the doorways between realms and exiling all the deities from the human realm. She's the reason we are trapped here. None of us will ever fight for Her."

Aurel's throat went dry. "There must be another way. You can't want this destruction."

"What we want matters not." The false Daimos's tone was quiet, distant. "This is the end of it all, human. We've all lost."

Evita dove at Zelle with the intent of tackling her to the ground, but the staff's magic flung her aside without Zelle herself sparing her a single glance. Evita caught her balance in midair, her cloak billowing around her.

Zelle stood like a pillar, unmoving, entirely consumed by the will of the nameless Shaper. She'd thought the two were sharing their minds and bodies, but nobody had mentioned if it would be possible for them to separate again. Evita was far from an expert on Relics in general, but if she was able to make Zelle drop the staff, it might weaken the Shaper's hold. It was worth a try.

Evita flew at Zelle, but once again, the staff's magic caught her mid-flight and pushed her backwards. When their gazes locked, a chill raced down her spine at the absence of any signs of recognition in Zelle's face. Had the Shaper blotted out her human memories altogether?

"Zelle!" shouted a hoarse voice.

Evita spun around, looking for the speaker. Rien stood on the pier, soaked to the skin, his Aestinian garb drenched with seawater and his hair plastered to his forehead. Blood dripped from his hands, completing the alarming image, but Zelle gave no signs that she'd seen or heard him.

Instead, she pointed the staff at Evita, who raised her hands placatingly. "I don't want to fight you, but all you're doing is hurting civilians. I thought you intended to destroy the Relics, not *people*."

"Why does it matter?" The voice that came from her mouth wasn't Zelle's, and it chilled Evita's blood. "They made their choice."

"Zelle!"

Rien might as well have said nothing at all. Zelle lifted the staff, and a large wave arose over the pier, drenching all three of them. Evita flew higher, spitting out salt water, but Rien stood his ground. So did the soldiers, who approached the seafront despite the danger from both the Aestinian forces and their own side. Evita flew down to Rien, who eyed the oncoming soldiers with a grim expression. "I think they're under the control of Invicten's fog."

"Shit. You're right." Evita took in their uneven gait and glazed expressions. "Where's Aurel?"

"I thought she was with you." Rien didn't look much better than the soldiers did, his staff bound to his hand by a layer of thorny vines that she could only assume didn't cause him any pain.

She went into the realm of the Powers. Her gaze skimmed the front of the city, which was a smouldering wreck thanks to the cannon fire from earlier, but the Shaper had caused just as much damage. Ruined boats lay scattered around the bay, their owners lying half-conscious in the water or scrambling onto the piers. As the tides receded, glints of light caught her eye. Relics. The Shaper hadn't been entirely focused on drowning everyone, but She didn't seem to care how many human lives were snuffed out on her quest to destroy Invicten's Relics.

Rien's gaze went back to Zelle, who'd faced the sea as if she—and the Shaper—was contemplating how best to deal with the mass of Relics she'd brought to the shore. "I need to get that staff away from her."

"I tried," said Evita. "Didn't work. You fought Daimos?"

"Yes," Rien answered. "We fought, and he fled into the deities' realm—who opened that doorway, anyway?"

"Daimos did. Somehow."

Rien swore. "No, there's a deity who looks just like him."

"That explains a lot," said Evita. "Where's the real Daimos, then?"

"I don't know." Rien's gaze followed Zelle, who began a swift stride down the seafront. "I'll talk to her."

He tailed her down the pier, catching her up as she neared the Relics strewn across shore. Zelle ignored his presence, pointing the staff at the gleaming Relics. White light flared, turning the scattered stones into dust and vapour. In an instant, the fog began to disperse, yet Evita felt no relief, only a sickening sense of dread.

"Rien," she called to him. "Get away—there's nothing you can do for her."

The distant sound of a cannon firing drew both of their attention to the sea.

"My allies are out there," Rien murmured. "I don't know if any of Invicten's Relics are left, but the Emperor's ships are following Daimos's fleet. I told his soldiers that most of the people fighting for Daimos were being controlled by Invicten's magic, but I'm not sure they listened."

"Are you sure they aren't coming to attack Zeuten instead?"

He shook his head. "If anyone attacks *them*, they might, though. I need to warn them off... Can I fly on Chirp?"

"Go ahead." She beckoned, and the dragonet descended, looking sadly at Zelle.

"If he drops her into the sea, she might snap out of it,"

Evita remarked. "No—we don't have time. Go and help your allies, Rien. She'll be fine."

Rien lowered his gaze. "I have to convince the army to turn back. I—I'm sorry, Zelle."

The dragonet crouched to let Rien climb onto his back, while Evita watched the soldiers stop mid-motion, looking around as if they were unsure how they'd ended up at the seafront.

That was one problem taken care of, but not everyone realised the spell had broken. Someone needed to tell Itzar's warriors not to attack Rien's allies, and since nobody else was available, it would have to be her.

Evita soared into the air, the cloak supporting her on either side. At least she had control over her Relic again, but before she reached the eagles, a curtain of rippling silver passed overhead, resolving into a circle of Changers.

"Gaiva's tits."

34

Aurel stared at the false Daimos. "What did you say? The Shaper's magic…"

"Yes, Her magic closed the doorways and trapped us here." The other two deities shrieked their agreement, causing Aurel to cover her ears again.

"That doesn't make it my sister's fault," she said defiantly.

"She was willing to sacrifice her very humanity to help the Shaper," said the false Daimos.

"To stop your boss," Aurel corrected him. "Daimos is never going to give you what you want. He won't give you access to human bodies, and I doubt he'll let you have your revenge on the Shaper either."

"We don't want revenge on Her," Kyren said thickly, the deity's manner still subdued in the aftermath of Aurel's unwelcome revelation. "It's not possible for any of us to do any harm to a Great Power. All we can do is watch Her destroy your realm."

"No." Aurel wouldn't accept defeat that easily. They

didn't even know for sure that the nameless Shaper had been responsible for closing the doors between realms and permanently banishing all the deities from the human realm, did they? Or maybe they did, given that the deities had lived for many centuries longer than humans did. If it was true, then it was wonder the deities had reacted the way they had when they'd seen her Book of Reading.

Speaking of which...

"What are you doing?" the false Daimos asked.

Ignoring him, she walked over to one of the odd, transparent pillars. Did that count as enough of a physical object for her to use her gift? She was out of any better ideas, and so she laid the Book of Reading on the cloud-like ground, pressed one hand to the indistinct form of the pillar, and leaned over the pages.

"Show me..." She faltered, unsure of her question. "I don't know if you can Read this realm like you can ours, but I'd like you to show me how the nameless Shaper came to be allied with my family."

Images filled her mind in a dizzying rush, far faster and more unexpected than she'd anticipated, and Aurel gripped the book hard with both hands to keep from being swept away in the tide.

In her mind's eye, she saw a large chamber lined with pillars—almost like the room she was currently in but without the cloud-like nebulousness overlaying every-thing and full of tall humanoid figures. *Deities.* This was the realm of the Powers, but as it once had been: a place of beauty, colour, and majesty. Open doorways stood at every corner, letting sunlight in... sunlight from the *human* world. The two were connected like rooms at opposite ends of a corridor, and both thrived.

As more images filled Aurel's mind, the room's vibrancy turned to darkness, and war engulfed the realms on both sides of the doors. Magic and weapons clashed, leaving settlements in ruins and forests burned to ash, and the doorways to the realm of the Powers allowed destruction to spread from one side to the other until the pillared chamber was left in ruins. Humans fled the destruction, unable to escape as deities flew back and forth from one side of the conflict to the other...

The deluge of images came to a halt in a sudden flash of light. When the light cleared, the deities were left in their ruined halls, and not a single doorway was to be seen. The distraught deities argued back and forth. Some conjured up windows through which they could see the human world, but no matter how hard they tried, they were unable to step through. Images of their distress reverberated in Aurel's mind, until a final image flickered into her head.

The image showed a mountain path, recognisable as the Range, and a group of weary-looking travellers walking up a steep slope through a driving storm. As she watched, they reached a cave in the cliffside. *The Sentinels' cave.* The lever system that existed now clearly hadn't been around because they walked right into the cave with no resistance.

In front of the gleaming black rock lay the staff of the nameless Shaper. The newcomers exclaimed, pointing, and a familiar blue light flared up when they drew closer—

In the same instant, the vision let Aurel go. She stared at the book for a few moments then lifted her head.

The three deities watched her warily, as if reluctant to

get close to the Book of Reading. The false Daimos spoke first. "What did you see, mortal?"

"I saw…" She licked her lips. "I saw the doors between worlds close…"

The false Daimos studied her face. "Do you believe us now?"

"I didn't actually *see* the Shaper close the doorways." She hadn't seen the Shaper at all, in fact.

"You *can't* see the Shaper," said Xeale. "Not if you wanted to keep your mind intact, mortal."

That might well be true. Zelle hadn't seen what was left of the Shaper's physical form, either, despite directly visiting Her prison herself, but the Book of Reading hadn't shown her anything about how she might convince the Great Power to let her sister go. There'd also been another notable absence in her vision.

"And the other Great Powers?" she asked. "I didn't see either of them either. Aren't they the ones who supposedly imprisoned the Shaper in the mountains?"

"They're gone," Kyren whispered. "The Shaper… She killed our mother."

"Gaiva." Her mouth parted. "How?"

"Don't tell the mortal that!" Xeale shrieked. "It's an insult to Her memory."

"If the Shaper closed all the doorways between realms, then how can She have ended up imprisoned in the mountains?" Aurel asked. "Unless… she was trapped on *that* side? In our world?"

"They all were." Kyren sniffed. "They fought, and our mother valiantly gave Her life in battle to stop Her."

Powers above. The Shaper had *killed* Gaiva?

"So did Invicten," said the false Daimos. "Nothing remained of him but a few fragments of His power."

"Relics." The Changers' Relics. *That* was how they'd ended up so close to the mountains… but from what Zelle had said, the Shaper had been unaware of their nature until recently. How? Of course, Invicten was the god of trickery and illusion, and the Shaper's perceptions were limited by her prison. "Why didn't they just *kill* the Shaper, rather than imprisoning Her?"

"We'll never know," Kyren said in mournful tones. "We were but youths when the doors between realms closed."

"You're still immortal." Yet this realm wasn't a pleasant place to spend an eternity in, she was willing to bet. "Wait —you met my grandmother, didn't you? Why didn't you tell *her* not to trust the nameless Shaper?"

"We owe her nothing," said Xeale. "She betrayed us."

"You could have stopped a war." It was hopeless arguing with them, though. Zelle had been backed into a corner when she'd allied with the Shaper. Aurel knew that as well as anyone.

"There he is," said the false Daimos suddenly. "At last."

Aurel spun on her heel. Another doorway opened in the air, revealing Saudenne's harbour—and a man who looked almost identical to the deity at her side. He was soaked from head to toe in blood and seawater, his clothes torn, and bore several deep cuts on his face. Rien had given him a real beating, but Daimos must have fled before he could deal the killing blow.

She propped a hand on her hip. "You're the real Naxel Daimos, aren't you? Running away?"

Daimos looked startled that she knew his name, unless

he was simply surprised to find another human in here. "Who are you?"

Daimos's Zeutenian was faltering—she guessed he didn't use the language often—but understandable to Aurel. "The Sentinel, and I've had two enlightening conversations with the deity who's pretending to be you."

Daimos's eyes narrowed, his hands gripping the crimson staff that must be Rien's former Relic. "You shouldn't be in here."

"People keep telling me that, but I bet I understand this place better than you do." She might not know the first thing about how to stop Zelle, but she was willing to bet Rien would appreciate her delivering his enemy into his hands.

She ran at Daimos, who swung the staff, but she ducked under his arm and ran straight into a wall of constructs. A claw swiped at her from the other side of the doorway, sending her stumbling back. Towering wraiths lurked within the fog, and so did smaller creatures—gremlins, rattler-imps, the sort of beasts she usually found at the outpost.

"What in the name of the Powers?" She stared, stupefied, as the constructs swept around the city of Saudenne in a tide of darkness that reminded her of when the Shaper had conjured up a storm of constructs to fight off Orzen.

"Look at your sister," said Daimos. "She's become a true vessel of the nameless Shaper, far beyond an ordinary Relic."

His tone sounded odd, almost reverent, and Aurel was willing to bet that he was already concocting a scheme to make use of this new development.

"You won't get at her," she warned. "I'll stop you first."

Daimos raised his staff again. "Will you now?"

Aurel reached for the knife at her waist. "Yes. I will."

———

Rien flew across the sea towards the ships closing in on the remnants of Daimos's fleet. It was easy enough to spot the official vessels, which flew official Aestinian flags and moved in an actual formation rather than Daimos's chaotic muddle.

Speaking of whom, where *was* Daimos? Hiding in the realm of the Powers? He must be, since Rien didn't see any signs of the crimson staff among the debris floating in the water and the soaking-wet Aestinians pulling themselves back onto their vessels. The fog had cleared, too, following the destruction of Invicten's Relics. The Shaper was efficient, he'd give Her that, but that didn't mean the war was over. The Emperor's forces were due to meet with Daimos's, and there was no guarantee that Zeuten wouldn't see both as the enemy and attack them.

Rien did catch sight of Reyes, drenched to the skin and dishevelled, clinging to the railing on the deck of his ship. Upon seeing him, Reyes yelled, "You're flying? What *is* that?"

"A dragonet." He flew lower. "The Emperor's army is catching up on you, if you didn't already see them. You need to get out of the way."

"We're trying, but it's hard to manoeuvre when the sea keeps unpredictably trying to drown us," said Reyes. "Is Zelle...?"

He shook his head. "She can't be reached, and I have to stop the fleet from sailing straight into a trap."

"Good luck."

"Stay alive." Rien took to the sky again, and Chirp cleared the distance between the two fleets with ease.

From the sky, Rien scanned the Emperor's oncoming army. A war vessel decked out in Aestinian flags led the fleet—and none other than Martzel stood at the prow. Had he managed to get through to the soldiers after all? Or had he come along to ensure nobody else perished unnecessarily? Rien flew lower, and Martzel watched his descent with wide eyes. "Arien? What are you flying on?"

"A dragonet, and that isn't the important part," he said. "Don't fire on those ships. Invicten's Relics have been destroyed, but some of Daimos's former allies might still be confused about whose orders they're following."

"Did you kill *him?*"

Rien shook his head. "We both fell into the water. I saw the deity who looks like him flee through a doorway, so perhaps he's hiding in there himself."

Martzel took a step back, his gaze fixed at a point somewhere behind Rien. "What in the name of the Powers is that?"

Rien twisted in his seat on the dragonet's back, his heart sinking at the sight of a dark mass spreading across the harbour. Was the fog back? He'd thought Zelle had already destroyed all the Relics, but Daimos might have had more hidden in the realm of the Powers. He wouldn't be surprised if he'd had an alternative plan in case his first failed.

"I'll go and see, but I wouldn't follow me," he warned. "Tell the fleet to turn back, if possible."

At Rien's prompting, Chirp turned around mid-flight, facing the dark mass of fog creeping through the harbour. Nebulous shapes moved within, ones that put him in mind of magical constructs, and this time the spell appeared to be concentrated at the very front of the harbour.

Where Zelle had been standing.

Rien flew closer, squinting into the grey haze. As he'd feared, a blue glare shone from the staff, and Zelle stood in the middle of a swarm of constructs that swirled around her like a storm.

———

Evita stopped mid-flight, surrounded by Changers, who'd formed a wall of rippling silver around her.

"I'm on your side," she told them. "Believe it or not. But the Aestinians—they were under a spell, and they aren't any longer. You don't have to attack them."

"They're our enemies." Briony's voice spoke from within. "You dare to try to stop us?"

"You again?" Kolt's eagle descended to hover beside Evita, the glow of Gaiva's magic shimmering in his palms. "You saw for yourself—the Relics controlling the will of Aestin's soldiers were destroyed. They are no longer a threat."

"Exactly," said Evita. "Zelle destroyed every Relic. We're all on the same side."

"Zelle?" said Verne. "She's on nobody's side, fool. Look at her."

Despite herself, Evita's gaze swept over the harbour, and her stomach lurched at the sight of a mass of greyness swirling around the area where Zelle stood. Dark shapes stirred within the grey, constructs born of the Shaper's magic. *What is she doing?*

Kolt swore in the Itzar language. "Is *she* doing that? Zelle?"

"I think she is," said Evita quietly. "Well, the Shaper is, but I don't know why. We've won."

They hadn't, though. Daimos was alive somewhere, and Zelle...

The Changers' formation broke apart as a winged form flew through their midst. The dragonet, with Rien riding on his back, soared above the harbour and headed directly for Zelle.

Zelle stood amid the swirling grey, watching the constructs take form into beasts with snapping teeth and claws. She was only vaguely aware of the screaming humans fleeing across the seafront and the boats lying in ruins in the water, but nothing mattered but the Shaper's need to be rid of everyone who threatened her, human or otherwise.

The Shaper hadn't relinquished control, not even when Rien had shouted her name, nor when Evita had leapt at her and tried to knock the staff out of her hands. Yet part of Zelle remained conscious beneath the Shaper's presence, screaming to be released.

What are you doing? She directed the silent question at the presence in her mind. The enemy was gone, Daimos had fled, and with the destruction of Invicten's Relics, there was no need for the Shaper to unleash horrors upon innocent people.

"Zelle!" Rien's voice echoed from above. Heedless of the constructs swirling around her, he jumped off the dragonet's back and landed on the pier. "Zelle, you have to stop this."

The Shaper watched him without emotion. "Haven't you killed Daimos yet?"

Disbelief flickered in his eyes. "What does it matter to you, Shaper?"

"I know how your quest for revenge has consumed you." Zelle's voice spoke, but the words weren't hers. "That's why I gave you that Relic. If you want to throw the favour back at me, then I can take it away just as easily."

No, she thought, but the Shaper moved her hands, reaching for Rien's staff. He took a sharp step back, his face pinched as if in pain, but the marks on his hands ignited crimson, and so did the staff, which he lifted into the air. Did he think he was a match for the nameless Shaper?

She'd prove him wrong. Pointing at him with the staff, she sent the constructs surging over Rien in a rippling cloud. He staggered, and in a sweep of wings, the dragonet swooped down and grabbed Rien in a claw, lifting him out of range. Swatting at constructs with his staff, Rien one-handedly clambered onto the dragonet's back. He looked down at Zelle from his perch, his mouth set in a grim line. "I'm sorry, Zelle. Chirp—grab her, and don't let go."

The Shaper made a noise of outrage, but the dragonet obeyed his command and grabbed Zelle around the middle, lifting her into the air—staff and all. Constructs surged upward at the dragonet, but the beast picked up speed, wings pumping with such speed that it was a wonder Rien didn't fall off.

"If you fight back, I'll drop you," Rien warned. "I doubt you can possess a corpse, Shaper."

"You wouldn't," said the Shaper from Zelle's mouth. "You care too much for her to risk her life."

Rien grimaced. "I care about Zelle. Not you."

Yes, thought Zelle, triumphant in the wake of the Shaper's fury. If she had to die, then so be it. Anything was better than the Shaper remaining in control of her body, and Rien ought to know that better than anyone.

They flew over the upper-class district and the palace and towards the lowest peak of the Range. Without any fog masking the view, the route was clear, and Zelle realised where he was taking her a heartbeat before the Shaper did.

"No!" Incensed, the Shaper fought to free the staff from the dragonet's grip, but his claws had locked around Zelle's arm, not the staff itself. Her fragile human body was no match for the dragonet, and if the Shaper kept pushing, She'd break Zelle's delicate human bones.

Rien leaned over to speak to her. "It's time for you to go back to prison."

"How dare you!" the Shaper screamed. "I will end you."

Constructs burst from the mountain in a tide of grey and black, but the dragonet flew too high for them to reach Rien.

"It's up to you," he said. "When I ask the dragonet to let go, you can either let her fall to her death and then wait for the next fool to offer themselves as a host for you, which might take another few thousand years... or you can save her."

With the latter option, the Shaper would remain in control of Zelle's body but only by enlisting the magic of the Range and bringing Zelle back into Her own territory. That might give her a fighting chance of wresting control of her body back, and while that didn't mean she'd succeed, Rien had enough faith in her to make one last gamble.

Go on, she whispered silently. *Let go.*

Rien squeezed his eyes shut then opened them again, a determined glint in his expression. "Do it."

The dragonet's claw released Zelle, sending her tumbling into the air. While she felt no fear at the mountains careening below, the Shaper's own thoughts began to seep into her own. Would waiting for another host truly be so terrible? If it took a year or a thousand, it made no difference... but it would deprive Her of the opportunity to make Arien Astera pay for his trickery.

As she neared the mountain path, the ground split open, and Zelle fell into the darkness. Her fall slowed, and a familiar void of emptiness cocooned her. A soft, suffocating sensation pressed on her from all angles that hadn't been present the last time she'd been inside the Shaper's prison.

Her prison. Rien had known that saving Zelle's life would have required the Shaper to bring Zelle to the one place she could fall into without her bones shattering against the hard ground... and the one place the Shaper Herself couldn't get out of.

"Did you grow fond of me after all?" Zelle was surprised when the words came from her own mouth without any resistance. "No, you're too vindictive for that."

"Speak for yourself." Not to be suppressed, the Shaper also spoke through her mouth. "I hope you're happy with your fate, then."

"What was the alternative? Let you use your constructs to attack innocent people?" Zelle said. "I thought you'd be satisfied once Invicten's Relics were destroyed, but you weren't."

If she had to live here with her own guilt for however long a human Relic's lifespan turned out to be, so be it. Anything was better than letting the Shaper walk free.

"They would never have let me live in peace," said the Shaper. "This land was *mine*, mine alone, for countless years before humans ever set foot here."

"You want *Zeuten?*" It sounded absurd, and yet the Shaper had been here for so long that it shouldn't be surprising that She'd developed a territorial streak. "You want to drive out all the humans? Really?"

"If I cannot return to my former home, then it's only fair that I am allowed to claim dominion here, in the lands I was imprisoned in long before your people set foot in these mountains."

"That isn't reasonable in the slightest." Not that it mattered to a deity, let alone a Great Power. "Was it all a ruse, then? Everything you did to help me—to help the Sentinels?"

"You always knew what I was," the Shaper said. "I never lied."

"You did. At least once." Hadn't the Shaper claimed that She had closed the doors between realms to spare humanity the wrath of the warring gods? "You made it sound as if you were unjustly imprisoned here for trying to stop humanity from being destroyed in wars with the deities, but I bet that's not how it went at all. Am I right?"

"My siblings' children did wreak destruction across both realms with their petty wars," said the Shaper. "You saw it for yourself."

"The Sentinels' cave is entirely under your control," said Zelle. "You could have fabricated any vision you wanted to convince me you had humanity's best interests in mind."

"Everything I showed you was true," the Shaper said. "You can choose to disbelieve me, but my imprisonment was a cruel act on behalf of my siblings."

"Maybe you're all as bad as each other, then." The Shaper was entirely self-interested, like all deities, but the betrayal left a cold, hollow sensation in her chest. "If you feel like telling me the full story, we have all the time in the world now."

No response came. Nor did Zelle have the energy to start another argument. The prison was rather like the deities' realm in a way; she felt no real earthly concerns like hunger or tiredness. Her exhaustion was more of a bone-deep weariness born of her resignation to an eternal future of solitude.

Moments passed, turning to minutes. Zelle fell into a stupor, and she didn't notice the face looking down at her until her grandmother cleared her throat.

Zelle startled. "What... Grandma?"

Her grandmother peered down into the Shaper's prison through what appeared to be a window, like a doorway into the realm of the Powers. When she saw

Zelle looking back, the Sentinel tutted. "Foolish girl. It *is* you, isn't it?"

"For now." Zelle gave a wry smile. "We're going to spend an eternity tussling over control over my body, or until I die, anyway. It's no more than I deserve for trusting the Shaper."

"I'm to blame as well," said Grandma. "I should have listened to my instincts."

"You did warn me. I should have listened." The Shaper might have been her ally—or to be more accurate, the staff had—but ultimately, She had had Her own agenda from the start.

"It's not over," said Grandma. "There's hope for you yet, but it relies on *you* staying in control, not the Shaper."

"Hope for me to do what, exactly?"

"Stop Daimos," she replied. "You didn't think he'd leave you alone to feel sorry for yourself in confinement, did you? I'd wager he's factored this development into his plans, and if he hasn't, he'll be scheming at how to get the nameless Shaper's Relic into his own hands."

"I'd like to see him try getting in here."

"I wouldn't tempt fate," Grandma warned. "Believe me."

Zelle raised a brow. "*Can* he get in here?"

The Shaper answered. "I cannot leave this prison, but any other deity can come and go as they please, assuming I let them."

"Then if Daimos comes here, feel free to destroy him yourself." She closed her eyes, weariness once again settling over her like a heavy cloak. "It might be the last bit of excitement either of us sees for a while."

35

I hope Rien knows what he's doing, Aurel thought, watching the dragonet carry Zelle away through the open doorway.

She'd taken her attention off Daimos, which was a mistake. Movement made her spin on her heel, but sharp thorns seized the knife from her hand and cast it aside, while Daimos grabbed her arm. When she fought, he twisted painfully, dragging her further into the realm of the Powers.

"Let me go!" she hissed, but his grip was like iron, and the wild look in his eye betrayed his fury that Zelle had been snatched from his grasp.

"Follow them," he ordered the three deities. "Now."

"They're moving too fast," protested the false Daimos.

"That isn't good enough." The real Daimos kept a tight hold on Aurel, jarring her injured arm, while she waited for an opening to break free of Daimos's hold.

None came. The deities argued back and forth, doorways opening in the air to show various views of the city and the mountains beyond. The dragonet had surely flown back into the Shaper's domain, and Daimos told the deities as much.

The bottom dropped out of Aurel's stomach when she watched her sister fall, tumbling over and over towards the mountains below.

"No!" She shrieked in pain when Daimos twisted her arm again. "Let me out of here."

"Do you want to fall to your death too?" His gaze was flinty. "Besides, she's not dead. Look."

Ignoring the spasm of agony in her shoulder, she saw her sister's fall had ceased an instant before she'd touched the hard path below. Instead, a thick mist arose to swallow her. *The Shaper... saved her?*

"Where is she?" Daimos hissed in her ear. "Where did the Shaper take her?"

"How should I know?" she gasped, dizzy with pain. "I can't see... ow. The mountains are riddled with passages and caves, you know."

"She wouldn't have survived that fall without help from the Shaper's source." Daimos yanked on her arm again, prompting another gasp, as he gestured at the other deities. "Find Her."

Aurel hung from his grip, trying not to pass out, as the view from the doorway shifted over and over—until Daimos let out a triumphant cry.

She lifted her head. A patch of whiteness dominated her vision, the doorway having opened on what appeared to be a deep pit smothered in thick mist. It had no floor or walls, nothing anchoring Zelle in place as she hovered in the air, suspended above nothingness.

"Zelle," Aurel whispered. "Don't—don't touch her!"

Pain ripped up her injured arm when Daimos shoved her to the ground and stalked towards Zelle.

"Clever of Arien, bringing you to the one place where the Shaper is weakened," Daimos called to Zelle. To Aurel, he added, "It looks as if your sister is back in control of herself. You should be pleased."

"Would you stake the lives of everyone on this planet on that?" Grandma's voice prompted Aurel to push upright, frowning in confusion. Her grandmother peered at Zelle through a window in the air, but instead of the realm of the Powers, she appeared to be in a cave. It appeared, in fact, as though her grandmother was watching the Shaper's prison through the surface of the Sentinels' rock. Which ought to be impossible, but who was to say?

Daimos didn't appear remotely surprised at her appearance. "Sentinel, I didn't intend for us to meet under these circumstances," he said, "but I can assure you that I have a plan to control the nameless Shaper's host and prevent any more unintended destruction."

"You can't control Her," warned Grandma. "If you remove Her from this prison, She'll kill you, and you'll deserve it."

"I disagree." Daimos reached into the pocket of his cloak with his free hand. "From the moment I learned the nameless Shaper was imprisoned here, I began searching for answers from the other deities on how such an event came about. It was obvious that the other two Great Powers combined their forces to do so, and while a mere human cannot hope to achieve such a feat, it can be replicated."

"What are you talking about, you foolish little man?"

Grandma scoffed. "Whatever the deities told you, the Shaper cannot be controlled."

"Your granddaughter isn't the Shaper," said Daimos. "She's a Relic. More formidable than the staff, I grant you, which is what I originally intended to use this for… but she's still a Relic in the end."

Aurel's heart lurched when Daimos held up a length of what appeared to be rope, the same glittering blue colour as one of Gaiva's Relics with a hint of the silvery sheen of the Changer's cloaks. Invicten and Gaiva's magic, melded into one. He must have taken one of Gaiva's Relics from Itzar together with one of Invicten's and forged this rope with the intention of neutralising the staff.

Would the same work on a human Relic? Aurel suspected he had no more idea than she did, but Daimos had no hesitation as he reached for Zelle's staff with the hand in which he held the ropes.

The staff ignited, but the blue glow faded in an instant, and Aurel gasped when the Relic fell from Zelle's hands. Daimos seized both of her hands, pulling the ropes around her wrists and tying them in a firm knot.

Then he dragged her through the doorway and into the realm of the Powers. The deities hastily shuffled away, as if they feared the Shaper even now, but Daimos showed no fear as he pushed Zelle to her knees.

Aurel thought she'd see the Shaper looking through her sister's eyes, but while Zelle wore a dazed expression, there were no traces of another entity. Instead, her eyes widened at the sight of her sister. "Aurel…"

"I won't lie—I'm glad to see you again." She'd thought the Shaper would ensure she never saw Zelle in control of her own body again… but this was different. Would

Daimos's handmade Relic hold up outside of the Shaper's prison? Even if it did, Daimos must know that a Relic alone couldn't permanently hold back a Great Power.

The doorway winked out of existence along with the Shaper's prison, while Daimos pulled Zelle upright again. The false Daimos, the only one of the three deities who'd stayed close enough to watch, met Aurel's gaze with frightened eyes.

"Please," Aurel whispered to him. "You must know nothing good can come of this. Help me stop him."

"Pay her no attention," the real Daimos told the deity. "Open me a doorway to the harbour."

In an instant, another window in the air appeared, revealing Zeuten's seafront. The mist had barely cleared, and the wreckage of Aestin's fleet was still visible in the water.

"Good." Daimos tugged on Zelle's hands. "We have work to do."

———

Evita watched from the ground, waiting for the dragonet's return, but a familiar flash of light signalled a doorway opening.

To her astonishment, Aurel emerged behind a man with a crimson staff—Daimos? Or his double?—who had Zelle at his mercy, her wrists bound with ropes. How could he have subdued the nameless Shaper? It had to be a trick.

Aurel hurried over to Evita's side, clutching her injured arm. "We're in trouble."

"I can see that." Evita sucked in a breath. "How... is that Zelle? Or the Shaper?"

Aurel grimaced. "Long story short, Invicten and Gaiva combined their magic and gave their lives to imprison the Shaper in the mountain. Daimos figured he could do the same with a pair of Relics in order to neutralise the staff, and he decided to try the same on Zelle, since she's effectively a Relic herself."

"Oh, Powers." As Evita watched, Daimos dragged Zelle by her bound hands, wearing the expression of someone contemplating a room full of great riches. "He can't get away with this."

"Where's Rien when we need him?"

"Good question." The last Evita had seen of Rien, he'd been flying on the dragonet to drop Zelle as far from the seafront as possible. In her absence, the constructs had faded, but in her current state, she couldn't use her magic at all. Daimos had her entirely at his mercy. "I can fly... but you can't."

Not without the dragonet.

"Well observed." Aurel clutched her arm. "Bastard threw me around, but I think I got off lightly."

Daimos had all his attention on Zelle. He wasn't watching either of them. *Think, Evita.* He might have the upper hand on Zelle, but nobody else was on his side, including both armies he'd abandoned. Or what was left of them.

Evita turned her attention to the newly clear sky, where the Changers formed a silvery blur above the city. "I think they're scared to get too close to the Shaper."

"Typical." Aurel peered up at the eagle-riding warriors circling in the distance. "We almost had the wielders of

Gaiva's and Invicten's Relics fighting side by side with one another."

Against the Shaper. An idea hit her. "I'll see if I can convince them."

"All right," Aurel said. "I'll cover your back."

"Thanks." Evita spread out her cloak and took flight, launching herself into the air. She let the wind currents carry her upward until she flew on a level with the gathering Changers.

"Hey." She addressed Briony and Verne. "It might have escaped your attention, but Daimos has captured the nameless Shaper and intends to use her power against us all. Did you plan on watching him do it?"

"We have no intention of aiding either of them." Briony spoke in a weary tone. "We've suffered enough losses already."

"He's one man, and you outnumber him," Evita pointed out. "Look—he's used that rope to counter the Shaper, but once he takes it off Zelle, Her magic will hit whoever is standing in her path. He doesn't intend to leave anyone alive. You won't escape."

Verne had gone pale. "We cannot fight the nameless Shaper."

"You can stall Daimos and stop him from setting Her free," said Evita. "In fact—where are your spare cloaks?"

"In the palace," said Briony. "Why? Do you mean to steal them for yourself?"

"No, but I'd say you need to replenish your ranks," she said. "Those cloaks of yours contain the power of Invicten, and there are Relics of Gaiva here, too, in the hands of the islanders of Itzar. Combined, those are the only two deities who've ever come close to subduing the Shaper. Just—think about it."

She didn't wait for a reply. Leaving the Changers in the air, she soared down to land next to Aurel.

"Any luck?" Aurel's attention was fixed on her sister and Daimos.

"I did all I could." A flare of silvery light overhead told her the Changers were on the move. "Let's hope some of them are going to the palace. I think we'll need those Relics of theirs."

"You have a plan?" Aurel said out of the corner of her mouth. "Do I want to know what it is?"

"Not really a plan," said Evita. "More of a last resort."

Aurel gave a laugh tinged with despair. "Isn't that all we have left?"

Rien sat on the dragonet's back as they circled the peak, checking to be sure Zelle and the Shaper didn't reappear. Once they'd ascertained that they'd vanished into the mountain, he directed Chirp to fly south to the capital again.

I made the right choice, he told himself, but that did nothing to quell the hollow sensation in his chest. He'd stopped the Shaper and lost Zelle in the process. That she wasn't dead didn't matter. He'd never see her again either way.

As he flew over the harbour, a familiar brightness caught his eye. A doorway had opened on the seafront, and out of the doorway came none other than Naxel

Daimos—and to his horror, Zelle was with him, her arms bound with silver-blue ropes.

Is that a Relic? It had to be—but how could Daimos have subdued the nameless Shaper?

A familiar pain throbbed in his left hand when Daimos looked up, seeing his approach. The crimson glow of his enemy's staff urged him to strike Daimos down, but Zelle remained at his mercy, and there was no sign of her own staff at all.

Daimos gestured at Zelle with his staff. "I suppose I ought to thank you for delivering her into my hands after all, Arien."

"You have no idea what you're doing." Did he even have a plan? Most of his army was in ruins, the harbour was a wreck, and from his casual grip on his staff, he didn't even seem to care about Astiva's Relic any longer.

"I have the nameless Shaper at my mercy," said Daimos. "If you attack me, I will set Her free."

"And seal your own fate," Rien said. "As well as everyone else's."

"Not at all," he replied. "She is a Relic, and I can claim her if I so desire."

"Then you forfeit Astiva." A spasm hit him, half pain and half hope, together with a jolt of anger from Zierne's Relic.

"It's not impossible to wield more than one Relic, you know." Daimos's mouth twisted. "That's just a lie Aestin teaches its Invokers to put limits on their ambitions. How do you think I killed you the first time around? I held your father's Relic when I struck you dead, as well as Orzen's."

Raw fear clamped over his chest. Daimos had lost his

mind, but what if he was right? If he truly could claim a piece of the Shaper as his own, then nobody would dare to challenge him again. And that wasn't even considering that he intended to claim *Zelle* too.

A silvery cloud passed overhead, and a stream of arrows rained down on Daimos. Rien startled, surprised to see the Changers had stayed, let alone continued the fight.

Daimos deflected their arrows with ease, crimson vines snatching each one out of the air, and a renewed surge of anger arose at the sight of his former Relic in his enemy's hands—but Daimos had also taken his eyes off Zelle. She looked exhausted, but her face was her own again, and Rien forced his attention away from Astiva's staff to hurry over to her.

Zelle gave him an accusing look. "You threw me into the mountain."

"It worked, by the looks of things."

She lowered her gaze, ducking her head as more arrows narrowly missed Daimos. "Not for long. If he removes this rope, then I'm his weapon to destroy whatever he points me at."

"Not if he can't claim you." Out of the corner of his eye, he watched as Daimos continued to deflect the arrows raining upon him. "How does he know it'll work? Claiming a human as a Relic?"

"He doesn't," she said. "He's improvising, and Powers help anyone who tries to talk sense into him. I can't get the rope off myself. It's made from a mixture of Invicten's and Gaiva's magic, like the Shaper's prison."

"That's how the Great Powers did it." Removing the rope himself would free the Shaper, which was out of the question, but he could at least get her away from Daimos. "Come with me—"

"Don't you even think about it, Arien." Daimos swung his staff and sent a wave of vines at him. Rien blocked with his own staff, Zierne's anger rising to meet his own —but the vines weren't aiming for him after all.

Vines snaked around Zelle's wrists, on top of the ropes. *Powers above.*

The ropes loosened, and Zelle stretched out her hands. Bluish light flared, and a wave of constructs surged up to the sky to meet the Changers. Her expression turned distant, intently focused, and when Daimos reached to grab the ropes from where they'd fallen to the ground, Rien hit him.

He didn't even bother with Zierne's magic, simply pounding the end of the staff into Daimos's skull. Daimos staggered, spitting blood, and fell back under a clawed, winged construct that detached itself from the swarm.

It didn't come as a surprise to Rien that the Shaper wanted Daimos dead despite owing him Her newfound freedom, but despite himself, he felt the urge to snatch his enemy out of the way. Zierne longed to destroy Daimos himself, but if Rien let the Shaper kill Daimos, he'd then have to tie the rope around Zelle's wrists with his own hands.

As if she sensed his thoughts, Zelle gave Rien a considering look. "I'm feeling generous. Go on, you two can finish your fight, and I won't interfere."

Daimos beat back the last of the Shaper's constructs, slowed by the injury Rien had dealt him. Zierne's magic roared in his hands, demanding revenge, but common sense told him to pick up the rope and trap the nameless Shaper before She tore the city to the ground.

Why not both? A crimson light engulfed his staff, and vines grabbed Daimos and reeled him in like a fish on a hook. Thorns lashed against thorns, a repeat of their first battle, but this time he was acutely conscious of how his staff's magic reacted both in accordance with and independently of Rien's own command, driving Daimos into retreat.

The ropes. Get to the ropes. He moved towards Zelle without ceasing his attack on Daimos, and when she looked directly at him, the inhumanity in her gaze made him falter. With Zierne urging him to destroy Daimos, did he look as much unlike himself as she did, with the Shaper in control of her actions? Had his Relic's anger been mingling with his own until he couldn't tell where his ended and Zierne's began? Maybe the rumours were true and Zierne's appetite for violence went beyond Rien's own need for retribution, but Daimos had to die, didn't he?

A doorway to the realm of the Powers opened in a flash of light, but vanished an instant later, and Zelle shook her head. "No running away, Daimos."

Daimos spat out blood. "I set you free."

"By enslaving me to your will." Zelle kicked the ropes with enough force to send them sliding down the slick surface of the harbour towards the ocean.

Rien backed down the seafront, ready to lunge for them, but Zelle advanced on him, casually swatting away both his and Daimos's vines as she might a swarm of midges.

"I've changed my mind." To Rien's confusion, she

turned to Daimos first. "Since you both imprisoned me, I think I should kill you both myself."

Extending a hand, she plucked Astiva's staff out of Daimos's grip. Rien's heart contracted, a spasm of pain striking his left hand even as Zierne's Relic ignored Zelle's presence and urged him to strike down his enemy while he was vulnerable.

A cruel smile tilted Zelle's mouth. "Ah, yes, the infamous sibling rivalry lives on even in your Relics. Look at them."

Zierne's Relic stirred in Rien's hand, vines lashing outward and gripping Astiva's staff. Daimos tried in vain to snatch it away, but Zierne's vines snaked up and down the other staff until Zelle released it, still wearing that horrific mockery of a smile. Astiva's staff remained suspended in the air, smothered in Zierne's vines. If the Relics truly did contain any hint of the real deities, then Zierne didn't want to help Rien reclaim his old Relic... He wanted to destroy it.

"Zierne," he gasped out. "Stop. Now."

Zelle tilted her head as if in fascination while Rien fought to regain control over the vines crushing Astiva's staff. "I expected this to happen sooner, truth to be told. When guided that Relic into your hands, part of me thought you'd give in to the struggle right away. You have more patience than most Invokers, more of an even temperament... but in the end, Zierne's Relic will have its way."

Daimos said nothing. He'd dropped to a crouch, right hand gripping his left wrist and moaning softly. *His Relic is breaking.* Zierne's magic was crushing his Relic, and if it shattered, so would Daimos.

And so would Astiva.

Zelle smiled widely, no traces of her true self visible through the Shaper's mask. Given the chance, would Zierne take over Rien's body the same way the Shaper had done to Zelle? There wasn't enough of him present inside the Relic to achieve that feat, surely, but it was plain to see that his Relic was no longer listening to a word he said.

"Stop!"

He wrenched his staff, *demanding* that Zierne's vines release the other Relic. Astiva's staff jerked in midair, and Rien's heart gave another agonised spasm. How could a Relic he'd lost still cause him such pain?

Unless... during his fight with Daimos earlier, Rien had been sure, for a short time, that Astiva's Relic had answered to his command and spared his life. He might be deluding himself if he thought Astiva himself had been present in any way, but it was the Relic he'd bound himself to, and the godsmark remained, broken but undeniable.

Rien focused on the ever-present throbbing pain in his left hand and imagined the glow of Astiva's Relic returning to the staff and fighting Zierne's hold. The two were siblings, equal in power, and if Daimos wasn't willing to make an effort to save his own Relic, then Rien would have to do it for him.

Pain shot through *both* his hands, as if Zierne objected violently to his intrusion—but Astiva's Relic began to glow brighter beneath the grip of Zierne's vines.

Rien staggered when Zierne's vines shattered, releasing Astiva's Relic. *Yes.*

Extending a hand, Zelle caught Astiva's staff in her

hand. "Allow me to rid you of your dilemma forever, Arien Astera."

With speed no human could hope to match, she reached out and seized Zierne's Relic, the staff tearing loose from his grip. With one staff in each hand, Zelle clenched her fists, which ignited with white-blue light.

Both staffs broke clean in two, the halves falling to the ground, and a familiar roaring agony ripped through Rien's arms, causing him to fall to his knees. A yawning cavity opened in his chest, and his strength gave out, his forehead resting on the harbour floor.

With his last shred of awareness, he reflected that if he had to die, at least he'd take Daimos along with him.

His vision flickered, but he could see that Zelle stood over him. Or someone did, a blurred winged figure that was surely a conjuration of his fading mind. His hands twitched on the ground, one palm brushing against a piece of Astiva's staff. He might not be able to see it, but he'd always recognise the sensation of the smooth wood beneath his hand. Grasping for the rest, his other hand found the end of Zierne's staff, still throbbing with the fury its deity had left behind.

Rien held on tightly to both as the last of the light faded to darkness.

Zelle watched Rien give one last desperate lunge towards the broken Relics before collapsing onto his front. Beside him, Daimos lay still enough to be dead already. Pity, really. She could have made use of him.

Not Rien, though. He'd keep trying to bring her back

to herself, and it would be incredibly tedious to watch. Better that he'd died fighting, the way he'd planned.

A bright flash drew her gaze upwards, where the Changers were putting up a valiant fight against her constructs. Helping them were several eagles, their riders wielding Gaiva's Relics. Evita was there, too—and Aurel, sitting on the dragonet's back. Did they not see their struggle was futile? No human could hope to match the nameless Shaper.

Upon seeing her sister standing over Rien's body, Aurel flew downward. "Bloody Powers, Zelle, you had to go and kill him, didn't you?"

"Aurel, get away from her!" Evita shouted. "There's nothing restraining the Shaper now."

The dragonet hovered without descending any lower, though the Shaper had no interest in taking his life. Dragonets owed their magical gifts to the era when the Powers had walked in the human realm, and while this one was a juvenile, the Shaper wouldn't destroy a remnant of the days in which She had been free.

Of course, She was free now, but the Changers would have to be dealt with. Raising a hand, Zelle was disarmed to see the constructs had fallen into retreat, driven back by the eagle-riding islanders. She'd have to deal with *them* first.

Aurel and Evita exchanged a few words, the latter gesturing at the Changers if giving them instructions, and Zelle lifted her hands to strike them down.

A bolt of blinding light surged towards Zelle from the islanders. She raised her hands to deflect their icy magic, which shattered on the seafront, only for someone to seize her shoulders from behind.

She jerked out of their grip, but a hood came down on her head, a fluid material that she nevertheless recognised. *Invicten.*

The humans dared to use Her siblings' magic against her? Enraged, she twisted around to shake off the cloak they'd thrown on her, but more icy magic rained down, cutting through her constructs and shattering against the pier. Changers flew around in circles, dodging her attempts to knock them out of the sky and further occupying her constructs.

By the time she realised the water coating the pier was freezing to slick ice, her feet had already slid out from underneath her. She hit the ground hard with a hiss that was more humiliation and anger than pain—and felt someone grab her hands.

A laugh escaped her. "Are you asking to die?"

"No." That was Evita's voice, speaking in her ear as she tied Daimos's ropes around her wrists. "You're bound by the magic of Gaiva and Invicten."

To her shock, the Shaper's influence withdrew, leaving Zelle reeling and sore. She struggled into a sitting position on the ice-slick pier, her hands bound behind her back. Evita hadn't tied her bonds as tightly as Daimos had, but as long as Zelle remained in control...

"You have to take me back to the mountains," Zelle warned. "Drop me back into the Shaper's prison."

It was only a matter of time before the Shaper found a way to break free again, and now Zelle knew that the Shaper had been the one who'd killed the other two Great Powers, and that the last shreds of their combined magic had seen to Her imprisonment, letting Her take control again was out of the question.

Aurel approached her, biting her lower lip. "Ah... Zelle. There's something you ought to know."

"What?" Her gaze followed her sister's, and then she saw Rien lying as still as the grave, clutching one half of each broken staff in each hand "Rien."

His eyes flickered open at the sound of her voice. "Zelle."

Both Evita and Aurel jumped, while pain pierced her chest, the realisation that she'd brought him to the brink of death crashing over her like a storm. Did he even realise he'd picked up half of Astiva's staff and the other half of Zierne's?

"I... I'm sorry." *Powers above.* "Can I fix this?"

The Shaper would know, but the Shaper was no longer an ally of hers. Panic flared like a torch inside her, and her pleading gaze sought Aurel's.

"I don't know," Aurel said. "Look, it's not my area of expertise. What do you want us to do?"

She cast a brief glance at the gathering Changers, who'd been joined by Gaiva's Blades and even some of the soldiers from the royal palace. Finally, everyone was on the same side—but united against her. Or rather, against the Shaper.

Rien stirred. "Not... your fault."

"It is." Her eyes burned. "I'll—make you a new Relic. I'll bully the Shaper into it if I have to. You know how to create a Relic, right?"

"Yes..." His eyes closed again. "It's too late, though."

Oh, Powers. She'd severed his link with Zierne, and he'd lost his connection to Astiva long ago. Maybe she could transfer the power to a new Relic, but who could say whether he'd be able to use it again?

"Never mind that," he whispered. "Get the Shaper back to Her prison before it's too late."

Right. It wouldn't do to let the Shaper take command again, and however badly it hurt her to leave him, Rien's dilemma didn't outweigh the fate of humanity. She'd willingly turned herself into a Relic and had only herself to blame for the devastation that had followed. There was no undoing the damage to Rien; the Shaper alone knew how, and why would She share that information with Zelle after her betrayal?

Aurel cleared her throat. "I may know someone who can deliver you directly back into your prison without the need to fly."

Zelle swivelled to a nearby doorway to the realm of the Powers. The fact that one of the deities on the other side of the door looked exactly like Daimos barely registered. She was too tired, too full of regrets. "You're sure they won't take me hostage instead?"

"They all hate the nameless Shaper," Aurel replied. "It's unlikely."

Zelle sucked in a breath, the pain of leaving Rien as acute as a missing limb, but she could do nothing but hurt him as long as she remained a Relic of the Shaper.

Before she could take another step, however, Grandma pushed her way past the deities and glowered at her through the open doorway. "I'm glad to see you're back to yourself."

"Only because the other Great Powers are keeping mine in check, but it won't last forever. Look, I need to go back to the Shaper's prison, unless you know someone who can get the Shaper's magic out of me without ending up dead."

If that was even an option, which she severely doubted. The sight of the staff in her grandmother's hand ignited a new possibility in her mind. *There's more than one Relic of the Shaper.* She already knew from talking to Rien that it was possible to transfer the magic from one Relic to another or even remove it; the families of Aestin did so all the time whenever they had too few or too many heirs to inherit their Invoker parent's magic.

Would transferring the Shaper's magic from Zelle to another Relic work? Even if it was possible, who could possibly achieve such a feat, save for the Shaper Herself?

Grandma studied her. "You have an idea?"

"A binding spell might do it..." She faltered when her grandmother gave a nod as if she'd confirmed some suspicion of hers. "No. Not you."

Grandma sighed. "Don't fight me on this, Zelle. Someone needs to cast the spell—not you either, Aurel."

Aurel made an indignant noise. "Why not?"

"Because you aren't used to working with the staff. I am."

Zelle shook her head. "The staff isn't just going to let you rip out my magic and put it somewhere else."

"I'll need some help, certainly." She pointed into the doorway. "Come on."

Zelle followed, not knowing what else to do, and her grandmother led her a short distance to another open doorway, this one leading into the Sentinels' cave.

"How were you able to speak to me in the Shaper's prison?" Zelle asked. "You were using the rock, right?"

"Correct," Grandma replied. "I bullied the rock into telling me how to access the Shaper's prison without going inside."

"Of course you did." It surprised her less than it should have that her grandmother had succeeded in bullying a Relic, much less accessing the most well-hidden part of the mountain. "Did you and the Shaper have a chat? The part that's left behind, that is?"

"Oh, there's not much of Her left in there," said Grandma. "She pushed as much magic into you as you could handle without your mind breaking into shreds, but a fair portion of Her is in the rock... and then there's the staff, of course."

No wonder the Shaper was able to use the rock to show Zelle a false vision of the past. "Where did you plan to put the Shaper's consciousness once you'd pulled it out of me?"

"The rock itself, of course," she said. "If that fails, we can find an alternative. There's plenty of possible Relics in the Reader's house."

But not plenty of time. Rien was dying, if he hadn't already, and she could hear the Shaper beating at the back of her mind, demanding to be free.

"Aurel, Evita, remove those ropes and then don't let her go."

At Grandma's command, Aurel and Evita each took hold of one of Zelle's arms. The material binding her loosened, and the Shaper came roaring to the surface. As she lunged for freedom, Grandma brought the staff down upon her shoulder. A shock of pain struck her, and she stumbled against the rock.

"I bind you, Shaper," Grandma said, her voice echoing in the cave. "I bind you to this Relic. In the name of all of humanity."

The Sentinel's rock glowed brighter. Zelle screamed, a

primal sound, as a torrent of power rushed out of her. The Shaper's magic ripped free like a scab from a wound, leaving a gaping emptiness inside her chest.

Her knees hit the ground, her shoulder throbbing. She was fairly sure the staff had broken a bone, but at least it hadn't snapped her in two, as she'd done to Rien's Relic.

Rien.

"Grandma!"

Zelle lifted her head at her sister's cry, and her mouth went dry. Grandma lay on her back with the staff in her hand, unmoving. She'd used her last vestiges of strength to perform the binding spell, and Zelle didn't need to listen for her heartbeat to know it had faded.

"Grandma." Zelle moaned, half in pain; the Shaper's withdrawal had caused all her hurts to come flaring back. Her knees ached, her shoulder throbbed, and yet none of it mattered. "Grandma…"

"She's gone." Aurel stepped over her and delivered a vicious kick to the Sentinel's rock. Cursing, she hobbled back to her grandmother's side. "Ow. That hurt."

"She…" Tears blurred Zelle's vision. "Why did she do that?"

"For you, of course." Aurel groaned. "Fucking *deities.*"

Evita cleared her throat. 'Ah—you should know you left the doorway open."

Zelle jerked upright, giving the staring deities a blistering glare. "What are you looking at?"

The false Daimos hesitantly walked out of the doorway, Rien's body draped in his arms. "He's alive."

The words slammed into her chest. "You'd better be telling the truth."

"We are, but he just put himself in debt to all of us

several times over on the condition that we kept him alive," Kyren said from behind him.

Zelle made a noise halfway between a laugh and a sob when the false Daimos laid Rien down, and the two pieces of broken staff rolled onto the cave floor. The crimson glow had almost entirely disappeared from both but not quite. "I... I'll see what I can do for him."

Rien's eyes flickered open. "I'm guessing the nameless Shaper won't give me another new Relic this time... but there might be another way."

"Oh?" She leaned closer to him, hardly able to believe he was still conscious. "Like what?"

Rien spoke slowly, each word pained. "You could... put the magic into me instead of a Relic. Make *me* the Relic."

Like the Shaper did to me. "I've never done that to a *person* before. If it doesn't work, you'll die."

"I'll die either way, won't I?"

Her eyes welled up. "Damn you, Arien Astera."

Could she bind a deity's magic to a person? Yes, she'd turned herself into a Relic for the nameless Shaper, but it was anyone's guess as to whether she was capable of doing the same to another person now she was no longer the Shaper's host.

She picked up the broken halves of the staffs, one in each hand. Remnants of power stirred beneath the wooden surfaces, but despite their visible similarities, each felt starkly different. One smooth and polished, one rough and sharp.

"Which Relic?" she asked of Rien. "One of these is Astiva... The other is Zierne."

"Either. Or both." His breaths were shallow. "It doesn't matter. The deity isn't the same as the Relic."

"I have no idea what you're talking about, but I'm not sure I can bind *one* Relic's magic to you, let alone two." She certainly felt the power running through the wooden sticks, but she couldn't grasp it in her own hands the way she had to the Shaper's power. She wasn't strong enough.

Her gaze fell on her own discarded staff. A steely resolve seized her as she reached over her grandmother's limp form and picked up the staff in her hand. "You. Owe me."

How dare you? The staff's voice sounded the same as usual—indignant and peevish. *I saved you from being the Shaper's host.*

"You *are* the Shaper, you miserable stick."

I am, and I am not. Part is not the same as the whole.

What was *that* supposed to mean? She held two broken pieces of different Relics in her hands, admittedly, but the Shaper was one entity, right?

The deity isn't the same as the Relic, Rien had just told her, and it was clear that what the Relics "wanted" didn't reflect the actual deities' wishes any more than they reflected her own. Yet she'd held a significant part of the *actual* Shaper's consciousness inside her own body, and she couldn't deny it hadn't felt anything like when she'd initially joined with the staff.

With Rien dying, she had no time to ponder on the difference. "I need to use your magic. You took my grandmother's life to save mine, so if I have to owe you another favour in return, so be it."

I didn't take her life. She gave it willingly. She told me so herself.

"I don't believe a word you say." But she needed a Relic to perform magic, and the staff was all she had. "If you're being truthful, then tell me every step of how to do this. If you lie, I'll throw you into the prison and tell no future Sentinels about you until everyone forgets you ever existed."

That's harsh. Fine, fine, but hurry up. He doesn't have much time.

Zelle extended the staff to touch Rien's shoulder. "Well?"

Speak the binding words. I will do the rest.

"I bind you... Asitva. I bind you to this vessel." Would that work? She didn't know, but Rien gasped, and a glow suffused his hands and arms, spreading from the two pieces of Relic. "Wait, you're binding both of them to him?"

Even if part of a deity wasn't the same as the whole, could a person survive holding remnants of two deities in their hands at once? Daimos had claimed as much, but Zierne and Astiva were hardly harmonious. She'd seen the struggle herself as Rien had sought to stop Zierne's magic from crushing Astiva's staff—but it was too late to undo the spell.

The glow dimmed around Rien's hands, his eyes closing again. She half expected him to fall unconscious, but instead his mouth tilted into a smile. "I knew you could do it."

"You're going to have to answer for this later, Rien, you know. You might have died."

"No... I trust you." Rien held Astiva's *and* Zierne's magic inside himself. That couldn't last, not without becoming dangerous to his life, but he didn't appear to be struggling the way he had when he'd fought to prevent Zierne's magic from ripping apart Astiva's staff.

He wouldn't have ended up in that situation if not for her. Powers above, how could he possibly trust Zelle after the Shaper had used her mouth to taunt and threaten him? The Shaper had even admitted that She had handed him Zierne's Relic out of a desire to see what chaos would unfold when he had to wield a Relic that refused to submit to his commands and whose deity and his were bitter enemies.

"You're a fool." A sound half sob and half laugh escaped her. "Before I get too close, are you going to get possessed by Zierne and try to fight me?"

"I don't think so."

His words didn't inspire confidence, but she found herself embracing him, tightly, in a way that said more than words could. He released a soft sigh when she buried her head in his shoulder, and when she reluctantly let go, Rien looked almost calm, despite the fresh thorn-like scars glowing on his left hand and spreading up his arm. Could he hear Astiva or Zierne in his mind, like she had with the Shaper? Unlikely, given that neither of his Relics had been conscious like hers was... but it couldn't be anything but harmful to be a Relic himself.

He dragged himself into an upright position. "My two Relics might be at opposing angles, but they were brothers, once, and they seem to be balancing one another out for now. I wonder... will you have to separate them out when you create a new Relic?"

Good question. "I wouldn't have said it was possible, but with the way Invicten and Gaiva's magic could be combined to work against the Shaper... it might be possible for both to be bound to a single Relic if they don't destroy each other first."

"It's worth a try." His shoulders slumped, as if exhausted, his eyes briefly closing. "I don't know why the Shaper led me to that Relic, or why the Sentinels brought it here to begin with. The stories aren't clear, and this might be a huge mistake."

"It might," Zelle confirmed, "but we never really know, do we? The stories are all we have, and they change based on the teller."

Rien inclined his head. "That's a wise perspective."

"I guess it comes from briefly sharing my body with a deity that lived before our world was ever conceived of. The wisdom of age, taken to an extreme."

A laugh escaped him, and she startled when his hand closed around her wrist, pulling her close to him. His lips brushed her ear. "I should have told you how I felt a long time ago. If I don't survive…"

"Enough of that." She released him, her eyes burning. "I'm going to fix this. I'd give you the choice of which object I should turn into your new Relic, but there's not much in here except rocks."

His mouth tilted upward. "Don't you have a scintillating collection of old junk in the Reader's house?"

So she did. "Yes, I do, but make your mind up fast before the staff decides to back out of helping you."

His eyes flew open, alarmed. "You know, I can alter a Relic into any shape I desire when I claim it, so a rock will work fine."

"Good, because I'm not walking all the way down to Tavine." She picked up a stone the size of her palm in her free hand and held the staff in the other.

It was time for her and the Shaper to cast one last spell together.

36

Aurel surveyed the cabinets in the downstairs room of the Reader's house, aware that she needed to dust them but lacking the inclination. Grandma had never bothered to clean, either, and keeping the collection of dust would also keep her memory alive. So Aurel told herself, anyway.

The burial had been a quiet affair, away from prying eyes, but Zelle had left for Saudenne shortly after, answering the summons of that ridiculous Crown Prince. He seemed to have left Aurel off the guest list altogether, which was insulting. Aurel was the official Sentinel now, though the title had never meant less to her, so it would have been nice to have a little recognition.

A prickling on the back of her neck warned her that she was being watched. Putting down the glass of wine she held, Aurel turned around to find a window into the realm of the Powers had opened in the middle of her living room. Two bird-shaped faces looked out at her.

"Have you always been able to do that?" she asked. "Make yourselves visible to me?"

"Yes, but we prefer not to have humans gawking at us," said Xeale.

"The feeling is mutual, believe me." She exhaled in a sigh. "What do you want?"

Since Zelle had left, she'd been at something of a loose end. It didn't help that her arm had taken a few days to heal from the beating she'd taken in the fight, so she hadn't been able to join Evita on flights on the dragonet or help her train with the cloak. Some of the warriors from Itzar had decided to stay for a few days, and she'd had a very pleasant night with Kolt at the local tavern, but everything else had been an annoyance. The Sentinels' cave had sealed itself against entry, and even the shortcuts across the mountains were no longer accessible to her. That meant the outpost was out of bounds until she could fly again, and while her arm felt better today, she'd declined to go with Zelle to the capital after the Crown Prince had so rudely snubbed her. The deities' appearance was the first piece of excitement she'd had all day.

Kyren popped up. "You know what we want."

"Look, I can't set you free," said Aurel. "Zelle can't, either, though you're a few hours too late to catch her."

"You can at least keep us company."

She sank into an armchair. "Why me?"

"Because you kept your promise," said Kyren. "You looked for our Relics."

"That doesn't mean I owe you anything else. And no, I'm not doing the same to every deity in your entire realm."

"All right, then," said Xeale. "We'll take our interesting information elsewhere."

"What information?"

"Oh, now she wants to hear us out." Kyren snickered.

"You can't expect me not to ask questions when you mention *interesting information*," she protested. "What is it?"

"You're a historian, aren't you?" Xeale asked. "Wouldn't you like to know the origin of *your* Relic?"

The words brought her up short. "I know where my Relic came from. The mountains."

"You *don't* know which deity's power resides within it," Kyren said. "It isn't the nameless Shaper."

"I'm sorry, what?" They had to be winding her up out of boredom. Aurel might know less about the deities than she'd realised, but the Book of Reading and the staff had been used together by Sentinels for countless years. The staff might have a few more practical advantages, but both Relics could be used to Read the history of an object or person.

"Ask it yourself," said Kyren. "If you don't believe us."

"Right…" She had nothing better to do with her day, so she decided to humour them. She picked up the Book of Reading and flipped it open. "Two deities claim your power doesn't come from the Shaper. Is that true?"

The pages glowed, and an image flickered into her mind's eye of the book, tucked under the arm of someone walking across the mountain path. More images showed the travellers crouching over the pages of the book, studying them.

But they hadn't found the Shaper until they'd already reached the mountains…

Aurel reeled back. "You're… who are you?"

Words appeared on the page in front of her. *Haven't you guessed?*

She pressed a hand to her forehead. "Our stories… We always thought our magic came from Gaiva, but the staff's power is the Shaper's. Right? Do you mean to say the original Sentinels were guided by Gaiva all along?"

Yes and no. They guided themselves.

They had indeed, and she was willing to bet that Gaiva had accompanied the original settlers from Aestin to Zeuten partly to ensure the Shaper remained in Her prison. The pieces of Invicten that had eventually become the Changers' Relics might have done the same themselves.

"You're welcome," said Kyren.

Aurel lifted her head. "Gaiva. No wonder I was still able to use the Book of Reading even after my sister pissed off the Shaper."

Its magic was nothing like that wielded by the people of Itzar, but there was no reason why Gaiva's power couldn't have been split between multiple Relics on different continents. Gaiva's rock might not have even known Aurel's Relic existed, as they'd never interacted before.

As for the staff, it remained where Aurel and Zelle had left it, in the Sentinels' cave. Zelle seemed to prefer it that way, and Aurel couldn't say she disagreed. She knew better than to trust anything connected to the nameless Shaper again.

Kyren snickered. "Our mother was always a step ahead of Her sister."

"Maybe." She closed the book. "I notice you waited

until after *my* sister left before showing up for a visit. She'd have wanted to know too."

"Your sister worked with the Shaper," Xeale said. "She cannot be trusted."

"We're going to have to disagree on that one." Aurel tucked the book under her arm and went to hunt down her boots amid the piles of junk in the living room. "She was put in an impossible situation. You'd have done the same."

"We would never have freed our mother's killer," Kyren said petulantly.

"She didn't *know* that. The Shaper lied to her." The Sentinel's rock, to be precise, which had shown her a vision that omitted a significant part of the truth. It also cast into question the veracity of the visions the cave had shown Aurel in the past, although none of those had come with such high stakes attached.

Had the Shaper always intended to use the Sentinels to free herself, or had She simply taken advantage of an opportunity? Those questions haunted Zelle more than they did Aurel, though she'd pondered on the subject briefly. Likely it didn't matter; centuries had passed since the original Sentinels' arrival, and given her family's decline over the years, she was inclined to believe the Shaper's possession of her sister had been more of a whim than a calculated move centuries in the making. Zelle herself probably felt differently, but who could blame her, given the ordeal she'd gone through?

Aurel tracked down her boots. As she was tugging them on, she saw that the deities were still watching her from their window. "What is it? If you want payment in exchange for the information you just told me, I don't have anything that would be of use to you."

"You have information," Kyren corrected. "Stories. Your grandmother told us stories."

Aurel blanched. "I thought she was a treacherous human and you never wanted anything to do with her kin again."

"That's true," said Xeale. "It's her fault Daimos tortured us."

"Yet here you are. In my house." Relatively speaking, anyway. "Asking for favours."

"No favours," said Kyren. "An exchange. We have stories of our own, you know."

"Stories are more Zelle's thing than mine." Aurel straightened upright. "I have other interests."

"Such as those artefacts of yours." Xeale eyed the cabinets behind her. "We can bring you more."

"In exchange for what?" Aurel ducked around the cabinet and hunted down her coat. "If you're trying to build up to me giving you unfettered access to the human world, you're going to be waiting a long time. It's impossible."

Their Relics had gone. The only other way for them to be allowed back into the human world would be if someone found a way to undo whatever spell the Shaper had used to seal off the realm of the Powers, which was both unlikely *and* unwise.

"Someday it might not be," Kyren said. "We're long-lived, human, and we've seen more impossible sights in recent times than we have in a thousand years."

"So you're courting favour with the Sentinels, then." At least they were being honest about their intentions, if nothing else. "In case someone figures out how to set you free, so you can rampage around causing havoc among humans like you used to."

"Not at all," Kyren insisted. "We wish to experience the wind on our faces and the ground beneath our feet again."

"You'll have to settle for watching," Aurel told them. "You might find it interesting to see my sister's face when I tell her I've been carrying one of Gaiva's Relics all along, though."

Evita was in the middle of practising manoeuvres with her cloak when a group of Changers swooped down upon the forest path near Tavine. Chirp sat and watched her, gnawing on the carcass of a large rodent he'd caught in the mountains and occasionally chirping encouragement at her. She enjoyed flying with him, but she couldn't deny she was making real progress on her fear of heights when she had wings of her own. Once, she'd even managed to come close to transforming into a bird. Well, she'd conjured up a few feathers, anyway, which was a starting point.

Landing in front of Chirp, she faced the silver-cloaked messengers. "What is it?"

"Evita." Briony spoke from the back of their group. "The Crown Prince has invited us to the palace and told us to invite you too."

The *Crown Prince* wanted to meet with her? Not to arrest her? Granted, Zelle had flown to the capital earlier that day herself, but Evita had imagined the palace guards' fear of retribution from the nameless Shaper would overtake their grievances with Zelle for the damage she'd wrought upon the capital.

"I suppose I can spare the time for His Majesty," she allowed. "Is that where the other Changers are staying?"

"For now," Verne said. "Briony and I have temporarily been put in charge."

That wasn't a surprise to Evita, since there were few other available options. The Changers had suffered a few casualties in the battle, but they'd lost so many people as a result of Daimos's meddling that it was no wonder they'd been desperate enough to look to someone else for guidance. Even a spoilt prince who'd spent the entire battle hiding in his palace.

"Well?" Briony pressed. "Will you come with us?"

As Evita considered her options, Aurel stepped out from behind a bush and answered, "Yes."

"What?" Evita startled. "How long have you been there?"

"Long enough," said Aurel. "I want to go to the capital myself. I just learned something *interesting* about the Book of Reading that I think my sister will want to know."

"Shouldn't you be resting that arm?"

"It's fine." Aurel moved closer to the dragonet, who dropped the rodent's carcass and let her stroke him on the nose. "Want to fly?"

After mounting the dragonet, Aurel flew alongside Evita, who spread her arms wide, soaring over the countryside. Even now, the fear of the drop and the exhilaration of the flight remained in a delicate balance, but she concentrated on the rush of the wind rather than the distance from the ground below. It helped that Aurel was on hand to distract her with the tale of the deities' unexpected visit to her house—and her revelation that her own Relic had belonged to Gaiva all along.

Before she knew it, they'd arrived in Saudenne, soaring over the high walls surrounding the palace. Some of the guards pointed arrows towards them before recognising them as allies—even Evita, though she remained on edge when their group landed and saw the increased number of guards waiting in front of the palace doors.

Aurel ducked her head. "I should probably wait outside. Let my sister know I'm here, won't you?"

Evita and the others climbed the stone staircase, and the guards ushered them into a wide entryway and told them to wait to be called along with their other guest. It was then that Evita spotted Zelle standing against the nearby wall, who gave her a wry smile. "You too?"

"You aren't being arrested, are you?" Zelle had left in such a hurry that morning that Evita hadn't had time to ask her if the visit was for a good reason or a bad one.

"No, but I probably should be," Zelle murmured. "His Highness isn't my biggest fan, but he promised me compensation for the damage my shop suffered in the battle."

"It was that bad?"

"Yes, but it's the least of what I deserved. I think the Crown Prince is too scared to arrest me, personally, in case the Shaper strikes him down."

Given the way the Chargers gave her a wide berth, they seemed to think so too. Briony and Verne waited with several novices Evita didn't know, and she couldn't resist posing a question. "Are you *all* staying here in the palace? Where did your spare Relics end up?"

"Here, of course." Briony indicated the wide hall. "The

royal palace took the cloaks of Changing as compensation for our actions when we were following Daimos's orders."

Her mouth parted. "What do they plan to do with those Relics?"

"That's likely what our meeting is about." Verne gave a brief glance at Zelle. "I don't know why he wants the Sentinel, too…"

"Zelle isn't the Sentinel. That's her sister—who's outside, by the way."

"She is?" Zelle blinked. "I should have guessed she came with you."

"She has something she needs to tell you. Good news, don't worry."

Before she could say more, a door opened, and one of the Emperor's guards beckoned to them. "Zelle Carnelian and Evita Govind, the Crown Prince wishes to meet with the pair of you alone."

Bewildered, Evita followed Zelle through several rooms until they came to one containing a high throne flanked by cabinets full of various objects. Not Relics, she didn't think, though she wouldn't know one if she saw it. Neither would the Crown Prince, according to Zelle.

The Crown Prince himself wasn't much to look at, despite his bright clothing and crown. Mousy-brown hair, a nervous expression… though the latter might be a result of his proximity to Zelle. He took care to avoid her eyes as he addressed the two of them. "Thank you for meeting with me."

Evita gave an awkward bow. "Your Highness."

Zelle made no movement at all. It couldn't be pleasant for her to be back in a place where she'd been held prisoner, and she didn't owe him any respect.

"Zelle Carnelian." He looked at her feet instead of her face. "I want to offer my apologies for how I treated you as a guest here."

"Apology accepted," Zelle said crisply. "I know it was Jarven's influence... mostly."

The Crown Prince flushed. Evita didn't blame her for taking the chance to get under his skin, considering that it sounded as if the Crown Prince had acted on his own when he'd tried to have her arrested, and his desire for an alliance with the wielder of the nameless Shaper had played at least some part in his behaviour.

"And you..." He turned to Evita next. "Evita Govind, I want to apologise to you as well, for failing to notice the enemy's influence on the Changers and for allowing them to treat you so abominably." He spoke in a precise manner, as if he'd practised apologising in front of a mirror for hours beforehand.

All too happy not to prolong their conversation, she replied, "I accept your apology."

"It's clear to me that the Changers can no longer exist in their current form," he said. "I intend to order them to disband."

Evita fidgeted. "I understand why, but I'm not one of them. I—also can't give up my Relic."

"Don't look so worried," he said. "You can keep the cloak. I intended to offer you a job."

Her mouth dropped open. "A job? Me?"

He inclined his head. "After disbanding the Changers, I intend to have them restructured, and I would like you to offer your expertise, as someone who saw their short-comings firsthand."

Evita shook her head. "I'm far from an expert. Ask one

of the Senior Changers... or even the novices. Someone who went through more training than I did."

"So you're saying no?"

Evita's heart leapt into her throat. "I meant no disrespect, your Majesty. I just don't think I can be of any help in that particular area. I, er, wasn't a very good assassin."

"Is there another position you'd prefer?" he asked. "I want to offer you compensation. Would you like to apply to work as a servant here in the palace instead?"

"Definitely not... Your Majesty," she added hastily. "I'm not much good at cleaning either. But I can fly."

"You can fly," he repeated.

"Yes. With the cloak." *Stop talking, Evita.* He might be a fool, but he was still a prince.

He gave her a considering look. "Would you be interested in the position of a royal messenger?"

"I..." He still wanted to offer her employment after she'd turned him down? Maybe he thought Zelle would strike him if he didn't. "You mean carrying messages from the palace to your allies?"

"Yes, but not just in Zeuten," he said. "It's clear to me that I failed to consider the other potential uses of the Changers' Relics, such as in crossing the sea to speak to our neighbours, and you certainly qualify for the job."

Aestin? He wanted her to go to Aestin? She wasn't opposed to the idea, though she'd have thought Zelle would be more suited to the job than she was. "I... I'll have to think about it."

She'd talk to Aurel before accepting any offer, though the Sentinel seemed to have dropped the idea of having Evita work for her. Evita had never intended to stay in

Tavine forever regardless, not where she'd spent her childhood dreaming of leaving her village.

"Good." The Crown Prince returned his attention to Zelle. "Am I right in thinking you no longer hold the Shaper's Relic?"

Zelle flinched, lowering her head. "Correct. The staff is… in the outpost. My sister and I have decided that the Shaper's magic should not be wielded by a human."

"Very well," he replied. "We also need to look into the training of new Invokers, but if you have no magic, teaching will be difficult, I can imagine."

"Yes," she said. "I'm not the right person to teach anyone to use magic. Nothing in my experience was typical."

The Crown Prince's shoulders tensed, perhaps in response to an unpleasant memory. "And… am I right in thinking you intend to return to your grandmother's house?"

Zelle gave a tight nod. "For the time being, yes."

Like her, Evita doubted Zelle would be content to stay there in the long term, but she knew better than to talk her out of it. The Crown Prince dismissed them with visible relief, and the two of them left the throne room. They continued to walk in silence until they reached the top of the stone stairs leading out of the palace.

Chirp sat waiting at the bottom of the steps. Evita didn't know what surprised her more—that he'd come back despite the archers outside or that the guards had actually let the dragonet into the palace grounds this time. Not to mention Aurel, who stood at his side with a wary expression on her face.

Evita hurried down the steps and gave the dragonet a

stroke on the nose. "Did you know he was going to offer me a job?"

"I had an inkling," said Aurel. "You, too, Zelle."

"Evita said you were here." Zelle caught up to them. "Are you going to take the job, Evita?"

"I…" She returned her gaze to Aurel. "I know you never officially dismissed me as your servant…"

"You're too loyal for your own good," Aurel said. "I don't need a servant. I also don't intend on staying in that house forever, but that's beside the point. Zelle?"

"You want my opinion?" asked Zelle. "Evita, I think you should take the job. If you don't like it, you can always ask for another."

"Don't you want to travel as well?" *To Aestin?* She managed to refrain from saying the last part, since she wasn't entirely sure where Zelle stood on the subject of Rien at the present time. Since he'd returned to Aestin, none of them had heard how he'd been received or if he intended to come back to Zeuten at all.

Zelle exhaled. "Yes, but I don't want to be beholden to the Crown Prince."

"I understand that." Evita's own loyalty was to her Relic, and while she doubted that she'd ever fit into a regular life again, she wasn't yet certain she was up to the task of being a royal messenger.

Aurel grabbed Zelle by the arm and began whispering in her ear, conveying the unexpected news of the Book of Reading's origin, while Evita considered the dragonet. "What do you think?"

The dragonet chirped, nudging her arm.

"Yes, I know you want to fly with me," she said. "Across

the ocean, even? You want to join me in running errands for the Crown?"

The dragonet made a chirping noise of confirmation, and she smiled. "We're *both* too loyal for our own good, but all right. I can't wait to see what's out there. Can you?"

———

Across the ocean, in another palace, Arien Astera waited to be called into the Emperor's throne room. While he had Martzel's reassurance that he wouldn't be arrested or taken to the dungeon this time, that didn't make him any less apprehensive at how he'd be received.

The Trevains occupied several of the cells themselves, assuming they hadn't already bought their freedom. Rien wished he'd been there to watch the palace guards fish the sopping-wet Luvid Trevain from the water and put him in cuffs, but he'd already been jailed by the time Rien had returned to Aestin.

Daimos, meanwhile, hadn't survived being stripped from his Relic.

Rien ran a hand over his staff as he waited, tracing the familiar smooth edges with his palm. It hadn't been difficult for him to reshape the new Relic she'd created for him into a staff, but it wasn't the same as Astiva's *or* Zierne's.

The godsmarks broken and whole on both his hands served as a reminder of the time when he'd held one then the other, and a fresh mark had spread up his left arm to his shoulder, a remnant of the time he'd become a Relic himself. Now the mark had faded a little, but it glowed whenever he used his staff, combining both Astiva and

Zierne's Relics into a unity they'd never experienced before.

During his brief time as a Relic, he'd heard no voices in his head the way Zelle had experienced while she'd shared her mind with the nameless Shaper, as the two Relics of Astiva and Zierne had never been conscious. That was likely for the best, because the two would have likely argued to no end. As it was, they had the chance to experience harmony again, of a sort.

The real Astiva and Zierne might have forgiven one another or not—he'd probably never know—but the Relics had been forged into a single entity that comprised both of his past Relics. Astiva, calm and loyal. Zierne, passionate and determined. Both were part of him, along with the scars they'd left. Maybe it was true that the deity to whom he'd always directed his prayers cared little for the wielders of his Relics, but whether Astiva was looking out for him or not, it was his Relics to which he owed his life, several times over.

Rien looked up when Devan Martzel and his two children walked out of the throne room. For some reason, the Emperor had asked to see them first, perhaps because it would take much longer to deal with Rien's own situation.

Reyes shot him a grin. "We're in the clear. Thank the Powers. I can't wait to get back to my workshop."

"You have other responsibilities too," Sanne reminded him. "To your nation."

"Sanne, enough," said Martzel, surprising all of them, including Reyes himself. "I think the current situation has proven the disadvantages of allowing certain Invokers a level of influence over our country's diplomacy. It's a wonder Zeuten hasn't closed their borders against us altogether."

Rien looked at him sharply. "Did they consider it?"

"I doubt that Crown Prince of theirs has ever considered anything in his life," Reyes remarked. "That plays in our favour. It helps that he was tricked, too, and by the same Invoker as the Emperor at that."

"He might still blame the nation that produced Daimos," Sanne pointed out. "It was our actions that led to his rise to power."

"I am aware, since I was one of those responsible for exiling him." Martzel's expression darkened. "We have decided to allow the Emperor to handle the punishment for the traitors alone rather than offering advice. It's a wonder he trusts any of us at all, after the Trevains abused their position so badly."

"Yet he still wants to see me."

"To apologise," Reyes clarified. "And to officially give you the title of Invoker, I don't doubt."

That made sense to Rien, but did he want to accept? His gaze shifted to Martzel, whose expression exuded reassurance. "You did Volcan proud. Never forget it."

Eyes stinging, Rien turned away. The Martzels departed, while the Emperor's voice rang out of the partly open door. "I would like to talk to Arien Astera alone."

Two guards came out of the room and flanked Rien on either side as he walked into the Emperor's main throne room. Gold filigree adorned the throne on which the Emperor sat, dressed in resplendent shades of red and gold. Tapestries hung on the walls, and a pang hit Rien's chest when he recognised the towering painting of a battlefield that he'd seen in Zeuten's royal palace as well.

A reminder of the ties between the two nations, before things had gone so terribly wrong.

"You have a new Relic," observed the Emperor.

"It's not exactly new," Rien replied. "That is… it's a combination of two Relics that broke during the battle, one of whom is the same deity who has worked with my family for a thousand years."

"I have no intention of taking your Relic away," the Emperor said. "Or testing your rightness to wield it. I never should have listened to Luvid Trevain."

"Daimos tricked us all," Rien reminded him. "He intentionally manipulated the other Invokers as well as everyone else."

"He was devoted to his revenge," said the Emperor. "As the person who authorised his banishment, I cannot help but take responsibility."

"It wasn't your decision alone," said Rien. "We all played a part, and we know how we can avoid making the same mistakes again."

"Daimos was able to gain the power he did because of those mistakes," the Emperor agreed. "I will talk with the other Invoker families about how to move forward, but I wished to give you the chance to decide how to proceed with rebuilding the Astera family, if that is what you desire."

Rien's mouth parted. He'd been offered what he'd always wanted: his position as head of the Astera family back. His deity, his Relic, and the support of his Emperor.

Yet there was one thing he wanted above all else, and it wasn't here in Aestin.

"My family's home was destroyed," he began. "I have nothing left but the foundation of what my ancestors started a thousand years ago, but before his death, I believe my father was attempting to re-establish links with the Sentinels in Zeuten. I think it would be valuable to exchange knowledge with them as my ancestors once did, especially concerning the deities and their Relics."

"Of course," said the Emperor. "If you want to go to Zeuten and talk to the Sentinels yourself, I'll gladly give you leave to do so."

"Thank you."

The question remained of whether Zelle would still be interested, or if he'd ruined his chances already.

———

Zelle tramped down the path through the forest, following a meandering route up the mountain. She'd hoped retracing the same steps she'd taken on that day several months ago when she'd gone looking for her grandmother and found Rien and the staff instead would give her a sense of purpose, but so far all she'd found were blisters.

The day after her visit to the capital, she found herself back at the outpost, having convinced the dragonet to ferry her to her grandmother's cottage in Randel. She'd got partway through tidying Grandma's possessions before giving up and walking into the forest instead. Not with any particular direction, but she'd been lost ever since she'd buried her grandmother and Rien had left for Aestin on the same day.

It would have been selfish of her to expect him to stay in Zeuten when he had as much of a mess to clean up in his home country as she did, but this time, it was hard to deny that he had no reason to come back. Daimos was dead, the enemy defeated, and he had a life waiting for him on the other side of the ocean.

As for Zelle? She'd rather chew off her own arm than accept employment from the Crown Prince, but it was starting to look like that might be her only option. Rebuilding her aunt's old shop wouldn't solve the problem of most people being too afraid of the nameless Shaper to want to buy from her, and besides, she couldn't bring herself to return to that life.

Aurel had returned to the Reader's house, while Evita had decided to accept the Crown Prince's offer of a job. Everyone had moved on, and Zelle had to do the same. She hadn't lied when she'd said teaching magic was most definitely not for her, but there must be some other option for the only person in Zeuten—in the world—to have been touched by a Great Power and survived.

On her walk up the mountain path, no would-be tourists disturbed her, and she reached the tower without running into another soul. After unlocking the door, she let herself into the lower room of the Sanctum. As far as she knew, the doors to the upper room were still barred against entry, as was the Sentinels' cave... but somehow, the staff lay on the floor, half-underneath an armchair.

A rush of disbelief flooded her, and for a moment Zelle wondered if she'd somehow been catapulted back to that day after all. How could the staff be here? Hadn't she left it in the Sentinels' cave after they'd removed her grandmother's body for burial?

Zelle reached for the staff. The instant her hand brushed the faintly glowing wooden edge, a shock hit her palm, forcing her to drop it. "Ow."

You deserved that for leaving me behind.

"How did you get out of the cave?"

The cave didn't want me around any more than the rest of you.

"That makes no sense, Shaper. You're the same person. You and the rock, that is."

A part is not the same as the whole.

"You said something similar before," she murmured. "Are you trying to avoid responsibility for everything the Shaper did? Or are you really… separate?"

The staff and the Shaper were one and the same, yet it had been the staff that had answered her grandmother's final wish and ripped out the piece of the Shaper's consciousness that had possessed Zelle. Yes, Grandma had had a certain level of influence over the staff, but the Shaper was a Great Power. Perhaps it was Zelle's reluctance to accept her ally had truly betrayed her colouring her perspective, but the staff hadn't defied her grandmother's wishes, nor had it left Zelle to live in eternal imprisonment as the Shaper's vessel.

I already told you the answer to that question.

"You aren't endearing yourself to me." Zelle sucked in a breath. "The Sentinels' cave showed me that vision of the past to make me believe the other deities punished you without reason. That was a fabrication, wasn't it? You omitted the fact that you—the Shaper—caused the deaths of both other Great Powers and then locked the lesser Powers out of this realm in a final act of vengeance. Which is the truth?"

I cannot show you myself. I did not lie when I told you the rock holds my memories, and I little expected the vision it showed you to erase part of the truth.

"You're the one who tricked me into joining my consciousness with the Shaper to beat Daimos."

Could you have achieved victory any other way?

"You nearly handed him the tools to destroy everything."

Why do you think I willingly aided your grandmother in reversing the spell? I hardly expected Daimos to be able to replicate my prison with a Relic of his own.

The ropes, as far as she knew, were in the Reader's house. They might not be needed again, but Aurel had insisted on keeping them, just in case. "That's what concerns you the most? Not the fact that you wanted to make Zeuten into your own personal paradise free from any other inhabitants?"

That is not my desire.

"You expect me to believe that?" She glared at the staff. "Prove it. Prove you aren't the same person."

The staff was silent for a moment. *When I urged you to join forces with me in the Isles of Itzar, did I ever force you to act against your will?*

"Binding myself to you didn't give you the ability to take control of my body."

Precisely. A Relic is not the same as the deity to whom it owes its existence. Take that friend of yours, for instance.

"Rien." He'd held parts of *two* deities, for a time, but it was plain to see that he hadn't been affected in remotely the same way as she had. Still... "His Relics weren't conscious. Not to the same degree as you are."

More than a Relic is needed to give a deity access to this realm. I thought you read those books of yours.

"What does that have to do with—?" She broke off. "Speaking of books, I'm guessing you intentionally manipulated the information I found in the Sanctum too."

Didn't you hear a word I said?

"You're being awfully rude for someone looking for forgiveness," she said. "What do you mean, more than a Relic? Are you implying the deity itself needs to be involved?"

That was precisely right. The *staff* couldn't possess Zelle, couldn't take control over her actions. And Daimos couldn't give every deity access to a human form. He needed their Relic… and he needed the cooperation of the deity themselves.

Fine. The staff and the Shaper weren't the same person. That didn't mean she forgave it.

"What do you want me to do?" she asked. "We teamed up to close the doors between realms, but if you think I'm taking you to Aestin to clean up the mess Daimos left behind, then you're mistaken."

You want to risk more deities escaping?

"There aren't *that* many." She hadn't seen the false Daimos since the battle, but he'd been considerably more help than Xeale and Kyren had, and she had no ill will against him.

Have you learned nothing from this? You might need my help dealing with him if he becomes a problem.

"*Your* help?" Zelle looked askance at the staff. "You want to wheedle your way into my hands again, don't you? The only reason I haven't thrown you off a cliff is because you helped prevent me from becoming a permanent vessel for the Shaper… even if you did let my grandmother die in the process."

That was no fault of mine. She made her choice, as did you.

"I've taken full responsibility for my decisions." She levelled a glare upon the staff. "You, however, have nothing but excuses and false promises."

Did you not notice that I released you from our bond?

Zelle's gaze dropped to her wrists. The marks remained, though they'd faded a little in the days since the battle. She'd assumed it was more to do with her no longer carrying part of the Shaper's consciousness inside herself than no longer being bound to the staff. "I'm not sure I understand your meaning."

I do not expect forgiveness. I wanted to give you the chance to choose to trust me again... on your own.

She exhaled. "I don't think that's going to happen."

You might need my help if anyone gets the same idea as Daimos did.

"You think someone else might try to set the gods free in this realm? I doubt most people can pull it off." Daimos had been an unusual sort, and Rien had told her of his intentions to prevent anyone from getting similar ideas upon his return to Aestin. No doubt he had a plan for safeguarding any doorways he'd left open, too, though it would be difficult to close them without the staff...

You have company. We'll finish our discussion later.

Zelle spun to the window, where she saw a familiar reptilian form descending on the path outside.

She hurried out of the tower without stopping to put the staff down, surprised to see Aurel looking down at her from Chirp's back.

"There you are, Zelle." Aurel waved at her. "Oh, you found the staff."

"I did." Holding it in her hand had erased some of the gaping sense of loss she'd felt since the battle, though she'd prefer that the staff itself didn't pick up on that thought. "The cave threw it out, allegedly. What are you doing here?"

"Evita's back from her first official trip as the royal messenger," she answered. "Want to fly to Tavine and meet her?"

"That was quick." Zelle looked between the staff and her sister, debating. "The staff claims that it acted independently when it helped Grandma set me free from the Shaper's influence. It also claims that I might need its help if any of the deities Daimos gave human bodies to come back to cause trouble."

"You mean Nahen? I don't think he's going to be an issue," said Aurel. "He's not the bloodthirsty sort, but I can ask Xeale and Kyren to keep an eye on him."

"You trust them?" It had been odd enough that they'd appeared to tell Aurel that the Book of Reading was a Relic of Gaiva, let alone this.

"No, but I can make it worth their while."

Her sister, at least, didn't seem to have qualms about bargaining with deities. "Do you think I should carry the staff?"

"Up to you." Her mouth twitched at the corners. "Evita brought a message with her from across the sea. You might like it."

"If the Crown Prince is trying to be nice to me again, then he can forget it."

Aurel simply laughed. "You'll see."

Bewildered but willing to go along with it, Zelle climbed onto the dragonet behind her sister. Their flight passed swiftly, and not a single patch of fog appeared as they flew over the peaks and the forest on the other side.

When they swooped down to land next to the Reader's house, Zelle found out what had amused Aurel so greatly. Rien stood on the doorstep, dressed in a long travelling cloak and holding his crimson staff in both hands.

Scrambling off the dragonet's back, Zelle hurried to meet him. "Rien."

Rien's brows shot up when he saw what she held in her hands. "You have the staff?"

"We have a temporary agreement," she told him. "Provided it behaves itself. Why are you here?"

"I'm here to visit the Sentinel… and her family," he said. "I convinced the Emperor to let me set up a connection between Zeuten and Aestin again. To restart what my family began."

"Is that all?"

"No." He released the staff with one hand and wrapped her in an embrace. She stiffened then returned the hug, swiftly pressing her lips to his.

When he released her, a flush crept up her face when she saw Aurel was grinning at her. Evita, meanwhile, was busy feeding something to Chirp, her gaze averted awkwardly.

"You…" The words tangled together in her throat. "You'll be around here a lot, then?"

"If you want me to be."

"Of course I do." Her breath quickened. "If that demonstration didn't convince you, then yes. I do."

"Good," he said, "because I haven't discussed the subject with the Crown Prince yet. I wondered if you wanted to come with me to convince him. Aurel said you already turned down a job from him, but I have my doubts he'll want to deal with Invokers without an inter-mediary."

"I don't know that he'd want me as a liaison either." Nor would the other Invokers, come to that. "I'll come with you, though. I'd like that very much."

"I thought we could spend some time in the capital."

Zelle thought. "Ah—we'd have to stay at an inn. My shop is a pile of rubble, and frankly, I don't think there's anything worth selling in there anyway."

"You had a generous payment for your part in stopping the war, didn't you?"

Not entirely deserved. "Yes, but... but I don't want to spend it repairing the shop. I'd like to travel for a bit, I think."

"I doubt the Crown Prince would deny you anything you asked for."

Zelle pulled a face. "That's partly why I want to avoid him. I never wanted to be notorious. I just wanted..."

"To hide in a room and read your books," Aurel inter-rupted from behind her. "Have you ever thought about chronicling our history? The Sentinels'?"

The suggestion made her frown. "Using what? I can't get into the Sanctum."

"Most of our family's history records are in my house, not up there," said Aurel. "Anyway, I'm sure you'll be able to convince the staff to help you."

"We'll be lucky if any Sentinel is ever allowed in there again." She rubbed her forehead, bewildered to find Rien smiling and nodding at her. "What?"

"That's perfect. I can't think of anyone who'd be better suited for organising the history of the Sentinels than you, Zelle."

"You do?" *Recent* history she could certainly write down, for the sake of future Sentinels. Her family's history, though, was as full of holes as the deities', albeit without any living witnesses to lie through their teeth about their own past.

There was still enough to work with, though, wasn't there? She'd start with the founding of the Sentinels' base —Aurel could help with that, since her Book of Reading had turned out to be a remnant of Gaiva, after all—and go from there.

A sense of certainty she hadn't felt in a long time slid into place like a missing piece of a puzzle. "There might be something to that idea."

"I thought so." Rien gave a satisfied nod, while she shook her head at him.

"I'm not starting on *that* for a while. Not until after we've given the Crown Prince another scare, anyway. And after I've gone to Aestin to get rid of any doorways Daimos might have left lying around."

The notion of returning to Saudenne was already more appealing now Rien was at her side, and the last of the uncertainty of the past few days began to fade as she imagined being free to show him around her favourite haunts at leisure, without the shadow of an oncoming war hanging over their heads.

Her life and Rien's had started in very different places. They might still diverge at times, but the Sentinels' old alliance with the people of Aestin would return through the pair of them, and Zelle was confident that this time, it would hold.

ACKNOWLEDGMENTS

Thank you to my editors at Red Adept Editing, my cover designers at Deranged Doctor Design, and to my patrons over at Patreon:

tripwire_mn

Sissy Satterfield

Carl

SunnySideDown

Deb C

Walter Schelsky

www.ingramcontent.com/pod-product-compliance
Lightning Source LLC
Chambersburg PA
CBHW030837190726
48285CB00004B/1253